Judy

LADIES CLUB BOOK
PLEASE RETURN WHEN READ

Lawrence Drain was born in London and educated in Buckinghamshire and Essex. In the late 60's he began a career in telecommunication; which eventually led to more than twenty years of expatriate life in the Middle East, Far East, Australasia and Africa. He has now withdrawn from travelling the world to follow his love of writing, which he does from a sunny hillside in Spain with his wife Linda, their Dachshund Cara and an unnamed but precocious laptop to type with.

ROSIE'S LOTTERY

Lawrence Drain

Rosie's Lottery

Chimera

A CIP catalogue record for this title is
available from the British Library

ISBN-13: 9781903136379
ISBN-10: 1 903136 377

*Chimera is an imprint of
Pegasus Elliot MacKenzie Publishers Ltd.*
www.pegasuspublishers.com

First Published in 2006

**Chimera
Sheraton House Castle Park
Cambridge England**

Printed & Bound in Great Britain

Dedication

To Lin

Chapter 1

My name is Rosie. Rose Alexandra Morgan to be precise, and I am dead. At least I think I am. Dying is not something that happens to one every day, is it? But I'm pretty sure my declaration is correct. If it isn't then I really do apologise but I know of no better word to describe my present state, other than dead.

As you can no doubt tell, I haven't been in this particular situation for very long, in fact no more than a few seconds... I think! Perhaps, in a little while, I'll be able to tell you more, to describe my condition with more clarity and hopefully with a far greater understanding. But first I feel an uncontrollable urge to tell you something about myself. To somehow share my existence with you. To prove to myself, that I really do... did, exist.

I'm a widow, and I've been widowed more than once. During my long life I've buried three husbands, an infant son and two dogs; Labradors, to whom I became rather uncharacteristically attached. In fact both the dogs departed with a far greater sense of loss than either husband number one or number three. Especially number three, who I'd forced myself to marry. Prostituted myself really, but one has to survive. The house and the estate would have gone under if I hadn't.

And my beautiful, innocent infant son, Robert? Well. My tears have long since dried and my melancholy and despair have faded and passed. Passed a long time ago, along with my childhood, my youth, my once coquettish beauty, all imperceptibly lost to antiquity, or so it seems to me know.

Had he lived, Robert would be fifty-one years old now.

Stop it Rosie! Dying is no reason to be maudlin.

So... The husbands? The dogs? Do I sound a little misanthropic? I suppose so. I know people regard me as a cynical person and I suppose I am, or at least was. I was born in 1917, and when one reaches eighty-three years of age cynicism should be, and is allowed. After all, as I reached the end, there is... was, little else left. But although I have spent the greater part of my life trying not to think about it, I have to admit that the loss of Robert did have a fundamental effect on my long tenure on this earth. Not the shock you understand, not really. Not when husband number two and I had been trying so unsuccessfully for a child for so many years. When I finally, gloriously, became pregnant, there was a problem,

11

inside. The doctors immediately advised me to abort. For my own health, they insisted, and especially that of any future babies. So the fact that Robert didn't survive really wasn't a shock at all. I had stubbornly refused to accept the doctors' advice, selfishly some might say, and Robert was born, arms, legs, everything perfectly formed, everything in its right place, everything except his life force, his will to live.

And me?

How did Robert's death affect me?

Well... I was rational... composed... pragmatic. I had given motherhood my best shot. I had performed the eternal miracle. Produce an offspring and failed. Only just failed however. It was like having one's horse win the handicap then collapse a head past the winning post. And I had paid the price. No More Children! Not Allowed!

Simply not allowed.

Strangely, none of that worried me. Not at all. If I am truly honest with myself, what has haunted me all my life has been Robert's thoughts. He lived for two days and just over nine hours. One thousand nine hundred and ninety nine minutes to be exact. Almost two thousand minutes; it sounds a lot longer that way – two thousand. But what did he think of for almost two thousand minutes? He hadn't been around long enough to learn or even to feel very much at all. Yet he had a soul. What happens to an undeveloped soul such as his? The thought has perplexed me throughout my life and still perplexes me now, into my death.

Death?

It's a subject about which, after watching almost all of my friends and peers pop-their-clogs, I had allowed myself to foolishly assume I knew something.

Well, I'm finding out now, aren't I?

I can tell you it's an unusual feeling, death. Do you know we are the only creatures on this entire planet who actually know we are going to die; eventually I mean. So much for being top of the food chain. I for one would rather not have known in advance. But I digress. Back to the way it feels. I mean of course it's an unusual feeling. Nothing in life really prepares you for it. Although, as soon as you are old enough to understand, death becomes present, an integral part of your life. But you simply cannot be prepared for its arrival. Never. Take it from me, dying is a once in a lifetime experience. A moment shared with no one else. A moment of utter

12

loneliness. Yet, strangely, my actual moment of death was one of complete and total surprise. Strangely that is, because I have...sorry...had been ill for almost a year – an unstoppable decline into infirmity. Each month my health failed me a little more, inexorably deteriorating until in the end I was quite desperate for death to claim me, to release me from life's terrible, avaricious bondage. And, this last month has been the worst, especially the doctor with his probing tubes and fawning bedside manner, and that overbearing Hagen who called herself an executive personal attendant. Sadists, both of them. Personal, highly paid, sadists. But at least this last month I've been at home and today, on the last day of my life, Frederick sent the nurse back to the dark crypt she undoubtedly came from.

During those long cruel months I had longed for death to take me, willed it with every pore and fibre of my body. I had lain for hour on endless hour focusing on dying. Long lonely frustrating hours, fruitless and ineffectual. At one point I had even tried to starve myself to death, but that had only resulted in the immediate insertion of further tubes into my peppered flesh. On reflection, I am hard-pressed to choose which was the greater loathing, the loneliness or the frustration? But I suppose they are one and the same really, delicately and demonically interlaced, gnawing at the substance of life. And although I now stand on the brink of answering the big question, of discovering if there is a divine presence, an afterlife, my fear of the unknown is sharply tempered by an overwhelming sense of anger. Not for the decay of my body, not for being subjected to those last five horrendous months as a human cabbage or even for meeting such an undignified end. Being deprived of the power to communicate, that's what really makes one mad. Not to be able to talk, write or even scratch a garbled note; dribbling from the corner of my mouth did not, in my estimation, constitute cutting repartee. If I could have at least communicated. Then, at the very least, I could have told the doctors, the hospital and the entire medical profession, exactly what I thought of them and their antiquated, medieval art. And as for that nurse, a dozen contracts on her head would have been scant retribution. But most of all, it was Frederick. He had been the one to make me really angry.

Frederick – Freddie to the family – is my half brother, an obsequious, miserable, biped, barely vertebrate and never upright in any sense of the word, who should be cast back into the primeval

13

slime from which he unquestionably emerged.

Strong words? Perhaps. But why should I care now? When I could I've certainly called him worst things to his face. And why did he suddenly become so caring and attentive? As if I need to ask... Yes, that was it. That was the bottom line, the last straw. That was the real suffering. No one could be more alone than I was with only Frederick as company, or more frustrated at not being able to vent my feelings at him.

Then there's the rest of the family, my kith and kin, my lineage. A collection of sycophantic, scheming, grasping, hypocrites and a blight on the face of humanity.

And there they are. In front of me now. Resplendent. The Loewen clan. Huh! Look at them all. Freddie, gnarled, stubborn, with a callous streak as wide as his shoulders, that has accompanied him all of his life. He's five years my junior and the product of my fathers second marriage. He's had a heart condition for many years and I have to admit it does stick in my craw that he's managed to survive me.

Then there's Christian, Freddie's bureaucratic, middle-aged son, whose tall scrawny frame and round protruding eyes give a countenance so removed from Freddie's, or Freddie's late wife Victoria's, that it leaves one with severe doubts as to his ancestry. And Lia, Christian's wife, much younger than her husband, extremely pretty but not quite tall enough to be termed a real beauty. Unfortunately Lia's a half-wit. No Rosie, that's not completely true. But Lia certainly is a dizzy, scatty creature, with an intellect that slides way off the bottom of any scale one cares to apply. I suppose that explains why she ended up with Christian – poor girl. Elsbeth is the old one next to Lia, a cousin, from my father's side of the family. She's a spinster of eighty-two years. A short, rotund, overweight, ignorant woman, weak in every aspect. To Elsbeth's far side is her widowed brother Thaddeus, with his gammy leg and ebony cane. His personality was cast from a similar but not quite as robust mould as Freddie's, who, although he is three years younger than Thaddeus, even in childhood was always the stronger. Finally, there's Thaddeus' praetorian son Charles and his stunning wife Helen. Charles is a plain looking man, and an unfortunate soul, totally devoid of backbone or fortitude, who wears a permanent scour of gloom and despondency – no doubt the result of his marriage to Helen. Helen, despite her vibrant looks is a scheming, miserly creature; I imagine her scraping her lipstick off each night before she goes to bed and then smoothing it carefully back onto the stick to use again the following day. She married Charles for his money. Why she thought he had any I don't know, but it must have come as quite a shock when she found out the truth.

One, two, three... yes all seven. Only Lisa, my goddaughter, is missing. She's the orphaned granddaughter of Elsbeth and Thaddeus' sister Margaret; her parents were killed in a car accident when Lisa was eight years old. I haven't counted Margaret in the family list. I should but her illness sadly precludes her. She has to live in a nursing home now, poor dear. Lisa visits regularly, and I used to when I could, but Margaret hasn't recognised anyone for at least four years. She just lives in a world of her own. Thank God for Lisa. Without her, her grandmother would have no one, certainly not the rest of the family. I would have been at a loss myself.

As I was saying... Lisa. The only one in the family with the more desired qualities of life, the only one with a virtuous character, with a normal quota of integrity and compassion. So of course they've deliberately kept her away. They don't want her to know what they're up to. They're frightened of her. They know she's a great favourite of mine. They'll want to split up the spoils without her, cut her out, give her a minimum share, a token, and that's if she's lucky.

Well, are they in for a surprise!

So I wonder what happens next, and why am I here now, in this room? I suppose I didn't really expect harps and a pearly-gate, cherubs and Saint Peter and all of that. I'm not sure what I expected. Nothing really. It's all rather a wonder, and a complete surprise. Especially considering my religious holdings, or lack of them. But there you are. I'm arrogantly assuming I'm in the middle of a religious experience. Isn't it amazing how pre-conditioned and indoctrinated even a confirmed agnostic like myself can be?

But enough of that. I'm sure to have the time for philosophy and theology later. Now is the time to explore. I should experiment. I'm here, now. I have a form and a presence that I can feel. But what can I do? Physically that is. I've been unable to move freely or unassisted for so long I've forgotten to even try.

Let's give it a go.

Ah! Well look at that. Yes! There! I can do it! I can move! Yes! Yes! That's my arm. Left. Right. What a strange sensation. I'm not actually doing anything, not in the muscular sense, there's no actual physical sensation. Yet if I think, instruct, want, feel, there's movement, and direction.

Wonderful!

Let's see if I can get right across the room?

Yes!

Right under Freddie's scrawny nose, and he didn't even see me. They didn't see me, any of them. Although Freddie flinched, I know he did. Let's try again.

Wheee! Great! I'm a ghost, a real ghost.

I wonder?

No... That didn't work, no shimmering reflection in the mirror, no shadow on the floor. Let's try lowering the temperature...?

That worked O.K. Not bad for a first try and I bet there's lots more I can do. Lots and lots and lots.

This is going to be fun.

Chapter 2

With the exception of Lisa, who was as yet unaware of her godmother's demise, Rose's entire family stood in the dimly lit makeshift bedroom, pressed around the cold, sparse metal-framed bed. Heavy lined curtains were closed across the windows, with the merest gap releasing a single shaft of light along the polished oak floor of the old music room and across the still warm face of Rose's body. The only other light came from the flickering illuminated dials of Rose's life support system and a sombre single bedside table lamp with a heavy Victorian brocade shade. The room had been temporarily converted into a bedroom, at Rose's request, before she had been admitted to hospital, before she had lost the power to communicate. Lisa had seen to it, seen that Rose's wishes had been met. But that kindness was lost now. Taken by the callous actions of her grasping family. Rose had loved the view through the broad French windows, out over the carefully manicured lawns and past the herbaceous border to the atrium at the far end of the inner garden. She would have been furious that they had pulled the curtains before pulling the plug; she had wanted to die looking at the view.

'Has she gone?' A wisp of grey-white hair hung across her sallow face as Elsbeth leant slightly forward, asking her question in a voice that was no more than a meek whisper.

'What?' asked Freddie. He was standing at the foot of the bed, straining to hear Elsbeth's question above the sharp electronic sound of the alarm that emanated from Rose's life support system.

Elsbeth's thin, watery eyes flitted frantically from side to side. She jumped back in alarm as Thaddeus prodded Rose's corpse with a horny, index finger. 'Yes. She's gone,' he announced brusquely, and receiving no reaction from his earlier prod he reached across the inert body again, pushing Rose's shoulder firmly. 'Thank God for that,' he added. 'I was sure she intended to hang on forever. Be just like her, wouldn't it? Cantankerous old bitch. She always had to have the last word.'

'Huh,' Freddie snorted. Clearly implying that **he** never let his half sister get the better off him.

Thaddeus gave Freddie a hard look, but didn't attempt to question his cousin's statement, however false it had been.

'So was I,' Elsbeth nodded in agreement.

'So-was-you what?' Thaddeus snapped at her.

'Afraid she would hang on forever,' Elsbeth replied, avoiding Thaddeus' cold glare. She stared down into Rose's lifeless eyes, which appeared to follow her as she backed away from the bed, glancing nervously at the life support system and its insistent alarm.

As if in commune they all stared at Rose.

Helen looked sharply at Elsbeth, her voice breaking the spell. 'Oh! Don't say that.' Helen took her husband's hand and squeezed it tightly, deliberately pinching his little finger with the edge of her wedding ring, demanding support. 'Poor Aunt Rose. How could you all be so disrespectful?'

'Don't include me,' Christian interjected hastily. 'I was never disrespectful to the old girl – wouldn't dare. In fact I had a lot of time for her, particularly her strength; no one talked down to Aunt Rose.' He looked directly at Freddie as he said this but turned away; as usual he was unable to match his father's stare.

'Yes'. Charles responded belatedly to his wife's prompting. He had discovered very early in their married life that it was always best to do so. 'Jolly bad thing to say Uncle. Jolly bad thing to sa…'

Can't we turn that damned noise off now?' Helen interrupted.

Thaddeus glared at Charles. 'Hypocritical young puppy. It was you and your scheming wife who were the first to suggest turning off this infernal machine. And you'll be the first at Brinker's office for the reading, won't you?' Thaddeus pointed the same skeletal index finger accusingly at them both.

Frederick stepped between them. Momentarily, before he could speak, a sharp acrid smell caught under his nose. He flinched, sniffed to clear his nose then spoke. 'Yes,' he agreed in a tone that immediately assumed command. 'Turn that noise off now and shut up. All of you.' He rubbed the underside of his thin, red-veined nose fractiously. 'This is no time for bickering. Cornwall-Thompson will be here soon and we have to present a united front. Remember, we need a Death Certificate and we need it now. Remember,' he repeated, then added. 'The doctor's supposed to be here at the moment of death, not ten minutes or two hours after. If, he insists on an autopsy, it could delay the reading of the Will for weeks, even push the whole thing into probate.' Freddie's tone reverberated with indignation at the word 'probate'. The same pungent smell caught beneath his nose a second time. He flinched again then turned his stooped frame towards his son. 'We're all relying on you for that, Christian. And it's a simple task, so don't mess it up. Old Cornwall-

Thompson's been the family doctor for over thirty years. He's our man. We know him well, far better than he likes. The doddering old fool shouldn't be a problem at all, and anyway, a couple of hundred should settle any objections. Remember, no bureaucracy. I know what you're like with your forms and procedures. If you have to remind him of that incident in Buckton last year, then do so. Just make sure he signs the damned Death Certificate before he leaves.' Frederick coughed and wheezed. Christian helped his father to a chair. The old man pulled an inhaler from the pocket of the course tweed jacket he was wearing and puffed its therapeutic vapours rapidly between his lips.

Beside Rose's bed, just to the side of where she lay, stood the life support system. It consisted of several black metal boxes mounted one above the other on a rigid chromium stand, linked by an endless stream of tubes and wires that had regulated Rose's heartbeat for the last five months and fed an exotic cocktail of drugs, food and stimulants into her failing body. Charles stood in front of the stand, inspecting the apparatus closely, the high pitched alarm it emitted was deafening at such close range. He didn't understand the dials, lights and gauges that flashed and flickered on the face of the boxes, any more than he could have assembled the column of high-tech wizardry, but he knew enough to know the whole thing was functioning properly – again.

'Is it OK?' Christian asked, holding his hands to his ears as he walked round the bed to add his personal inspection to the situation. 'I didn't know these things made such a racket.'

'Yes. It's all right,' Charles answered, pointing to the centre of the column. 'Look. The scopes just showing a straight line. That's because the old girl's gone, that's why the alarms buzzing.' He crouched and flipped the main power switch off at the wall socket, and the room dropped to a sudden, deathly hush. 'Can't stand that noise,' He added. 'I'll turn it all back on as soon as we hear the doctor arrive.'

Helen shivered. She wrapped her arms across her chest and rubbed her shoulders vigorously. 'What was that?' she asked timidly. 'It was as though something brushed past me. Why is it so cold?'

The temperature in the room had dropped noticeably. Lia, who was wearing a heavy woollen long-sleeved dress, rubbed her arms as well. 'Why didn't we wait for the doctor before we turned off the machine? She asked nervously.

They all turned towards her. Involuntarily she took a step backwards, away from the bed.

'Stoopid bitch.' Helen clenched and unclenched her fist, stepping towards Lia angrily, the manicured edge falling from her carefully practised accent, revealing a brief hint of her original London, east-end, roots. 'We should've turned off your machine as well.' She dabbed at Lia's forehead with the flat off her hand. 'Is there anyone in up there? Anyone at all?'

Christian grabbed Helen's arm and pulled her away. 'Don't talk to her like that Helen,' he ordered. 'Just leave her to me. Leave her alone.' He took his wife's hand and led her to the door. 'I'll explain it later, dear,' he said as he led her from the room.

'Remember Christian. She's your responsibility. Remember,' Helen called after him, her temper still ringing in her voice.

'Remember. Remember. Remember. Is that the only word this family knows?' Christian threw the words back over his shoulder.

Helen looked fleetingly at Rose's corpse. 'Let's get out of here. That gives me the creeps.'

Charles ignored her. 'Complex, isn't it?' He twisted two of the knurled chrome knobs. The first appeared to do nothing at all, but the second increased the volume of the alarm so he turned it back until the buzzer dropped to a faint hum. 'There. That's fixed it.' Buoyed by his apparent success he twisted the third knob. The straight green line that traversed the face of the scope in front of him gave a sudden blip.

Helen jumped and immediately turned back towards Rose's corpse, suspecting that it had miraculously regained life. Her heart drummed in her chest. She grabbed at Charles, pulling him away from the life support apparatus. 'For Gawd's sake leave it alone.' She took a deep breath to compose herself. 'Let's just turn the bloody alarm back to where it was and close the doors behind us.'

Charles did as he was told. The room filled with the sharp strident sound of the alarm. Thaddeus pulled the sheet up and over Rose's face. He stared as the white linen fell across her face. 'Yes. Let's go,' he agreed.

'You thought she'd come back to life, didn't you?' Charles gloated.

'Don't be stupid,' Helen responded tersely, then added, 'I need a drink, I don't know about anyone else. Helen led the way from the temporary bedroom, through the main hall, with its capacious twin stairways sweeping upwards to the mezzanine floor above, passed generations of Loewens, immortalised in oils and mounted like trophies upon the flock-papered walls.

The main entrance hall of the house was by far the largest room in the building, quite disproportionately so. It was the result of a specification laid down by Rose Loewen's great great grandfather, who had a passion for stag hunting; in the days when stags and the very forest they habituated, still existed nearby. It was in the Great Hall, as he chose to refer to it, that he would entertain his fellow-sportsmen and their favourite hounds. Lia, squashed between Thaddeus and Christian, shuddered as she crossed the stone-flagged floor of the hall. She had never liked the house and in particular it's sombre, brooding entrance hall. The smell of age and the glare of Loewen ancestral eyes – every pair of which seemed to follow her as she crossed the hall – gave her, in her own words, the willies. Helen led them into the library where Freddie opened the doors of a large mahogany cocktail cabinet – commissioned by the same great great grandfather who had insisted on the cavernous entrance hall. The cocktail cabinet was set perfectly into the wall-to-wall, floor-to-ceiling, sculptured mahogany bookshelves that covered eighty percent of the room. This room, like the rest of the house – except, temporarily, Rose's present bedroom – smelt of distant times, of ancient paper, of age; something Freddie's presence did little to dispel. He poured himself a large brandy from a crystal decanter. 'Anyone else?' he inquired. Thaddeus joined him but the others abstained.

Chapter 3

There you have it. Murder. That's what it is. Cold, callous and premeditated. Bless them. I'm not enraged by their actions. Turning off the machine was a blessed relief, a release from the torment of dying slowly. Besides it would do me little good to be angry now, it's far too late for that. Old Cornwall-Thompson will be here soon enough. He'll sign the Death Certificate, that's for sure. He won't want his skeleton dragged out of the cupboard and he knows Freddie won't hesitate to expose him. He's known the family for years, he knows their characters as well as anyone. He won't go against them. Although he may hang out for the two hundred pounds Freddie mentioned; Cornwall-Thompson has always been a pragmatic individual.

What skeleton?

Huh. It's rather a long story but, bear with me. It was Freddie you see. Freddie who helped him cover up the scandal, arranged for the private clinic. Because, Cornwall-Thompson is a pervert. Oh yes. He's been one all his life, although, up to the time he was forced to seek Freddie's help, he'd managed to keep the fact a secret. But one shouldn't make him sound too awful, his perversion was not in the incest sense, or involving small children or anything nasty like that. No, he's into sexual games, or at least he was. One of his favourite games was to persuade his wife to twist a metal tube – taken from the centre of an old surgical syringe that his wife had once used to do fine filigree icing patterns on their children's birthday cakes, with a different nozzle, of course – into his rear end. This would expand that particular orifice so that a long, thin feather-tickler could be inserted to stimulate the inner walls of his anus.

I know it's hard to believe, but it's true. After it all went wrong his wife was in a terrible state. She came to see me, to ask my advise, then broke down quite uncontrollably; which is something I hate people doing. She didn't tell me everything mind. Not the grim details. But I wheedled the rest out of Freddie. You see, on that fateful day, the feather tickler, a wire stemmed brush made from Swan tail-feathers, had got stuck. The binding on the feathers had parted causing the stems to splay. This had an effect similar to the barbs on a fishhook. All Mrs Cornwall-Thompson's efforts to pull out the tickler were met by screams of pain and curses of retribution from her stricken husband. So she stopped; just for a quick peek

22

inside the tube, to locate the cause of the problem. It was very dark inside the tube. She told her husband she would have to find a torch, to see properly. This made him shout even more vehemently. How could she think of leaving him in this predicament? She searched around the bedroom, not knowing what she was looking for, until she spied the box of matches that lay with the other contents of Cornwall-Thompson's trouser pockets, on top of his bedside cabinet. Back with her prostrate husband she struck a match, just for illumination. The effect was instantaneous. A pocket of intestinal gas, released by the internal activity of the feather tickler, immediately ignited, consuming the dry Swan tail feathers and scalding both Mrs Cornwall-Thompson's left eyebrow and the inner walls of Mr Cornwall-Thompson's lower intestinal tract.

Freddie arranged the treatment for Cornwall-Thompson and a divorce lawyer for Mrs Cornwall-Thompson – her partition was centred around mental cruelty and was not contested. No mention of her husband's obscure sexual proclivities was ever made public. Freddie had bought himself a personal, free-of-charge doctor, for whatever service he needed.

So now you know.

***

Claire shivered. Last night she had slept in one of his old tee-shirts and now, as she stepped outside of the warmth of their bed, it was far from adequate; especially with the heating turned down to minimum. Her dressing gown lay across the chest-of-draws beside the bed. She slipped her arms quickly into the thick towelling and pulled the cord as tight as she could around her waist. That felt better. She picked at the bobbled edges of one sleeve. The dressing gown was getting old but it would have to do, there was certainly no money around for a new one. He'd bought it for her that first Christmas, the year they moved in together.

'Five years,' she whispered at the mirror.

She brushed her hands down her sides, feeling the dip of her waist and the curve of her hips.

'At least I've still got my figure,' she said, staring at the mirror defiantly, challenging it to dispute her statement.

For how long, she thought, as she pulled the gown tighter around her middle and patted the flatness of her stomach. The towelling warmed her, but only a little. She swept her long dark hair out from beneath the neck of the dressing gown and reached towards the mirrored wardrobe door in front of her, then hesitated, her hand hovering over its chrome handle. 'Come on, Claire,' she said in a whisper. Her hand began to shake a little. 'Come on!' She repeated in the sternest tone she could muster; it was still hardly more than a whisper. She gripped the handle then slid the door open. At the back of the wardrobe, behind her dwindling collection of hanging clothes and buried deliberately beneath two shoe boxes, lay two envelopes; one long and buff coloured with a bold crested water-mark stamped in its upper right corner, the other short, unpretentious and white. She looked at the envelopes for several seconds, turning them around in her chilled delicate hands, afraid of what they contained, afraid to pass that on, but it was Sunday, and she'd deliberately left it till Sunday. From the bottom draw of the chest of draws she took a soft white Teddy.

Andrew sat at the breakfast table, his square, solid frame covered by an old red jumper and a pair of tracksuit bottoms. He looked up from a mug of steaming tea and stared at the ceiling above him. The splattering of the shower had stopped ages ago and he wondered what she could be doing for so long. Then he heard her, padding down the stairs. She had to be wearing those fluffy mules her mother gave her for her birthday; nothing clip-clopped on the stair boards as they did. He brushed a hand through non-existent hair, still unable to come to terms with the ultra-short crop Claire had talked him into; only modesty prevented him from accepting that it really did make him look like a false, Hollywood action hero or a Premier League footballer. Still, she liked it and that was good enough for him.

Claire paused at the foot of the stairs, staring at the two envelopes in her hand, uncertain what to do next, then pushed the white envelope back into her pocket; that would have to wait for a better time, perhaps next Sunday. The buff envelope seemed to stare back at her, demanding to be read. Not that it was that bad really, but Andrew wouldn't see it that way.

The envelope was postmarked four days earlier and had arrived the day before yesterday. She could have given it to him that evening, when he returned from work but she was too frightened. Not of Andrew. He wasn't a violent man; he wouldn't shout at her or strike her. Despite their problems and anguish, he never had and she knew that whatever happened, however bad, he never would. She was frightened for him, not of him. She looked at his strained, anxious face, her vision blurred by the moisture in her eyes. It wasn't fair. Their situation wasn't really their fault. It certainly wasn't their fault that the company folded so dramatically, or that they both worked at the same company. Andrew's promotion had seemed so deserved but, his success had been their undoing; they'd bought a house. Everyone had told them to buy the biggest one they could afford, to buy big; 'house prices are on the way up'. So they gave up the semi they were renting and bought a large detached just outside London, with a mortgage to match. They even took a holiday, so Andrew wasn't actually there at the end. But that didn't matter; he was employed by the company, part of the company and, as the most junior, the least able to defend himself. Tarred was the word he used. Not implicated or indicted for criminal negligence and even embezzlement, as some members of the board were, no, just tarred for life, untouchable. Then the house sale fell through, twice. But life is like that. 'Just as one door closes, another slams in your face'. When he was alive, that's what her father used to say and she had always thought it quite a funny line, but it wasn't funny any more, not funny at all. For a while, after it all happened, while they were still trying to sell the house, as they watched the mortgage eat away their savings, their overdraft and eventually take them deep into debt, forcing them to take a short-term loan that they now couldn't afford to pay; self-pity had threatened to engulf her. Then slowly, over the last eighteen months, she had found the strength to accept their situation, to cope with life. They were both working now. Andrew had struggled to get another job. Tarred as he was, he wasted several months vainly chasing similar positions to his old one. When he did find a job, she didn't think it would last. She didn't think he would be able to cope with such a huge step downwards. But they knew he had no choice, and now, even though he hated the job bitterly, he was still there; she was so proud of him.

'You all right?' Andrew called out from behind the door.

His voice made Claire start. She'd been standing there for ages. She pushed the kitchen door open rather harder than she meant to, it clattered back against the refrigerator.

Andrew was starring at her, his face puzzled. 'You all right?' He repeated.

'Yes. I'm OK. Just something in my eye,' she lied without conviction as she stepped into the kitchen.

The room was small and cramped. She hated it. She hated the entire apartment. She longed to go back to the bright spacious detached house that their creditors had taken away from them. She waited in the doorway, holding the door open, reluctant to enter the room. Andrew knew she was lying and could see that she was upset. Her bottom lip quivered slightly, her gorgeous green-grey eyes began to water. She was on the very edge of tears and he was about to ask her 'what was the matter', then he noticed the envelope in her hand. The question froze on his lips. He recognised the envelope at once. Not as a particular letter from a particular person, or company or organisation, but as trouble, official trouble, more trouble to heap upon the mountain of trouble they already had to bear.

Claire slid the letter slowly across the melamine top of the breakfast table.

'Another one?' He asked in a resigned voice.

'The building society.'

'Leeches. They've taken the car and the house. What more do they want, blood? Bastards!'

'Andy that's not fair. They only took the house, the bank took the car.'

'Only took the house! Wasn't that nice of them?

'I didn't mean it like that. You know I didn't.' She hated it when he was sarcastic with her. She pulled her dressing gown even tighter around her and the Teddy he didn't know she was wearing, and won't know if he carries on like that, she thought.

'Helping themselves. That's what they're doing,' Andrew continued. The envelope had already been opened, he slid out a single sheet of paper and opened it flat on the table, unfolded it and began to read, his lips moving unconsciously.

'They've agreed to give us another twelve months. Ironic really,' she added softly.

'Shit! Shit! And double shit!' He exclaimed loudly, screwing the single sheet of paper up into a tight ball. He launched the paper ball across the kitchen and into the sink. It landed with force, fixing itself between the soiled plates of last night's dinner and the frying pans in which the meal had been cooked.

'Andy!' Claire extracted the paper from the unwashed utensils, opened it up, and tried to smooth it out on the only available clear area of worktop. The residue of food on the unwashed crockery and pans had stained the edges of the paper, its crumpled appearance seeming to reflect their current existence – crushed and defeated.

'An extra year. Great! At an extra half a percent.' Andrew looked across the table at Claire; she looked strange, different. For a moment he thought his outburst had frightened her, she looked frightened or at least nervous and that wasn't like her, she had become the strong one, stronger than he could ever be. The thought passed, he sat back in his chair and returned to the crumpled letter. 'They'll be another one. You watch. Just as we start to get on top of this they'll present us with another year, 'that nice man at the bank' he'll write and say that for a mere additional half a percent we can stay in debt for one more year, or perhaps a decade or so. Claire, when are we ever going to get out of this?

Claire moved behind him, bent and folded her arms around him and pressed her cheek against his beard. He felt a warm tear trickle from her eye to his. 'We'll find a way darling. I know we will,' she whispered. Another tear dropped, and as it did she could feel the tension across his shoulders slowly ebb. He pulled her round so that she sat across his knees; he could never cope with her crying. He began to kiss her cheeks, whisper to her, comfort her, apologising for his rage. She nuzzled into him, moving her bottom into his lap as he kissed her left eye and then her right, gentle kisses, lifting the tears from her cheeks with the tip of his tongue. His lips brushed the tip of her nose then met her lips, the merest touch, a simple brushing of his lips against hers. She moved her bottom again, a circular motion, deeper into his lap, then slid her hand behind his neck and pulled his lips to hers, parting them with her tongue, searching inside for more than just passion.

Andrew closed his eyes; the letter and the bank began to slip behind him.

Claire pulled at the cord of her dressing gown, wanting him now, wanting their love to remove the pain she felt, give her the courage she needed but didn't have.

His hand caressed her neck, his fingers stroked the hair behind her ear, fondling the lobe then drifting tantalisingly down beneath the folds of her dressing gown, barely touching her flesh. Her back arched, pushing her breast into his palm. She could feel the effect of her bottom in his lap. Their kissing had become deeper now, urgent and demanding. His hand reached between her legs, softly massaging her inner thigh, climbing upwards, fingers exploring beneath fabric, feeling, parting her flesh, sliding inside her. He began to softly massage that one spot that he knew she couldn't resist. The faintest of murmurs squeezed from between her lips. She grabbed his hand and pulled it away.

'Remember exactly where you were,' she said breathlessly,

jumping from his lap and pulling him towards the kitchen door.

'I'll try.'

'You'd better do more than try,' she grinned, pointing up the stairs. 'Bedroom! Now!'

***

Joan studied Martin's back as he stretched a tight pair of cycling shorts over the solid girth of his thighs. He was tall, a tad over six foot, well-built, and even at the end of a long cold winter, tanned. Even if his shoulders were slightly rounder now than they had been before, and he had lost a little of his stature, he was still handsome. Handsome in the way film stars manage to look on the screen; as if they were at least ten years younger than they really are. Except that Martin didn't need make-up for the camera and he always kept himself in top condition, even his hair refused stubbornly to fall out or even grey, red-heads have that kind of luck. He would be off to the back bedroom now, to work-out on his boys-toys, his rowing and cycling machines and that weird contraption of wires and weights that banged and crashed as he strained against them for exactly twenty minutes every evening; except for Sundays, when he preferred to work out in the morning. Sundays had a depressingly repetitive regularity that they both detested but would never admit to each other. They had, in fact, just finished doing what Andrew and Claire had just started to do with such passion; although there had been little passion in Martin and Joan's coupling. There hadn't been passion in their relationship, in any shape or form, for at least three years. They barely went through the motions once a week, and then just to keep up appearances to each other. Martin saved his passion for Chloe, his much younger and extremely voluptuous secretary. Joan saved hers for Liam, her sympathetic and loving watercolour tutor at the local evening institute. Fortunately, both Martin and Joan were ignorant of the existence of the other's paramour, each blithely assuming they were the only one in the marriage conducting an extra marital affair. Consequently both felt equally guilty and ashamed.

Martin accepted his indiscretion as simple mid-life crisis. His fiftieth birthday, coming and going two years earlier, had triggered something off, something deep inside him, the feeling that the next milestone birthday – sixty – would bring an end to his charm, his sex-appeal, his charisma. Vanity and conceit began to consume him.

Panic crept into his life, a deep routed fear that had to be assuaged, something that crept up on him and demanded to be satisfied. In short, he was ready for Chloe and that's when he met her.

Joan would be fifty later this year and Martin had promised her a special holiday as a birthday present. Somewhere exotic, with lots of sunshine. A tropical island, somewhere Caribbean. It was while doing the research for the holiday that he first met Chloe. She was working at the travel agents in the High Street and had steered him very competently through the maze of catalogues available; cruises, hotels, beach-side cabins – the choice seemed endless. He couldn't say that there had been an instant attraction, certainly not on his part. He'd noticed the brightness of her eyes and the sweeping shape of her body, but only in the vague way that all men notice beautiful women. He had found her smile particularly beguiling but had assumed it to be her customer-smile, no more. He simply remembered her as an attractive blonde with big boobs and hazel eyes; not particularly tall, a little over five foot with a cute round face and a button nose, that wrinkled to discourage him against a particular location or hotel. Later, on reflection, he could see there had perhaps been something there, something deep, subliminal, alluring. After all, he didn't usually remember casual acquaintances like that in such detail. He had taken a selection of brochures home to Joan and spread them across the dining room table. They covered the polished wood from end to end, with gleaming white beaches, hammocks strung between coconut palms, endless photographs of colourful exotic fruit awash in lakes of blue liquor that threatened to burst from bulbous glass containers if not pinioned firmly by a fluted straw and twizzle stick. Eventually they decided on a cruise – six islands, starting from Kingston Jamaica, then to Saint Kitts, Martinique, Saint Vincent, Granada and ending in Port of Spain, Trinidad. Martin couldn't remember the last time he had seen Joan so excited. It was almost as though they were a couple again, but only almost. That night they had both gone to bed feeling more guilty than ever before. They actually made love, midweek.

Martin returned to the travel agents the next day and placed a deposit. To his great disappointment, a dark haired, mousy woman in her mid forties served him.

After six weeks, the initial excitement of the cruise-holiday had paled quite significantly. They had a further six months to go before Joan's birthday and hadn't yet made the final payment on the holiday. Joan had increased her watercolour classes at the institute.

There was a new tutor, she said, who brought the best out in her. She had started to go three times a week. It was the only time that she appeared to be happy with her life. Martin hadn't minded at all. He enjoyed the freedom that being alone three nights a week gave him. On Mondays he would stay in and watch the live match on the telly, without interruption, without that awful feeling of monopolising the evening and boring Joan to death. Then on Wednesdays he'd started to play darts with some of the lads at the Copper Spigot in Church Street. He hadn't been able to do that for years, but sadly discovered that he'd outgrown such nights. The novelty soon began to wear off. But then there was Fridays. The best night of the week. Joan had a double session of watercolours on Fridays. It was perfect. Martin could indulge in his major passion – foreign films. Joan hated foreign films, especially old ones. She simply didn't have the patience to read the sub-titles or to appreciate the subtle plots serious cinema could offer. She liked her movies from Hollywood, with stars whose names she recognised from the glamour magazines and romantic plots that didn't tax the imagination too much. She also hated darts and football.

It was at a particularly moving and somewhat disturbing showing of 'Cineima Paradiso' that Martin met Chloe for the second time. He was reading the forthcoming-attractions posters, outside the cinema, Chloe was doing the same; they literally bumped into each other. He recognised her immediately. She recognised him. The die was cast. They started chatting. She was also a foreign film buff and especially loved the older films which, she said, had far more charm and depth than the modern versions; she had seen 'Cineima Paradiso' on at least two previous occasions. Without consciously asking if he could accompany her, he found himself sitting next to her. He hadn't seen the film before and was deeply impressed by its depth and pathos. Chloe seemed to enjoy it equally as much as he did, even though she knew the plot intimately and insisted on leaning over repeatedly to whisper a comment, a trait that he found enticing, surprisingly. Her girlish charm was simply captivating. They left the cinema in deep discussion of the moral issues the film addressed and it seemed quite natural to continue their conversation over a drink at the pub down the road. Martin discovered that Chloe was thirty-two years old, divorced and struggling to raise twin five-year-old boys on her own. That she lived in a small, one-bedroom flat near the office and that her ex-husband had vanished overseas, as had his maintenance payments.

Although they didn't formally plan to meet the following week, they both turned up at the cinema at exactly the same time. It just seemed a natural coincidence. Martin hadn't mentioned Chloe to Joan, and now he never would.

Much to his surprise, it was Joan who first mentioned cancelling the holiday. She said it would be too expensive and they couldn't afford it and she was worrying about the cost. Martin was extremely relieved. Keeping up the pretence of happily married life was becoming a strain and the stress of planning for the rapidly approaching holiday made that worse. Joan was right. They really couldn't afford it, especially now that his new double life with Chloe had to be financed.

To help Chloe cope with the cost of single parenthood, and to be nearer to her as much as possible, he arranged for her to get a job at his company; his position as personnel manager made that easy. It was at the same time that he transferred Chloe from the word processing office to be his personal secretary that Joan suggested less expensive and separate holidays. She wanted to go on a trip from the evening institute, painting flowers in Wales, and she knew that he had always wanted to go to one of those stupid foreign film festivals in France. Feigning reluctance, he agreed. He didn't have anything planned for those two weeks, yet, but something would turn up – something with Chloe. It never occurred to him that two weeks was an awfully long time for a watercolour-painting trip from the local evening-institute.

Joan had tried to analyse the reasons for her indiscretion with Liam, which were many and varied. Boredom came high on her list. Boredom with her own life as well as the life Martin chose for them both. Dissatisfaction came a close second. Dissatisfaction with her lot in life; there had to be more, which sounded trite beyond words. Then there was lust. Simple, unadulterated lust. Something she could never experience with Martin. They had been together too long and they hadn't changed or adapted with the passing of time. They'd simply stayed the same, except for getting older of course, which was another element to consider. Liam was thirteen years younger than her and she often wondered what he saw in her. It certainly wasn't her money, she didn't have any. She knew that she still cut an attractive figure, she was tall and had always been slim and she dressed well, but in a sensible forty-nine-year-old way. Liam said she had untapped inner beauty. He could see it in her eyes and in her painting. He had said these things to her before they became lovers. He said similar things to all of his students, and he was a very demonstrative sort of man.

From the very first lesson he gave she had sensed his attraction to her. At first she was flattered and found herself changing little things about her appearance. Her hair had been short and rather severe, so she let it grow out and had it tinted a darker brown to hide any trace of the grey hairs that had started to appear. She began to realise that her gradual transformation was not limited to her outward appearance; inwardly changes began to occur, particularly the way she felt when in Martin's company, and the way she felt at classes with Liam. She became frightened. The feelings she was developing towards Liam confused her, so she gave up her classes, stopped going to the evening institute. That had been the turning point. After not seeing her for three weeks, Liam telephoned her. He was worried that she might be ill, he said. She had lied, agreeing that she had been. A week later he came to her house. She had made them coffee and they had talked. An hour later they were in her and Martin's bed making the sort of love that she had only ever read about in books. She had never felt so guilty in all her life – or so good.

***

Alan sat on the edge of the bed, scratched his balding head and stared at his limp, flaccid form in the tall trestle-mirror his wife used for dressing. His beautiful wife Ann was sixteen years his junior; an interval that had always given him concern. 'Never marry a beautiful woman', the expression goes, but he hadn't regretted marrying her for one second. He used to love watching her in that mirror. Love watching her dress. Dress or undress, it didn't matter, the wonderful folds of her body still drove him crazy, even after he'd passed the magic age of sixty, even after twelve years of marriage. Not even the ravages of time could dampen his ardour. Ann had loved that as well, loved the affection, the attention, and the worship.

He sat completely naked and was, on his own admission, not a pretty sight. Several rounds of fat vied with each other to cover his navel. His arms were soft and wrinkled and his hands blotched with purple. He surveyed his body from stooped shoulders to veined feet, stopping with a disgusted grimace at his manhood, limp between his legs. 'No use to anyone, are you? Poor useless bastard,' he said, addressing his fallen member. His voice faltered and cracked. 'Sunday bloody morning. Sunday.' He aimed the words at the mirror more than to it, his frustration hanging heavily and pathetically in the void between his lips and the glistening glass. 'Sundays used to be so good. A bit of rumpy-pumpy, a cup of tea in bed then down stairs for a full fried breakfast and the Sunday papers. Smashing,' he added woefully.

'Stop talking to yourself and put some clothes on,' Ann called out to him from the bathroom. She wouldn't come into the room while he was undressed. Ever since they had found out about his complaint, that they couldn't, shouldn't, do it anymore, she had made a point of removing all temptation. She dressed and undressed alone and insisted that they both wear pyjamas and slept in single beds and she still didn't know who to believe. Almost two years had passed since he had received the hospital's diagnosis. A pretty miserable time. But the worst thing of all was the doubt, not knowing. The doctors said that it was possible to contract herpes that way, and thrush was such a common complaint, and so were cold sores, but she still had her doubts. She would never know of course, not for sure, but the longer time went on, the more she suspected, the more she doubted the entire, flimsy excuse. Anyway it was too late now. Especially now that she had met someone else. She had even thought of leaving Alan, allow him to rot away alone, but she hadn't done that, it would have been too disloyal, particularly as he had lost everything, and besides, she had to try out her own remedies. What did doctors know anyway? At least that's how things had been for what seemed a lifetime.

But lately...? Lately, she was beginning to have serious doubts. Beginning to find excuses – it was Alan's fault, he had brought them down, down so far that they could never rise, at least not together. Alan had played the markets. He had lost all of their money, he had lost their lovely house, the car, everything. Black Wednesday they had called it. Black it had certainly been. What right had he to gamble everything in that way? He had been so sure. So sure. Then he went missing. She came home one night and he wasn't there. But he'd left a note on the fireplace. She had been frightened to open it in case it was a suicide note, but she should have known better, she realised that now. Alan? Suicide? Never! That took a kind of courage he simply didn't posses. It was when he returned that the other problem started. He wouldn't tell her where he had been or what he did. He just said that he had got drunk. But he had been gone for a whole week. Alan? Drunk for a week? A likely story. She'd the police out, everybody looking for him, and when he finally returned he said he couldn't remember a thing. If she ever found out for sure that it was then, while he was on his binge that he contracted that awful disease, she would kill him. She knew she would, and she knew how.

She wiped the steam from the mirror in front of her, its plastic frame rattling the door of the plastic cupboard it was mounted in. They had been planning to redecorate the bathroom this year, with the latest fittings and a new bath – one of those spa-baths that massage you as you soak – that wouldn't be happening now, not with Alan on social security payments. Redecorating in general had been put on hold, permanent hold. The plastic bathroom cabinet and everything else in the house would have to last for a lot more years. She swept her hair back with a heavy wooden handled brush, pulling it into a short bushy ponytail.

'To young, my dear,' she mumbled. Since they had taken up separate bedrooms she had adopted the bathroom mirror, it was a new friend that she spoke to daily. 'You may be a lot younger than him in there', she said to the tired face looking back at her, 'but don't forget you're the wrong side of forty.' She brushed her hair forward and down, back to the style she had been wearing for the last two months, the style that her new man preferred. Her new man... the thought buoyed her, the face in the mirror began to show some colour, the tiredness dropping from her brow, a tinge of glitter appearing in her green-grey eyes. She opened a small glass-stoppered jar and sniffed the fragrant contents. Inside the jar was a bouquet-garnet of herbs and dried wild flowers which had been crushed to a fine powder. She tipped a moderate measure of the powder into the palm of her hand and peeked around the bedroom door.

Alan was half dressed. The trousers of the shell suit he liked to wear for watching the television were deep green, with a stripe of tiny red crescents, one above the other, down the seam. Ann walked into the bedroom as he pulled his arms into the matching top. Her fist was clenched as if she was grasping something cherished. She shook her hand flamboyantly in the air in front of her, releasing her grip on the precious powder as she did so. It showered from her palm. She blew it out in a fine cloud that dusted the centre of the room. Immediately the air smelt of dried leaves and petals – Coltsfoot, Bitter Velch and Wild Celery.

'Ann!' Alan batted his hands at the translucent cloud of

powder and mumbled grumpily from the room. 'Stupid…' the only word she caught.

***

Eric looked up from his newspaper. 'It say's here that I need multivitamins. "Energin MV for the middle, middle-aged". Can you believe that? What's middle, middle-aged for Christ's sake? Why can't they just say fifty or fifty-plus or something? I don't know?" he added, and returned to the newspaper.

Norman stared vacantly out of the window, only half listening to his partner. He scratched the dark stubble on his chin. 'I've seen that advertised,' he replied rather vacantly, 'on the underground, on my way to the clinic.' He took half a step back from the window, further passage blocked by the edge of the bed, then slumped backwards, spreading his long thin frame across the duvet and announcing in a mystified voice, 'Homo! You never hear that word anymore. Do you?' his question was directed across the tiny bed-sit, to where Eric sat in a worn armchair.

'Pardon.'

'Homo. You don't here it used any more.'

'What's that got to do with multivitamins?'

'I'm not talking about your middle-aged ecstasy, I'm making a meaningful observation, you're supposed to come back with a meaningful response, even on Sunday mornings.'

Eric folded the newspaper into his lap. 'Hadn't really thought about it,' He replied wistfully. 'Why?'

'Well. I was thinking about hypocrisy.'

'What the oath. Doctors and all that?'

'No. Not Hippocratic. Silly old codger. *Hypocrisy*. The act. Being hypocritical.'

'Less of the old,' Eric replied indignantly, sweeping his thinning blond hair back off his face and rubbing his eyes sleepily. 'Anyway, I'm not with you.'

'It's just that it used to be the common word. Before gay became vogue. Of course it was a derogatory term, as was gay originally but now gay is accepted. Gay this, gay that, it's commonplace. In fact most people, embarrassed by our mere existence, seem to fall back with relief on the term gay They even regard the word homo as bad, like a swear word. Doesn't that strike you as hypocritical.'

35

'You're too intense Norman. Lighten up.' Eric rose from the chair and stepped to the dresser in the far corner of the room. He pulled down the front panel of the dresser to reveal a kettle and one saucepan on a double electric ring inside. He shook the kettle. Satisfied that it contained enough water, he turned on one ring. 'Tea or coffee?'

'Coffee. Thanks,' Norman replied, still ruminating on the sanctimony of the straight world.

Eric tipped level teaspoons of coffee into two mugs, but no sugar. They had both given up sugar and in fact this would be their only intake of caffeine for the day. 'If you want something to worry about my beautiful boy,' Eric said, 'then worry about where we're going to live in a couple of months time. The lease is up and we won't find another place as cheap as this again. I'll tell you, I'm fresh out of ideas.'

Norman gave Eric a reassuring smile. He held out his hand. 'Now who's an old worry-guts?' he said. 'It'll work out. You see if it doesn't. Something will turn up. It always does.' He took the mug of coffee that Eric offered, cupped it in both hands and sipped noisily

**

Stuart sniffed and cleared his nose. The large stately room smelt of mothballs, old and stale. Heavy, lined curtains were pulled across the windows, the only light coming from the hooded lamp on the floor next to him. Stuart changed the drill bit for a larger size, and began re-drilling the four holes in the safe door, slowly boring out the hard steel. This was the fourth drill he had used – a 6mm, an 8mm, a 10mm and now the final 12mm hole. There were three more holes to finish. Each had consumed the same number of drill bits. The drill ground at its slowest speed. Slow speed reduced the noise level considerably and posed no anxiety for Stuart who was an extremely patient human being. He hummed the theme tune from 'MASH', as he ground out the first two holes, then switched to 'Lara's theme' from 'Doctor Zhivago' for the last two. On the floor beside him sat a small, ornately decorated wooden box. The lid of the box was inlaid with polished soapstone and, like the rest of the box, was made of camphor-wood. It had that camphor-oil smell that always reminded him of his holiday in Kashmir. That had been many years ago, back in the days when you could go to that northern Indian state in safety. He had bought the box from the boat-boy who had acted as both his guide and his cook on his rented houseboat. The boat-boy had charged him twenty dollars for the box, probably two or three times the real price but it had been worth it. Since owning the box, he hadn't had any bad luck, not a single moment of concern in his professional or private life – except the incident with the Rottweiler and of course love.

He opened the box, revealing four glass phials, each set perfectly into a cushion of velvet covered foam sponge. Gently he measured one of the phials into the first 12mm hole. A perfect fit. He secured the phial with putty and repeated the exercise on the remaining three holes. Satisfied with his work he broke into 'Raindrops keep falling on my head' and connected the detonators.

He tapped the lid of the camphor-wood box for luck, reflecting as he did so that his earlier thoughts had been misplaced. Love hadn't been a problem, he'd divorced, that's all. Not badly. Not with both parties kicking and screaming while the lawyers rubbed their hands with glee and counted the zeros on the cash register. No.. Theirs had been an amicable divorce. An amicable marriage which had lasted ten years; six very good years, three uneventful years with the last one more distant than acrimonious. And they were still friends. So then, the only black spot had been the Rottweiler, he thought as he tried to switch to 'The Sting' but couldn't get it right.

The explosion, muffled by the two mattresses placed against the safe door, was relatively soft and certainly inaudible outside of the walls of the old house. Stuart pulled the burnt mattresses away from the safe and tugged at the twisted door with a thick wad of cloth. The hot metal gave way and the door fell forward, off its hinges.

This was always the best bit. The bit where the adrenaline flowed fastest. What would he find? He was expecting a good selection of jewellery, perhaps some cash and a few bonds and that's exactly what he found. He broke into 'All I want for Christmas' and began examining his haul. Two strings of pearls, at a couple of thousand a string he assessed. A good Cameo broach but not very valuable. Matching pairs of his-and-her Rolex and Cartier watches. A tray of rings in gold and stones. A bundle of bonds, all neatly wrapped in a yellow ribbon, and a thick pile of cash. He would count that later, when he got home. Not bad for his last day's work he mused.

This was going to be his last time, yet despite the satisfaction he felt from yet another perfectly executed, professional job, the jewellery and the bonds weren't much of a Swan song. But he'd been thinking of retiring for a while and knew that scaling walls, traversing roofs and climbing through windows had to stop; he'd been doing it since he was a teenager, almost two decades before. The near disaster of three weeks before had brought the point graphically home.

He'd broken into the penthouse with little difficulty and had blown the old safe just as easily. But had been totally unprepared for the Rottweiler. How people could keep a dog that size in an apartment was beyond Stuart's comprehension, but it was there. The stupid dog hadn't been concerned at all when Stuart broke into the apartment. It hadn't barked, and it must have loved the muffled noise of the drill – certainly hadn't attacked him. In fact Stuart had been totally unaware of the dog's presence. That is until the explosion. The safe had been cleverly concealed, built into the front panel of a large old oak desk and anchored to the floor. The dog was asleep behind the desk. Even while he'd been drilling the safe out, the dog hadn't moved, hadn't so much as growled. Then he'd set the charges and blown the door. That woke the brute up. Stuart had taken it as a sign. Stuart took everything as some sort of sign or omen, and manic Rottweilers woken from the sleep of the dead by the combined explosions of four phials of nitro glycerine was a sign if ever he had seen one. He had decided to retire.

In reality, he had been thinking of retirement for a while. He had a fair bit put aside and quite fancied a quiet little place in the country, Sussex or Hampshire seemed nice. He had made meticulous plans, set up a new identity, new passport, National Insurance number; nothing was impossible if you knew the right people and had enough money. Plastic surgery was the part he wasn't looking forward to. At least he called it plastic surgery. It was only a nose job. Simple really, he kept telling himself. As a youngster Stuart had been an amateur boxer, nothing serious, but enough to get his nose broken a couple of times. As a result, his nose was both his least redeeming feature and his most recognisable. A friend of his, Darren, had also been a boxer in his younger days and, like Stuart, his nose had been badly flattened. Flattened all over his face. But recently he'd had a nose job done. The first time Stuart saw him, after the operation, he couldn't believe the difference in his appearance. He just didn't look like the same person. His build, the colour of his hair, nothing had changed, but Darren's appearance had changed completely. Only the eyes remained the same. Stuart wore contact lenses, so if he wanted to he could change the eyes as well. Stuart was sold. He would have the same done to his nose, change his appearance, take a new identity and vanish from the face of the earth. He would retire in style, incognito. Go somewhere where no one knew him.

***

Maureen hung her head in despair. 'Reggie darling. Please?' Frustration streaked her face as she tried to push the inert form of her husband backwards into the cramped rear seat of their hatchback. She began to get angry, very angry. 'Reggie! Get your damned legs into the back. Why do you have to do this every time? I mean every time! It's Sunday. Couldn't you take at least one night off?' Reggie gurgled something unintelligible at her. His feet slipped forwards, out of the car, draped loosely from the knee towards the kerb-side. She kicked him sharply across his shins. 'Drunken sot!' she hissed through clenched teeth. She gripped his legs again but she couldn't budge him. 'That's it,' she announced angrily and almost in tears. 'I've had enough. If you don't help me I'm getting a taxi. You can just rot here alone all night.' She kicked him across the shins, gripped his ankles and pushed once more. Reggie groaned again. Maureen rubbed the spot on his shins were she'd kicked him. 'Please Darling,' she repeated.

Although she was young and healthy, she was only five feet tall and rather slight of build. Reggie, in his present state, was almost too much for her. She pushed Reggie's shoulders round, so that he was facing across the car then gave one last heave, using the belt in his trousers as leverage. Reggie slipped forward. His face scraped across the worn fabric of the seat, allowing his torso deeper into the back and his legs to be finally bent across the rusty door seal. Maureen slammed the door shut with relief then climbed into the driver's seat. She sat for a moment, regaining her breath, looking at the shambles she'd married, his face buried beneath his arched back, his legs twisted at an almost impossible angle beneath him and his rear thrust ostrich-like into the air. She fumbled in her handbag for the car keys, slipped them into the ignition and turned them sharply. The old car responded sluggishly, coughing deeply but eventually gurgling into life. Maureen breathed a sigh of relief. She looked back at her husband's bundled form, sighed, then engaged gear and pulled away.

She drove slowly and carefully. It was late, after midnight, and a full twenty miles to their tiny two-bedroom semi. The last thing she wanted was for the police to pull her over with Reggie in that condition. It had happened once before, and what a disaster it had been. That night she had managed to get him into the front seat and belted in; it had seemed the right thing to do, but turned out to be a stupid mistake. Reggie hadn't been totally gone, completely comatose like tonight. He had woken up and his arms had been everywhere. Covering his eyes against on-coming lights, waving fists at imaginary adversaries, shouting directions. Eventually his right arm had caught her across the nose, drawing blood, making her swerve badly and brake hard. Of course this had happened in front of a parked police patrol car. Maureen had been fined ninety-five pounds for reckless driving and the police had wanted to book Reggie with a charge of drunk and disorderly. As it turned out, this had been impossible to do as Reggie was deemed to be in the confines of his own car. A technicality that Maureen didn't understand and deeply regretted; a few nights in a cell might have done Reggie the world of good. Sorted him out a bit.

Her thoughts drifted to sorting him out, as they always did. She had made a decision. He had forced her to it but the decision frightened her. She would go through with it though. She knew she would, that she had to. He had to have help, more help than she was capable of giving. He had refused to go to alcoholics anonymous, refused help from whatever quarter. But once the house was sold, once they had nowhere to live, once they were broke with no money for the drink he so desperately needed, then he would have to do as he was told. She would hold all the cards. Maureen held that thought. If only it worked out, she would hold all the cards.

The rehabilitation centre had assured her that six to nine months would be enough. At three thousand a month she had no choice; the house had to go. She would go to live with her mother. Reggie couldn't follow her there. Her mother wouldn't let him in and he knew it. He knew how much her mother hated him, blamed him. But that wasn't fair. It was true that Reggie had been driving, and he'd had a drink, but only the legal limit. Not like now. They had all been wearing their seat belts, even little David in the back. Reggie hadn't jumped the lights, the other guy had. It hadn't been Reggie's fault at all. But that's where her mother and Reggie were so similar. Neither could handle David's death. Reggie had turned to the bottle, blaming himself for not taking evasive action; as if there was any that could be taken in the centre of a crossroads. Her mother had blamed Reggie for the death of six year old David, her only grandson, simply because she had to blame someone and the driver of the other car was a stranger, distant and somehow beyond her direct hatred, plus he was sober. In short they had both broken down to a point of no return and utter disregard for common sense or reason.

She glanced at her face in the rear view mirror, round, framed with a curve of light-brown hair and with a turned up snub of a nose that lent a cute, whispish air. It was a pretty face that had always belied her age. But not any more. The stress of David's death and the pressure Reggie's illness brought to bear had started to line the smoothness of her skin. She was ageing before her time. She knew that she couldn't go on like this any longer.

Chapter 4

Marios Branchman placed the high-powered rifle at an angle against the wall. He knelt beside it and flicked the quick release beneath the telescopic sight. He clasped the slender matt-black stem of the scope with his left hand and twisted, releasing the scope from the barrel, then lifted the scope to his eye and balanced it in both hands. Cautiously he looked over the rim of the windowsill. The telescopic sight magnified at 12 x 12. 'Little beauty,' he murmured softly to himself. 'From this distance I could pick out a zit on a flea's arse.' He swept the telescopic sight in a slow arc, being careful not to let the end of the sight drift over the edge of the windowsill, and scanned the pandemonium in front of him.

'Beelzebub!' He congratulated himself.

Barnes slid his not inconsiderable bulk off of his charge. Beneath him, the senator spluttered weakly, his life ebbing away onto the cold, stone flagged sidewalk in a growing pool of blood that surrounded his head and saturated the elbows and cuffs of Barnes' designer suite jacket. A gaping hole pulsated in the senator's throat, oozing blood and bile – his lips trembled, vainly struggling to mouth words, small fleeting motions bubbling with pink froth. Then he gave one last gurgle as his entire muscular system relaxed. Fluid seeped from his lower body, soaking the knees of Barnes' designer-suit trousers. Barnes crawled away from the dead senator on his hands and knees then turned and sat on the cold flagstones beneath him. He rubbed his elbows and was about to rub his bruised knees but change his mind. 'Always knew he was full of shit,' he commented ruefully to no one in particular. In fact, only Barnes' boss, was there beside the body. The three other bodyguards and several of New York's finest, were otherwise engaged struggling to hold the burgeoning crowd of on-lookers at bay.

Barnes' boss took the senator's wrist.

'No pulse,' he announced unnecessarily. 'The bastard's gone.'

'Where did the shot come from?' Barnes inquired. He had taken a large white handkerchief from his pocket and was using it to wipe as much as possible of the senator's disgusting residue as possible from his knees.

'Half a block down. Third floor. You were facing the wrong

way but from my side you couldn't miss the flash. Must have used a frigging elephant gun – frigging Fourth of July!' He slid his hand under the senator, lifting the dead man's neck and shoulders from the ground to wrench free his jacket. He pulled the tail of the jacket over the senator's head, laying it across his face and gaping neck. 'The Secret Service boys have gone in after the guy,' he added dispassionately.

'Good luck to them,' Barnes replied. 'He'll be long gone.'

Marios spread the component parts of the partially dismantled rifle across the floor beneath the window. He pushed the aluminium stock a little further out to his left and flicked the trigger guard sideways, separating the last of the major components, then stepped back, considering the collage of high-tech metal and high tensile plastic before him. Satisfied with his arrangement he took one last look through the scope. One of the Secret Service men had reappeared from the building across and down the street. It was time to go. The synchronisation of his radio-controlled decoy had worked perfectly but there was no sense in pushing his luck. 'And besides,' he thought, looking at his watch, 'my flight leaves in two hours'.

***

Sidney Brinker brushed his plain dark blue tie flat against his shirt, adjusted the lapels of his hand-sewn suit and surveyed the scene through his office window. As he looked down the gentle rise of the old village common towards the expanse of the golf course and the fifteenth tee, he took a moment to reflect on the swing of the golfer teeing-up, then returned to his desk and the silver tray in front of him. He tapped the back of his hand against the silver teapot on the silver tray and felt the sharp sting of the hot tea through the shinning metal. He smiled in satisfaction then slowly poured a full cup of the deep tan liquid. He added a splash of milk, just as he liked it then took a biscuit from the plate next to the teapot and slowly dunked it halfway into the tea. Gently he bobbed the biscuit up and down three times before removing it – three, not four or five times. If you did that the biscuit would break and spoil the tea. He hated it when that happened. On the third dip he retrieved the biscuit, cupped his free hand under it, lifted it to his mouth and ran the softened portion across his tongue, separating that half neatly from the remaining hard portion. He licked a sheen of tea from his lips, then turned the biscuit through ninety degrees and repeated the process. He held the remaining quarter to his eye and admired it as one would a precious gem. There was a loud rap on the door. Sidney popped the remains of the biscuit into his mouth and crunched, irritated that his morning ritual had been so rudely disturbed.

'Yes,' he called, his voice edged with annoyance. 'Come in.'

'Sorry to bother you so early.' Ronald Briskin the other half of Brin, Brinker and Briskin, Solicitors – Brin, county squire, senior partner and founder of the firm had died three years earlier – stepped nervously into the dimly lit office. Briskin cast a guilty glance at the teacup in front of Brinker and the small, uneaten stack of biscuits on the china plate. 'The second Death Certificate has arrived,' he said. 'The doctor concurs with old Cornwall-Thompson. Natural causes. The old buffer was a bit eccentric, wasn't she?' he concluded ambiguously.

Brinker looked sternly across the top of his pince-nez at the younger man. Not for the first time he wondered at the sanity of old Brin, appointing him to the partnership. Of course he had to admit that fate had given Briskin good looks. Dark black hair, good build, tall and rakish. He also dressed well and was a real snapper with the female clients. Yes, he was good for public relations and company image, but Brinker thought him a complete and utter fool, a cretin of the first order. He also had a sneaking suspicion that he was not quite right, not quite cricket, not first order; these had been the terms he had used to express his doubts to his wife, which was about as far as his politeness would allow. Of course, Briskin was Brin's nephew and Brin's family still held the controlling interest in the partnership. He would have to suffer the young twerp. God save us from yuppies. Brinker kept the thought to himself. He took a deep breath and replied. 'She was afraid that they would try and do her in. She had become quite paranoid towards the end. The second doctor's opinion was to protect her from being buried alive.' He removed his glasses and glared at Briskin who in turn stared back vacantly. Brinker's patience snapped. 'To say she was old is a correct statement, I congratulate you on your awareness and acute powers of observation. But to say that she was an old buffer, graphically reconfirms my previously, minimal, assessment of your intelligence quotient, removing a further ten points, reducing you to the sub fifty moron bracket. Moreover, you're statement grossly misuses the English language. Then, to say that she was a bit – a bit! – eccentric, is to display an understanding of the situation which is absolutely singular in its misplacement and stupidity.'

Stunned by the fervour of old Brinker's onslaught Briskin fumbled for a reply. This hadn't been the first time that Brinker had dressed him down and Briskin suspected that it wouldn't be the last. In fact it all seemed a bit pointless to him. He hadn't wanted the job in the first place. The family had just pushed him into it – especially his mother, who was convinced that being a solicitor was simply a matter of wearing a dark suit and filing musty old papers. He would never make the grade in old Brinker's eyes, and he didn't care. Besides, he thought, my IQ's one fifty-eight, probably twice as much as yours. Rallied by the thought, he smiled inwardly but decided to say nothing at all. He just placed the paper he was carrying on Brinker's desk, then he beat a hasty but silent retreat, making a mental note as he did so never to disturb Brinker during his early morning tea again – ever.

Without a second glance at the document, Brinker took the Death Certificate and slid it inside a buff card-folder with the name 'Loewen' hand written in black ink on its face. He grunted with disdain. 'Clever old Rose. You weren't anywhere near as eccentric as you appeared,' he chuckled to himself quietly. 'With a family of roaches such as yours, you had real reason to fear.' Brinker returned to his tea and digestive biscuits, lifting the cup in silent salute to his recently deceased friend.

Brinker's secretary, Mary Little, looked up from her computer screen. 'I told you,' she said with that air of superiority she so loved to use on young Alex Briskin. 'You should have waited another fifteen minutes. Never underestimate the power of the digestive biscuit.' Briskin's face was pale, his general pallor flaccid. Serves him right, she thought gleefully. She really detested the spoilt pup, as she always referred to him. She resented his position as a full partner and the smooth actor's looks that made her feel physically sick, especially his style of charm that inexplicably attracted the younger girls.

'Wouldn't have made a jot of difference,' Briskin answered truculently. 'Old bastard hates me anyway. If I told him I had just signed up the Pope he'd just chew me out for anti-Semitism.'

'Language, Mr. Briskin,' Mary Little rebuked. 'Language. When you get back to your office you'll find a photocopy of an estate agents' flyer. Mr. Brinker wants you to read it and return to his office at ten forty-five. She returned to her computer screen, dismissing Briskin with her usual off-hand disinterest.

Briskin's office was large, wood-panelled, and rather grand in a cloistered sort of way. It was quite similar to Brinker's, very similar in fact; Briskin's position demanded that. But the view from the window was from the side of the building, down onto the narrow courtyard where the dustbins were stored. The amount of available floor space was severely curtailed by the slope of the underside of the staircase that ran up one wall and the indentation of the storage cupboard from the hallway, unlike Brinker's office which was large and square and spacious and looked out over the golf course. Dejected, Briskin flopped into his mock Chesterfield swivel chair, a personal touch that he was extremely fond of; he knew that its fake, leather upholstery annoyed the hell out of both Brinker, and that frustrated old prune Little. 'If only she could see what I've got!' He mouthed the words silently, then lifted his knees and spun the chair round twice.

'One debaucher... two debauchers,' he chanted with each revolution, in a rasping voice. He spoke aloud but not loud enough to carry to prying ears. He smiled fervently and glanced towards the painting of his great uncle Eustace that hung, resplendent, above the mock Adam's fireplace. Another proud fake that he had installed since the death of his bucolic uncle. Behind the old painting was an equally old, cast safe. Inside the safe was an envelope full of photographs. Briskin's smile broke into a malicious grin, then a grimace. Got to be careful, he thought, not for the first time. Got to get the timing right. He looked distastefully at the brown envelope lying on the desk in front of him, the one Mary Little had placed there earlier. 'Back to work,' he sighed.

The envelope was sealed by a fine white string that had been twisted furiously between two pressed studs. Inside the envelope was a thick document. He counted the pages. Twelve. The first page carried a colour photograph of a building, a very large, grand building, a mansion house. The full-page photograph was of the building's front elevation. He stared at the Victorian façade complete with its four column central pediment and brace of six canted bay windows to either side. Each window was identical to its neighbour and precisely placed to be exactly equidistant and prismatic in its appearance.

'Ugh!' Briskin hated period houses. He had been brought up in one, a lot smaller than this, but identical in style and character to the picture in front of him. It reminded him of loneliness and separation. It reminded him of parents that were never there – at least not for him. It reminded him of an endless series of nannies who seemed to have one singular common denominator; the good ones, the ones he liked, never seemed to stay for very long. The others seemed to be there forever. Briskin shivered and turned the page.

The second page was full of text, under the general heading of 'Southgrim Manor'. The name rang a small bell but not enough for recognition. He read on.

Historic period property. The family seat of the Loewen family. Built 1841-1843 by Sir Archibald Bluit of Downpaddocks Wiltshire (designer of the west wing Southchester Cathedral, advocate and patron of the Dimsdale philanthropic housing programme, 1862).

Briskin read on with renewed interest. Of course he remembered the house. He had been there on at least three occasions as a boy. Loewen. He knew that name very well. The Loewens had been with Brin, Brinker and Briskin forever, almost since the partnership started, and it had been Rose Loewen's second Death Certificate that had caused such animosity earlier.

The remainder of the page summarised the details of the manor house. Eighteen bedrooms. Twelve bathrooms. Four receptions. Library, billiards and music rooms. Kitchens. Cellars. Servant's quarters. Seven acres of woods and gardens that included a small lake, separate Japanese and Rose gardens, and an enclosed swimming pool with attached steam room, both of which had been added twenty years before and, according to the paper in front of him, had been maintained to the highest order.

Briskin's slender, manicured fingers flicked through the pages as he quickly read through the details listed for each room – they covered the next eight pages, including a full inventory of the building's contents. The mansion was a masterpiece, a meticulously detailed museum to the Loewen family. Rare Chinese porcelain, Persian rugs, grisly animal heads hunted on long forgotten safaris in the wilds of Tanganyika and the Congo. The paintings were endless and there was even a genuine Adam's fireplace alongside the Steinbeck in the Music room. The details nauseated Briskin.

The next four pages contained diagrams, which were obviously related to the manor house. Briskin rotated the first diagram, trying unsuccessfully to orientate it to the main building. He separated the four drawings and laid them on the desk in front of him. Realisation dawned slowly. He moved the first drawing next to the third then the second below the first. 'No!' he exclaimed aloud, slapping the palm of his hand hard onto the desktop. 'No. It can't be. Who would allow it? Who?' Briskin drew a deep breath and held it, calming the sudden rush of adrenaline that threatened to lift him bodily from his seat. All recollection of his original reaction to the outside of the house vanished. This… these, designs on the desk in front of him, made his sort of house, the sort of house that he knew he was made for. What he wouldn't give to live in a place like that. This was a scheme with more irony than he had imagined possible. She wasn't such an old buffer after all, he thought ruefully. A trample of heavily shod feet rumbled up inside the staircase that invaded his room, breaking his thoughts and making him curse. Perhaps it was time to pull the plug on old Brinker. Move him out. Take his nice big quiet office with its golf club views. Let the lady out of the box.

***

For the second time in three days the entire family were together, again with the notable exception of Lisa. They sat in a semi-circle around a polished wooden coffee table that separated them from Brinker's desk. On the coffee table lay seven envelopes, each identical to the one Briskin had opened and read earlier.

Frederick Loewen's reaction to the diagrams he found in his envelope was very similar in its duration and pace to Briskin's, although with an entirely different conclusion. Frederick had taken the envelope Brinker's secretary handed to each of them, with considerable trepidation. He knew his half sister well and fully expected that she would try to cheat him, even from the grave. But he was ready for her. He already had his own lawyers standing by and fully primed. She wouldn't get the last word, not so long as he was around.

Beside him, Lia was studying her picture of the house intently. 'It's just like Aunt Rose's,' she exclaimed. Christian sighed, embarrassed by his wife's foolishness. None of the others took any notice.

Thaddeus was the first to object. He tossed his envelope across Brinker's desk angrily. 'What's all this rubbish, Brinker? I warn you. If that vindictive old crone has been playing games, she won't get away with it. We're ready for her. We're not going to let her cheat us out of what is rightfully ours. And we're ready for you too,' he added menacingly.

Brinker gave him the same look he had given young Briskin

earlier. 'Thaddeus,' he replied evenly. 'I know you all, each and every one of you, most of you for longer than I care to remember or would want to remember for that matter.' Frederick, Thaddeus and Charles bristled at the snipe. Christian, Helen and Elsbeth just smiled. Lia looked at her husband quizzically, and was about to ask him what she had missed. He reached across and squeezed her hand tightly. She recognised the look he flashed and the question froze on her lips.

'And what are all these diagrams?' Thaddeus continued. 'Looks like she intended to divide the place up into flats.'

'Apartments actually. Self-contained modules. Ultra modern. Three bedrooms, one-and-half bathrooms, lounge, dining room and a modular kitchen in each,' Brinker replied in a level tone.

'In each what?' asked Christian, finding his voice for the first time since the initial etchings of realisation had begun to dawn on him. If Aunt Rose has bequeathed this madness we'll have to move fast to get a restraining order or whatever we need to do to stop the builders moving in. The thought sent shivers of panic down his spine. He knew how resourceful his aunt could be. After all, she had managed to stay ahead of his Father and Uncle Thaddeus throughout their entire lives, something he considered to be no mean achievement at all.

'What's modular?' Lia asked, totally mystified but desperately wanting to make some contribution to the proceedings.

Helen rounded on her sharply, throwing an exasperated look at Christian as she did so. 'It means chipboard and Formica, stupid.'

'You can't talk to me…' Lia ruffled.

'Apartment,' Brinker interrupted decisively, ignoring the exchange between Lia and Helen, answering Christian's original question. He lifted a single sheet of paper from his desk. 'I have in front of me an agenda. It is dated twenty-eighth of March last year and was attached to a letter of instruction from Rose Loewen. She chose to use her maiden name and had in fact filed to change her name back to Loewen by deed pole. Unfortunately that process was still incomplete at the time of her death and…'

'Agenda for what?' Helen interrupted.

'For today,' Brinker snapped. 'For this meeting.'

'Get on with it then,' chorused Thaddeus and Frederick.

Brinker gave them both a withering look, which they returned with equal passion. 'It's a simple list of five items, as follows. Number one, pass each of my beneficiaries the envelopes addressed to them. This I have done, with the exception of Miss Lisa. Rose warned me that she didn't expect Miss Lisa to be here today, but that I was to continue anyway.'

Lia's mood changed abruptly. She grinned at Brinker excitedly. She understood the word beneficiaries, it meant money and it was the only word she had really digested so far.

Brinker continued. 'Two. Read my last Will and Testament, dated April 17th 1997 and duly witnessed by, Mr. Sidney Ambrose Brinker attorney at law, Ms Marry Little, and the Right Honourable Norman Hewlett-Temple MP.'

'Crafty cow!' Elsbeth whispered under her breath. Hewlett-Temple was the local golden boy. He had served for years as a local justice of the peace, he had stood for parliament and after a brief spell as a junior member of the cabinet had risen to the dizzy heights of foreign secretary at the last reshuffle. Brinker caught the response and hesitated but refrained from looking up.

'Three,' he resumed. 'Explain the terms and conditions of the lottery. Four. Explain the terms and legal tender of the Rose Loewen Trust, and five – and a rather nice gesture I thought – serve seven strong coffees and brandies.' Brinker placed the agenda carefully back onto his desk and looked at each of them in turn, wondering who would be the first to react. He didn't have long to wait.

'What lottery?' Thaddeus demanded.

'What trust fund?' asked Elsbeth.

Christian, Charles and Helen just stared at each other. Frederick's eyes glazed a little, a deep thoughtful frown creasing the wrinkles on his brow.

'I'd like a coffee. Thank you,' added Lia.

Brinker ignored them all. 'I'll go straight to the terms of the Will... I'm certain that you are all anxious to hear who benefits,' he added. 'And please, please! Do me the courtesy of not interrupting until I have finished reading.'

All seven Loewen's looked at each other and then at Brinker. Frederick nodded curtly and the others followed suite.

Brinker took a deep breath then started to read. 'I Rose Alexandra Morgan – nee Loewen – hereby state my last will and testament...' Brinker read through the legalese of 'witnessed by' and 'hereby state', enjoying every protracted moment. It wasn't until now that he really came to realise just how much he despised them all. Oh Rose you darling! I can't wait until I get to the lottery part. The thought buoyed him. He finally reached the bequeathments. 'To my Goddaughter Lisa Loewen I bequeath two hundred thousand pounds, to be used entirely at her discretion – I know she will use it wisely.'

Frederick's frown deepened. It wasn't enough. He had expected Rose to leave her favourite more. Much more.

'To my nephew Charles Loewen I leave my father's entire collection of Chinese porcelain. Despite the contempt that I hold Charles in, I feel certain that his vanity will prevent him selling the finer pieces and that in a rather perverse way they will have gone to a good home. To Charles' mendacious wife Helen I leave the desk from my private study. I am sure that she will find it, as I did preparing the lottery trust and this Will, a solid base to hatch future plans. To Christian Loewen I leave the cars. They have considerable value, but I do hope he has the decency to keep the Lagonda. For his wife Lia I leave my diaries. There are thirty-six volumes covering three quarters of a century. I have left them for Lia as she is the only one of you that will be able to read them with an open mind – it is truly her best and only asset. That leaves the elder Loewen's. I see little point in leaving a great deal to you, not that I've left a great deal to the younger ones, at least not in the material sense. To Elsbeth I bequeath the Mayslip-pearls, the three diamond cluster broaches, the lion's head signet ring and the gold and sapphire necklace that Grandma Octavia wore at her wedding. All of this jewellery belonged at one stage to our Grandmother and as the only surviving female of our generation; I feel that she has a right to it. For Thaddeus and Frederick I had great difficulty selecting anything at all. Neither has given a single thing of any value to me throughout my entire life, including love, affection or support, and neither deserves to be rewarded for their disaffection. However, after considerable deliberation I have decided to leave to their responsibility, the entire contents of my estate, excluding the bequests listed above.'

Thaddeus clapped his hands loudly. Frederick gaped in total amazement. The house and grounds, the furniture, the rugs, the tapestries, the paintings, the remaining jewellery… the list was endless. The old girl really must have gone off her trolley towards the end, he thought. The frown had vanished from his forehead completely.

'That's not fair!' interrupted Elsbeth, unable to contain herself. 'I get a few measly trinkets that she freely admits were mine anyway, and you two receive a small fortune each.' She struggled from her chair, turning towards Frederick. 'Especially you Freddie. She hated you with a passion. Why?'

As if on cue they all began talking at once.

'Please, Ladies and Gentlemen, please.' Brinker had stood and was leaning pointedly across his desk. 'Miss Elsbeth, please sit down. I haven't finished yet... not by a long way.'

There was something about the way that he spoke. A chill level of sarcasm that sliced cleanly through the uproar. Elsbeth sat. The frown on Frederick's forehead returned and Lia looked to her husband for explanation.

Brinker sat, picked up the Will and brandished it across the desk at no one in particular, or all of them in particular, depending on each person's viewpoint. 'Your heedless interruption was totally misplaced and completely misleading. I will continue,' he bristled indignantly, returning to the text in front of him. 'I have decided to leave to their responsibility, the entire contents of my estate, excluding the bequests listed above,' he repeated. 'They are to sell each and every item and will be allowed to keep one quarter of the proceeds to be shared equally between them. The remaining three-quarters I bequeath to the Rose Loewen Trust.' Brinker placed the Will squarely on the desk and sat back. Now for the good bit, he thought mischievously. A quiet grin eased from the corners of his mouth and slowly spread into a broad smile.

Frederick's frown deepened again. He knew of Brinker's feelings towards them, they'd been made quite plain to all of them today and Frederick couldn't remember the last time he'd seen Brinker smile or even grin. The other six had started to argue again. He held up a gnarled hand. 'Silence!' he demanded, glaring at each of them in turn. Lia giggled, Frederick always made her laugh when he got angry. It was the mole beneath his left eye, it twitched at right angles. As his eyelid lifted up and down the mole slipped in perfect unison to the left on the up stroke and the right on the down. It had fascinated Lia since the first day she had been introduce to her father-in-law. It did not have a similar effect on the others.

Frederick had always been the strongest, the leader and the meanest. 'Listen to me,' he continued. 'Look at that smile.' He pointed towards the lawyer. 'When did you last see him smile at all, let alone like that. Something is not right. Not right at all.'

They stopped their bickering, looking alternately between Frederick and Brinker.

'What's the catch? There has to be a catch. I mean, apart form the three quarters bit; but we can contest that, she obviously wasn't of sound mind when she made that one up. And what's all this lottery and trust rubbish? Is there more to the Will? Is she trying to set up a Trust with our inheritance? Come on. Out with it man!' Frederick challenged, his horsewhipping tone not affected but straight from the hip.

Pointedly, Brinker relaxed further into his chair. 'There is no catch. None at all,' he replied, curtailing a smirk. Each of the bequests is genuine and perfectly within Ms Morgan's right to leave. If I may return to the agenda laid down at the beginning of this engagement?' He paused to allow them to settle. He certainly had their attention now, he mused. He took a second sheet of paper from the desk. 'The lottery will be divided into six equal sections, each section consisting of one hundred tickets and each ticket costing one thousand pounds.'

Six hundred thousand. The thought made Frederick squirm in his seat. This was more like Rose, but he liked the sound of it even less than the sound of the Will.

'There will be three draws in total, the first two will take place on the 1st and 15th of the second month following my death. This will be July,' Brinker interrupted himself. 'The first draw will reduce the tickets from six hundred to sixty tickets and the second from sixty to twelve. The final draw will be on the 1st of the following month, at precisely midday. At this point, six of the tickets from those remaining from the previous two rounds, will be drawn as the eventual winners. Each of the draws will be made in-camera, in the library of Loewen House, and under the adjudication of the Right Honourable Norman Hewlett-Temple MP – a guest list is attached. The results of the first two draws will be published in late editions of the local and national evening press on the same day. For the final draw the twelve final ticket holders may be present if they choose and be accompanied by a friend or relative, but no press or media will be allowed into the draw. Each of the six winners will be handed keys, deeds and a leasehold contract for signature. They may take possession immediately conversion works are completed.' Brinker looked up from the paper and everyone tried to speak at once.

'Possession of what?' Helen asked.

'Six? What conversions?' echoed her Husband.

'Can she hold a lottery? Don't you need a licence or

something?' Elsbeth queried suspiciously.

Thaddeus waved her down. 'Of course you don't need a licence.'

Charles disagreed. 'But you must do. Mustn't you Christian? You're the bureaucrat. You must know.'

Christian shook his head and turned to his father for support. The frown on Frederick's brow had grafted itself into a deep furrow. 'Silence', he called for the second time in ten minutes. His voice was raised and agitated. 'Listen you fools! Listen to what the man's reading. Don't you see? Haven't any of you realised what this is all about?'

'I know.' Lia smiled happily. 'It's the house. Aunt Rose is playing housy-housy.' Frederick's mole almost did a polka, but Lia's giggle was cut short by his response.

'Precisely,' Frederick agreed.

Lia gaped, shocked to have someone actually agree with her. Usually they either ignored her or scoffed. Apart from Brinker, Lia was the only one enjoying the day so far. She couldn't wait to read Aunt Rose's diaries and now Frederick was paying her compliments.

'She intends us to sell off the house.' As he struggled to control his anger, Frederick almost lost command of the words he spoke. 'She expects us to sell the house, all the contents and then leave seventy five percent to this cock-a-maimy trust she's set up.'

Thaddeus was the first to respond. 'Like hell we will! She's not giving away a million or more of my money. Oh no!' Thaddeus turned to Christian, his short-temper soaring to the surface. 'You've done the figures, Christian. What's the bottom line here?'

Christian produced a small leather bound notebook and read from the first page. 'The house and grounds are worth well over ten million, but finding a buyer with that amount of money could take forever. If we really wanted to sell, and quickly, then it should go for between seven and seven and a half million. Then there are the paintings, another one point three million. The furniture, ornaments, rugs etc., should fetch around six hundred thousand. So, leaving out the Chinese porcelain, I'm not sure about that…

'We'll see about that later,' interrupted Elsbeth and Thaddeus respectively.

Brinker said nothing. He would allow them to let off a little steam before he delivered the punch line.

'As I was saying, leaving out the Chinese porcelain,' Christian continued pointedly, 'should result in net proceeds of between eight point nine and nine point five million – let's say approximately six million less taxes and duties of course.'

Frederick huffed at Christian's last comment. He had even less time for the tax man than he did for his late sister, and he didn't intend to let too much of that six million slip through his fingers to the government or anyone else for that matter – including family.

Helen nudged Charles in the ribs. 'Don't just sit there. Say something!'

'Yes. It's not fair,' Charles responded lamely, his eyes averted from the gaze of both his father and uncle.

'That's right,' Helen added. 'Six million and it's not fair that just you two should share it. Is it auntie?' She questioned Elsbeth directly, looking for the support her husband denied her, assuming that Frederick and Thaddeus would contest and eventually share the full amount and not the quarter bequeathed to them in the Will.

Christian held up a hand. 'Excuse me,' he said, in his usual flat unruffled monotone. 'I think there may be more. Mr. Brinker still has that smile on his face father and he hasn't completed Aunt Rose's agenda yet. Have you Mr Brinker?'

'No,' Brinker replied. The grin across his face was starting to ache now. They where right about one thing, he couldn't remember the last time he had smiled so much and for so long. 'If I can just have your attention for a few moments longer.' He pressed a button on his telephone, lifted the handset and spoke into it. 'Mrs Little, could we have that coffee and brandy now? Thank you.' Brinker replaced the handset and paused, allowing the tension to build a little and their full attention to return to him. Again Frederick nodded and the rest followed suit.

'The trust was set up by Ms Morgan three years ago, with an endowment of just over one million sterling – one million, three hundred thousand, nine hundred and fifty seven pounds thirty two pence, to be precise.'

Frederick, Thaddeus, Elsbeth, Christian, Charles and Helen looked at each other.

Lia said, 'That's a lot. Isn't it?'

'Before you ask,' Brinker edged in quickly. 'That was the entire amount of cash then to hand, plus six hundred thousand pounds that she raised in mortgage from the bank. Ms Morgan literally put all her money into the trust, down to the last penny.'

'The cantankerous old bitch,' Frederick sputtered, his face

livid with anger. 'She's done for us. How can I...? If the bank has its fingers...?' Anger and frustration surged within him as the full extent of Rose's strategy opened before him. He was lost for words, and both sentences remained incomplete.

Brinker's gaze panned over them, as through he was looking at someone else at the back of the room. 'It is my opinion, for what it is worth,' he added thoughtfully,' that Ms Morgan's action's were directly made to preserve Southgrim Manor in, or as near too, its original glory, in perpetuity. To that end she has instructed that the residence is to be divided into leasehold apartments, and modernised internally. I must add that one of the conditions of the trust is that the external facade be maintained as originally built. She has, by nature of the trust and fund established, ensured both legal and financial security for the house on a very long-term basis. She has also effectively ensured the continued tenure of the Loewen family seat, while eliminating both the potential disruption of a Loewen household or – her worst nightmare – that you would all agree to sell off the house. A ninety-nine year lease will ensure that at least three generations of Loewens will come and go before the house passes back into family hands. A remarkable lady. Quite remarkable.' Brinker nodded, then switched his gaze back to the family in front of him.

They had been staring directly at him but then, as usual, turned to Frederick. They were lost for comment, confused by Frederick's totally unnatural display of defeat. Elsbeth broke the silence. 'But how did she live? Food, the house, all those medical bills? She asked, clearly mystified.

'Ah. Yes. I almost forgot that,' Brinker replied. 'Just a little more patience, please.'

With a soft knock on the door, Mary Little entered the room carrying a bottle of cognac and eight crystal glasses on a large tray. Behind her followed one of the office juniors similarly laden with a tray full of steaming coffee cups. Mary placed her tray on the near end of Brinker's desk; the junior placed his on the coffee table in front of the family.

'A very good question indeed, and one that I am pleased to answer,' Brinker responded, 'as it dovetails neatly into the situation at hand. One of the Trusts prime directives concerned Ms Morgan's welfare. That is, food, staff, her day-to-day expenses, running cars, entertaining; everything she required would be paid by direct invoice to the Trust. Sadly, the final costs placed on the Trust for

Ms Morgan were the medical expenses you referred to Elsbeth.'

Elsbeth gave him an I-told-you-so smirk.

Brinker continued. 'Now, before you get carried away with your assessment of the value of Ms Morgan's Estate, there is one more vital piece of information. I must advise you all that although the contents of the house remained inside the Estate's assets, the house and grounds were gifted to the trust immediately after cash payment had been made.' Brinker sensed the instant of shock his statement induced in his audience. He got to his feet and put up both hands to quieten the first wave of protest, adding quickly, 'The Trust is to be administered by a governor. A person appointed by Ms Morgan at the inception of the Trust. Miss Lisa Going, daughter of Margaret Going – nee Loewen. ' He sat, exhausted by his delivery. 'Who would like coffee and who would like brandy, or both?' he inquired, totally ignoring the tirade that had broken out in front of him.

***

The Ouija board in front of Maureen and her mother, Diane, was antique, an original 1902 William Fuld. Yet as old as it was, its rich, golden coloured bird's-eye maple veneer still glistened as though it were brand new. Maureen and Diane sat hunched over the ancient board, Maureen's slim unfettered fingers in stark contrast to Diane's heavier, bejewelled extremities. Their middle fingers barely touched the planchette as it whizzed across the board, picking off, in rapid succession, the numbers from the line across the bottom, and the characters from the two arcs of letters above. The top corners of the board carried the words YES, to the left side and NO, to the right. The planchette was also a collector's item but not antique. It was a standard Heskelite from the mid-forties with the classic withered witch's finger as its pointer.

Maureen held her breath. She could feel her mother opposite her, her equable frame tensed, the cheeks of her round, jovial face flushed in a similar heightened state of anticipation. 'Are you sure?' Maureen asked hesitantly.

The witches' finger didn't hesitate. It flashed to the word YES. Then, just as abruptly and slightly rudely, switched to the letters G and B 'Good-Bye'. Both Maureen and Diane exhaled, their fingers still firmly on the now dead planchette and board. Diane glanced at her daughter's face, raised to the ceiling, drained, her eyes inflamed and slightly distended; a look that her mother mistook for exhaustion.

'He certainly likes you,' Diane said, breaking the tension that had hung, shroud-like and tangible, dominating the room only a second before. 'In all my years as a medium I've never met one so determined to help, so persistent. I don't understand it?' she added as a question that Maureen, her head still raised silently towards the ceiling, completely ignored.

Diane stood from the table, shaking her head, and walked to the window. She opened the heavy curtains with more force than was necessary. Her annoyance at her daughter's persistent refusal to confide in her showed, openly. Light flooded into the room from a brace of double-glazed patio doors, the outline of Diane's flowing kaftan in silhouette against the neat, trimmed herbaceous-bordered lawn and garden on the far side of the glass.

'You can't tell me that there's not a connection, and it has to be from your past.' She gave her daughter that same annoyed but knowing look she had been using since Simon had first visited them six weeks before.

'I've told you mum. I don't know who it is.'

'Rubbish! I wasn't born yesterday. It isn't unusual at all for a spirit to seek someone out, in fact it was quite normal, but not with the determination that this one displays. Not unless there's a very, very strong connection and an equally strong reason.'

'I've told you mum. I don't know who it is.'

'You sound like a stuck record,' Diane replied.

'Mum. I don't know.'

'I'll find out, young lady. I will.' Diane turned towards the door that led to the kitchen. 'I'll put the kettle on,' she added somewhat obtusely as she left the room.

A tear rolled slowly down Maureen's cheek, dropping from her chin to the breast of her yellow cotton blouse. She reached into the pocket of her jeans and pulled out a white handkerchief. She knew that her mother knew she was lying; she would have had to be deaf and blind not to notice. The thought stole through her mind like a cheap comedy routine 'I know she knows that I know she knows, but does she know that I know she knows I know?' But Diane must never be allowed to know the truth, it would simply be too much for her. She wouldn't be able to handle it. This was something that would be sure to come between them, in spite of their deep bond of love. The thought terrified Maureen. Life without mum would be totally unthinkable. Mum was the only comfort she had in life, what with Reggie and the bottle. No.. Simon had to remain a secret.

When he had died, Maureen had understandably assumed that was the end of her torment. But now he was back. Back from the grave. Haunting her through her mum, his presence getting stronger and more menacing with each sitting. The man had been a chauvinistic pig during his lifetime and, as soon as Maureen realised who he was, it puzzled her that he showed the sensitivity and presence of mind not to let his true identity slip out, in front of her mum. In fact, that unexpected trait had thrown Maureen at first. When he made first contact and identified himself as Simon, Maureen had been as misled as her mother had, and as curious. It was his insistence in talking only to her, and his abruptness each time her mother asked a question, that fanned the first strains of suspicion. Maureen then began to load the questions. Carefully of course. A few small enquiries about his habits, his likes and his dislikes, had enabled her to probe with questions that meant nothing to her mother; except to raise a curious eyebrow every now and then. By the third session Maureen knew. His exaggerated agnostic views had always made him unpopular. Maureen's final question had been about the religion, last rites to be precise. This had elicited the expected response, almost exactly word for word as she remembered him saying it to her, just before he died. It was a quotation 'there are no atheists in foxholes'. She had read it in a book when she was a young and impressionable teenager. He had laughed at her and called the quote gibberish. From then on he often quoted it, mocking her. She had always wondered if he was being cynical when he whispered it on his deathbed. Or perhaps?

During the last week Simon had started to visit Maureen directly, without the presence of her mother as medium. At first Maureen thought that she had suddenly received 'The Sight', which she found very exciting; she would love to have her mother's gift. But when she tried to open her mind, to speak to other spirits, nothing had happened, just emptiness. She tried several times but stopped after the last attempt, because he caught her doing it and rushed in with a force that was almost physical, almost tangible. She realised now that this was what he wanted. It was like the film she had seen – what was the title? She remembered only the horrible story – a widow who had been repeatedly raped by the devil. And the film was based on fact. How could she forget? She remembered the anguish the women had suffered when no one would believe her and that even when she was able to convince people that it was true, their pathetic attempts to help her had failed. The film ended with the women having to come to terms with the nightly visitations of the devil.

Maureen knew it had to be true because, that's what he had done to her when he was alive and now, wanted to do to her again, even after death. When he died, she thought she was finally free of him and that the torment had come to an end. But she was wrong, he was back. He wanted her again and he would have her. She knew she couldn't stop him.

'Tea.'

'Coming, Mum,' she answered, relieved at the cosy normality of the word.

***

Another new experience…

I suppose everything will be like that for a while, so much to discover. But this experience was different. It left me a little breathless. It wasn't just another New Experience. No… It was quite unlike anything else so far. This one has left me with a rather bewildered and uneasy feeling. I'll try to explain, but first of all you will have to consider Time. What I mean is that I hadn't really given it much thought, at least not when I was alive but I now know that time is totally different when you're dead. Since my death I haven't felt the need to sleep at all and I really haven't been conscious of night or day or time. There are no meals to tell the time by, no daily ritual; I've simply lost my body clock. Everything that happens now is just an event, or to be more precise, a continuous series of events. For instance, on that first day, when Freddie led the family into the library, I followed. When they had all finished arguing and finally started to leave, I stayed with Freddie and Thaddeus. Then, when those two returned to Thaddeus' house, to hatch out their pathetic little scheme – a counter-move Freddie called it, pompous old fool – again I just followed. But followed is the wrong word.

I'm sorry but I'm just not explaining myself properly.

You see, one moment I was with them in the library – I had tired of making Freddie flinch with nasty bitter smells under his nose and had started experimenting with Thaddeus, I really enjoyed the cough and the sneeze, but the twitching moustache was the best – then they left, and I was with them when they reached Thaddeus' *house, but there was no in-between, <u>I was just there.</u> For me there was no travelling in-between.*

I began to amuse, and often annoy myself, following the family around, listening to their plotting and scheming, and occasionally having a little fun at their expense and as I did so I could feel my powers grow, especially my ability to control. I can now move smallish objects like ash trays and vases freely and easily, and I have even managed to heave that great heavy old portmanteau – the one that I had wanted to throw out for years – up the steps from the cellar. I lost control at that point, dropping, as-it-were, the thing back down the steps, where it broke into several pieces. Freddie called out the police, assuming we'd been burgled. They're now looking for a gang who specialise in decaying old luggage. And that is how it has been so far, following, listening, moving things around... Except for this last event. This was completely different.

This time I didn't actually go anywhere, at least not in the physical or terrestrial sense. I was just conscious of a change of environment. I was no longer in the house, or at Freddie's or any of the family's homes. I was in a new world of colours, totally surrounded and engulfed by colours. Lots and lots of colours mixed together, not quite a kaleidoscope, more of a swirl of soft, intangible, vaporous colours covering harder, prime reality. A little like a Turner painting, picking out Brighton Chain Pier from the luscious oranges of the sky. Now I know that this all sounds rather abstract and ethereal but there was some reality. The hardness behind that soft pastel percolation was daunting, intimidating, very real, and left me with an absolute sense of foreboding. If I was capable of feeling cold or of shivering, then I'm sure that I would have done so. Sounds rather morbid doesn't it? A morbid ghost? In one sense that's rather ironic. But I'm rambling now so let me return to events so far. Let me bring you up-to-date.

The family have arranged to bury me on Thursday, that will be six days after they pulled the plug. The day after tomorrow is Thursday and I'm really not looking forward to it. Most of all I'm worried about things changing. Is burial the end? When they commit me to the ground, will my ghostly presence change? I hope not, there's so much to do before I move on and I must admit that I am really quite enjoying it all.

The family didn't tell Lisa for two days. Frederick made the excuse that because she was out of the country he couldn't reach her which was absolute rubbish – he never tried, and she was only in

Dublin, not deepest Africa. It was all part of his and Thaddeus' little scheme, in which, unbeknown to the rest of the family, these two geriatric charlatans had decided to cut not only Lisa, but everyone else out of my wealth – including their own children. Nice people, aren't they? Thaddeus explained to the family that he had a friend, from his army days, who was a top probate lawyer. Using Frederick's gender, the male line, he would contest the Will in Frederick's favour. He would argue diminished responsibility and senility on my part, rendering the Will null and void and Frederick the natural heir. Of course he would need the support of the rest of the family to prove me off-my-head and proposed to protect everyone's interest by signing an agreement. This document would disperse my wealth equally amongst them all – except Lisa. Naturally the agreement wouldn't be worth the paper it was printed on. This was ensured by Thaddeus' probate friend employing the services of a somewhat dubious colleague called Terrance Whet, a rather mercenary member of the legal profession, who usually specialised in criminal law, on the side of the criminals. Thaddeus set up a meeting between Frederick, Whet, Christian, Charles and an extremely suspicious Helen. This was held in the private dining room of a local pub, two days after my death, and I had great fun crinkling Frederick's nose and twitching Thaddeus' moustache. Unfortunately for her, Helen's suspicions were not enough to overcome her husband's naiveté or the pressure from his father and uncle, but her unease caused her to comment on the sniffing and twitching antics of her older relatives, so I switched my attention to her and Christian. I went for itching. Helen found herself scratching behind her ear and in the small of her back, and I can only guess at the discomfort of Christian; I believe crabs is the common term used. His normally pallid face was a picture; red, flushed, lip-bitten and perspiring. I suppose I was a little hard on him, but the depths they were prepared to go to and their unrelenting greed, had really annoyed me. Charles I let off with a rather minor twitching of the head.

That's when the colours returned. There has to be a link. Each time I bond with the living, switch them, make them scratch or wriggle, a spell of 'The Colours' follows. The greater the interaction with the living, the longer the colours stay with me. It's as though I have to pay for the use of this power. Perhaps I'm being paranoid. The colours may just be charging my batteries, as it were.

***

Lisa stepped from the shower, wrapped a large, white hotel towel around her body, folded its edges tightly above her breasts, then took a second towel and began to rub her hair vigorously.

'Chuckles,' she mouthed the name at the mirror as she gently touched the faint, reddish stain that sat almost imperceptibly beneath each eye – it was four days since Aunt Rose's death, and two since she had stopped crying openly. She smiled at the thought of Chuckles, the big gruff Australian with the strange accent, who she had met just three days before. Was it only three days? She thought. It seemed a lot longer. She stopped rubbing her hair, scooped it from behind in both hands and coiled it on top of her head, securing it turban-like with a fresh, dry towel, then bent to retrieve the toothpaste, toothbrush and plastic beaker that she had brushed to the floor earlier.

Above the refrigerator, in one corner of the bedroom, sat a kettle. She poured bottled mineral water into the kettle and switched it on, thinking about the events of the last four days as she prepared a cup of Earl Grey tea.

The first day had been the worst. Brinker's telephone message had caught up with her at five o'clock that evening, six hours after Aunt Rose had passed on, and a full thirty–six hours before Uncle Freddie had deigned to phone. It had hurt her deeply that she had not been at her godmother's bedside and annoyed even more that she hadn't been in when the phone call came through. The fact that Aunt Rose had insisted that Lisa be away, at the end, hadn't eased the pain at all. Similarly, Brinker's insistence that she stay away until after the reading of the Will had left her with an empty, desperate feeling that she really had trouble handling. But the instructions had been specific, and although the second had come from the lawyer, she knew that both had originated with her godmother, and therefore she had no choice but to obey. Then she felt even worse, because of Chuckles. She glanced at her watch.

'One-twenty. Damn!' They were meeting for lunch at one-thirty. She dashed back into the bathroom.

Chuckles was already downstairs in the coffee shop of their hotel, waiting. He was in his early forties, tall, slender across the shoulders, with a friendly open face that needed little encouragement to break into laughter. He was an Australian. At least he claimed to be an Australian, but had the strangest accent for an Australian that Lisa had ever encountered. His proper name was Charles O'Donnell. His father had been a minor Australian diplomat of Irish decent, his mother was Swiss and spoke five different European languages. It had been under his mother's tutelage that he had developed his own multi-lingual abilities. During his childhood the family had travelled extensively, including a long spell at the Australian Embassy in Washington were he had picked up the nickname Chuck.

Chuckles glanced at his watch, one-thirty-two. At least another eight minutes, he thought to himself, smiling. He had taken a small square table at the far end of the restaurant, with his back to the wall, facing the entrance. In the centre of the table sat a single yellow rose in a fluted glass vase. He moved the vase to one side. He understood why restaurants decorated their tables but would never understand why customers bobbed from side to side of such adornments to make conversation. This was to be their last lunch, and in the place where they'd first met; an irony that Lisa had commented on as he had left her bedroom in the early hours that morning. She had thought of that old film, where the couple met at the railway station. 'Brief Encounter' had been a great favourite of her Aunt Rose's she'd informed him tearfully.

The seminar that brought Lisa on the ferry to Dublin a week ago, had finished this morning and Chuckles own wait for *oversees instructions* had ended with a long-awaited telephone call the previous night. He had skipped breakfast and spent the morning booking a seat on the 7.50 to Paris for himself, and the 8.15 to Stanstead for Lisa; she'd refused his offer to pay for the ticket and he hadn't pressed her as he didn't want to give the wrong signals. The tickets were in the breast pocket of his blazer. He could feel the weight of the plastic pouches that the travel agents had insisted encasing the tickets in, pulling ominously at the fabric of his pocket. He touched the tickets with his right hand, and felt the hollowness deep in his stomach that had plagued him all morning, swell. His feelings mystified him.

Lisa pulled the flesh back from above her left eye, stretching her eyebrow to a thin, plucked horizontal line. She peered closer into the mirror, searching for the almost invisible scar, the result of a childhood accident in the school playground – an altercation with the cross-bar of the schools climbing frame during a game of tag, which had resulted in a half-inch cut across here left eyebrow, requiring three stitches. The cut had healed quickly and neatly, you would almost need a magnifying glass to see it now, but ever since then the hair along the scar line had stubbornly refused to grow.

Recently, she had thought of having her eyebrows tattooed, but thinking about it was as far as she'd got, for now an eyebrow pencil was the only answer. She hated having to use one. She had the habit of folding the stubby pencil between her fingers and inside the palm of her hand while she peered into the mirror to inspect her work. Occasionally she would fold the pencil the wrong way and flatten the soft tip against the mirror. Today she had managed to dab her nose instead. She reached for the pink face-cloth on the sink, depositing the tube of toothpaste, her toothbrush and the plastic beaker back on the floor as she did so. The plastic beaker made a dull flat sound as it came into contact with the mat on the tiled floor. Lisa ignored it. In her experience things often fell to the bathroom floor and she had long since ensured that all her toiletries came in plastic containers. Vigorous rubbing with the face-cloth did the trick. She moved her head from side to side, checking for any further smudges. The face that looked back at her was gentle and kind, with a glint of sharpness and strength behind the eyes that belied her obvious physical clumsiness. A face that, despite her enforced use of the eyebrow pencil, was almost perfect. Her nose, a touch red from rubbing the eyebrow pencil off, was slim and slightly angular but not too long, a nose belonging to a far-gone classic era. Her cheekbones were high, her mouth full and her eyes an enticing honey brown that complimented her glistening full length brown hair.

Lisa knew where Chuckles would be sitting and waved automatically at the far end of the room. Chuckles rose from his chair as she approached, wincing as the swing of her shoulder bag narrowly missed the coiffured head of an elderly lady dining at a table, apparently, directly in Lisa's path. His sudden look of apprehension, as her bag narrowly missed its mark, reminded her of their first meeting. That had been in the early evening of the day after Rose died and at the point when the redness around her eyes had been all too apparent. He had obviously noticed. She had felt him looking at her. He was good-looking, with that soft, faraway light in his eyes that some men have that makes them look like bemused school-boys. She sensed, more than knew, that he would approach her and contemplating what approach he would use had been a welcome pastime as, for a few fleeting seconds, it had temporarily distracted her from the remorse that had threatened to overwhelm her. In the end she had inadvertently made the first move for him, by sweeping her purse off the table and across the divide between them, as she waved a hand for a waiter, and a third cup of espresso that would ensure she wouldn't sleep at all that night; the thought of dreaming had frightened her thoroughly.

Her purse had almost landed in his lap.

'Thank you,' he'd said as he passed it back to her, 'but I think you're supposed to tip the waiters, not the other guests.'

'I am so sorry…'Lisa had begun to reply.

'No problem.' Chuck had interrupted as he stood to pass the purse back to her.

He had then introduced himself as Chuck, in a slightly over-loud voice that had caught the attention of all the other diners around them. Lisa's immediate impression was that he had to be American. An impression he instantly dispelled by adding the word g'day. Which had been followed by a bright, cheerful and totally disarming laugh, that had spurned the name Chuckles in her mind.

'Look,' he had said, I'm dining alone and you seem to be as well, and I could sure use the company. Perhaps…? He had then held out his hand in the direction of the vacant chair opposite Lisa. She knew he was lying, he was far too self confident to be in desperate need of company, but he had correctly assumed how much she was.

She had been on the point of rejecting him, and could see that he had spotted the doubt in her eyes, then she replied, 'please do,' almost in defiance of herself. Within minutes she was glad that she had. Chuckles had a natural warm charm that was totally disarming. Almost immediately, Lisa had found herself talking to him as though he were a favourite uncle and not a total stranger who she had known for just a few minutes and of whom she knew nothing at all. He was just what she needed.

Lisa reached their table without incident. Chuckles held a chair back for her. As she sat, he slid his fingers beneath the thin leather strap of her shoulder bag. Deftly, and without comment, he removed the bag to the safety of a spare chair.

'I'm sorry,' she said. 'I'm late,' Lisa's voice carried a faint and incongruous strain of coyness that she knew was the direct result of the previous night.

Chuckles dismissed here apology with a smile. 'How are you today? He asked, with a tinge of apprehension in his voice that pleasantly surprised him.

'I'm fine,' she replied, 'don't look so worried. It looks so out of place, so unnatural.'

Momentarily, Chuckles considered giving a – don't know what you mean – reply, he wasn't worried about anything. But something stopped him. Something akin to the feeling he had been experiencing all morning.

'It is,' he said, 'I have to admit that.' Chuckles' reflective reply was interrupted by the appearance of a waiter with two menus.

'Would you like a drink? Chuckles asked.

'Just mineral water for me, thanks. Still, not sparkling.'

'And a G and T for me. Lots of ice.'

'Charles?' Lisa asked in a whisper as the waiter moved out of earshot, 'was I a one-night-stand?' The frankness of her question took him completely by surprise, but before he could answer she held up her hand, her middle finger to his lips. 'No. Don't say anything yet. It was unfair of me to put it like that. What I really mean is, I don't mind. Being a one-night-stand, that is. But I do mind terribly, if I don't see you again. I desperately want to see you again and I'm frightened that once we get on those planes tonight and fly off to different parts of the world...'

'I'm only going to Paris, not Outer Mongolia.'

'I know but hotel romances...' Lisa let the sentence trail off, unfinished.

'People have to meet somewhere,' Chuckles laughed. 'What's wrong with a hotel? It could have been in an office, or at a party, or as a blind date arranged by mutual friends, or...'

'I know. But we're getting off the subject.'

'The one-night-stand,' Chuckles teased.

'Yes,' she replied tersely. For the first time since she had met him she felt herself annoyed by his light-hearted chuckling manner. What I'm trying to say is that I want you to understand that you where not a one-night-stand either.'

'Pardon.'

Lisa flashed a contented smile. 'Good,' she said. 'That got your attention. Look. When we first met, here, four days ago, I was overwrought, distressed, desperately needing a shoulder to cry on, and there you were. You listened. You let me ramble on about my Aunt Rose and the Trust Fund and the Will and everything. You where wonderful.' Lisa reached across the table to take Chuckles' hand in hers.

'Only after you'd got my attention,' Chuckles replied with a chuckle, referring to the way Lisa had launched her purse at him that first night.

'You said thank you, when my purse landed in your lap. Then you said – you're supposed to tip the waiters, not the guests – that made me laugh and I needed to laugh, desp…'

'Desperately?'

'Yes! And I needed to talk, and to listen. I needed to hear your story, your life, someone else's problems.'

'So you have been using me,' Chuckles teased.

Lisa pinched the back of his hand between the tips of her fingers. 'Stop it,' she said. 'I'm trying to be serious. You see, I didn't intend to see you again, not after that first meal, not with Aunt Rose and all. The last thing I needed was romantic involvement. When you asked me to go out with you the following evening I said yes simply because I was too nervous to say no. Then, the following day, after all those telephone calls with Aunt Rose's lawyer, his insistence that I should wait here for two more days. I felt far too down to even think of leaving my hotel room, let alone go on a date. I just wanted to go home. I was about to call you and cancel when your flowers arrived.'

'Wonderful things Roses.'

'They were Carnations.'

'Oh! Really.'

She pinched his hand again, harder. 'I'm trying to be serious.'

'I know,' Chuckles said softly. I could see that you weren't looking at me as a possible suitor. You never even asked if I was single, I had to tell you. And believe me, when a guy of my age meets a beautiful young girl…'

'Thirty three and divorced hardly qualifies as Girl!'

'You let me be the judge of that. And as I was saying – are you married? – although it's not always put as directly as that, is usually high on the list of questions asked.'

'Well. Are you married?'

'Didn't you believe what I told you the first time, was it all a story to win you over, get you into bed?' he teased.

'It usually is. All that simplistic – I've been too busy working and travelling the world – crap. Really. What's a girl supposed to think?'

'Girl?'

'Woman then. You've probably got a wife and three kids back in Australia.'

'And another in Hong Kong, and Manila and…'

Lisa kicked his shins under the table. 'What I'm trying to say is that I hope you haven't got a wife and kids back home. But if you have, although I'll never forgive you, I still want to say thank you for the last three days, thank you for helping me survive them.'

Chuckles put her hand to his lips and kissed it.

'Thank you,' she replied.

'Again.' She gave him a puzzled look then laughed as she realised what he meant. 'Look,' he continued, 'stop thanking me, I understand how you feel. The uncertainty is understandable – Is he telling the truth? Will I see him again? Will there be a future for us? – And what can I say except, yes. I'll be in London early next month, I'll call you as soon as I arrive and then we'll see if this was just a temporary fling or the real thing. After all, I caught you at a very vulnerable time, tearful, soft, vulnerable…'

'I may be clumsy. People say that, I've heard them.'

'Really?'

'Yes, they do. But I'm level-headed, methodical and much tougher than you've seen me this week,' she interrupted.

'Precisely, after a couple of weeks back on your own turf you may suddenly realise that I'm not quite the dashing Australian hero you see now.' He chuckled as he finished his speech and Lisa kicked him again under the table. The waiter arrived with their drinks.

Chapter 5

True to Thaddeus' word, Terrance Whet produced the agreement for the family to sign, on time. I know this because I was at Freddie's when Whet called. That was yesterday. Now, this evening, I'm at Thaddeus' house. All the family are, except Lia. She's at her own home, reading my diaries. She's really hooked on them, and I'll have to keep a special eye on her.

Why, you ask?

Well. I may have underestimated nephew Christian's dopey wife. I mean she's a harmless soul and I know she loves to read; always got her nose buried into a huge tome. Usually a romantic saga of three volumes at least. Do you see now why I left the diaries to her? I've led a full, and even if I do say so myself, interesting life. During which most things have happened to me, certainly dramatic changes of fortune, a turbulent love life and a tenacious will to outlive everyone else – husbands that is. And isn't that what that style of book is all about? So I thought Lia would simply have a good read, perhaps I might even go up in her estimation and that would be that. But no.

I dropped in on Lia and Christian yesterday. To check on them as it were. Christian was going on about 'it' not being fair, and how I had tricked them all and that now he was worried that his father and uncle intended to cheat them even further. He was right about that one. He was in one of his someone-has-to-do-something-about-it moods. It bored me to death. Oops! Sorry, it bored me witless. That's better. And must have been doing the same to Lia. It was then I got my first inkling that I may have got my niece-in-law's character slightly wrong. It was the way that she answered her husband 'Yes dear. Of course dear. What ever you say dear' always pandering to him, always giving him the answers he needed to hear at exactly the time that he needed to hear them. That takes understanding. It's like lying; don't start unless you know what you're about, and can keep it up till the very end. That's asking a lot if you are talking about a lifetime of marriage, isn't it?

Intrigued, I stayed for a while. Christian rambled on about the will, probate, coroners and lawyers. He dissected my lottery scheme. Put up theories, propositions and increasingly irrational counter measures that would restore what he saw as 'his fair share'. Through all of this Lia never missed a prompt, the platitudes rolled out endlessly, always on cue, always at the right time, and throughout it all she read the diaries. None stop. Impressive?

You still don't understand my concern. Of course you don't. But you haven't read the diaries, especially the dismissal of my third husband's trial and the aftermath of that event. You see the truth is in there, in the diaries. Not in straight direct language, but between the lines. Lines that Lia is now consuming so avidly. Subtext that I thought was beyond her simple understanding. I may have been wrong. Perhaps I want to be wrong.

Anyway. Back to the meeting.

This was the meeting to convince the rest of the family to accept the cousin's lame scheme. I stayed only briefly, just long enough to see them all arrive and to hear Thaddeus declare that Frederick wasn't feeling too well that evening and sent his apologies. Well! I didn't believe a word of that and set off to find him. He was at his home. He lives in an apartment block on the edge of the old town centre. It's a converted inn and stables, beautifully done and rather expensive. I've often wondered how Freddie manages to afford it. His apartment is three bedroomed and on the ground floor. I found him in one of the bedrooms; he'd converted it to a small library with three walls of books and a mahogany desk to the one clear wall. He was entertaining the perfidious Mr Whet. I witnessed the signing of a separate agreement, drawn up in Frederick and Thaddeus' favour, ensuring my entire estate into their avaricious hands. They toasted each other with glasses of single malt whisky. Smiling huge, friendly smiles that deluded neither of them.

Naturally, all of this scheming, wheeling and dealing, was based upon the assumption that my previous bequeathment of virtually my entire fortune to the trust fund, could be rendered null and void. Both the probate lawyer and the devious Mr. Whet had assured everyone that this was the case. The lawyers would come out on top anyway. To win would mean an extremely sizeable fee, but losing would be expensive as well, and therefore profitable. Unfortunately for the family, they would lose.

I have actually based the whole lottery idea on a magazine article that I read several years ago. A Yorkshire lady, a certain Mrs Hunt, living just outside of Leeds, had set up a trust fund for her cats; she shared her house with more than thirty of her feline friends. Her first step had been to set up a home for the cats and a small trust fund to support the home. This she did a full two years

before donating her entire fortune to the fund. She lived for a
further four years and, after her death her family contested her will
and sued the trust fund. The case went all the way to the High Court
and House of Lords. The family lost, and an unshakeable precedent
was set for me to exploit later. I freely admit to plagiarising Mrs.
Hunt's idea. I also admit that selling the house by lottery was not
my idea either. There have been quite a few houses sold that way in
recent years and even the odd Hollywood movie has been made,
based on the concept. What I can lay claim to is putting the two
ideas together. What a clever girl?

By the way, the family have agreed to meet again with their
lawyers next week, after the funeral, to discuss the action they
intend to bring – that's one meeting I shan't miss.

***

Carlo stood back from the long, sleek limousine, rested his
corpulent frame against a convenient workbench and admired the
metallic glow from the deep black paintwork in front of him. He
flicked at an invisible speck of dust with the soft cloth he held and
snapped his fingers loudly – his usual ritual to announce that yet
another vehicle had been given the 'Carlo car conversion' – the
catch phrase he used on local TV to advertise his limousine valet
service. He glanced at his watch. He was running a little late, which
was not surprising, as his entire staff of five had all called in sick
with what appeared to be an epidemic of food poisoning. As a result
he had been forced to cancel two of this mornings appointments, but
not the limousine in front of him, which, apart from the fact that it
was the first appointment of the day, was Elena Mazzi's car. Elena
Mazzi was the wife of Paulo Mazzi, the last person in New York
City that Carlo ever wanted to disappoint. In fact, in spite of the
additional staff the success of his valet business enabled him to hire,
he still insisted on preparing Signore Mazzi's car personally.

The sudden sharp noise of a telephone bell made him jump.
The telephone was in the office; a simple glass partitioned box in
one corner of the workshop. Carlo refused to have a telephone in the
workshop itself. If staff wanted to make a call they could come to
his office where he had control, not on the shop floor, where they
could be calling anyone for as long as they liked. The bell, mounted
high on the back wall of the workshop, was very old and spluttered
inconsistently but it was still extremely loud and effective. Carlo

72

muttered under his breath. He didn't need interruptions this morning.

Marios Branchman watched Carlo waddle towards the office. He slipped quietly across the workshop floor to the far side of the limousine and opened the rear passenger-side door. The deep bottle-green upholstery gleamed at him, the heady aroma of polished leather momentarily distracting him. He pulled down the central armrest, exposing the rectangular recess. The back of the recess was covered by a leather flap, held into place by Velcro tape. He peeled the flap forward and removed the plastic panel behind it, revealing a second, smaller recess, then a metal flap identical to the plastic one except that it had a small chrome lock securing it. The lock didn't interest Marios. This vehicle, like thousands of others, had the facility to open a trap between the boot and the cabin of the car, so that long objects such as skis could be slid through. Although why people would go skiing in a limo totally baffled Marios. What had interested him when he began researching this particular contract was that, although this particular limousine had been especially constructed, with bullet-proof glass etc., the small recess between the armrest and the locked trap door still existed. He placed the explosives he was carrying into the recess, pushing them firmly against the metal trap until he was confident that the mastic on the back of the package had stuck firmly. On the front of the explosives was a small, slim plastic box with a single yellow button and three coloured LEDs. He pressed the button. The LEDs glowed, the red centre one flashed rhythmically. Satisfied, Marios replaced the plastic panel, smoothed the leather flap into place and pushed the armrest back into the deep fold of the rear seat. The entire operation had taken less than twenty seconds.

From his vantage-point in the hospital car park Marios could see the hospital casualty entrance quite clearly. He scratched at the bridge of his nose, the only outward sign of agitation he ever displayed, and looked for the fifth time at the digital clock on the dashboard in front off him. They're late, he thought, a little concerned that he may have miscalculated. He had been given so little time between the last job and this one, and this made him anxious. His preparation over the previous five months had been meticulous, as always. He had taken three contracts at the end of the previous year; each with a programme dictated by the client. Marios had advised each client that he would not be held to rigid schedules or time scales; his very survival depended on his own control at all times. Of course he had to respect and work with the clients general time scale. He couldn't accept a 'Political' required before the opening of the British parliament or the Israeli feast of Yom Kippur and carry them out after the events had occurred, but experience had taught him that working to a client's specific date or even worse, specific venue, just simply didn't work. You ended up with failure, a disappointed client and the very real possibility of personal tragedy. Marios always insisted that the planning and execution of each operation would be his alone and the first the client would hear of the hit would be on the television news.

For this year's contracts, initial planning and research had dictated that three be completed within an incredibly short period. He had originally planned to do Senator Frankman in the early spring, but had been thwarted by the senator's appointment to a presidential committee on world malnutrition and a four-month programme of travel with US Aid. Which meant Africa. Marios had only worked in Africa three times throughout his entire career. Each event had been fraught with unavoidable and unacceptable difficulties, which had led him to the firm conviction that what ever sum of money he was offered, Africa wasn't worth the risk. After all, there was plenty of work in the western world. Why complicate your life in countries without efficient infrastructure or predictable and civilised social practices that could be monitored and used in your favour? But, his programme was now dangerously compressed. The client's cut-off date had forced Marios to act quickly, striking at the first public appearance the senator was to make after his return from Africa.

In fact the entire year had been one of frustration for his normal delicate planning. The Mazzi job would go ahead as scheduled, but the third target – a European industrialist, had to be brought forward since the sudden announcement of a multi-national merger had sent the client into a panic for immediate action and had shot Marios' fee up by a full one hundred percent. The end result was that he would carry out all three contracts within the space of fifteen short days, the last two back-to-back. Now he was being offered a forth contract, this time in the UK. He liked working there, especially mainland England. Good infrastructure to work with. The money was good, well, at least reasonable, but the late receipt of the order and the clients short cut-off date meant working again, just a couple of weeks after the industrialist job and, unlike the first three, he hadn't yet carried out the advanced planning he knew the job required. His response to the client was to carry out a survey of the situation and then either agree to take the contract or not. The client hadn't been happy with Marios' answer and had at first rejected it. So Marios was quite surprised when one week later the request was repeated, subject to a successful survey, and a substantial bonus offered if the cut-off date could be maintained.

Over the total of five previous visits Marios had made to Chicago, he had noted several of the regular traits that the Mazzi household followed. The valet service had seemed to be the most fortuitous. Every second Wednesday, at exactly seven thirty in the morning, the Mazzi's chauffeur drove the limousine to Carlo's premises. He then spent an hour over breakfast at a nearby diner before collecting the limousine and returning to the Mazzi residence. At nine-forty he drove Mr and Mrs Mazzi down town to the St Christopher hospital where Paulo Mazzi was checked over by the senior heart surgeon; Paulo's heart condition was well-known, as was his wife's dedication to him.

The central set of double doors feeding the casualty department entrance opened, to reveal a cluster of dark-suited heavies surrounding a rather diminutive figure in a wheel chair and a tall, elegant blond in her early fifties – Elena Mazzi. The black limousine slid to a halt in front of the group, the chauffeur stepped from the limousine and opened the rear door. Elena and one of the bodyguards helped Paulo out of the wheel chair and into the rear of the limousine. The chauffeur shut the door firmly and escorted Elena round the rear of the car to the far side passenger door. He reached towards the passenger door handle.

Marios pressed the button on the remote control unit he held in his hand. The receiver unit in the rear seat of the limousine clicked once, making Paulo look round. There was a split-second between the click and the explosion, minuscule but just enough for Paulo to realise. Then the explosives reacted.

The limousine pitched violently forward on its suspension, the rear wheels lifting momentarily off the ground. There was a dull thud, and then it was all over. The roof of the vehicle had buckled upwards and the rear panel and boot area had buckled outwards, but apart from that the vehicle remained intact. The bullet proof glass didn't shatter and contained the explosion in a manner that would later give great satisfaction to the vehicles manufacturers but had a devastating effect on its single occupant; Paulo Mazzi was quite definitely dead.

Marios put on a pair of dark sunglasses, started his car and pulled slowly out of the car park. The whole event had gone particularly well, better than he could have hoped. He had no compunction over killing. It was his stock and trade, but he always tried to avoid taking unnecessary lives and today's had been particularly gratifying. Not only had he avoided killing the wife, but the chauffeur as well. Quite an achievement he thought as he eased into the downtown traffic.

Chapter 6

'It's 'posed to be Mondays that you 'ate, ain't it? Not Wednesdays.' Trevor arched his long thin back as he spoke, ran his fingers through his thinning hair and yawned.

Andrew listened, staring listlessly into his half empty mug of stale tea. Dark, cold, thoughts drifted across his mind. Criminal thoughts. Stupid, desperate, thoughts that showed too clearly on his open face.

Trevor, his partner and co-driver leaned across the white canteen-table that separated them. He replied in short, anxious lowered tones. 'For Christ's sake Andy, you've gotta snap out of it. You know what they're like.' He glanced nervously over Andrews shoulder at the glass-partitioned door that led back into the main office area. 'If they'd 'eard 'arf the crap you've been coming out with lately they'd 'ave nailed your little pecker to the wall already. Now come on. Let's go.'

Trevor eased his chair backwards, as quietly and unobtrusively as he could. Andrew reflected, then carefully did the same, mimicking his friend's actions sheepishly. He knew Trevor was right. Failsafe Securities would fire him in an instant if they knew of his financial status. They would show him the door even faster if they got a hint of his depressed state of mind. It wouldn't be legal of course. You can't fire someone for depression or for just being broke, but that wouldn't be the official reason given. Failsafe were past masters at removing people who they felt threatened the integrity of the firm.

Andrew squinted at the bright sunlight that greeted them outside the canteen. Trevor pulled down his cap. A heavy metal door shut behind them with a double click and the faint pulse of an electric motor. Andrew retrieved his pass card from the lock in the centre of the door and replaced it in his Failsafe-wallet. Trevor did the same. The company computer registered them both out of the canteen at 10:56am, exactly twenty one minutes after they had entered.

In front of them stood three gleaming armoured vans, all a deep shade of bottle green, with the simple double-padlock Failsafe logo printed in the centre of the rear panel. They used their cards again to swipe the locks along each side of the second vehicle. A flap opened in front of Trevor and he punched in a six-digit code.

The computer recorded them entering 'Unit 16' at 10:57am.

Inside the vehicle, in the face of a small box mounted between the seats were three slots, one long one across the top and two shorter identical ones to each side. They placed their cards into the shorter slots. This would be the last time they used the cards until they reached their destination. The cards activated pressure plates under their seats – if they left the vehicle without removing the cards and following the correct exit procedure, the vehicle would automatically lock its doors, immobilise its engine, initiate an alarm procedure within the vehicle and transmit directly to both the police and the Failsafe head office. Andrew and Trevor sat in silence, waiting. All the other drivers did the same, not trusting themselves to talk until they had received their instructions and were in motion, out of reach of the prying eyes of the company compound.

The box between their seats began to whirr gently. A coil of paper printout chattered from the top slot in the box. Trevor tore the paper out of its holder, read it and passed it to Andrew. Without saying a word Andrew started the engine, slipped the armoured truck into gear and drove towards the compound gates, they opened eerily, seemingly without instruction. Andrew signalled right, checked both ways and pulled across the road into a gap in the flow of traffic. At the next junction they were stopped by a set of red lights. Trevor flicked a switch on the dashboard in front of him. 'Western Avenue and Church Street,' he announced flatly, then flicked the switch back to its original position. They wouldn't have to call in again until they reached the destination given to them on the printout; the company's GPS tracking system was automatically relaying their position, fifteen times a second, back to the Failsafe computer. They both breathed out. Now they could talk.

'If they do boot me out, at least I can get back to some sort of reality.' Andrew sighed, taping his fingers impatiently as he waited for the lights to change. He dabbed at the box between them and changed the subject. 'This latest gizmo obviously impresses the bosses but it must really give the crooks a bloody good laugh. I mean, they're just going to follow us, fancy gizmo or not, and we never know in advance where we're going or if we're carrying the crown jewels or sacks of old notes for the furnace. The bad guys always get that info from the office. I mean it wouldn't come from us, would it? Our Cheryl would be the one, not me.' Trevor's sister Cheryl worked in the dispatch department. 'Everyone knows that.'

'Grey panel-van,' Trevor stated abstractly, 'four lengths back, pulled out as we left the depot.'

'Got him,' Andrew replied, fixing the van in his rear view mirror. They drove on in silence for the next three minutes, passed the first two sets of traffic lights along the high street. At the third set, the van signalled left and pulled out of his line of sight. 'Clear,' Andrew stated flatly. They were trained to watch for any vehicle that followed them for more than a few blocks and especially ones that picked them up as they left base.

Trevor spoke first, returning to their earlier topic. 'And,' he exclaimed, 'what the 'ell will you do if you quit?' Although only Andrew's senior by three years, Trevor's voice rang with a parental arrogance that he usually reserved for his four year old daughter when she had been particularly naughty. 'You'll be right in it, up to your neck. And don't forget the Christmas bonus, you'll lose that.'

'That's weeks away,' Andrew replied defensively. 'If I can't get my hands on some readies now, immediately, and lots of them, then there won't be any Christmas. Not this year or for the next dozen. I've had it Trev.' Andrew reached into his jacket pocket and pulled a folded brown envelope. 'This arrived this morning,' he said. 'The building society again. They've agreed to extend the payment time on our second loan. Another nine months; at an extra half a percent of course. We've got no choice but to accept, which means that next year – when we've fallen behind again – there'll give us another nine months and another. We're just paying interest really. The capital never seems to go down at all.'

Trevor scrutinised the paper. 'Gotcha by the short-n-curlys. Bastards!' he said softly. 'What you going to do now?'

'What can I do? I've not got a lot of options, have I?'

Trevor tried to answer but was stuck for a suggestion.

'All I've got is three choices,' Andrew continued. 'Drive this hi-tech cash box home and attack it with a tin opener, throw myself off the roof of Failsafe House and go for the insurance money, or prey for a frigging miracle.'

'Go for the insurance,' Trevor replied, with a quiet laugh. He leaned backwards towards the rear of the truck and its cargo. He cupped his hand to his ear. 'It sounds like loose change to me.'

A grin began to appear at the corner of Andrews's mouth; Trevor always could make him laugh. He punched his friend on the arm and swore at him. 'We're there,' he said. Trevor flashed his lights at the gate man and signalled through the portal of Grunthorpe's Building Society and Friendly Bank. Behind them, its nose just visible around the edge of the next corner, the grey panel-van pulled quietly to a halt.

***

'Just going to the archives Miss Cooper.' Martin flipped the key he was holding in his hand into the air, then caught it. He gave Chloe a broad wink as he closed the office door behind him, and whistled cheerfully as he strode along the corridor towards the lifts.

Two years before, on his appointment as personnel manager, he had been given the responsibility for the archives and the sensitive documents they contained. He had the only key, except for the chairman, whose own office was in a different building all together; the risk of the chairman arriving to visit the archives, unannounced, was simply nil. The situation was perfect.

The lift came to a halt at the basement. The doors quietly rattled open, allowing a draught of cold, slightly dank air to invade Martin's nostrils. Directly in front of him, across the corridor, stood the entrance to the archives. Martin let himself in and closed the door behind him. The lift doors quietly rattled closed behind him, as the lift was called back to a higher floor. He placed the key back in the lock, but didn't turn it. There was no point, she would be here soon.

The room was large. Its walls were lined from floor to ceiling with heavy, wooded-slatted shelving, stacked with neat, labelled document boxes. In the centre of the room stood a long polished table and two plain metal chairs. Martin sat and waited. After exactly four minutes there was a gentle knock on the door.

'Come,' he said perfunctorily.

She loved his voice. It was one of the first things that she had noticed about him, outside the cinema, so deep and even and controlled. It was no wonder that he was the office heartthrob, and the fact that he was unavailable only added to his allure. Several of the office girls had made a pitch for him, especially the new Scottish receptionist. She had gone completely over the top at the last Christmas party and had nearly lost her job as a result. None of the girls had been successful in ensnaring him. Martin's reputation as an untouchable, happily married man, remained intact, and that's the way Chloe and Martin wanted to keep it. This was their own, well guarded secret.

The door swung open. Chloe caught the edge of the door with a practised swing of her foot and pushed it back behind her until it

80

clicked resoundingly shut. She turned the key in the lock then walked across to where Martin sat, waiting. Her high heals clattering on the hard, tiled floor. She lent forward to kiss him, her lips full and welcoming, freshly painted with the latest shade of lipstick. The top two buttons of her blouse had been undone, revealing the full depth of her bosom; she had nothing on beneath the blouse. Martin smiled gently, then reached a hand inside the blouse and cupped one breast in his palm. He kneaded the breast slowly, rolling the nipple between his thumb and forefinger. Chloe closed her eyes then withdrew the hand gently. She leaned further towards him, until she could run her tongue fleetingly up the side of his neck and behind his ear. She nibbled his ear briefly then pulled away.

'No you don't. Not today,' she said firmly.

Martin raised an eyebrow in surprise. The open blouse, the lipstick, usually meant they would go all the way. It was Thursday after all, and Thursdays was the day of the company production and scheduling meeting; as personnel manager he wasn't needed for that meeting. Thursdays had the hidden advantage of tying up just about everyone who would normally want to see him. Thursdays was a good morning.

'Don't look so forlorn,' Chloe added, pouting at him. She languidly did up a button, then, on reflection, she slid into the chair opposite him, protected by the full width of the desk. 'I'm sorry about that darling. I shouldn't have enticed so much, but we can't keep on pushing our luck, we're bound to get caught.'

Martin sighed. He knew she was right. As safe as the archive room was, people were bound to notice eventually. Regular trysts, every week at exactly the same time, was asking for trouble. It was stupid and dangerous, but that's what made it so exciting, so stimulating.

'I've got a surprise for you,' Martin said, pulling a folded newspaper clipping from his jacket pocket. 'Have you seen this?' Chloe opened the paper and read the headline that he was pointing to – Loewen House to be sold by lottery. 'Yes,' she replied, puzzled. 'There's been talk of nothing else all morning. But how does it affect us?'

'You're going to buy a ticket.' He grinned mischievously, knowing what her next statement would be.

'I can't afford that,' she laughed. 'Where would I get a thousand pounds for a ticket? I wouldn't take the risk anyway,' she added, her voice tinged with the first touches of annoyance; she hated having her hopes built up fruitlessly.

'But you are going to buy one. You see, I still have the money left over from the cruise holiday that Joan cancelled. Joan would notice immediately if the next bank statement came in a thousand short, but I put it away in a separate account. She doesn't even know that I had it put aside.'

'But the risk Martin. It says here that six hundred tickets will be sold, and the house will be divided into six apartments.' She paused to calculate the odds. 'That's one hundred-to-one.'

'Ex… actly,' he replied, a grin breaking out across his face. 'Listen. One hundred, a thousand or even fifty – whatever the odds, they're infinitely more winnable than the state lottery or the pools.'

'I can see that, I'm not stupid. But it still doesn't guarantee that we'll win, or that we won't lose money that I couldn't afford, even if you can.' She reached to her throat and fastened the top button of her blouse, annoyed at his cavalier attitude towards so much money.

Martin tapped the side of his nose, knowingly. 'You don't have to worry about the odds darling. I have a friend. And he owes me a big, big, favour. He's on the inside, the very inside. Believe me we can't fail.'

Chloe stared at him. He had never lied to her before but there was something about his last statement that she didn't trust. 'A Friend. Who?' she asked accusingly.

'No one you know. Some one from way back, long before we met. Don't worry that pretty little head.'

'Don't patronise me Martin Welland don't lie to me. I…'

Martin slipped quickly around the table and knelt at her knees, raising his body until their faces were level. 'OK,' he said. 'He's not exactly a friend, more of an acquaintance, a contact. But he is on the inside and if the race is going to be fixed then its better to be in than not. That's what I say.' He kissed her squarely on the lips but she didn't respond. She pushed him away.

Half of her wanted to jump for joy. Her own apartment. A luxury apartment with no mortgage or rent. A home for her and her boys. And the article in the paper said that all the services were covered by this 'Loewen Trust' that had been set up. The other half of her quailed. It all sounded more than a little illegal to her. She loved Martin dearly. But she wasn't going to end up in prison for anyone and it showed clearly on her face.

He read her thoughts perfectly, realising she wasn't ready for this type of risk, that her background and upbringing made his proposal sound immoral to her. 'OK,' he said again, pulling back, retrieving the situation. 'We didn't have this conversation, and I won't buy a ticket in your name. But in a few weeks time, I intend to bring a huge smile to that beautiful face of yours.' He reached behind her head with one hand and pulled her face to his, with the other he slid her body off the chair towards him, forcing her knees apart. The hem of her skirt slid upwards as she wrapped her legs around his waist 'Now where were we?' he asked. His fingers deftly reopened the buttons of her blouse, his hand crept back inside and his eyes challenged her to resist.

Why do I always fall for the chauvinists? She thought quiescently.

***

At thirteen, Crystel wasn't quite old enough to understand Chloe's attraction to chauvinistic men, but she was old enough to have her own opinion on the subject of chauvinists and it was quite the opposite of Chloe's. Crystel hated chauvinists. Jingoists, was her mother's name for them, and she had good reason for hating them too. Crystel's father had been a dedicated jingoist throughout her entire life, and an alcoholic.

His death, just a few days before Crystel's tenth birthday, was an accident – he was blind drunk when he locked himself in the garden shed and the shed caught fire. Everyone knew it was an accident. But only Crystel knew how much of an accident it really was.

The garden shed had been Crystel's third fire, following the waste-paper bin at school and the pillar-box on the way to the corner shop. She had executed the first two in quick succession, and would have completed a third immediately after, but she was nearly caught setting the third and that had frightened her. It was almost a year before her next fire, the garden shed. That year had been miserable. The need to plan and set a new fire, gnawed at her consciously, growing stronger every day, slowly overtaking her fear. Besides, she knew that she was safe with the garden shed, it was old and rotting, and in their own garden. She decided to do it during the Easter holidays, the Tuesday after Easter Monday.

When the day came she had the house virtually to herself. Her father was back at work and her mother was asleep, ill in bed with a late dose of the flu. It was a fascinating game to her. She had made her plans meticulously. The back wall of the shed was in urgent need of repair and several boards had almost rotted through. Using an old chisel she easily pushed a hole through one of the boards, a hole large enough to push three of her fingers through without covering them in splinters. The old shed was a treasure trove of materials for lighting fires, weed killer on one shelf, a can of paraffin on another. Fertiliser was stacked in half opened polythene sacks against a side wall and a catch of pesticides, half abandoned, occupied a dark recess under the workbench her father had used, before he discovered the bottle. For a brief while she considered abandoning her plan and looking for a new target, using the old shed as a source of supply for future ventures. But she hadn't the patience. That gnawing feeling inside had become unbearable and had to be satiated.

She decided to use the fertiliser as the catalyst for her fire, dragging the heavy sack to the back wall beneath the hole she had made before smothering its dry contents in weedkiller – to ensure success. She also placed the can of paraffin and the half empty tin of weed killer beside the sack, unsure as to the result of her actions but hoping for a small explosion at least. She covered the sack and the paraffin can with a piece of oily sacking. Then, her preparations completed, she went back into the house to make her mother a cup of tea. Much later, after the fire, and the firemen, and the ambulance had gone, she remembered seeing the bottle of whisky on the workbench in the shed. But it hadn't occurred to her then that her father would choose that particular time, in the middle of a working day, to come home for a crafty drink.

When she reached her mother's bedroom, she found her mother awake and coughing badly. The bottle of cough medicine on the bedside table was empty, so she offered to go to the chemist and buy another. Her mother told her what a good girl she was, then gave her some money for the medicine and some extra for sweets for herself. Crystel felt elated as she jumped down the stairs two by two, she loved compliments and attention, and her mother never let her down.

Half an hour later she was back, with a fresh bottle of cough medicine clasped in her hand and half a box of matches stuffed into the pocket of her jeans. She couldn't hear her mother coughing. The house was quiet and still as she tiptoed up the stairs. The only noise she could hear was the call of the matches in the box in her pocket as they rattled against each other. Her mother had dozed off. Crystel placed the new bottle of medicine softly on the bedside table, carefully closed the bedroom door behind her, then she went back to the shed.

This time she hadn't gone into the shed, but around to the back. She had taken three double sheets of an old Hello magazine and rolled them into a loose bundle, which she stuffed into the hole in the rotten board. Then, hands trembling, eyes shining, she had lit a match.

At first nothing happened. She watched with concern from a safe distance behind the old apple tree that grew at the far end of the garden. The sheets of magazine flared and slowly disappeared smoking through the hole, but the shed had shown absolutely no sign of burning. She was just about to come out from behind the tree, when the flames inside the shed, creeping along the oily sacking, reached the paraffin. Vapour, produced by the heat from the burning sacking warming the paraffin can beside them, had met the flames on the sacking at the same moment that Crystel stepped out from behind the tree. Two explosions rocked the otherwise peaceful afternoon – the first, the paraffin can, followed almost instantaneously by the second, the liquid weed killer.

Crystel was totally mesmerised. And she wasn't too young to understand the rush of adrenalin that surged through her body, or that this was the greatest thrill possible. She was hooked, nothing could replace this! The force of the blast had ripped the shed apart and almost toppled Crystel off her feet, but she really hadn't stropped smiling, and certainly wasn't aware of any danger to herself. Splinters of wood had shot past her face and ears but miraculously missed her, as did a metal plate from her father's tool cupboard that whistled past her head and into the apple tree, burying itself two inches into the trunk. A box of screws and bolts had taken on the appearance of a nail bomb and peppered the back of the house, leaving a shower of holes in the stucco. The shed had been peeled open like an orange, in four smouldering segments. Her father was found pitted with shrapnel, a three-inch bolt lodged in his windpipe. Accidental death. Crystel had noticed none of these things. She had just stared, lost in the glory of the burning twisted timber.

That had been three years earlier, she was thirteen now and a veteran of a whole series of fires. None of which had been quite so explosive as the garden shed and the accident that had killed her father, but each one became progressively more intricate than its predecessor, and each required an ever expanding knowledge of the arsonist's art.

Not surprisingly Crystel was excelling at school in the sciences, especially chemistry. The chemistry-lab had been an obvious target, one she had carried out with meticulous planning and stunning results, but it had attracted too much direct attention. She decided not to attack the school again. The police tended to ignore sweet, innocent, freckle faced, blond haired young ladies when a kiosk or newspaper night stand are set ablaze, but a fire at the school draws attention directly to the children who attend it.

In the three years since her father's death, Crystel had perpetrated eleven more fires. The smaller ones, two pillar-boxes, six dustbins and an abandoned chicken coup, were fun, just to keep her amused and try to satisfy the longing she felt deep inside, but they were not enough. The real rush had come from the last three. The derelict house had been relatively easy. It was open, unguarded and full of rotten, bone dry, timber beams; her carefully poured paraffin had hardly been necessary, a single safety match would have been enough to set the place ablaze. But the next fire, the railway wagon, was far more difficult. The wagon was of the boxcar type, with its superstructure made almost entirely from wood, but not dry or rotten wood. This wood wouldn't burst into flames like the derelict house. Weeks of planning had gone into the operation before she was ready. Siphoning off the required petrol from the tank of her mother's car a cupful at a time, so that she wouldn't notice the loss. She had to lug a full gallon of petrol across the railway sidings to soak the floor of the wagon. But all the planning had been worthwhile. The wagon caught like a tinderbox and burned so fiercely that the fire spread to the wagons either side. Crystel was stunned by the enormity of her achievement and swore that she was never going back to thinking small again.

Her last fire had been her only disappointment so far. She had simply chosen the wrong target. The post office was comprehensively alarmed and the post-master lived only two doors away from the post office. She couldn't get into the building and had to spread her mixture of weed killer and sugar on the outside. As a result, she produced more smoke than fire, the alarm was raised, and the fire brigade arrived before the fire had any chance of catching hold. But she had learnt a valuable lesson. The fire brigade were **the** enemy.

It was during the last three fires that she introduced her

pseudonym. After each fire she sent a simple note, printed on plain white card, to the local evening paper. She used an old printing set that she'd been given as a Christmas present five years before, and signed the cards with her left hand – *Jenny Hellfire*. Now she was busy planning her next fire. It would be her biggest and best so far and, had the additional element of a deadline that had to be met.

Chapter 7

As the aircraft banked sharply Marios gazed vacantly out of the window, reflecting on the events of the last few days. The white caps of the Alps began to break and disperse below, as the Boeing 737 approached the low country south of Zurich. The triangular shadow of the Boeing, that had chased them across the snow capped landscape for the past twenty minutes, was abruptly severed as a thick bank of cloud barged between the airliner and the ground with unerring stillness. He stared at the cloud, sensing the gloom that it passed across the valleys below, then smiled to himself. Nothing could depress him today, he felt extremely pleased with himself. The third of his contracts, the industrialist, was completed and with what competence. This was the one that had worried him, the one that he felt uneasy with. Yet the industrialist had made it all so simple for him. Industrialists didn't always do that he recalled, remembering an earlier contract in Canada. The target there had obviously suspected that he was in danger and had gone to extraordinary lengths to protect himself. Marios had eventually completed the contract but implementation had been messy, not the usual surgical isolation that he prided himself on. Not by any means; he had to take out two body-guards and the poor guy's wife as well. But there had been no such complications this time. If the man had any idea that he was in danger, he certainly hadn't shown it. In fact, quite the opposite – flitting from luxury hotel to luxury hotel, dividing his time equally between business, the card table, and expensive prostitutes, was hardly precautionary behaviour. He was so intent on his own pleasure that he simply didn't know it was coming.

Marios always utilised the maximum time available to him to study a target and had kept tabs on the industrialist throughout the year. He already had a comprehensive folio of his behavioural patterns and travel habits. So when the time came to action the project, a couple of basic telephone calls where enough to track the target down. Marios caught up with him in Prague, but he didn't make his move there. He spent the entire two days that the industrialist was in the beautiful city, studying the man's movements, reconfirming the picture that he had already formed.

On the first day Marios followed his quarry to a factory, fifteen miles outside of the city. For three hours Marios sat waiting, drinking coffee from a flask and snacking on biscuits – whenever he passed through the UK his duty-free spending was always on biscuits. In his opinion British biscuits were the best. Digestives Ginger Nuts and Short Bread in particular.

After his visit to the factory the industrialist, accompanied by people in dark clerical suits, took lunch at a nearby restaurant. It was a long lunch with several courses and as many bottles of wine. After lunch the other suits returned unsteadily to their factory amidst great shaking of hands and slapping of backs – their order, Marios assumed, securely signed to a contract. The industrialist dismissed his car and driver and then made directly across the city by taxi, not to his own hotel, but to a small, slightly seedy hotel facing the river. Marios spent a further hour waiting before the industrialist reappeared, looking slightly jaded but indescribably pleased with himself. The last part of the day was spent at the Casino and ended in the small hours of the morning. Marios wondered whether killing the guy was really necessary; if he lived life as destructively as this all the time, he wasn't going to last much longer anyway.

On the second day the industrialist rose late and took breakfast at his hotel before attending a meeting at the central bank. A second meeting, at a firm of management consultants, bridged another boozy lunch and completed the industrialist's working day. He then returned to his own hotel on the north bank of the Danube. Marios knew that the industrialist was booked on an evening flight to Bucharest but wasn't at all surprised when his target returned directly to the casino for a final fling before the flight. It was this obvious addiction to the casinos that decided Marios to break with recent tradition and do this one directly, hand-to-hand, and what better place than Bucharest, a city that he was very familiar with, and at the casino, which was an old haunt.

Marios completed the contract inside the casino, in the men's lavatory, using a long thin stiletto blade that slipped effortlessly beneath the cranium at the back of the neck, the industrialist dead before he hit the elegant marble tiles at their feet. Marios was at the airport less than forty minutes later.

The aircraft banked steeply to the left, spilling Marios' thoughts back to the present.

'Excuse me sir.'

One of the stewardesses was staring straight at him; he could hear the words, but didn't register clearly. He looked back at her, questioningly.

'Your seat belt sir. You have to fasten it. The captain has announced our approach into Zurich.'

Marios grunted and fumbled with his seat belt; the male half had slipped down between his seat and the vacant one next to him and appeared to be irremovably lodged there. He fumbled awkwardly but his own body weight pinned the belt firmly in place. The stewardess leaned forward. 'Allow me sir,' she said. She tugged at the belt and when it didn't move knelt forward with one knee on the empty seat, to get better purchase. The hem of her uniform skirt rode up tightly, revealing a slender inner thigh. She pulled hard at the belt, tugging it free. Her breast heaved with the effort. Marios became aware of a subtle perfume that appeared to rise in intensity, in harmony with the rise and fall of her breast. He gave her his best smile. She smiled back at him and leaned further forward, her left arm on the top of his seat supporting her body weight. 'There,' she said, passing the liberated belt to him.

'Thank you Meloni,' Marios replied, reading her name from the black and gold lapel badge, so recently close to his face. 'Tell me?' he asked. 'Can you recommend a good hotel in Zurich? I've never been there before and I hate arriving alone in a strange city.'

Meloni smiled softly. 'There's a hotel reservation desk at the terminal sir. Company policy doesn't allow us to make recommendations for passengers I'm afraid,' She leaned closer to his ear. 'But I can tell you that the crew stay at the Ambassador.' She turned quickly away and continued her inspection of the other passengers and their seat belts. There was something about Mr Heinkel in seat 5A. Something about those devastatingly sexy eyes. There was a charge in those eyes, a plethora of irresistible emotions that she felt unable to resist. She stopped between rows seven and eight and took a deep breath, feeling her pulse gradually slow. Anyway, she told herself, he was probably only flirting with me. She wanted to look back, to see if he was still watching her, but didn't.

Marios was savouring the aftermath of her perfume in his nostrils, and fighting to suppress a smile. The one that he really couldn't control, the one driven by adrenaline, sexual and physical, the one that he could never intentionally repeat, although vanity had forced him to try on many occasions. It was the same smile that followed a successful kill. It came from a deep recess inside him and hid all of the malice and darkness of his soul.

The aircraft lurched through the heavy cloud hanging low

above Zurich airport; Meloni tripped back down the aisle between the seats. She gave Marios a knowing glance as she passed seat 5A then scurried forwards towards the crew seats next to the galley, steadying herself against the top of each seat she passed.

With his seat in the upright position Marios could just see the bottom half of Meloni's legs, slender feet and ankles, protruding from the galley bulkhead. He wondered how early she was leaving in the morning. Perhaps he would extend his stop over in Zurich by an extra day. Meloni would do him good. Clear his head for the last contract of the year. Especially as this one obviously fell into the personally motivated category. They were always the worst. A gang killing, a political or even the industrialist – who had obviously made the wrong deal with the wrong people – were always safer, always professional; nothing personal was the cliché that sprang to mind. But a contract let for personal reasons invariably meant that the client wanted to interact. Sometimes even literally wanting to witness the kill. Marios always denied them this pleasure of course. The kill had to be on his terms and definitely without an audience, but you never knew to what lengths a client would go for personal gratification and how much unwanted attention that would draw to the kill.

The Boeing bumped firmly onto the tarmac beneath them, both engines roaring with reverse thrust. By the time the aeroplane had reached its parking bay, Marios' thoughts and attention had returned firmly to Meloni, who was busy stretching to retrieve the hand-luggage of an elderly passenger two rows in front of him from the overhead lockers. She would do very nicely indeed, he thought

***

It's amazing, isn't it? The way that the press are incapable of reporting anything accurately or at least honestly. They claim to be so virtuous, but in my opinion they don't even try. I know my scheme for the house is a little unusual. OK.. Very unusual if you will. But if I'd wanted to conform I would have just left the lot to Lisa and then let them all fight it out. No... I wanted to preserve the house and the family name. The present crop of Loewens may not be worth much, which is an understatement if ever I heard one, but that hasn't always been the case. We've been like any other family, some good apples, some rotten apples, but overall, mostly good. That's why I let the house go to the trust at such a low price. The six hundred thousand that the lottery will raise may only be a fraction of the house's value, but by devaluing the property I've ensured that the trust will easily be able to financially administer the estate. I mean, the collaterals still in the house. It's still worth four and a half million and, eventually, that wealth will pass back to the Loewen family. Yet yesterday, one of the newspapers informed the world that I had deliberately reduced the house's value to avoid paying tax and death duties. What rot!

Then today's article about my poor family being cut out of their inheritance. What do they know about my family? Have they ever had to live with Frederick, put up with his continual bickering and backbiting, let alone his bad side? No... I had to stop Frederick and his band sullying the Loewen name forever and the only way to do that was to separate them from the family seat. Permanently.

The other thing the press seems incapable of, is printing without sensationalising. 'Rosie's Lottery' they've called it and now it's reached the nationals, who have already started to dig into my past for skeletons. I just know that they're going to dig up Harry. Not literally of course, but Harry was my third husband, my greatest mistake, and no great loss to mankind when he passed on. Of course, it all came out at the trial, all the sordid details, so it won't be difficult for them to find. It'll be in the papers before the end of the week, I'm sure of it.

At least they can't come after me this time.

Perhaps I should visit a few of the editors? Shake them up a bit.

I've been doing a lot more experimenting. It's been fun. I've now got Charles flinching when I pass near him and Elsbeth sneezing as soon as I enter the room. They had another family meeting yesterday, the first time they had all been together since the funeral. It was hilarious, twitching, scratching, sneezing, flinching. I'm afraid I've always been a bit mischievous. I had to concentrate as hard as I could to tone it down a little. I had to keep myself in check as they were all starting to look at each other suspiciously.

Now they've drawn up a contract, 'memorandum of understanding' they called it. Letter of conspiracy more like. It's all a complete waste of time of course, but they have to do something I suppose. Their lawyer, Whet, is aptly named a total crook. I spent a few hours listening to him making telephone calls. He's got his sticky fingers into all sorts of grimy, fetid pies. The children don't know that of course and neither does Elsbeth. That part of

Frederick and Thaddeus' plan seems to be working and I find it quite incredible that the rest of them are falling for it. I thought that Helen at least would have smelt a rat. Still... give her time?

So... I have to tell you about the funeral.

First of all, I had been worrying unnecessarily. I experienced no dramatic changes or ethereal reaction. As you can tell, I'm still here. Still 'dead but kicking'. The funeral I actually found quite moving. I've been cocooned by my immediate family almost totally over the last year, so it was so nice to have other people, friends old and young, people that I love and will certainly miss, around me for one last time.

Much to Frederick's annoyance, I left strict instructions for the entire day. He moaned a little when Brinker told him but soon relented when he discovered that the foundation was footing the bill. The service, the hymns and the reception at the house afterwards, if I do say so myself, all went off very well indeed. Even Frederick's obsequious arrogance – he gave a nauseating eulogy in his newly-assumed role as head of the family – couldn't spoil the serenity of the occasion. My only regret was my choice for the last hymn. In fact not a hymn at all, just a love song. But a special love song. Lisa's father had dabbled as a songwriter and written the song for Margaret – his wife and Lisa's mother. It was his one–and–only commercial success and a great favourite of mine. But I hadn't allowed for the effect it would have on Margaret. I had assumed, incorrectly that Margaret wouldn't actually know what was going on. I'd only included her in my guest list out of courtesy to Lisa and I'd made it perfectly clear to Lisa that it was her decision whether to include her grandmother or not. I was not the only one unprepared for Margaret's reaction. At first she sat in the pew where Lisa had put her, quietly staring around the chapel, vacantly gazing at everything and nothing, everyone and no one, all at the same time. She didn't react at all when the service started, but got to her feet with everyone else for the hymns. I should have realised then that something different, unplanned, was about to happen, but I didn't. As soon as her song started, Margaret seemed to come alive. For the first few bars she listened, her head lolled to one side like a dog's. Then her lips began to move to the words the congregation was singing. Then she began to sob. She wailed and cried in ever increasing spasms until she broke down completely, inconsolably. Lisa tried her best to calm her. She was inconsolable. Then the song finished. Margaret stopped crying immediately and as if switched–off by some invisible hand, she returned to her insensible, unperceiving norm. During the song, I had tried hard to reach her myself. I thought I might be able to generate comforting or soothing thoughts, to calm her down, but I failed. Now I wish that I hadn't tried. It was while I was concentrating so hard on Lisa's mother that I noticed 'the colours' again. The first were spots of blood–deep crimson that trickled like rain droplets into the periphery of my vision. It was tangible. I mean, it was there, this strange vision. But somehow it wasn't. I know that I'm not making any sense but since then it has happened three more times and each time it appears it's larger and more developed, an entity in itself, somehow threatening. The last time it appeared there were two additional colours, a pulsating gold and a misty smoky sapphire. Three interwoven shapeless colours, each a variation of a primary colour. For the first time I could actually feel its presence as well as see it, and it wasn't a pleasant feeling at all. This was a basic, primitive energy, ominous and foreboding. For the first time since my death, I felt cold and alone. Totally alone.

***

Chapter 8

Mary Little sat opposite her boss waiting while he read through the three-page report she had just passed him. He read quickly, scanning the pages, picking out the salient points with a precision that always impressed her.

'Three hundred and seventeen thousand pounds,' Brinker observed, as Mary Little smoothed the hem of her grey skirt flat across her knees. He flicked the rectangular desk-calendar in front of him from April to May, sucking on his bottom lip reflectively. Less than two weeks to go to the first draw. Will we make the target? That's the question! What do you think, Mary?'

Mary smiled; she loved the depth of his voice, always had. 'People love to gamble, sir, and new applications for tickets are arriving every day – almost fifty yesterday. We'll be turning them away by this time next week.' She loved to gamble, it was her one true vice. Rosie's lottery had captured both her imagination and her pocket book with a vengeance. Unfortunately, as an employee of Brin, Brinker and Briskin, she was excluded from participation but circumnavigated the problem easily by buying a ticket in her stepdaughter's married name. Her stepdaughter didn't share her enthusiasm, or her love of gambling. She had tried very hard to talk Mary out of spending, what she described as a 'huge amount of money'. Mary had simply told her not to interfere. She could easily afford it. She had her husband's life insurance payment, which had lain untouched in the savings bank since his death five years before. A thousand from that wouldn't do any harm. Her stepdaughter had capitulated, she had never had the strength to stand up to her for long

'I do hope you're right, Mother. I really do,' her stepdaughter had sighed in submission.

Beside Mary, on the floor next to her chair, lay a thick ring binder file crammed with papers. She reached down to pick it up. 'These are the application papers, sir,' she stated, opening the heavy file onto her lap. 'I've filed them alphabetically and each contains the data requested by the foundation for every participant. The second and third pages of the report you're holding, list the applicants as they are filed in here, in alphabetical order.' She tapped the file on her knees.

Brinker folded the first page back and began to sift again

through the names listed on pages two and three. There were no Loewens of course, the immediate family were not allowed to participate, but several times names came up in pairs; tickets were limited to one-per-household. 'Have you checked these ones with the same surname?'

'Yes sir. They're simply coincidences. Each applicant's address has been checked against his or her local electoral roll, the eight pairs and that one triple all check out.'

Brinker eyed the document suspiciously then grunted his assent. 'Who's doing the checking?' Brinker asked.

'Mr. Briskin, sir,' Mary replied. Her tone non-committal.

'Hmm! Well he should be able to manage that without too much of a problem.' Brinker passed the report back to Mary. 'Keep this in your office, Mary, but make sure it's locked safely away and be sure to update me every day. The sooner this is behind us the better if you ask me.'

Mary didn't. She placed the report in the file and, suppressing a little smile, walked out of his office.

***

Briskin's path was blocked by two large florid men each clasping a glass of beer in hands that made their pint glasses look like small tumblers. Briskin took a deep breath. 'Excuse me please,' he said in his most determined voice. The man to his left took half a step backwards and held his beer up high so that Briskin had to almost walk under it. The tray that Briskin carried wobbled alarmingly as he squeezed through. Beyond the two men was a round, wooden, polished table supported by a pedestal centre on three clawed feet. Sitting at the table were two men in business suits. One, Terrance Whet, was stocky and slightly rotund. Briskin knew him to be in his early fifties even though his balding head and poor complexion made him appear a lot older. The second man had been unknown to him until introduced five minutes earlier. He was, by contrast, broad shouldered and muscular, with a strong, film-star face. He appeared to be in his mid forties but Briskin correctly assumed that he was actually several years older. Unlike Whet, the second man had a full head of hair, rich red hair. His name was Martin Welland. Briskin placed the tray of drinks on the table and sat opposite the two men.

'Here we are,' he said. One gin and tonic, one vodka and tonic and pint of best for me. Cheers!'

Both Whet and Martin nodded politely, although in Martin's case obviously nervously. It had taken all of his courage and resolve to attend the meeting at all, and now that he was here he badly needed the drink to steady his nerves. He didn't consider himself a model person – his affair with Chloe was clear evidence of this – but he had never actually committed a criminal act and couldn't even contemplate doing so. Yet here he was, about to commit grand-fraud. Still it wasn't his fault, not really. The thought buoyed him. It was circumstances that had driven him to it. His life in the last week had been completely turned upside down, revolutionised. Although he had to admit that he had been approached by Whet before last week, before he'd told Chloe about his foolproof scheme for Rosie's lottery, before he discovered his wife with that arty ponce from the evening institute. But it had been little more than talk then, bravado, a pipe dream. And then there was the matter of the money. He'd told Chloe that he had the thousand pounds for the ticket and that was true, money wasn't a problem but he hadn't told her that his Friend, who owed him a favour, was a slight exaggeration. Whet was in fact paying him. One thousand now, a further two thousand after the first draw, then seven on the successful completion of the final draw, with a ten thousand bonus in five years time – on completion of the transfer of ownership. There was a clause in the trust-fund contract which stipulated that the new owner has to retain ownership of the lease for at least five years before he or she could sell it on. Now he had taken the money there was no turning back. Especially not with the underworld associates that Whet had recourse too. No. It wasn't his fault, or even his decision in the end. It was Joan's infidelity that had tipped the scales and given him that final, indignant, dash of courage.

He had all the evidence he needed, Joan had hardly been discreet. He'd felt quite ridiculous taking photographs of them going into the man's house, like a cheap private detective. But that had been enough. Once he showed those photos to Joan she was sure to break down – he knew her well enough, and a divorce would follow easily. Then he would have at least half of the value of their house; half of almost two hundred and fifty thousand. Minus his share of the mortgage, still over seventy thousand, plus the money from Whet and a nice little nest to share with Chloe for the next five years. He began to relax, a broad grin appearing on his face. Whet's voice interrupted his thoughts.

'Martin? Martin? Are you alright?

'Yes. Sorry,' Martin answered, who was staring at him intently.

''Thought we'd lost you there for a moment.'

'Yes. Sorry. I was thinking.'

'I'm sure you were, but day dreaming won't help, and if you can't concentrate on this then the deals off. I can find plenty of others. Plenty,' Whet concluded angrily.

'Look, I said that I'm sorry. And don't you threaten me. We're in this together. Till the end,' Martin added dramatically.

'Please. Please. Calm down. Both of you,' Briskin intervened, glancing anxiously over his shoulder at the two large men behind him, who were looking curiously in their direction. He lowered his voice. 'It's all set up. The first draw is the week after next. Six hundred tickets will be reduced to sixty. And, Martin, remember, when that happens you must keep a low profile. The names have to be made public, so the press will be after all of you. Remember that you don't expect to win, that's all you say. You'd love to win but you don't expect to. You're nervous. Show a little regret, like you're getting cold feet. You know. Beginning to feel you've wasted a thousand.'

'Mr. Briskin,' Martin replied, refusing to be drawn into the familiarity of first names. 'I'll play my part. You just make sure that you do yours.' Martin's smile returned, it was part of his charm and always disarming. 'I assume that this will be our last meeting?' he stated abruptly, then finished his drink in one swallow and rose from the table. 'Thank you very much gentlemen. I'll leave you to your drinks. I've an appointment in London this afternoon. Good day.'

Whet and Briskin sat in silence until Martin had left the pub. Whet spoke first. 'That's all six now,' he grinned. 'And quite a bonus. I expected the family of course, even though they are contesting the will. I've known old Freddie for years, and Thaddeus, and it was no surprise when Charles approached me. Although I suspect it was that wife of his, Helen, who was pushing him. Still. Whoever. It doesn't matter, it's all good money.'

'Quite,' Briskin replied. 'But I'd better be gone as well. I'm seeing the guy with the box. He should be finished this afternoon and he'll want his money. You know, I still can't believe old Brinker gave me the job. He obviously can't see the importance of it. He never gives me any of the important jobs – thinks I'm incapable of getting anything right.'

'The man's a fool,' Whet replied disparagingly. 'An honest man, therefore a complete fool. In his eyes he hasn't given you an important task at all. Simply arrange the lottery box. A child's job.'

They raised their glasses together. 'Here's to children,' said Briskin.

***

So there's a twist. Freddie and Thaddeus' contest-the-will scheme is a front. The family get together, listen to Freddie spout on about family-support to prove me loopy, while all the while he knows he can't. The rest of the family agrees, just as a show-of-face but they don't believe him. Then Whet gets involved, finds Briskin, the junior partner at Brin, Briskin and Brinker, and sets up a scam to fix the draw using stooges to buy the winning tickets. Now, if I understand what I've just heard correctly, Whet and Briskin intend to double cross Freddie and the family. They'll let them finance the whole thing, take their money and then move in on the six apartments themselves. And it all works because Whet has underworld contacts and he's made sure that the stooges are people who know that fact. By the time Freddie and co. find out, it'll be too late. Clever.

I had better find this lottery-box. Find out how it's been fixed and see what I can do about it.

Now there's a thought...

***

Lisa enjoyed the first draw; it was a real success, even if it was rather an anti-climax. She had worked hard to ensure that everything was carried out as denoted in Rose's Will. The draw was held strictly in *camera*, with just the family and a selected few members of the press present, plus Brinker, Briskin and Brinker's secretary Mary Little, to carry out the draw and adjudicate. The MP, Hewlett-Temple, wasn't required to draw the two preliminary rounds, just the final.

There had been a tremendous amount of hype and build-up in the press, blowing the whole thing up to almost National Lottery status. Brinker and Lisa had only just managed to calm things down, and the trust fund had to pay out for a private security company to keep unwanted press and public away. The TV people had been the worst. Lisa eventually agreed to let the cameras into the house in the morning, to take background footage, but she insisted that they were to leave by midday, before the draw. She had two wooden platforms erected; one in the entrance hall of the house, where the draw was to be conducted; the second, outside, where the main driveway formed a circle at the house. This is where the press were to mount their cameras; it had a canopy, in case of rain.

The preliminaries were tedious. Six hundred balls were counted out, with the number on each publicly noted and recorded by Mary Little on a neat, efficient clipboard. The job of calling each number was given to Briskin, who took it upon himself to lighten the tension a little by introducing a few fairground bingo calls, which delighted the selected press inside, and the non-selected press outside, who, despite Lisa's best efforts, had managed to secrete microphones inside the house and were avidly recording every word said. Briskin's antics did not, however, amuse Brinker or the family at all, except for Lia, who had to ask what legs-eleven meant and what was so obviously rude about the number sixty nine. Every one breathed a sigh of relief as, finally, Briskin called ball number six hundred. He had placed all six hundred balls in a clear plastic drum, which he sealed with press pleasing ceremony. The drum was supported on a rectangular base, also of clear plastic. The interior of the rectangle was designed to catch the numbered, Ping-Pong balls as they were released from the drum above, lining them up neatly before allowing them to drop into the final receptacle, a large glass bowl which would catch the sixty first-phase winners.

Brinker stepped forward to the edge of the platform. 'Ladies and Gentlemen, members of the press,' he began solemnly. 'As you have witnessed, the contestants,' he waved his hands at the six hundred balls in the glass bowl as if they were indeed the actual ticket holders, 'have been counted and verified. We are now ready to draw the sixty, first round winners. 'He paused, giving his announcement time to settle.

'Boring old fart,' Freddie muttered to Thaddeus, who nodded in agreement.

Brinker was still talking. 'I will ask Miss Lisa Going, Chairperson of the Rose Loewen Trust, to spin the drum.' He stepped back, full of his own importance. Lisa, smiled at the gathering, leaned forward and spun the perspex drum quickly through several revolutions. The balls rattled around noisily inside, bumping and hopping over each other. Finally satisfied that all the balls had been thoroughly mixed, Lisa stopped the drum then began to rotate it in the opposite direction. The entire room held its breath. A tube inside the drum caught the first ball and dropped it neatly into the centre of the rectangle below. There was a rattling sound as the ball rolled along a short track and then into a channel inside the clear plastic rectangle before dropping into a large glass bowl below. It was number 427. Martin's number. A second ball dropped then a third. Briskin stepped back several feet behind Brinker, counting out loud as each ball dropped into the glass bowl.

'Sixty,' Brinker announced, slightly out of breath.

***

What a frustrating afternoon. All that concentration and nothing to show for it. This morning I spent some considerable time studying that contraption that dispensed the first sixty balls. There was nothing wrong with it, at least not as far as I could see. It's constructed entirely of clear plastic. You can see the movement of each ball as it passes from the drum through the box below and into the bowl underneath. It all seemed foolproof, at least until the first ball dropped. Then it suddenly became deadly serious. They had done it, were doing it, openly, in front of everyone. In front of me. I knew that I could, should intervene. I knew that I was capable of moving the balls, moving them physically, controlling the outcome, and eliminating the six balls selected by Mr Whet. But I didn't know which ones they were. I have to admit that I was more than a little frustrated. I know all about the trick lottery box, about the designs of Freddie and Thaddeus. I've been privy to the meetings with Whet and Briskin and to most of Freddie and Thaddeus' private discussions. I know who one of the fraudulent winners is – the man Martin, from the pub meeting who was now legitimately into the next round. But I haven't a clue how it's being done. And I've no idea which five of the sixty were the other conspirators. That's what makes it all so doubly frustrating. Now, how am I going to find out?

***

The dining hall of the Melanie Masters Rehabilitation Clinic was a spacious steel and glass extension to the main building, and the product of a generous donation by the family of a previous patient. The Mathew Collins Hall had been completed just six months earlier and was now the pride of the clinic. A coffee bar and serving counter occupied the main-building end of the room, with two swinging doors – one marked IN the other OUT -giving access to the kitchens. Dining tables were placed at regular rows, and interspersed with clusters of potted plants, each neatly aligned and gleaming with daily washed and polished leaves.

At eleven-thirty in the morning, in the lull before lunch, the dining hall was almost empty. Reggie and Maureen sat at the far end of the room, three tables away from the only other couple present, a middle-aged man, holding the hand of his wife and talking to her in soft, deliberate tones. The table separating Reggie and Maureen was long, shiny and synthetic, a composite plastic-fibreglass surface with rounded edges supported on stainless steel legs. Reggie found the table-top indicative of the clinic. Rounded edges. Nothing sharp or angular or dangerous. Everything carefully controlled. Even the furniture had to conform to the rules. To Reggie, the clinic was nothing more than a well upholstered prison, all settees, TV lounges, musac and Dettol-swabbed reception areas, with bedroom doors locked at night, tighter than a ducks rear, and during the day as well if THEY wanted them to be. He was the inmate. Sentenced to life was how it felt, and Maureen was the gushy prison visitor. The do-gooder, trying to cheer him up.

Reggie looked across at his wife. She was talking, twittering on as she always did. An endless monologue of trivia interspersed with comments from her mum. But there was something different about her. Even in his present state of self-pity and despair, he could see that. She was dressed in blue-jeans and a cotton blouse, which was normal. The beige, lightweight coat draped across the chair next to her was two years old and that was perfectly normal as well. But there was something in her face, in the set of her eyes, a determination, a purpose. Because today Maureen wasn't 'twittering on'. Today Maureen had something to say. He wasn't listening. I NEED A DRINK! The words screamed inside his head.

'They had an open day yesterday,' Maureen continued. In the morning. For the press. Then at midday it was the draw.' Maureen's excitement did not transmit to her Reggie who shook his head in despair. Unperturbed, Maureen continued. 'That Newit-Temple man from the government, you know the one on the telly, on the news all the time, didn't do it though, they're saying...'

'Hewlett-Temple. It's an 'H' not an 'N',' Reggie corrected.

'Anyway, Newit, Hewlett, whatever. He's just doing the finals. Too busy to do the other rounds, I suppose. I've been reading about him in the papers. They say there's going to be a shake up now that he's foreign secretary. They say the Prime Minister is against him, that in private the Prime Minister refers to him as a fascist, but that Newit-Temple is so strong they have to give him the job, it's upset the Americans terribly, and my mum says....' On that slightly incredulous note she paused for breath.

Reggie looked at her. Perhaps it was the surroundings, or his depression. Perhaps it was Maureen's new-found power, the firm hold she now lorded over him. Whatever it was, this was a new Maureen, a very, different Maureen. Even if she did still sound the same, twittering on about politics she barely understood and always cross-referencing to her mother. Perhaps she should write a book – The Thoughts of Chairman Mum, by Maureen Chambers. All the twittering wives all over the world would read it. It would be a best seller. Think of the hours of relief it would bring to thousands of ear-battered husbands; who no doubt also NEEDED A DRINK!

But now, over the last two weeks, Maureen had changed. This wasn't his Maureen. This wasn't the half-witted blond that he led around by the nose. From behind that facade had appeared a new Maureen with an inner strength that he would have never dreamed she possessed. And a deviousness, a subtle cunning that had really caught him unawares. Getting him to sign those committal papers had been easy. He knew that getting drunk as often as he did, left him vulnerable for anything like that; including the house-sale papers. But setting the papers out the way she did was quite brilliant. At least if you wanted to make them absolutely broke it was. Where did she get it from? That thought had plagued him continuously, ever since he'd been admitted, ever since Maureen had first shown him those papers and explained what they meant, ever since he'd been sober enough to think.

'Hewlit-Temple's not a fascist,' he stated. This observation proved superfluous.

'You see it's all for the best.' Maureen enlarged. 'My mum says...'

Reggie tried to switch off, to push Maureen's voice into the background. He clenched his teeth. I NEED A DRINK! A DRINK! A DRINK! He closed his eyes and concentrated. Ice tinkled against a crystal glass. Golden droplets of whisky dribbled between his parched lips and warmed the back of his throat. 'Another sir?' The hiss of a soda-siphon as the barman poured his third. He reached towards it...

'And then my Mum said...'

Ahh!

Reggie screwed his eyes shut, as tightly as he could. Shutting out the bright sunlight that invaded every corner of the dining hall. He took a deep breath, and another, and a third. The level of Maureen's chatter began to diminish, eventually reducing to a barely audible drone that gnawed quietly at his nerve ends. He concentrated on the situation she'd put them into. They were almost broke. Maureen had put all but a small ten percent of the money from the house-sale, into his treatment. Over fifteen thousand pounds of over-priced, over-rated so-called treatment, and they hadn't actually treated him at all. Most of the time there was only one doctor on the premises the rest were all counsellors, most of them ex-alchi's themselves. And what good had it done him?

I NEED A DRINK!

The thought screamed at him. When he opened his eyes, Maureen was leaning towards him. She held both his hands in hers. His hands shook so violently that she couldn't control them completely. Tears welled in Maureen's eyes. 'It's alright darling. I promise it is. You'll be better soon. You'll see.' Despite the strong sunlight, Reggie's pupils were dilated, his cheeks began to flush and beads of sweat broke out on his forehead. His breathing quickened to a short rasping cadenza. Maureen looked anxiously over her shoulder. The middle aged couple were just leaving the hall. The door marked IN swung gently on its hinges. They were alone.

Maureen moved round to Reggie's side of the table and sat beside him. She pressed his hands into her lap, releasing one of her own so she could draw his head into her chest. She hugged him as firmly as she could, trying to absorb the shaking into her own body, to share the pain he was going through. 'Don't worry,' she said. 'You are getting better. It's wonderful the progress you've made. Really. It is.' She began to rock gently from side to side. Reggie's trembling slowly subsided. A thin steam of tears moistened the front of Maureen's blouse. 'Don't cry, Reggie. There's nothing to cry about. And don't worry about the money. We were never happy in that house. Anyway, it was a huge millstone around our necks, what with the mortgage and everything. And now we're going to win this beautiful flat, in a country manor, in beautiful grounds, and everything paid for. No bills Reggie. Just think of it! And it will happen. He told me.' She rocked him backwards and forwards, whispering into his ear, 'It's going to be alright' and 'I love you,' repeatedly. His body began to relax. Eventually she was able to lift his face to hers and kiss him on the lips.

'Better now?' she asked. She stared into his eyes, looking for recognition, for understanding. 'Just think of it darling. Our own luxury flat,' she repeated pressing Reggie's head back into her chest.

Reggie was thinking of it. He had to admit that since she'd gone crazy and bought the ticket, the thought that they might have a fighting chance of winning had helped to get him through the days without a drink inside him. But the last part, the – *he told me* – had connotations that he didn't want to go into too deeply. He didn't believe in all that mumbo-jumbo stuff of course. But he had been around during the seances with her medium-mum. For a laugh, he'd even attended them, listened to all the stupidity they came out with. No... He didn't need all that rubbish, didn't believe in it. Not at all. He pulled back from Maureen and looked up into her face. 'I love you,' he said. 'I don't understand... can't believe what you've done. I don't know why, but I do love you.'

Maureen smiled and kissed him gently on the forehead. She wasn't certain whether he meant that he didn't know why she had sold the house or didn't know why he loved her, but it didn't matter; he did love her, that's all that mattered.

'I've got something special to tell you,' she sniffed as she dabbed at her eyes with a paper handkerchief. 'I was saving it.'

'What?' asked Reggie suspiciously, recognising something deep in her voice, something that he had heard a lifetime before.

'Well two things actually and they're both marvellous.' She paused allowing a little tension to grow, elevating the moment to the place it deserved. 'First of all, the draw for Rosie's lottery was published this morning...

'And?'

'And! ...and we're through.' The excitement tore at her vocal cords, her voice cracked to almost a screech.

'What?'

'We're through! We're through! Look.' She pulled a newspaper from her handbag and laid it on the table. 'Here,' she said, dabbing at the print where she had circled her name in red biro. 'Isn't it fantastic!?

Reggie stared blankly at her. Through! He thought. If I don't get a drink now. Right now, then I'm through. That's what I am.

She was pushing a newspaper into his hands. 'Read,' she said.

'Read the story. It's in all the newspapers. 'Mrs Maureen Chambers, that's me, ticket number Four Four Eight.'

Perhaps… The thought began to gel in Reggie's pickled brain as he stared at the line of print above her finger. 'Eight's my lucky number,' he said.

***

Stuart fidgeted in his seat. He wanted to leave, to run away from the table, get as far away as possible from this madness, but he couldn't now. He was too far in and he was beginning to regret that fact, deeply.

His last job had gone as smooth as clockwork – not a Rottweiler in sight and it was supposed to be his last job, yet here he was, planning the next. This new one was definitely going to be his last, ever. His Swan-song. But it was getting out of control. The fact was that greed had brought him to this table. A greed that he had fought against successfully throughout his long career. He knew it was discipline that had always been the secret to his success. Discipline, plus guidelines, rules that he set himself and always abided by. Until now he had always worked alone. He had always prepared meticulously. He had always targeted worthwhile marks but never gone too far, never gone out of his league. Now that was no longer the case. Fourteen million pounds net had put pay to that.

The safe he'd blown so sweetly on his last job had paid out a good dividend. Its contents were exactly what he'd expected to find in the house of a wealthy businessman, no more, no less. Then, by pure chance, he had discovered the other safe, the one that was so cleverly hidden. It really wasn't fair to call it a safe at all, and on reflection, Stuart could see that is wasn't actually meant to be a repository, in the strong-room sense, more in the keeping-out-of-prying-eyes sense. It was little more than a tin box, very cleverly set into the back of a video cabinet. He wasn't a ransacking type of burglar and would take great umbrage if referred to as a burglar at all. Stuart was an old fashioned, dime-detective-novel safe-cracker. A specialist. A pro. He cracked safes, took the contents and left the premises. But he was still human and therefore couldn't resist a little look-around. It was while he was looking-around, bending low to inspect a rather fine porcelain vase that he dropped a coin from his pocket. The coin rolled right under the video cabinet. Fortunately for him, as it turned out, he noticed the coin fall. The video cabinet was made from expensive polished Rosewood. It was very heavy and not mounted on casters. He cursed himself for his carelessness. He was a pro and pro's don't make that sort of mistake. What was the point of wearing gloves and plastic hair caps to stop fingerprints and catch follicles of DNA abundant hair if you left a coin behind you'd been carrying for days that was covered in your prints and DNA; you might as well just leave a stamped addressed envelope. He had to scrabble on his back on the floor to retrieve it, his arm at full stretch and the coin tantalisingly just out of reach of his finger tips. That's how he discovered the metal box.

It wasn't a safe, it was really just a custom-built cash-box with a lock. Didn't even have to blow it. He simply picked the lock.

Inside the box he had found a letter, one that didn't make sense at first, but intrigued him enough to make him want to read it again. He sat comfortably in a deep studded-leather Chesterfield chair, beside the blown safe and the picked tin-box and reread the letter – three times. Gradually the enormity of its contents began to dawn on him.

Being a crook himself, the thought that other people – people purporting to be upright citizens – pillars of the community – committed enormous crimes all the time, naively struck him as rather odd. But there was no getting away from what he read, this was a biggee! Fourteen million pounds of smuggled, uncut diamonds was big by any standard. Big if you put a legal front on it, and gigantic if, like Stuart, you were just a simple honest small-time safecracker.

He rewrote the letter on a piece of headed note-paper from the bureau next to the blown safe in the study, then replaced the original where he had found it and relocked the tin box, taking care to recover the coin that had led to this discovery. He read and reread his copy of the letter every day, for a full week, before making the decision that eventually led to today's meeting. His decision to step out of the environment he understood and could control, into the hostile environment of his new colleagues across the table.

Their names were Phil and Mal Barnes. Which was short for Philip and Malcolm. They were thirty-two years of age, from the east end of London with accents to match, and they were twins, identical in every respect except for temperament.

Phil was the older by a matter of minutes, but by several years in maturity. Both brothers were highly intelligent and frighteningly sharp, but Mal had a vicious streak and a certain recklessness about him that worried Stuart. There was also a dependency that threatened the security of the job – Mal never did anything without Phil's say-so. What made it worse was that even after three weeks of planning and surveillance together, Stuart was still having difficulty telling the two brothers apart. A situation that wasn't helped by the brothers identical stubby short hair cuts and natural selection of the same clothing; unless they actually spoke, Stuart struggled.

'And this contraption works?' Stuart prodded the black and silver control unit that sat on the table between them.

'Oh yeah. It works all ryht,' Phil replied. 'It's simple, and the crazy fing is that it's a common piece of equipment that anyone can buy in any electronics shop.'

'Well wash it past me again,' Stuart said, finding the earlier, highly technical explanation Phil had given far from simple. 'And try and put it in layman's terms this time. Real simple like.'

Phil grinned at his brother, he was enjoying this. Stuart was the senior of their new-found partnership, it was his idea, his job and, his authority and obvious experience had left the twins a little in awe, but it was their plan and they were the electronic experts; it was good to have the upper hand for once. 'GPS, Global Plotting System,' he started. 'Each of the Failsafe armoured vans is fitted with it.

Mal nodded in agreement, reinforcing his brother's statement.

Now.. As soon as a van leaves the Failsafe depot, the GPS is activated. Remember?

Condescending little prick. Stuart's smiled assent belied his thoughts.

Phil continued, his tone ever superior. 'The military developed GPS to enable 'em to track troop and equipment movements, and to pinpoint targets, so its been around for years. What it does is lock onto a series of satellites, taking readings from each satellite, constantly cross-referencing them. So you can imagine, it's extremely accurate.'

'That's were Failsafe have made a big mistake,' Mal interrupted excitedly.

'And it's that mistake that we're gonna exploit, yes?' Stuart asked.

'Precisely.' Phil tapped the side of his nose. 'This is the clever bit,' he continued. 'Like many uver cump'nies moving into the hi-tech environment, they've forgotten the old adage of not putting all their eggs into one basket. It's amazin' how many small-to-medium cump'nies have bought themselves computer systems with all the computers linked to one server, without buying all the additional gear needed to protect the server and the system. The server goes down and all the PCs tumble with it. It's commonplace occurrence and, it's exactly what Failsafe have let themselves in for with the GPS.

They've got the GPS to do all the tracking. The drivers used to call in at every uver road junction – they had a sort of black-box arrangement like the airlines and a signalling procedure that preceded each call the drivers made. In uver words, they not only knew where their trucks were but they received that information from the drivers themselves. If anyone nabbed one of their trucks they knew about it as soon as the next call-in and signal failed; say… within no more than three minutes. Now, they rely entirely on the GPS. The drivers call in as they leave the depot or as they leave their drop-off point but not in-between.'

Phil paused to let his explanation sink in.

'OK,' Stuart responded. 'So far I've got that.'

Mal took up the momentum. 'Well.. The GPS units are mounted on the vehicles, where the information is no good at all to the driver – he already knows where he is. And the fact that Failsafe HQ know exactly where the truck is offers no protection at all, does it?'

'Now you've lost me,' Stuart admitted, shaking his head. 'It was much better this time. Much simpler than all that differential-calculation-to-offset-deflection crap you came out with before but, from the drivers point of view, what difference does it make what this GPS sends back to Failsafe? As you said, he already knows where he is!'

'Precisely. You've got it now. The driver knows where he is, ergo he knows where the truck is because he's in it, but Failsafe, they only know where the signal's coming from. That's the point.' Phil sat back and lit a cigarette, satisfied that he'd explained the whole thing as clearly as could be. Mal nodded again.

Stuart thought for a moment. 'So you're saying that we intercept the truck, disconnect the GPS and then what? Put it in another vehicle so that Failsafe think their truck is still on schedule?' Stuart looked at them both quizzically, uncertain of his comprehension of the situation

'Almost. Except that we're cleverer than that. You see. Failsafe have to get that information back to their central control, to monitor where each vehicle is and for that they're using a radio link, GSM, just like a mobile phone. That's their weak point.' Mal tapped the control box lovingly. 'And this little gizmo can intercept that signal.' He nodded his head, inviting Stuart to agree.

'OK. So we intercept the signal from the mobile phone in the truck. What then?'

'We send our own signal. We literally tell Failsafe where their truck is.'

'But it isn't.'

'Precisely.' Phil was grinning widely at their ingenuity and, not for the first time, Stuart saw a glimpse of madness behind Phil's eyes. That hint of the insane that is often associate with genius.

'That's better,' Stuart replied thoughtfully. 'I got it that time. All those giga-hertz and differential readings you spouted on about before lost me completely. But all the same, I'd like to see this baby in action.'

'No problem. I'll set it up with an antenna in our van and we can try it out this afternoon. Don't worry, it works. Failsafe will happily track their vehicle all the way to its destination, except it won't be their vehicle, will it? In fact, it won't even be ours. It'll just be a little programme Mal and me wrote, being transmitted back down their own communications system. Beautiful ain't it?

'As simple as that.' Stuart could see the logic, the simplicity of the plan, but was loath to rise to their level of enthusiasm for it.

Mal rubbed his hands gleefully. 'You gotta a'mit we're frigging geniuses, ain't we?' He threw the question with a grin and a challenge across the table at Stuart.

'You had better be,' Stuart replied, a little reluctantly. 'And what about the other gizmo?' Stuart jerked his question at the rack of black boxes in the far corner of the room.

'Would you like another demonstration?' Phil asked.

Stuart held up his hands in horror. 'Not bloody likely.' He remembered the first time the brothers had demonstrated their little electronic toy. He had thought his ears were going to burst. 'But don't forget the timing. That's all-important. Miss the spot and we're done. Nothing. Zilch. Ten million…' he snapped his fingers dramatically. 'Puff,' he added.

'OK. OK. We got your point.' Mal took a 1:50,000 ordinance-survey map from on top of the black boxes and spread it on the table. He traced his index finger across the map, following the line of a winding B road. 'Here,' he said. 'is the Barwick Village Road.

At this point the road splits. We know that the jewels will be moved to this house, Bridewalk Manor, a big, quiet mausoleum of a place hiding away in acres and acres of land.' He indicated the fork to the left. It's supposed to be a secret, but thanks to you Stuart,' Stuart gave a bow, 'we know that the basement of the manor house has been fitted out as a high security vault for the diamond company. To get to Bridewalk Manor from the M1 is a forty-minute journey, so we intercept the van here, at this point.' He pointed to the same B road, but at the point where it spurred away from the larger A road that led directly to the main motor way.

'We simply block the road with our broken down car. We don't threaten, or even look menacing, we're just simply broken down. So... because we are blocking the road – and therefore the path of the armoured car – the crew will radio into their HQ; it's their standard operating procedure, and...' Mal paused. 'just as they sign off, we intercept.' Phil interrupted smoothly, as though there hadn't been a break in the conversation. This was the second time Stuart had witnessed the brothers melding. Their reputation was not based entirely upon a sound and ingenious knowledge of electronics, as good as it was, their real talent lay in their uncanny, almost telepathic, understanding. Under pressure they changed. No longer just twins who looked and acted alike, they elevated themselves to a higher, almost telepathic level, one harmonious single unit, thinking, speaking and reacting as if they were joined at the hip. 'We can hold their channel open while their control disengages. Neither party will know, and that's when we hit them. The pitch from this baby slams the eardrums like a sledgehammer. It's impossible not to clamp your hands over your ears. The pain's incredible. You can't avoid screwing your eyes shut.' Phil offered Stuart the headphones that were connected to the rack of black boxes. 'You sure you don't want to try?'

Stuart shook his head. 'I think I'll give it a miss.'

'Once we've zapped them it's over to you,' Mal continued. 'Both crew'll be out cold. It should happen that way. But whatever... they'll be totally incapacitated for at least thirty seconds.'

'And I'll have their emergency call frequency blocked... No problem,' Phil added.

'It sounds good,' Stuart replied. 'I don't need that long to blow the driver's door. Ten seconds will do, fifteen at the most. But don't forget the pressure plates under the seats. We have to get the sandbags on before we shift the guards off.'

'Don't worry.' Phil pointed to two bulging Hessian sacks stacked in the corner. Fifty kilo's each,' he said. 'I weighed em out, meself.'

'So we're a GO then?' Mal stated more than asked, excitedly.

'We are bruv,' Phil added looking hard at Stuart, challenging him to disagree.

'Yes, we're on,' Stuart replied to them both, feeling less than fully comfortable with the statement. 'Now let's go over the map again, and the decoy break-down, and where we take the van.'

All three bent forward over the map of the target area. Stuart began to softly whistle the theme from Mission Impossible.

Chapter 9

'I don't hate him enough. In fact I don't hate him at all.' Eric slumped dejectedly into their one tatty armchair. 'And don't forget. Although he doesn't know it, he was the one that brought us together in the first place.'

Perched at the end of their bed – the only other comfortable seat in their tiny, tawdry bed-sit – Norman threw his arms out and round, encompassing the entire room in one simple gesture. 'Look Eric. Look at what we've got... Bugger all. Nothing. Except bills... In fact we're very strong on bills. And it's his fault. Not all of it of course, but most of it. He should have stepped in and spoken up for you. You'd have kept your position then and wouldn't be living like this now. Would you?' He threw the last question at Norman in pure exasperation, fighting back a frustrated tear.

Eric crossed the small room to him, sat on the bed and put his arms round him. He stroked Norman's thick mat of brown hair gently. 'There. There. Calm down. You're right. If he hadn't let me take the blame then I'd still be there. Earning a princely wage. But I wouldn't have met you then. Would I? And no Prince wants to live without his Princess He turned Norman's face up towards him, as you would a child's. 'Listen to me,' he said soothingly, kissing him softly on the forehead. 'We've been together long enough for you to know that I would never threaten or attack a friend in that fashion, especially one that had been a partner; it could be you.' Eric's eyes began to water. 'Even if you hurt me, really hurt me,' he added. 'I could never hurt you. You know that, surely.'

Norman nodded his head meekly. Eric continued. 'I agree that he could have done more, a lot more. It's hypocrisy that held him back. The same hypocrisy that we accuse the straights of, but in reverse. Even in today's liberated society we have to face reality. His position would be extremely difficult; totally impossible if his sexuality became public. I couldn't do that to him... But I will ring him, see if he can help.' Eric paused to look around the room himself. The old Regency-Stripe wallpaper peeling off the walls, the damp patch behind the bed-head that threatened rheumatically every time it rained. 'Your right,' he said. 'We can't go on like this.'

***

Well it's been a few days since the first draw and I've been rather busy, successfully so, if I do say so myself. Exhaustingly so. Not in the physica... Oh listen to me... You've had all that Not-in-a-physical-sense malarkey more than enough times to know what I mean. It's just worn me out trying to keep tabs on all of them, but it's paying off.

I'm up to four ticket numbers now. 62 that was the first one. That was that ginger haired guy from the pub, with Whet and Briskin. Martin's his name. Martin Welland. Smooth piece of work he is. The sort of man I used to fall for. Just like hubby number three. He's got a girl friend. That's why he's got himself involved. Needs the money to set himself up again. Money and five year tenancy in one of my new apartments. A nice little love nest. We'll soon fix him.

Ticket numbers 237 and 439 have been bought by women. Both young, hard-bitten, painted individuals who Whet led me too. He's supplied them with the thousand pounds each for the ticket and he's paying them two thousand more to front for him. But they're not going to live in the apartments at all. Whet's going to sub-let them on the Q..T.. No taxman no pack-drill. I kicked myself when I heard that because it was an obvious loophole I should have guarded against. Unlike Martin Welland, the girls didn't even think of taking up occupancy. They just took the money no-questions-asked. By the way, neither of them are virgins. If you get my meaning.

The forth ticket is number 501. Whet went for a more direct approach on this one and I wouldn't have found out about it at all if I hadn't latched onto his sister, Teresa, last Friday afternoon. There was something about her that intrigued me. I don't know what it was but it proved really opportune. Teresa has number 501. Teresa Stamp ticket number 501 it says in Mary Little's register. Yes. Stamp. She's Whet's half sister. Same mother different fathers. Which probably explains Teresa's looks. He must have been an unsightly so-and-so 'cause she's uglier than a pantomime witch.

So that's four out of six and I'm still working on the other two.

Then there's the family. I've been watching them as close as I can. Freddie and Thaddeus are as thick as the thieves they are. Almost inseparable at the moment. And they worry me, terribly. I'm having trouble accepting that those two are just going to leave it to Whet and the probate lawyer to contest the Will. That may be OK for simple minds like Charles and Christian. Even Elsbeth may have convinced herself that it'll work; after all they're no other options

114

on the table for her. Are there? But not the terrible-two. And don't forget Helen. Freddie and Thaddeus aren't about to let her into their confidences but I'm sure she's not going to just lie back and take it. So I've been trying to follow them all, and it's not working.

So. I've had to take a chance with the nephews and Elsbeth. I've just told myself that I've been too clever for them and that they're beaten, finished, not a threat. That goes for Elsbeth as well. I made that decision the day before yesterday and it made an enormous difference. I'm not worried about Lia, obviously. So that leaves me watching Freddie, Thaddeus, Helen, the lawyer Briskin and Whet; Teresa I've ruled out as well as I already have her number.

I'll keep you posted. Gotta go…

***

Liam stretched, pushed his feet clear of the crumpled bedclothes and wriggled his toes. He glanced at the clock on the bedside cabinet. 'Three minutes,' he mumbled to himself, pondering briefly on the unwritten law of nature that decreed he should always wake up just before the alarm went off, even if he changed the setting. He sat up and tussled his thick black hair between long elegant fingers. The third finger of his left hand was stained along the base of the cuticle; acrylic paint, a pale cerise from his last lesson the previous evening. Thursdays were always a late night. He'd missed the painted nail when he'd washed up, 'and now it's Friday,' he announced to the world in general, swinging his legs off the side of the bed and searching blindly for his slippers with his toes. His right foot struck something soft, then his left. He slipped his feet into the sympathetic padded slippers and sat on the side of the bed, staring idly at nothing at all. After what to Liam, seemed to be quite a long time, the alarm clock suddenly erupted into a cloud of jangling noise, making him jump from his temporary stupor. He clenched his eyelids firmly closed and focused his attention, visualising his lecture calendar for the day. Pre-Raphaelite masters at 9.30, a free period at 11.00, lunch, Impressionism verses Cubism at 2.00 and Art as a political statement at 4.00 – the thought depressed him. He thumped the plunger on the top of the alarm clock, skidding the offensive contraption onto the bedroom floor. The alarm stopped, in mid flight. The clock plopped onto the floor, its fall cradled by the thick shag-pile carpet. He always found that giving three lectures in

115

the same day was too much, no time to compose and prepare oneself in between. Thank God there's no Evening Institute class tonight, he thought, as he replaced the alarm clock on the bedside cabinet, completing what was a regular morning ritual. He staggered half-lidded to the bathroom.

Liam's bathroom was floored from wall to wall and floor to ceiling, with the highest quality Italian sculptured tiles. Predominantly blue, a mixture of azure background and stronger blue highlights, with picture tiles in the centre of the wall above the bath; three intertwined and slightly erotic cherubim's. The bathroom, as with the rest of Liam's one bedroom flat, was quite compact, but the extra care with which he had decorated, his determination not to stint on the quality of materials and his artist's eye, had served to produce an appearance of comfort, lightness, and freedom. Liam considered that the moonlighting he had to do at the Evening Institute to finance such luxuries, more than worthwhile.

He placed his razor on the marble top of the vanity unit that stood against the opposite wall to the bath, and rinsed shaving foam off his face, then wiped it with a towel and stared closely into the mirror in front of him. He tweaked the tip of his nose between his thumb and forefinger, inspecting every visible pore for signs of grease or dirt. Eventually satisfied, he smiled at the mirror. The mirror smiled back. It was an old friend, the only piece of furniture from the entire flat that wasn't new or at least purchased during the two-year period he'd lived there. The mirror was a family heirloom that his father had often threatened to take to auction; claiming that it had been brought into the family by his great-grandfather, and that the frame was over one hundred and fifty years old. Liam didn't doubt his father's claim but he suspected that the assumption that the intricately carved wooden and gilt frame was worth a lot of money, was merely wishful thinking. He actually preferred not to know, why spoil the myth?

Between the gilt and the glass, at the inside edge of the top of the frame, was wedged a small metal sprung clip holding a photograph of himself and a woman embracing each other affectionately. The woman was blond, tanned and in her mid forties. They both wore swim wear and stood on soft sand, framed by dancing white surf and a crystal clear blue sky. He was standing behind the woman, with his right arm wrapped around her, cupped below her breasts, lifting them to point straight at the camera. Liam unclipped the photograph carefully. 'Madeline,' he whispered as he

116

kissed the woman's face tenderly.

The sink was underpinned by a slim vanity unit that wrapped itself around the pedestal that supported it. Down each curved side resided small gold-handled draws. Liam pulled the top one all the way out and reached into the recess behind it, retrieving two similar photographs, each of himself with attractive, slightly older women; a different woman in each photograph. The first of the two photographs was again on the beach. But not the Caribbean beach of Madeline's picture, this was a much more recent photo, taken on the English south coast, with a pebble beach and goose pimples for a suntan. Unlike Madeline, Joan wasn't wealthy and so far he'd only managed to get her away on one occasion; a weekend at a small quiet hotel in Bournemouth. But Joan would have to wait. He slid her photograph on top of Madeline's and replaced the small drawer.

The last of the three photographs wasn't a beach scene at all. It was just of him and a woman alone against a stark white studio backdrop. She was seated, obviously posing and, although not completely naked, wearing just a length of translucent silk material draped from her shoulders to her legs, finishing in a curl around her ankles. Liam stood behind her, his upper torso bare, oil glistening on his chest, the lower half of his body invisible to the camera. She was blond and of a similar age to Madeline and Joan. All three women were attractive but Ann clearly stood out from the other two.

Ann was his latest triumph, a by-product of his Tuesday night class at the nearby Rochforth Arts Academy. As with all his conquests in recent years she had been cropped from an art evening class and just like the others she was about ten years older than him.

Apart from their age and their adoration of Liam, all three women had one simple common denominator; they had all taken up an artistic pursuit to stave off boredom or neglect and, in doing so, had found a romance inside of them that they hadn't realised existed. A romance that longed to escape, that demanded to be set free. A romance waiting for deliverance. Unfortunately only Madeline had shown any real artistic talent. Joan could at least hold a brush correctly and, with a lot of supervision, could outline a profile so that it was at least recognisable as human – although gender was often a complete mystery – but poor Ann had absolutely no talent at all except an inexhaustible energy to paint watercolours of wild herbs, which wholly entranced her. That hadn't mattered, the inner beauty that each tried to express on canvas or in clay, was clear to Liam, obvious, unmistakable, it was more beautiful than a Rembrandt, more powerful than a Caravaggio, more mystifying than a Picasso; it drew him to them inexorably.

For his part, Liam didn't fully understand what the women saw in him. Certainly they were all from the same age group, all older than him, all reaching back, trying to fold back the years a little, but that was only a minor part of the equation and they each had very different personalities and completely different backgrounds which tended to fog that particular commonality. He was good looking. Dark Mediterranean. Even sultry. But that wasn't really enough. It was the passion that they all shared that bound them into similarity, a passion that related directly to their need to paint or sculpture, their need to express themselves, to be individuals. There was also simply a need within each of them to escape. Liam had learnt how to nurture and develop that inner passion that they all so desperately wanted to release, to put onto canvass or into clay; that sense of the incomplete that they needed to fulfil. Even if he didn't really realise it, that was what drew them to him. He simply understood them and wasn't afraid to show it.

Madeline had been his first, almost ten years before. She had just split with her husband when they first met. For six months they had a torrid and stormy on-off, extremely physical relationship. Gradually the physical side had cooled and they found time to talk to each other, to actually get to know each other. It was during this time that Liam learnt the advantages of consideration, equality and respect. With Madeline's unconscious help he developed a strong sense of perception, awareness and comprehension. But most of all, an ability to listen and understand. Their affair lasted for almost a full year. Madeline finally called it off. She told Liam that she attributed her final reconciliation with her husband to their love affair. She claimed to have found herself, to have 'released herself from herself' she had said on the day she moved out of Liam's flat and back into her expensive detached house in stockbroker Surrey. At first Liam had felt used, indignant. But after a while he began to understand what she meant. That was the strength that she had given him. And he still saw her occasionally, perhaps three or four times a year. She called him her tonic. 'I need a Liam and Tonic' she joked, each time she rang him.

Liam slid the photograph of Ann under the clip on the mirror, Ann would expect to see it there, they all expected to see their photographs on the old mirror. He smoothed the photograph flat against the glass and looked longingly at it. Ann was special. He had met her in the same way as all the others, and for the same reasons, but there was something very special about Ann, something apart from her beauty. He couldn't explain what it was but it made him shiver, even frightened him. He rubbed a squeeze of gel into his hair, then quickly washed his hands before the mild black tint in the gel took a hold on his skin. As he pulled a dampened comb through his hair the flecks of grey that haunted him every morning, quietly vanished… A splash of cologne and he was finished.

He blew himself a kiss.

***

'Crystel! I'm leaving in five minutes, whether you're ready or not,'

Crystel pulled her hair back into a dishevelled ponytail and secured it with an elasticised band of fluffy, multi-coloured cotton material. 'OK. Mum. Ready,' she replied enthusiastically. She liked Saturdays. She was allowed to work on Saturdays. With her mum.

Her mother Stephanie, worked as an assistant with an outside catering company. She'd had the job almost a year, and apart from one week, when she had been ill, had taken Crystel to all of the weekend functions. This week it was a wedding in a rather posh village about twenty miles from where they lived. Crystel loved going along.

'Crystel! Right-now! The van's waiting!'

'OK! OK!' Crystel replied dashing out of her bedroom and thundering down the stairs. 'Ready,' she announced breathlessly as she tumbled to the bottom.

Stephanie looked at Crystel's hair and tut-tut-ted silently with her eyes. 'Out you go young lady. I'll sort that hair out in the van.'

The van Stephanie referred to was the property of the catering company. It was a dull green with a garish red logo on the side, an interwoven S&Y followed by the words Sansted and Yaul Caterers, and a brief text telling the world that S&Y were the areas leading outside catering company; a rather tacky exaggeration for a company that barely managed to hold its head above water.

Crystel's mother locked the front door to their house as the driver of the van tooted and waved out of his window at them. 'Stephanie,' he called to Crystel's mother, who waved back enthusiastically. Crystel's heart sank. Bob…. That was the driver's name and although he hadn't actually asked her mother out yet,

Crystel could clearly see the signs. Bob would be the fifth since her father's death and Crystel had been morosely jealous of each and every one of them. One by-product of her father's demise was the lavish attention she now received from her mother, attention that she cherished and harboured, that she wasn't prepared to share with anyone.

Bob was out of the van now, sliding the large side door back to reveal the inside and its myriad contents of pots, utensils and packages. He leant forward and unclipped a pillion seat that was folded back against the inner wall. Crystel stepped into the van, ignoring Bob's outstretched hand of support and sat on the unfolded seat. She pulled her pony-tail across her left shoulder and clipped the lap safety belt, that was fixed to the seat, across her stomach, then closed her eyes and cupped her hands to her ears as Bob slid the side door closed with a reverberating bang.

Stephanie climbed onto the passenger side of the van's bench seat, pulled down the sun visor in front of her and began to fuss with her own hair in the mirror that had been clipped to the visors underside. She pulled the hem of her black skirt tightly down across her knees as Bob bounded enthusiastically into the driver's seat beside her. 'Here we go,' he said, clapping his hands and rubbing his palms together. 'Another culinary conquest.' Crystel's mother pushed the sun visor back into the ceiling of the van, satisfied with her last minute preen.

'And how are my favourite young ladies today,' Bob continued, giving Crystel's mother an enormous wink in the process.

'We're fine. Aren't we Crystel?' She replied, but Crystel only mumbled morosely in response.

'No change then?' said Bob, casting a shrouded glance over his shoulder towards Crystel.

Stephanie shook her head and frowned a look that said change the subject – Now! She didn't want to risk an upset, not with the company struggling so, and everyone talking about cutbacks; she mustn't give them any reason to fire her. But she knew that they were heading for an upset, a major upset, she could see it coming. Crystel had changed. Obviously she was no longer the sweet little girl of a few years before, she was a teenager now, and a teenager who had lost her father in terrible, tragic and disturbing circumstances. Stephanie could still vividly remember her own adolescence, it wasn't that long ago, and the memories frightened her. But she had been so much more advanced than Crystel. At thirteen her entire bedroom had been decorated with posters and pictures of her favourite groups. Rock stars had dominated her every waking moment; which had led to terrible arguments with her father over homework and studying and that-racket-that-came-from-her-bedroom. Then there had been boys. She had enjoyed her first intimacy two days after her thirteenth birthday, not sex, that wouldn't happen for another four years, just a hand down her blouse and a quite revolting tongue in her mouth, that all her friends told her was the thing to do. She stole a quick glance back at Crystel who still had her eyes shut and appeared to be in a dream world of her own; which was another trait that worried Stephanie. I'll leave her hair till we get there, she decided in desperation. She had taken a book on adolescence out of the public library but regretted the action. The book was very good, the author really appeared to understand children, especially teenagers, but its frankness had frightened her. The book identified things that she really didn't want to have to cope with, even if she knew that as a single parent she had no choice. Moroseness carried an entire chapter, cheerfully announcing that parents shouldn't be unduly worried about such traits in their offspring as they were commonplace. At that point she had re-checked the name of the author who turned out to be a man. The book had gone on to tell its readers not to contest or challenge, but to try to steer and encourage. She could see the sense in that, her own memories of confrontations with her father were living proof that the parental stick didn't work. The book had also covered the subject of late development and juvenile tendencies. Here she could see Crystel clearly; the thought of Crystel behind the bicycle sheds with a spotty fourteen-year-old was really quite ridiculous. Crystel definitely hadn't reached that stage yet. Fortunately, late development certainly didn't apply to her studies, that was a paradox that the book failed to cover at all, Crystel was by far the brightest child in her class. Stephanie had taken the book back after a week, having decided that patience was the by-word and that Crystel would emerge safely, just as Stephanie had finally emerged twenty years before.

'A penny for them?' Bob leaned towards her. They were stopped at a set of traffic lights, waiting on the red.

'Oh. Nothing really. Just thinking.'

'Worrying. More like,' Bob replied, putting the van into gear as the lights turned green. He glanced knowingly into the rear-view mirror towards Crystel then back to Stephanie and received another change-the-subject look in return. 'What about this lottery business then,' he asked.

'Lottery?'

'Yeah. The old bird over at Southgrim Manor. You know, near Stepdown-Links. Come on Steph. You must know. It's in all the papers, and on the telly.'

A faint glimmer of recognition began to dawn on Stephanie. She didn't take a daily newspaper, and the only lottery she had seen on the TV was the national lottery. She never watched the news programmes or any of that current affairs rubbish because it was far too depressing, but she did listen to the local radio station in the morning, over breakfast, and she seemed to recall the DJ going on about something at Southgrim Manor.

Frustrated by Stephanie's lack of positive response, Bob shook his head and sucked air through the gap in his front teeth. Stephanie hated it when he did that. 'OK,' she said testily. 'Tell me all about it. As if I could stop you,' she added churlishly.

'Well. This old girl, Rose the papers called her, Rose Morgan. Was the lady of the manor and she obviously didn't get on with the old kith-n-kin. According to my paper she hated most of them on sight, kept an Elephant gun by her bed and threatened to blast the first one that stepped across the lawn to smithereens. Although I'm not sure I'm convinced about that last bit. Anyway... you must have seen the picture of the cousin, Teddy or Thady or something? Anyway.. He fair laid into this reporter, the one that wrote the article, with the Elephant gun an all. They're talking of suing. He must be all of ninety-five. Landed the reporter a beauty across the ear with his walking cane.'

'Who must be ninety-five?' Stephanie asked, recognising the heightened pitch of exaggeration in Bob's voice.

'Teddy or Thady, you know the old guy, the brother.' Bob gave Stephanie an exasperated stare then looked back quickly, touching the van's brakes as a cyclist wavered in front of them waving his right hand and glanced nervously over his shoulder. Bob eased the van to the left and slowed, allowing the cyclist to complete his manoeuvre.

'So how old was the reporter?' Stephanie asked.

'How the hell...' Bob began, then stopped himself from rising further to the bait. 'Eleven or twelve I think,' he concluded sarcastically. 'Now would you like to hear the rest of the story?'

'Yes. Please,' Crystel replied from the rear.

Startled by her sudden interest both Bob and Stephanie looked at each other. Bob smiled. A bit of a breakthrough his eyes said to Stephanie. She gave the slightest, almost imperceptible, nod of agreement.

'Well,' Bob continued. 'Apparently, the old girl wanted to spite her family so she cut them out of her will, but in a clever way. She sold the manor, which was the bulk of her wealth, to a trust fund that she set up herself. Then she made up this lottery thing to sell off the manor house as apartments. But not sell as such. Anyone who lives in the county can buy a lottery ticket and the lucky six winners each get a brand new apartment on a ninety-nine year lease. She must have got on with one of her relatives though, 'cause she left her niece in charge of the trust fund. Then of course the papers found out that her second husband was Herbert Rice, she was married three times in all. So the proverbial really hit-the-fan then.'

'Who's Herbert Rice' Crystel asked, her intrigue heightened by this new piece of information.

'Before you were born Crystel,' Bob replied, and continued with the story without offering anything more on Herbert Rice. 'The tickets are a thousand quid each and they reckon that they were hotter than cup final tickets by the end. I've heard that they went at two and half times that on the black market and sure to rise higher than that by the end of the last week. The first round draw was last Saturday. That took the number down from six hundred to sixty. God knows what those last sixty tickets are worth now.'

'Never mind Bob,' Stephanie patted his knee gently, sensing his disappointment at not being able to afford a ticket himself. 'Think how bad you'd feel when you lost. Lost a whole thousand.'

'And why should I have lost?' Bob pouted but he knew she was right. He loved to gamble but always came out the worst-for-wear; that's what cost him his first marriage.

'Who's Herbert Rice' Crystel persisted.

'We're there,' Bob said, and steered the van through a set of wooden gates to the rear entrance of the ivy clustered Upper-Stodten village hall.

Chapter 10

There is nothing more earth-bound than a headache, and therefore nothing less conceivable than a ghost with a headache. But until I move on from here – and the conviction that I will eventually move on grows increasingly as time passes – I just have no other point of reference or terminology to draw a more descriptive word from. I wonder if there's Esperanto for ghosts? Let me bring you up to date on what's been happening and perhaps then you will be able to see why I am so convinced that I will not only be moving on but more importantly, that there is somewhere to move on to.

Now... Slow down... I didn't say heaven. Did I? And I've no intention of doing so; at least not yet. Someone or something will have to do a lot more than perpetuate me in this patrimonial state of suspension that I find myself in, before I do.

Of course I'm not blind, and I'm not stupid. In fact I have never felt more aware in my entire life...

Sorry... existence.

The ability to see in both the physical sense and the telepathic is a wonder beyond explanation. So this morning, for a couple of hours, I took a break from the machinations of Freddie, Thaddeus and Whet; of whom I'll tell you more in a minute. But as I said, I took time off and played Dr Doolittle. Not like the famous story, I didn't actually talk to the animals, let alone sing with them, but I did communicate. I made contact. I was able to become one with them, follow their feelings, their emotions and their perception of life. This was by far the most wonderful experience; wonderful, marvellous, terrifying and utterly awesome. Most feelings and emotions that animals suffer are terrifying in their raw simplicity; eat or be eaten. But it's the animals perception that makes all the fear and hunger worthwhile; the cat's total conviction that no obstacle is too high; the terrier's certainty that he is bigger than any other dog, irrespective of other dog's size; the birds effortless leap into a nothingness that can carry it anywhere it likes to go; all of these things are known to man, but never has a human experienced them as the animals do, at least not a live human. I know it sounds a little corny, leaping over tall buildings in a single bound and such-like but believe me, when your turn comes you'll see and don't forget that it was me who told you to try.

The actual bonding process took a little while, which really just came down to my inexperience; I was trying too hard. Eventually I relaxed enough to bond with a terrier from the village; the one that belongs to the postman. It was wonderful. It was as though I was an integral part of him, inside him, at one with him. As he moved I moved, he jumped I jumped etc. Tremendous stuff. But the really exiting and frightening experience was my first commune with his emotions. We were walking, idly jogging along the road that leads out of the village, when a large mongrel suddenly appeared before us from a gap in the hedgerow. The mongrel, a Labrador-Collie cross was more than twice our size. It turned and lopped towards us, its tongue lulling stupidly from the side of its mouth. The static fairly crackled from the heckles of our neck, pulses of pure aggression reverberated up from the bowls of our stomach to broadcast to the entire world – and believe me, to us, it was the entire world – that WE were here and that no puny mongrel, what ever his size, was going to intimidate us. We shot forward.

Now I have to explain that the human side of me was still conscious. My attachment was strong but not total. I still had vision and perception of my own and it screamed at me that charging a brute twice our size, stupid expression or not, was foolishness bordering on the kamikaze. It was at this point that I made my first attempt to communicate with the terrier's consciousness, to tell it not to be so stupid. This proved to be a pointless exercise as the mongrel was now also full tilt towards us and the gap between us down to a few feet. Suddenly the mongrel stopped. More than stopped, it was stopped. Attached to its collar was a thin length of black nylon cord and attached to the far end of the cord was a large round robust man who I can best describe as farmer Giles.

The sudden and literal suspension of active by what we were now totally convinced was **the** enemy, didn't interrupt our singular intent at all. The mongrel's violent horizontal shift to the left as the black cord yanked his neck back, forced his upper torso to rise sharply and his whole body to pivot on his hind legs and totally spoiled the trajectory of our first lunge. We had to be content with a well placed snap at the mongrel's tail that elicited a mouthful of fur tinged with a tasty splash of blood.

Farmer Giles burst through the hedge with creditable speed for a man of his considerable bulk and grabbed at his dog, who had now realised that our intentions were less than friendly. His teeth were bared, his eyes crazed and he was just about to retaliate when *the farmer lifted him bodily from the ground. The mongrel resisted, struggling as best he could, but the farmer's bulbous arms had a firm lock under its chest, just at the point where the legs join the body. The farmer had obviously, and fortunately, carried out this manoeuvre before because as he scooped the mongrel up in his arms and tightened his grip on the thrashing animal he had the presence of mind to bury his own head deeply down the side of the mongrels body forcing the dog's head out above his own shoulders and the now menacing, growling teeth to snap harmlessly above his head.*

From his entrenched position the farmer was unable to see little more than a blur of wriggling black fur. He lashed out with his left foot, striking as best he could in our direction and shouting a string of words that sounded like the grating of a trucks gears peppered with expletives that my human side preferred not to recognise. This was our moment. I sensed a fleeting snatch of memory as several pictures of past triumphs flashed before our eyes. I winced at what I saw. We made our move. Two steps to the farmer's blind side, ducking under his lunging boot as we did so, an almost imperceptible shuffle of our hind legs to fine-tune our position, then we leapt. Our target was the testicles. Dangling fleshy orbs that cried out for mutilation but we missed. To be more precise we were right on target but the instability of the farmer, as he swung another welly-booted lunge at the point where we had been, literally knocked us off target. Instead of the testicles we locked firmly on the mongrel's left hind leg, at a point six inches above the knee. Our teeth sunk deep into the other dog's flesh, ripping and tearing then slid smoothly down the leg until the knuckle of the knee halted further downward movement. We hung there, suspended, our hind legs clear of the ground as the farmer who, unable to bear the sound of the mongrels screaming in his ear, risked facial laceration to look up and take stock. He then, inadvertently, did the only thing he could to retrieve the situation, he fell over.

As the farmer hit the ground we released our grip. The mongrel bound off of the farmer's upper chest, using the farmer's face as a springboard, his mangled tail firmly between his legs. We backed off several paces and barked resoundly at the farmer, just to make sure he realised we were not to be intimidated like that ever again. Maintaining the same distance and retaining the same depth of verbal chastisement, we circumnavigated the farmer's immense girth then, quite satisfied that our duty had been executed to the full, we trotted off in our original direction.

After a few moments my human side began to regain some composure. The mixture of the terrier's raw emotions and my fear and wonder was a heady cocktail to take, and one would have thought that it should have been enough, even for a fledgling ghost such as myself. But it wasn't. I wanted more. Which takes us back to the point were I started to tell you about my new found telepathic insight. I had seen inside the dog's mind. I had seen those flashes of past triumphs. If I could do that then surely I could communicate with the animal, talk to it telepathically. So I tried, and I failed. I tried several times but it was hopeless, at least it was until I realised how the terrier really felt at that moment. It wasn't elation, a sense of conquest or triumph. He did feel all of those things of course but that wasn't all, far from it, there was a deeper emotion, one of duty, of liability, or of an obligation exorcised. He had simple done what he _had_ to do.

So I congratulated him.

He stopped dead in his tracks. Fear surged through his every fibre and amidst a tirade of growling and barking contact was broken. The terrier thrashed in circles, gnashing at shadows, lashing out in total horror but its actions were blind, it had no physical sense of where I was standing, the terrier was literally terrified. The brief moment of direct contact had been total; the dog's reaction was proof enough of that but obviously its ability to handle the situation was beyond its mental capabilities.

So there I was, armed with a new skill but far too unprepared to try it on another animal, let alone a human. However, that's just what I did. Buoyed by what I saw as 'my success,' I took the next opportunity to try it out on Freddie. My reasoning was that as Freddie was just, and only just, a bit higher in the evolutionary scale than the terrier, he would be able to cope with the shock. He'd seen enough suspense, horror and ghost films in his time. It should be second nature to most people surely?

I spent the remainder of the morning playing with my new skills and with new friends, especially a bird, a pigeon; soaring high and free. I could write a whole book about that. Believe you me. But there isn't time. Suffice it to say that by limiting myself to the purely attachment level – I wouldn't try direct communication with an animal again – I had a truly wonderful time.

I played with the animals longer than I should have but eventually tore myself away and went in search of Freddie and the *family. Charles and Helen were dining out with friends from the local council. I was tempted to stay and see what mischief they were up to but five minutes was enough to ensure that it didn't involve me or the lottery. Elsbeth was asleep in front of a soap on the telly, Christian was playing squash and Lia – bless her – was avidly reading my diaries. With the minor players behind me I went in search of Freddie with Thaddeus and, guess where I found them.*

With that creep Whet, they're discussing their plans to refute the will and lottery.

This is more like it.

Chapter 11

Freddie, Thaddeus and Whet were at Thaddeus' house, sitting around a flickering, open fire. Each had a Crystal tumbler of Thaddeus' aged, single malt whisky in his hand.

Whet jingled the half melted ice in his glass, apparently listening patiently to Thaddeus, as he had been doing for over forty minutes of totally meaningless discussion. Thaddeus had dominated the conversation, presenting an endless string of futile suggestions, each of which Whet put down firmly; although in such a way as to leave open the endless possibility that a solution was possible. He had no intention letting go of the gravy-train, that's for sure.

'That really isn't possible,' Whet responded. 'To present a case against Miss Going in that fashion would have to be retrospective.' Having been comprehensibly denied the possibility of having Rose declared clinically incapable at the time of signing her will, Thaddeus had been suggesting that they try to have Lisa declared unfit to manage the trust. Whet, again deflated the proposal. 'Any notion against Miss Going would have to be based upon previously documented evidence. We can't just go to the court and say that now, after we've discovered the existence of the will and trust fund, we want to challenge the competence of the fund's appointed manager, because **we** think she's incapable. Not unless you can produce some deep, dark skeleton from Miss Going's cupboard.

Com'n Freddie. Thaddeus' completely run out of steam. What've you got to say. Or is that it, you're throwing the towel in.

Freddie pondered his empty glass, He shivered slightly. He felt just a little cold and momentarily pondered the fact that lately he had been feeling cold at the most unlikely times. He studied the fine prism of light formed by the reflection of the fire and the base of his glass. The prism darted from side to side as he rolled the last remaining droplets of Whisky spirally round the glass' hand-carved base.

'What if?' he'd said, then paused to think again before he started to talk.

'What if we conduct a spoiling campaign, legal interaction, partition the court, all that stuff? If we could delay the directive that the trust is bound to, especially the conversion of the manor house into apartments, by taking out an injunction against the trust, dragging it through the courts and appealing if we lost. Wouldn't the trust eventually default on its commitment to the new apartment leases? Then if we could get control of one of the winners, a nice hefty back-hander should do that, we could bring an action against the trust. 'Surely,' Freddie added. 'that would bring down the whole deck of cards.

Whet considered Freddie's suggestion for a moment before breaking into what Freddie would describe as a leer. Whet considered a smile.

What's going on now? I understood the words and I can see where Freddie's going; and I don't like the sound of it at all. But why's that leech Whet looking so pleased and smug; if Freddie's scheme goes through, Whet's six ticket-stooges could be held up in the courts for ever. There's no profit in that for Whet, so why's he smiling.

'Freddie,' Whet replied, his angry reply hung with arrogance, 'theoretically it's a possibility. There is jurisprudence. But it's not going to do you any good at all. It'll be like hitting your head against that wall. I'm afraid the Will and the Trust are too well put together.

The colour in Freddie's face rose to a climax, glowing as bright as the fire that reflected off it. He couldn't contain himself any more. He swung his cane in an arc above his head and with all his force smashed it down on the floor in front of him. Silence swept across the room. Freddie began to breathe very hard. He could feel each beat of his pulse, plainly and singularly as the chimes of a clock.

Freddie's breathing began to ease.

Phew. For a moment there I thought he was going to have a heart attack. I'm not sure that I'm ready yet for a face-to-face encounter with my baneful brother.

Slowly Freddie lifted his head to stare directly at Whet. The malice on Freddie's face was frightful. He pointed the split end of his cane at the lawyer. 'What ever it takes,' he said. 'What ever you have to do. I will have that house. You understand.' A thin trickle of spittle glazed the front of his chin.

***

Why's he so pleased with himself?

Whet of course.

Look at him. Look's like the cat with the cream. Slimy sycophant.

Let me in!

130

Com'n. Let's see what nasty little scheme's inside that twisted mind of yours.

Terrance! Terrance Whet. Let me in!

There. There you are. Just through there. Now what…

***

Thaddeus had argued almost to the point of violence over the pointlessness of a second meeting with Whet just one day after the last pointless meeting. Whet had telephoned Freddie that afternoon to call the meeting, and Freddie – with the same opinion as Thaddeus held now – had told Whet he wasn't interested any more. Something in the tone of Whet's voice had convinced Freddie the meeting would be worthwhile. Eventually his character prevailed over his less rational cousin. They travelled down together, by car, a long and tedious journey through London's dense and, at times almost impenetrable, traffic. However the journey served a purpose, as in the confines of their own vehicle they were able to freely discuss their repeat meeting with Whet. And discuss it they did, endlessly, for the entire two hours it took to fight through the traffic; the result was zero, a big fat nothing. Again, Thaddeus had been the most prolific of the two, re-offering the same endless stream of suggestions, with his aggressive nature barely kept in check by the authoritative hold of his stronger cousin; most of Thaddeus' suggestions were instantly deemed by Frederick as preposterous, ridiculous or at worse, beyond sensible reply. Their one hope remained the comment that Whet had made as he had left Thaddeus' house the night before. He claimed to have the solution but needed just one final confirmation before he would tell them.

They parked the car in a pre-paid multi-storey car park and slowly walked the remaining quarter of a mile to Whet's office in Kenilworth Street, looking to all intents and purposes like two out-of-uniform Chelsea pensioners taking an early evening stroll. An ancient church stood at the junction that led them into Kenilworth Street, its gardens bedraggled and untidy, neglect showing on its moss latticed stonework. The outer boundary of the church was firmly secured by a high wrought iron fence with arrow tipped spikes pointing aggressively towards the heavens above. Beside the church, running coldly along its northern wall, lay a small cemetery and an unkempt garden. The cemetery itself was little more than a short narrow strip of land, a thirty-foot corridor of nine meandering headstones irregularly staggered. Two graves in from the dark recesses at the far end of the church, lay a freshly dug grave, waiting, its opening loosely covered with fractured planks of wood.

Thaddeus stopped. The first gravestone was less than three foot from the fence in front of him, a tall slim obelisk of marble set in an untended splash of dusty grey and brown gravel. Set in the centre of the gravel were the remains of an empty metal rose bowl, its wire-mesh cap long rotted away. Thaddeus looked at the headstone and then at the fence in front of him. Half of the body must be buried under the pavement, he thought, mentally counting back one flagstone under his feet to where the tip of the coffin must have been laid and where presumably the boundary of the church must originally have fallen. He read the inscription on the headstone. 'Agnes Moorhead 1865 – 1927 Loving Mother Grandmother and Great Grandmother. Rest in peace.'

Thaddeus puffed. 'Not much of a tribute is it. Rest in peace. Why can't people use a little more imagination?'

Frederick wasn't listening. He had never shared his cousin's fixation with graveyards. He was more immediately concerned with the group of four youths that had emerged from Kenilworth Street and were now converging upon them. He reversed his grip on his umbrella so that it could be used as a club and raised it defensively, its dull point at half-mast.

The first of the youths was a tall spindly lad with a pallid sallow complexion and hair cropped to a stubble. He wore heavy high sided boots and a long dark overcoat that, despite the chill of the evening, flapped open as he swaggered, revealing a crumpled red tee-shirt inscribed with the simple phrase 'Fuck Off' in equally tall spindly white letters. He noticed Frederick's defensive gesture and responded with a deep throaty laugh that belied his lack of body weight.

'Hey. Back off granddad,' the youth said, holding his fingers out in a cross in front of him, as though to ward off an evil spirit. The three other youths, all much shorter and obviously younger than the first, stopped, forming a half circle around both Freddie and Thaddeus, their posture one of anticipation more than aggression. The tall youth blithely ignored Frederick's rampant umbrella, stepping round him to tap Thaddeus lightly on the back. His head dropped loosely over Thaddeus' shoulder. 'Visiting relatives?' He asked. His voice a soft hissing whisper in the old man's ear.

Thaddeus, who until then had been blithely unaware of the youth's presence, gave him a startled and uncomprehending look, retreating from the taunting face with a stumble. 'Pardon?'

'Sorry granddad,' the youth mocked, holding his hand to his mouth like a trumpet. 'I'll shout. Visiting relatives? How old are you anyway? The youth continued without waiting for an answer to his first question. 'Bet you fought in the war?' He pronounced the word war with an extra 'r', mimicking an aged and cracked voice.

'Cheeky pup,' Thaddeus straightened himself as best he could, bristling with indignation, the frustrations of the previous two hours arguing in the car welling within him. 'If you must know,' he continued, 'I'm eighty-one, an age you're decidedly unlikely to attain.'

'Decidedly unlikely to attain... eighty-one..,' the youth mocked. Behind him his friend's began to giggle, they'd seen this joke go down many times before and it always worked with stupid old farts like these two.

'Eighty-one,' the tall youth repeated, looking pointedly at the open grave beyond the marble obelisk. 'Not much point in you going home then. Is there?' He looked down seriously at Thaddeus but could only hold his expression for a moment before bursting into laughter, barging past Thaddeus, and swaggering off at the head of his sniggering gang.

Thaddeus cursed his ageing body. His mind had reacted instantly, with all the venom of his youth, but physical reaction was painfully slow, and his turn towards the youths with his own cane raised in anger was easily barred by a single parry of Frederick's umbrella.

'Don't be stupid,' Frederick snapped.

The youths, already more than twenty yards away, turned back towards Frederick and Thaddeus, their faces contorted in laughter. The eldest made a gesture with his arm that matched the wording on his tee shirt, while the other three turned in silhouette, stooping, holding imaginary walking sticks and making crackling noises in the backs of their throats.

'Look,' said Frederick. 'Isn't primeval the word that comes to mind?'

Begrudgingly Thaddeus snorted an 'Hmm!' Then fell in faltering step behind his cousin as they rounded the corner into Kenilworth Street.

Whet's building was the third in a long row of tall slim three storey Victorian town houses, fronted by a set of pointed iron railings not dissimilar to those that maintained the privacy of the church behind them. Steps led them upwards to the ground floor level of the old building, forming a bridge across the airy, the well at the foot of the building that provided light to the bottom rooms of the house, which would other-wise be simply a cellar. Frederick inspected the column of bulbous, yellow light buttons that announced the occupants of the building.

The top floor simply said 'Private', and was, as they were to discover later, a bachelor flat that Whet kept ostensibly as his town residence; that was often used for more nefarious purposes. The second and first floors were labelled T.H.E.Whet and Reception, respectively. The buzzer for the airy beneath them had a rather poignantly grubby label announcing the 'Alamo Inquiry Agency' that to Frederick, conjured up an instant picture of nineteen thirties Hollywood and badly pressed trench coats, all in black-and-white. Frederick pressed the buzzer marked Reception.

After just a few seconds the door opened. An extremely officious looking dark haired woman greeted them. Her face looming at them, long and scant of flesh, with an angular nose that separated thin watery eyes. Her smile was flat and straight, and devoid of any greeting. Frederick stepped back half a pace, then checked, peering directly into the woman's face. There was something there that he recognised, something about the set of the eyes and the shape of the nose that seemed familiar. The woman beckoned them in.

'Good day gentlemen,' she said, in a thin seedy voice that matched her appearance. 'Mr Whet is expecting you. I'm Teresa, Terrance's sister and secretary,' she added, neatly solving Frederick's puzzled thought. She led them up a straight set of stairs and through a pair of glazed double doors into Whet's private office. Whet rose from behind a large modern grey desk to greet them.

'Frederick… Thaddeus… Welcome.'

He shook both men by the hand with a firm but exaggerated grip. Frederick held the grip a second longer than necessary, using the time to stare intently into Whet's face. He could see the family resemblance clearly but couldn't define it. Whet's sister had obviously had all the bad luck. Frederick had to admit that although Whet was hardly tall, well built, fair haired and blue eyed, in fact quite the opposite, in comparison to his sister he was positively handsome. But there was a resemblance, there, in his facial caste, just under the skin, in his expression. Whet gave Frederick an enquiring look, then a knowing smile. They both recognised a kindred spirit and trusted each other all the less for it.

'Whet,' Frederick said in greeting. He never ever used forenames in business or with people that he didn't particularly like; which meant that he didn't use a great deal of forenames at all. Whet's sister's reference to Terrence had in fact quite thrown him, he had completely forgotten the lawyer's first name.

'Whet'. Thaddeus added, following his cousin's terse example.

'Please take a seat.' Whet gestured to two tubular steel chairs that had been placed in front of his desk. 'Teresa? Will you organise some refreshments please. Some coffee or tea and a Cognac I think.' He looked towards Frederick and Thaddeus.

'Coffee,' they both replied. Neither deeming it necessary to confirm the offer of brandy.

Whet returned to the far side of the desk and composed himself in the upholstery of a large swivel chair. His face assuming a smug look that immediately angered both Frederick and Thaddeus.

Thaddeus was the first to react. 'Waste of bloody time,' he said, the blood quickly returning to the tips of the vessels on his face, from where it had barely retreated after the recent episode at the church. 'Bloody hours to get here, traffic everywhere, those cretins at the church, having the life frightened out of us at your front door, and now you sitting there with that stupid grin on your face, all a bloody waste of time.'

The reference to the church puzzled Whet but Thaddeus' crude reference to Teresa brought a smile to his face, conjuring the memory of their childhood when they had hidden with friends, in the dark, in the cupboard under the stairs, and shone torches under their chin's to make frightening faces. Their friends only did it the once. The sight of Teresa, even as a child, with a pencil of yellow light from her chin to her eye brows would instantly reduce other children to tears.

'Thaddeus. Please. There's no need to be insulting. And besides, you of all people should appreciate the benefits of family loyalties. Especially in business transactions such as ours.'

Whet accepted that Thaddeus' Hmm, was as much of an apology as he was going to get and continued. 'The coffee and brandy will be here in just a moment. Teresa is very efficient as well as loyal.'

As if on cue the doors behind them opened and Teresa entered carrying a large wooden tray; either the coffee had been stewing on a hot plate, or Teresa's efficiency included telepathic foresight. They waited in silence while she poured each of them a cup of coffee and a large balloon of brandy, only speaking to acknowledge her offers of sugar or milk. With the coffee poured, Teresa retreated with soundless steps, sliding the doors behind her closed.

'Now,' said Whet. 'While you sip your brandy let me explain this stupid grin, as you call it Thaddeus.' He opened a drawer beside his chair and removed a large manila envelope. 'This gentlemen is a copy of the Deed of Trust for the Rose Morgan Foundation,' he said, waving the envelope at them, 'and after long and careful examination I have found a flaw in the deed, a serious flaw. It is our loophole gentlemen, our gilt-edged loophole.' He paused to let the impact of his statement take hold.

'And?' Frederick asked, his aggravation at Whet's theatrical manner clearly evident.

Whet pulled a cardboard covered file out of an envelope and opened it across the face of his desk. 'You will recall,' he began, 'that Mrs Morgan deliberately set out to create a vehicle to administer the management, control and execution of her estate, in a manner that would preclude all but the parties named by her, from its affairs.'

'You mean that she deliberately cut us out,' Frederick stated.

'No. No. Not just cut you out. She was much more subtle than that. In fact subtle is probably entirely the wrong word. Ingenious would be more apt.' Whet tapped the file in front of him with his fingers. 'This, gentlemen, is a very well thought out and cleverly crafted scheme to preserve the family name, to preserve the family seat, and what Mrs Morgan obviously perceived to be the family's reputation, while deliberately cutting out the present generations and skipping onto future generations in the next century. In ninety-nine years to be precise. Long after we have all ceased to be.'

Frederick and Thaddeus both sipped at their brandies. 'This much we've worked out for ourselves, thank you,' Frederick responded. 'And that is why my cousin here is so upset and belligerent today. We have discussed every aspect and every angle that we can see and nowhere do we see an opening. I never liked Rose. Never. But I always respected her. She was nobody's fool, and this Trust thing of her's proves that. So where's this great loophole? And how come it wasn't there last night.

136

'In time. In time,' Whet repeated. 'I'm not gloating. I promise you. And the loophole was there last night. It's always been there, but there are other considerations, other pieces to fit into place. Then last night you both gave me a clear indication of your position and the lengths to which you would go. So this morning I was able to fit the last piece in, so to speak. However, it is necessary that you fully understand the legalities of the situation. You see, Mrs Morgan could not set this up on her own. She had to have assistance from people that she trusted and even then she engineered the management of the trust so that those people did not have open control of anything that should be termed cashable. Of course she then left each member of the family a gift in her Will. This really was the masterstroke. She tied up the Trust Fund while she was unquestionably sound of body and mind, and made out her last Will and Testament at the same time, including in the Will everyone from her family who she felt threatened her scheme, she left no one out. By doing so she removed any possible chance of any of you contesting the Will or the trust fund.'

'Your going nowhere Whet,' Frederick interrupted. 'Last time you told us that we were going to contest the Will. Now you're saying it's a waste of time.'

'It is and we are,' Whet replied.

'Pardon? Frederick and Thaddeus responded unanimously.

'It is a waste of time to contest either the Will or the Trust, but we're doing it anyway. You see, the legal system of this country has an often misplaced philosophy. 'An overall commitment to fair-play'. Now I know that fair-play is a rather hackneyed expression, more applicable to a game of cricket than the country's courts of law, but the fact remains that if you have a disagreement with your neighbour over the size of his privet-hedge, or of the loudness of his dog, you have the right to take him to court. We have local assizes, small claims courts, justices of the peace, a veritable plethora of legalese and bureaucracy, and ours is not a petty claim over a tiff with the man next door. Ours is a claim involving an estate we will value in the millions. And that, gentlemen, will buy us the time that we need.'

'Why?' Thaddeus asked. 'Why do we need time? The lottery is about to have its second draw. Nothing's changed, has it?'

'Nothing at all. The draw goes ahead on schedule, and that's exactly what we want it to do.

Freddie and Thaddeus glanced at each other, puzzled by Whet's statement. Whet took a sip of his coffee. He had been talking for too long, the coffee was cold. He switched to the brandy. 'Now,' he continued, 'to the exciting bit. There are many forms of trust fund that can be set up, most of which are repetitive documents dealing with often recurring issues, Children's education, charities etc. But others, such as Mrs Morgan's deal with individual situations that are singular in their conception. Quite simply, no one has ever done this before, at least not in the same way. Therefore this Trust is a little unique, and that is where they made their mistake.'

'I don't see how making that brat Lisa a trustee can be construed as a mistake? Because that's what you're saying isn't it? Frederick asked, his forbearance stretched to the limit.

'Who are the trustees? Whet asked.

'Lisa,' Frederick answered.

'Just Lisa,' Thaddeus added. 'There are no trustees, in the plural, just one, that brat Lisa.'

Whet took another sip of his brandy. 'Not quite,' he replied. 'Miss Going may be the only trustee, but there is another controlling party included in the Trust document. Namely Brin, Brinker, and Briskin.' Whet turned the Trust file around so that Frederick and Thaddeus could see what was written on the open page. 'This is the signature page. If you look you will see the signature of our friend Brinker; for, and on behalf of, Brin, Brinker and Briskin.'

Frederick and Thaddeus leaned forward. Thaddeus adjusted the position of his glasses on his nose while Frederick retrieved his reading glasses from his jacket pocket and placed them across his own nose. Brinker's signature was clear and bold, almost gothic in its strength on the page. In front of the signature was typed the words 'for the Settlor'.

'What's a Settlor? asked Frederick.

'It's the person, or in our case the company, Brin, Brinker and Briskin, who are named as the body responsible for the appointment of trustees.'

'You mean Brinker, or Brin, Brinker and Briskin, can appoint additional trustees, with equal rights to the brat?' Thaddeus asked suspiciously.

'Not directly,' Whet replied. 'You see, in this particular case the Settlor would only appoint a new trustee if the incumbent trustee had to be replaced.'

'You mean, kick her out?' Thaddeus asked.

Whet clasped his hand in front of him and leant his chin on his interwoven knuckles. This was the moment of truth. He was certain that he hadn't underestimated his two clients, but what he was about to suggest would test that assumption to the very limits. 'No,' he said slowly and deliberately. 'I mean if she wasn't there and had to be replaced.' He breathed out slowly between pursed lips, his gaze fixed upon Frederick, understanding the influence he held over his weaker cousin.

Weaker or not, Thaddeus was the first to react. 'But that means…?'

'Precisely,' Whet replied.

'So your suggesting we replace both Lisa and Brinker?' Frederick's question was phrased in a manner clearly indicating that he had passed the point of decision, that for him Lisa's fate was sealed.

'Not necessarily. We have Mr Brinker in our pocket, believe me,' Whet smiled. They had accepted the proposal without flinching. Evil old buzzards. He'd wipe the smile off their faces when he explained the new terms he would require.

'But the brat? How?' Thaddeus asked.

'I've already taken the liberty of making some preliminary arrangements. You see, I spotted the fault in the Trust document as soon as I saw it, but needed some time to carefully cross check. All necessary arrangements for Miss Going have been in place for some days, they just need final authorisation.'

'And Brinker? How is he in our pocket?' Frederick asked.

'Ah. Yes. The upright, principled, pillar of the community, Mr Brinker. He, I am pleased to say, has a skeleton in his legal cupboard. A large jangling skeleton.

Chapter 12

'See you next Tuesday then. Bye!' It was a statement, not a question that the young man threw over his shoulder as he walked out of the master bedroom of Norman Hewlett-Temple's wife's London apartment. Norman sat up and listened to the sounds of the young man closing the outer door of the apartment and the dim ping of the lift bell as the elevator was summoned to the eleventh floor.

Norman collapsed back into the soft pillows behind him, his mind in turmoil. 'Damn,' he said aloud, throwing the word at the ornate, eggshell plaster on the ceiling overhead. He knew there would be no 'next Tuesday' but he hadn't told the young man that; Norman would be in Brussels on that day, speaking to the world. The young man would see the news during the week and understand. Their relationship had been opportunistic ever since it had started four months before. But now things had changed. The Prime Minister had appointed Norman 'Foreign Secretary' six weeks ago, and in doing so had completely changed Norman's life. Not that he didn't want the job, quite the reverse; he had gone after it like a terrier after a rat. But he knew that his bisexuality and the title Foreign-Secretary did not sit well together; the party already had several prominent gays, even a couple of token gay MPs, but they had come-out before their appointments and were even welcomed by the party, in order to show its open-minded attitude. That was not the same as being forced to come-out after being appointed to the number three job in the entire country, that would mean scandal and resignation, that is what would happen if he continued meeting his current, beautiful, young man.

But Norman wouldn't be a hypocrite. He had hidden his sexual proclivities simply to avoid hurting others, not because he was afraid for himself. And besides, there were far too many lovers in his past for him to be able to hold down such a high profile job for long without discovery. The Americans knew. They had already tried to block his appointment, to stop his controversial, conciliatory policy on Iraq and the Middle East. But he didn't need long. Once he had opened the doors the Americans would never be able to close them again. Then he would resign. He would take his moment of glory and make a dignified exit. Then his life could return to normal. Six months should do it, eight at the outside. He just had to hang on that long.

***

It's all right.

I think I'm OK now.

Just.

It was quite an ordeal though. At one point – more than once to be true – I really thought it was all over. I thought it was going to destroy me. But it won't happen again. Not if I can help it. Oh no.

I only slipped in for a second. And I had to work hard to get in at all. But then Whet's mind opened; just a tiny crack but it was enough. I slipped in and wasted no time at all.

What were the numbers of the six fraudulent contestants?

What were the plans of the opposition?

What scheme did Freddie have up his sleeve?

Whet's mind didn't exactly spring into response. There was a mere crack in the outer armouring and a brief point of light, but it was there, a beginning. Then, before I could start, it happened. My own consciousness was invaded, charged, stormed, violated by a surge of power, of darkness. Invaded by a power that thrashed and writhed inside me, growing and expanding at an exponential rate with all the eruption of an exploding universe and it was about to tear me apart, until Whet saved me. My earlier assumption that his consciousness would be controlled by a mind superior to that of the terriers was begrudgingly true. Whet winced, startled by my threat of intrusion, and as he did so he glanced around, as though I had just whispered into his ear from behind. The combination of Whet's movement, his instantaneous sub-conscious questions – what? why? who? – and the aggression of the attack on myself, broke contact. My whole being slumped exhausted in a mental, not physical way that I won't bore you with by describing. Then again, from the periphery of my perception, the colours formed. This ever more present entity that I have tried to describe before. And it was no longer a singular colour, but many more colours, all mixtures of colours that grew in greater, increasing numbers. Frightening in its enormity.

I wasn't going to try communication with a human again if it meant letting IT into my consciousness.

Oh no!

Pardon?

What did it want?

Me. Of course.

The rain fell incessantly against the expanse of windows along the north wall of the office canteen; a room of modest proportions, to the point that every day lunch had to be taken in two separate sittings; even though the workforce only numbered one hundred and eleven. But that simple restriction of space served admirably tonight, to create exactly the right atmosphere for the annual company founders-day party; incongruously held three weeks after the actual anniversary of the inauguration of Varny and Darling and sons; irreverently referred to by the employees as VD day. It was also the day that Messrs Varny and Darling, or at least the now present management, declared the company report and paid out the annual bonuses to the staff. This year the rag-trade had been good. There had been none of the lay-offs that had plagued so many other industries. High street spending had been up for three of the four quarters and even during the forth had held its own. VD had managed to maintain all its major contracts, especially the highly lucrative big-three high street retail outlets; everyone was happy, and virtually everyone was there at the party.

All but three of the dining tables had been rearranged from their usual lunch time spacing. The three that had been left in their original positions formed their usual protective barrier in front of the indoor plants; that were considered necessary to enhance the workers' inner calm, while eating their midday meal; the plants were set in concrete plant boxes, too heavy to move. Ann sat precariously at the first of these tables, absently fingering a plump, bushy variegated ivy.

'Ssssh poisonous you know.' Ann ran her thumbnail along the thin purplely veins of the bright green and mauve leaf, as if to emphasise the point, then took another sip of her gin and tonic smiling ruefully at Derrick, from purchasing, who sat opposite her.

'Really,' he replied, thankful that she had her own topic of conversation to follow and didn't expect him to furnish the small talk; drunken married women did nothing for him at all.

'Sss-true,' Ann blurted out.

Derrick leaned forward cupping his lips with his left hand.

'Pardon,' Ann shouted back at him, her response cutting through the din of the music, laughter and high spirits of the party in full swing behind them with a force that Derrick's whisper had completely failed to muster.

'I said,' Derrick replied at a volume that he judged to be just below reception at the next table. 'Don't you think that you've had enough?' He cringed slightly as Ann made to reply, her eyes roundly exaggerated and bloodshot, uncertain what to expect. This was an Ann that he hadn't seen before, that he never knew existed. She had always been a little strange; all that herbal crap she spouted had given her an almost witch-like reputation in the office. But it was a reputation willingly implied by others, not self-imposed by Ann. Apart from the herb eccentricity; she was so quiet and placid at work that he doubted if anyone in the office had ever dreamt she could get in this state. Her present conduct transmitted an almost Jekyll and Hyde behaviour. Not what he had expected when he'd asked if he could sit with her. He had simple thought her ready for the plucking, an easy lay. She was obviously unhappy in her marriage, the entire office knew about 'Alan's little problem', it seemed that the entire world knew about Alan's little problem. Ann had made the mistake of telling Mandy Sinclair from accounts; which was tantamount to a public broadcast.

What really ticked Derrick off, as he sat there, by the potted plants, stuck with Ann, was that he could have gone after the redhead from his own section. He had been making a lot of progress there and was sure he could score. But no, Ann had always fascinated him, the married ones always did. And she was great to look at and, with 'Alan's little problem,' she couldn't have had it for months and months; it was a sure thing. But now it was all looking rather sour. He was facing the prospect of not scoring at the company-anniversary do, for the first time in six years. Amongst other more obvious things it was a matter of bitter pride and the upkeep of a reputation that he was singularly proud of.

'I'm gonna be shik.' Ann announced. Her elbow gingerly grasping on the edge of the table as she slapped her chin fortuitously into the palm of her hand. Her head began to sway from side to side slowly, her blond hair alternately covering then uncovering her face to reveal spent eyes that she clenched and unclenched tightly, fighting to retain equilibrium. She opened them suddenly, fixing Derrick with a manic stare that demanded attention and made him physically flinch. 'Wa-ter,' she demanded in two distinct syllables. Her head slipped from her hand and slowly slunk sideways onto the polished surface of the table. 'And don't you dare think of slinking off,' she added sleepily. 'I know what you're after. It's same every year, and this year's my turn. I'll make a fuss if you slink off,' she concluded, lifting a half dead arm from the table to wave at him in emphasis.

The water that Derrick brought was sparkling, the bubbles tickled her nose and made her sneeze so that Derrick was sure she was going to be sick at the table. But he was wrong, she held on and then demanded another glass. By the time Derrick returned with the second glass of water, she was looking a sight better, definitely an unhealthy pallor, but at least her head was up, her elbows maintained a semblance of sitting steadily on the table top. She was holding a small white paper bag and poured its content, a fine grey powder, into the water glass.

'What is that?' Derrick asked looking hesitantly over his shoulder, worrying who may have seen what she did.

'Ssss alright. Ssss from the garden,' she explained, as if it should be obvious to everyone, even Derrick-from-purchasing. 'Sit down. I'm going to tell you a little story.' She giggled at the phrase. Derrick sat immediately. What had appeared to Ann as a giggle was in fact hoarse enough to carry to the dance floor and Derrick could feel people beginning to take attention.

Ann continued. 'It's Alan. My Husband. He can't get it up. Won't let him. Nooo way.' Ann stared directly at Derrick, the colour in her cheeks very slightly noticeable, her eyes less bloodshot and bruised.

Derrick shushed at her, flicking his fingers in a motion indicating she lower her volume.

'Sorry,' Ann replied. For the first time in almost three quarters of an hour, she appeared to have some idea of where she was. Derrick breathed a sigh of relief. What ever that stuff is, he thought, it's certainly good stuff.

'Sorry. But I got to tell you. You see you're the one. I picked you, because… Well because you're the right one.' She'd picked him because he was the office lounge lizard and what he considered to be his reputation as a Don Juan, was to Ann mean, selfish, heartless and despicable. Last year's girl had been Ann's friend. In fact she had been the only girl in the four years that Ann had worked for V & D that she could really call a friend. Derrick had dallied with her for over a month, then just simply cast her aside like a broken toy. The girl had resigned shortly after and Ann hadn't seen her since. Revenge was what Ann had in store for Derrick, but revenge at a penitent price.

'Ann.' Derrick squeezed her hand; she had drifted off in a world of her own again, just as he thought she was getting better.

'Sorry. Sorry again. Where was I? Yes... Alan's thing... Useless it is. In fact more than useless, it's bloody dangerous. One tweak of that and its good-bye sex life.'

She paused to give emphasis to the point, and Derrick found himself trapped. He was about to hear the real story and it enthralled him. 'Go on.' He urged.

'Well, it was a couple of years ago. He said he was depressed, went on a drinking binge, couldn't remember where or what he did. But he went to Bangkok – Bang-bloody-cock. It was a cheap package deal, and old Alan, stupid old sod, thought he would treat himself. A rather late mid-life crisis I suppose. Didn't know anything about it till last week. A letter arrived, one of those junk mail ones, asking him if he wanted another bargain holiday. Bargain! Anyway, it was a few weeks after the business trip that it started. Horrible. Really horrible. Just rotting away in front of his eyes.' Ann grinned broadly at the thought. 'At first I was sympathetic, especially when he told me that the doctor said he had caught it from me – women's problems,' she added, staring down at the table. 'But then I did some digging, some research. I found that in theory it was possible, but a visit to our doctor put that lie right. Alan had lied. He still hasn't told me the truth, and never will, no doubt. But I know. I know that he got up to no good on that trip, that it was then that he caught it.'

Her eyes were much clearer now and the strength of her complexion grew with every statement she made. She finished the last of the murky water, dabbing her lips carefully with a paper serviette that lay on the table between them.

'He lied to me about the money as well, and the house. Investment broker. Huh! Whoever he went to was a crook and the stupid old fool couldn't see it. I think the rot had left his dick and attacked his brain. He lost the lot; savings, pension fund, endowments and now the house. The only way we keep the house is if he dies, and soon. They're threatening to repossess within two months.'

Derrick realised he had lost her again. She was staring absently over his shoulder, mumbling softly. He leant forward, his ear to her lips. 'Insurance. Insurance is the answer.' She repeated the words several times before he gave her hand another squeeze to bring her around. 'Don't you think it's time I took you home?' He asked.

'No. Not really,' she replied positively, her attention directed back to him, her eyes clearing as she spoke. 'It's time you took me to your home. Isn't it? After all it is the night of the annual party, there are reputations to consider.'

Her sudden candour and the amazing way she had appeared to recover, took him completely by surprise. 'Yes,' he replied meekly. 'Of course.'

The drive to Derrick's apartment was conducted in draughty silence, the cool night air whistling between the loosely fitted convertible hood and the bright red paint-work of the car. Ann kept her thoughts to herself. She could hardly share them with Derrick, anyway. Derrick didn't speak because for once in his impertinent life, he was incapable of thinking of even the most glib comment. Ann had got to him. He couldn't explain how or why, but she had. It was amazing, that what seemed like just a few moments before, she had been the most disgusting, unpalatable thing he had ever had the misfortune to be saddled with, yet now she was almost perfectly sober, clear eyed and upright. There was still a trace of tiredness about the eyes, but even that appeared to be fading each time he glanced at her. Plus there was an assuredness about her, a determination. There was no doubt that she was in complete control and obviously had as much intention as he did of enjoying a full night of sex, even her chest had grown. She had good round breasts, firm and well presented. They had been the first thing he had noticed about her. He drove carefully, it gave him time to think, to anticipate, and besides, too much drink at the party would ruin their evening if the police stopped him.

By the time they reached his apartment, Derrick's thoughts had begun to take a grip of him, it was all he could do to hold back long enough to pour them both a drink and he had already removed Ann's dress before doing that. She stood there in just her underclothes, waiting as he filled two glasses with whisky, her breast gently lifting with each controlled breath. If Derrick had been less aroused and more attentive he would have noticed that her air of self assurance was no longer as evident, that she was beginning to look decidedly nervous.

Derrick cupped the two whisky glasses in one hand and with the other led her into the bedroom. He placed both whiskeys onto a bedside cabinet then turned to her, embraced her and in doing so expertly unclipped her bra. She felt her heavy breasts drop onto his chest. His hands scrambled with the neck of her pantyhose and untidily slid them and her panties to the floor. When he kissed her navel, flicking its core with his tongue, she stiffened, unable to control her fear. Pictures of Liam crashed across her mind in great waves of guilt. She dug her nails into Derrick's shoulder blades for stability, fighting back the near uncontrollable urge to run from the bedroom. Run and run and run, until the shame fell from her body. She ground her teeth in desperation, letting a muted murmur of determination escape from between clenched lips. Derrick, unable to see the expression on Ann's face, took this as a sign of pleasure and began to explore the area immediately below and between her legs. Ann gripped even tighter, her short nails about to cut into his flesh. 'May God help me.' Her agonising thought came out as a dull enticing murmur. She bit her lip, keeping her thoughts inside, away from Derrick. This is it. This is the penance you knew you would have to make, to get close enough, to be sure it worked.

Derrick laid her naked onto the bed. He removed his clothes slowly, as though this would arouse Ann even more. The last items of clothing that he removed where his socks. This seemed rather incredulous to Ann, and not a little humorous. She had always thought Alan looked ridiculous only in his socks but now came to realise that all men looked equally ridiculous with a raging red-veined erection and a pair of dark blue socks. The thought made her want to giggle, and relieved the tension that had built inside her. Derrick offered her one of the whiskys and began sipping his own. Ann took a sip then replaced it on the bedside cabinet. 'No,' she said, placing a hand over Derrick's drink. 'One sip's enough. We'll drink after.' She pulled the glass from his hand and placed it next to hers, then she pulled Derrick down on top of her.

After their love-making had finished she took her chance. She rolled Derrick off of her and leaned across him, smothering his face with her copious chest. She had held the small tube of powder clenched fast in her palm while he had undressed her and led her to the bedroom, then slid it deep under the pillows out of sight. She flipped the cap off the tube and poured its contents into Derrick's drink. For a few seconds it refused to dissolve. Panic began to well inside her. She couldn't hold Derrick down like this any longer, after all suffocation wasn't her intention at all. She flicked the whisky round inside the glass with her middle finger. That seemed to work. She breathed a sigh of relief. 'Up you get,' she said, extracting his face from her breasts.

Derrick snorted and sat up. 'Damn. I thought I was a goner

then. Those things should have a licence,' he added, cupping both breasts in his hands as if to weigh them.

Ann passed him his drink then took her own. 'Bet you can't?' she said.

'Can't what?'

'Down it in one.'

'No contest.'

Ann watched his Adam's apple bobble as the harsh tasting whisky slid down in one gulp. Satisfied, she copied his act, almost choking in the process and coughing much of the drink back up in fine spray of frenzy.

Derrick burst into laughter. 'Some Red Neck you are,' he teased and got up to pour another. 'Want one?'

'No thank you, I have to go.'

'Already.' Derrick looked back at her. What a strange woman. One minute blind drunk, the next lust-personified, then suddenly this little-girl-lost look... Once was enough he thought to himself.

'I'm sorry,' Ann added. She could see the confusion in his eyes and knew it was best to go now before things became even more complicated. Besides she had achieved what she came here to do. He had taken the potion and now all she had to do was wait. Ten days should do it, perhaps six. She knew that if she'd got the dosage right it would be untraceable in the blood or under post-mortem for that matter, but she had to be sure. Derrick and Alan where almost identical in build, so their body weight would be the same, as would the effect. It was the blood pressure that was the problem. Blood pressure and heart rate. The higher they are, the smaller the dosage. Alan's heart rate was always up. It was a side effect of his medication, and sex had been the only way she could think of to ensure that Derrick's heart rate would equal Alan's at the time the potion was administered.

'You've gone again,' Derrick said shaking Ann gently by the shoulder. 'Let me drive you home.'

Ann took a taxi; she didn't want to go anywhere near her home in the company of Derrick. It was bad enough that the entire office had seen her leave with him, but at least they could see she was blind drunk. She would own up to Mandy Sinclair; that she had collapsed in his car, beyond consciousness let alone sex. Derrick had done the gentlemanly thing and packed her off home. The next thing she remembered was waking up in a taxi outside her own front door, her honour in place. That should do it. She would be the laughing stock of the entire works but it didn't matter. If there were any questions asked, by the Police, later, when he became really sick, and there shouldn't be, but, if there were, then there would be no connection to Ann, no motive, no opportunity, no risk.

***

Lisa hadn't thought of herself as a suspicious person at all, but recent incidents at the manor house had begun to chew at the edges of that certainty. The furore that the press had raised with their Sunday-Rag articles had forced Lisa to request the assistance of the local police; who had been most reluctant to assist until Lisa dropped the name of Norman Hewlett-Temple in their laps. It was on their very first patrol that the police caught a woman digging a hole in the lawns to the front of the house. Not a huge hole, just a small one, about the size of a biscuit tin. The woman concerned was in her early fifties, well dressed and, according to the police; apart from digging up the lawn, she was apparently perfectly law-abiding. There had been six such incidents so far, each enacted by ticket holders who felt that burying a lucky charm or amulet in the grounds would secure their eventual success and win them an apartment. The local papers made a lot of capital out of each story, and Lisa suspected that they might have even been responsible for one or two of the plantings. But not this last one. That had been different. The lady that the police caught, was a Mrs Diane Ajot who, technically, hadn't actually been caught burying anything. She had buried the small wooden amulet, that the police caught her with, one week earlier; at the time she was caught she was just exhuming it to turn it over. When the police questioned her she explained, quite emphatically, that the amulet had to be turned three times then covered again before the next draw. Mrs Ajot's daughter was a ticket holder and had won through the first round. Fortunately this had all taken place while Lisa was in the house, waiting for the rest of the family to arrive for a family meeting, as Thaddeus had described it. The police, with commendable acumen, had taken Mrs Ajot directly to the house to ask Lisa if she wanted to press charges.

Lisa took to Mrs Ajot straight away. There was something deeply motherly about the woman that attached itself to Lisa like a missed opportunity suddenly recaptured. Diane Ajot was relatively short, relatively round and particularly homely, the sort of solid person that bakes cakes and knits yards of Arran sweaters. But it

149

wasn't just her appearance or her safe, matriarchal hue that drew Lisa to her. It was her presence that initiated the bond. A presence that transmitted itself from Diane Ajot to Lisa almost telepathically.

Lisa dispatched the police, thanking them for their consideration and for keeping the incident away from the press. She wouldn't be pressing charges and she had hired additional security in the form of a local security company to patrol the grounds at night for the last few weeks' run into the final draw. Satisfied, the police left, even offering to give Mrs Ajot a lift to her home, or to ensure that she left the premises, Lisa wasn't sure which. Lisa intervened at that point and invited Diane to stay. It was an impulsive act that Lisa couldn't explain, but one that Diane appeared to accept as perfectly natural.

'You feel it? Don't you? Diane asked.

Lisa nodded lamely, not quite knowing why. But she did understand, at least a little. Without another word or any form of explanation, Diane walked back to the garden, to the still-open hole in the centre of the lawn and resumed her rite.

Elsbeth was the first to arrive for the family meeting. Lisa saw the lights of her car swing slowly up the drive and went to the front door to meet her.

'There's another of those maniacs digging up the garden,' she announced by way of greeting. 'Ghoulish looking women. Caught dead in the middle of the headlights. What use are the police if crackpots like that are allowed out in public? Where'd you think she escaped fro...

'That's Diane,' Lisa interrupted. Then added. 'My friend.' It was a soothing thought – my friend. Yes Diane would be her friend. It was obvious.

'Fiend. More like.' Elsbeth squinted her eyes across the lawns to where Diane, who had returned to her amulet turning, knelt on the grass and appeared to be praying. 'Voodoo, is it?'

Lisa laughed. Of all her relatives, Elsbeth had always been the most likely to make her laugh. Not because the old lady was funny, witty, or even possessed a sense of humour. Quite the opposite in fact. The laughter came from the singular mind of Aunt Elsbeth, whose grasp of any given situation was apt to be bias, critical and negative. Plus, once fixed on a problem, decision or opinion Aunt Elsbeth became entrenched to the point of absolute intransigence. To Aunt Elsbeth a spade would always be a spade and more often a devil-like pitchfork, and once established as such was best left firmly locked in her overcrowded cupboard of prejudices.

As Elsbeth stared at Lisa, wondering at the sanity of her great-niece, two other cars arrived in convoy. Charles and Helen in Helen's metallic-grey diesel Citron. Christian and Lia in the Jaguar saloon that Christian had recently acquired in a less than respectable deal involving the liquidation of assets from a recently bankrupt local builder.

The second and third cars arrived just as Diane crossed off the lawns and onto the driveway. Diane reached the front door as Charles skipped lively round the large Jaguar to open the door for his wife. Helen stepped out from her car, glanced at Diane then looked straight through her. Diane took a position beside Lisa, as though she belonged and had always done so.

'Have we been introduced,' Elsbeth asked virulently.

'Oh no dear. Not yet. But we always would.' Diane's rotund comely face smiled up into Elsbeth.

'Always would? What the hell does that mean?' Elsbeth's question was lost in the rapid exchange of greetings between Lisa and her four relatives. This was the second time they had met since the funeral. The first had been cold and hostile; on the part of Helen in particular. But this time all four greeted Lisa with a warmth and affection that momentarily, quite surprised her.

'And who's this?' Helen asked of Diane.

'She's my friend. She's helping with the foundation. Aren't you Diane?' Lisa wasn't quite sure why she had drawn Diane into the fold but somehow it seemed quite the right thing to do. She prayed that Diane would accept the implied offer and play along.

Diane gave Lisa the same kind smile that she appeared to reserve for just about everyone and replied. 'I always knew I would be.'

'Talks in riddles,' stated Elsbeth. But no one was listening to her. 'Digs holes in the garden, like a mole.'

'Moles dig up through the garden, not down into,' Charles clarified.

'Shut up.'

Lisa led them all into the music room, which had been cleared of Rose's deathbed and restored to its original purpose, with the grand piano resplendent in front of the French windows. Diane squeezed Lisa's arm tightly. 'This is where she died.' It was a statement, not a question.

'Yes. She loved this room, and the view,' Lisa replied. 'When they have finished the modifications and divided the house into its six apartments, this room will not be included. Aunt Rose designated certain rooms in the house as utility; storage for maintenance etc. And one room, this room, as the manager's office. I intend to keep it as near as possible to its original appearance.'

'You weren't here when she died were you.' Again, Diane stated more than asked.

'No. Sadly I was away. I didn't actually know she was dead until two days after.'

'You mean they didn't tell you?'

'Of course we told her,' Christian interrupted curtly. 'But she was travelling. We couldn't reach her.'

'Of course you couldn't.' Diane swept a glance at Christian, Charles, Elsbeth and Helen. 'You were all here though. Weren't you?' Around the bed. She stated, her smile adjusting slightly to a hint of knowledge. Especially you.' Diane pointed an index finger at Charles and dabbed it up and down as though she were operating a light switch. It was a slight movement that no one else caught except Charles who turned a deathly shade of white. He stared open-jawed at the medium, frightened to speak.

'I was here as well,' Lia added. 'It was horrible,'

Diane walked quickly across to Lia and took both her hands in her own. 'Oh no dear. Death is never horrible. Dying… Yes. That can be awful. But not death,'

'Told you. She talks in riddles,' Elsbeth said.

'Who does?' Freddy and Thaddeus had arrived and entered unnoticed but in time for Elsbeth's latest observation; successfully managing to startle everyone except Diane.

'You were here as well,' she accused, then walked away to stare out of the French windows.

'Before you ask Uncle Freddie, Diane is here with me. I felt that I needed a little support. After all, the last time none of you were particularly happy to see me, were you?'

'Come. Come. My dear. Don't take on like that. You have to understand that Rose's Will came as a bit of a shock. We didn't expect her to let the manor out of the family's control, and all this housy-housy stuff quite knocked us for six. But it's better know. We have all got over the shock.' He swept his arm around the gathered family troop in a resigned fashion. 'That doesn't mean we agree to it though. Not at all. Far from it. Bloody stupid idea, if ever I heard one. But it's not a criticism of you dear. Oh, no. You just have to

152

understand that with such a peculiar Will, we have had to take legal advice. Strong legal advice. And I perfectly understand you wanting a friend along. We have no objection. Do we?' He directed his question at all the family. They all nodded, on call, enthusiastically, except Elsbeth who was still muttering to herself.

'She's probably one of those occult types, or a noony or what ever they're called,' Elsbeth concluded in a forlorn mumble.

Suddenly, and without warning, Diane dropped to her knees. She gave a low sigh then held her head back at an acute angle and placed her fingertips together, gently touching pouted lips.

They all turned towards her but only Lisa and Lia appeared able to move. Thaddeus, who had refrained from either greeting them or joining in the conversation about Diane, was sitting in a deep Chesterfield chair, his knee twitching vigorously. He gave an embarrassed, sideways look towards the others, expecting them all to be staring at him – the twitching knee had reached unbearable levels recently, forcing him to speak to his doctor about it – but what he saw was not the ridicule or unsympathetic impatience that he had come to expect from his family, they were all otherwise occupied. The woman, Diane, appeared to be praying, although why she would do so at this time of the day totally mystified him; perhaps she's a Muslim? The thought slipped fleetingly across his mind, evicted by a renewed spasm of twitching. Lia and Lisa had reached the woman and were bending over her. Charles had taken a step towards them then stopped dead, his head flicking repeatedly from a central position to one almost ninety degrees to his left. Helen had turned away from the window and seemed totally intent on removing her ears with her own hands by scratching them off. Freddie stood stock-still with his back to Thaddeus. He also appeared to be in some discomfort, his left hand gripped white-knuckled across the ivory handle of his walking stick and his right hovering in front of him as if to remove a swarm of invisible insects from his face. But the most outlandish of them all was Charles, who had ripped open his fly and appeared to be attempting a two handed masturbation through the material of his underpants.

Chapter 13

Variety. That's the spice of life.

I never really appreciated the full extent of that simple metaphor before. Perhaps the original author had his or her own run-in with someone like me. If not they should certainly meet Charles. Look at him. Serves him right though.

'Stop it! Stop it now!'

'Pardon? Pardon?'

'Pardon? No. Not at all. Pull yourself together.'

'But. Where are you? Who are you? What's your name?'

'I'm down here of course and my name's Diana. Newling. Diana.'

'Diana Newling?'

'No. Diana. Just Diana. You're the Newling. The new spirit. It is Rose I assume? Rose Morgan?'

'Well... Yes, Rosie,' she added inadvertently.

'Good. It would have been a little awkward if it had been the other one.'

'Other one. What other one? What do you mean?'

'Oh don't you pretend. You know what I mean, you're not that much of a Newling, are you? So don't be flippant with me. The other one. The other spirit, and remember, he's not a Newling. Oh no. Not a Newling at all.'

'He? He who?'

'Later.'

'How do you know that I'm here? Are you a spirit as well?'

'No. Not a spirit, not yet. Although I am rather looking forward to it when the day comes; there's a few bogus mediums that I'd just love to put a really good fright into. No. I'm just a medium. I'm here to help you, and by the feel of things right know you need all the help you can get.'

'But I don't understand. Why do I need help? You make it sound as though I'm in danger. I'm dead for goodness sake. You can't get further in danger than that... can you?'

'Oh, don't be so juvenile Newling. I've got to go now. I can't stay open like this any longer, not here, not in his territory. And don't call out for me, it's too dangerous, I don't know just how strong he is yet, but he's bound to be powerful, after all those years, powerful indeed.'

'But?'
'Go! Leave the room! Now!'

***

One quick visit to the school library and an hour mulling through the back issues of the local newspapers proved sufficient time for Crystel to discover the full history of the Herbert Rice case. He had been posthumously found guilty of murder forty years ago and for thirty of those years had been a regular character in the schools local history curriculum; which was why his name was so well known to both her mother and Bob. Herbert Rice's story had eventually been dropped from the school curriculum when the school received a healthy donation from a wealthy widow, to pay for a new swimming pool – Crystel had gleaned that information from Bob.

A child had been found molested and strangled in a spinney close to Southgrim Manor. Police suspected that the crime had been committed by someone local and had found a pocket watch not far from the crime scene. The watch belonged to one Herbert Rice, the husband of Rose Rice whose maiden name was Leowen. The Loewen family was the ancestral owners of Southgrim Manor, and prominent members of the local gentry. Herbert Rice had no tangible alibi for the night of the murder and when bloodstains of the group matching the dead boy's were found on discarded clothing that had belonged to Rice the police, not surprisingly, made their arrest.

What seemed like an open-and-shut case suddenly crumbled at the arraignment, when it was revealed that Rose Rice's blood group was the same as the dead boy's, and that she claimed the clothes were smudged with her blood following an accident pruning in the rose garden. This cast doubt on the prosecution's case and Rice's application for bail was approved. His suicide had the opposite effect. He was found two days after being released, lying in a pool of his own blood at the foot of the house, beneath the high gable. He had apparently climbed into the loft area at the highest point of the building to throw himself out of the small light in that end wall – to gain the maximum altitude for his death leap. Bob had also told Crystel that there was some local speculation that Rose Rice had found out that Herbert had actually carried out the murder, and having lured Herbert to the loft on the pretext of recovering some

155

lost heirloom that could be sold to raise cash to assist in his defence, she had pushed him out of the window herself. Apparently these rumours had never been seriously followed by the local police who took Rice's death as simple suicide to avoid the indignity of the gallows; the case was officially closed.

The death of the poor child had absolutely no effect on Crystel's ever increasingly callous view of life. To her, the child was simply the catalyst to an important event. However, the calculated finality of Rice's suicide was, to her, perfectly understandable. She could see how he had killed the boy because, to him, it was necessary, something that he had to do. Something inside of him that had to be set free. And when the police arrested him, quashed that freedom, he wouldn't tolerate their unwanted interference. He had to be in control. Death at his own hand was perfectly acceptable. Death at the hands of others, under the rules and control of others, was unthinkable. Crystel really felt that she understood Herbert Rice. She added the clippings she'd stolen from the library to her scrapbook of fire-clippings.

Crystel's plans for the Lottery Draw buffet where coming along nicely. She had spent over an hour roaming the grounds around the house while her mother and Bob had discussed the catering arrangements with the lady who was running the house now and the strange, older lady, with the eyes that seemed to look straight into you; not through you, but deep inside of you. Crystel couldn't remember the name of the first lady but the older one was called Diane, she remembered that. Diane frightened her. It was as though she knew what Crystel was thinking and that wouldn't do at all. Diane had to be avoided.

The high gabled end of the house was the best place to start. This was the place where Herbert Rice had jumped. Crystel had spent several minutes staring at the spot where he must have fallen, imagining the impact, the broken bones, torn flesh and sinew. She inspected the ground for signs of bloodstains but after forty years there were none. This was where she would do it. She recognised a deliberate irony in her preference, although the actual choice had been simple; this was the older part of the building and heavily inlaid with ancient and highly flammable materials. She would destroy at least a third of the house before the enemy from the fire station had half a chance of getting to the scene.

She made her plans meticulously. Her greatest danger lay in applying a suitable flammable compound to the timbers of the window frames, gable and roof beams. The wood was dry in a way only wood of excessive age can be, and the heavily layered paint that covered the wood would give added speed to the ensuing fire. But this was the highest part of the building, the pitch of the roof above was a full twelve or thirteen metres above the ground; how was she going to apply a flammable substance to that height? The answer, as it turned out, was very close to hand. A semi-circle of low trees, interspersed with thick Hawthorn bushes, swung in an arc across the end of the building, at the far left of these bushes and trees, stood a gardener's shed in which she found a collection of pesticides, weed killers and rat poisons; all materials she readily recognised and knew how to use. There was even a pressurised insecticide spray gun with a hand-pump; she would be able to spray flammable liquids up the side of the building with that. She found some water to poor into the bottle of the spray gun then pumped up the pressure as rapidly as she could. It held. She gave a little prayer that it was in good condition, especially the rubber ring inside that made the pressure seal; she knew that they were the first things to rot. Finally there was a small, half filled drum of tar; presumably used by the gardener to cauterise the severed limbs of pruned trees and shrubs. The tar drum sat conveniently inside the tray of an old wheelbarrow, its sides caked in hard crusted globules of black tar. The trees outside were full of late spring blossom; this was not the pruning season, the tar and its barrow should still be where she'd found them when she returned a couple of weeks later. Satisfied, she went back to the house to find her mother and Bob.

***

Claire knew that she had become slovenly, that she really should do better, keep the place tidier, cleaner but it had just all got on top of her. She hadn't always been this bad, never good, she admitted that, but not really that bad. She just couldn't handle the depression. Nothing would go right for them. Nothing had gone right for them. When Andrew got the job with Failsafe Securities they had thought that things would improve, and for a while they had. But then the overtime was cut and the mortgage rate went up and everything else seemed to go up at the same time. They were simply not earning enough to pay the bills. Less coming in than going out, that simple. Every week they dropped further and further behind, and now she had Andrew to worry about as well. He had started to go out at nights. She had told herself not to be silly. It had only happened twice so far, and he never came back drunk or anything. He certainly wasn't spending any money; in fact it would be easier to handle if he did. He just went out, at around seven thirty, every Tuesday and Wednesday, and came back at eleven. He wouldn't tell here where he'd been, just said it was a surprise and that she should be patient. Now he had announced that he would have to be up at four o'clock every morning, including Saturdays and Sundays. She knew that he was as desperate as her, more so. That's what really frightened her. What was he getting himself into?

The kettle began to gurgle and boil. She pulled a mug from the jumble in the washing up bowl and rinsed it under the tap.

Even a cup of tea was depressing. It was the cheapest she could find. A thin film of tea dust floated on the top of the pale brew. She sipped at it. At least it was hot. Tears began to roll down her cheeks, first one, then a second, then an uncontrollable flood. This morning had been just too much. This was the final straw. How would she tell him? This was something that she'd wanted so much. From the day that he first proposed to her. From her childhood really. She had always thought that telling Andrew would be the most wonderful thing. Watching his eyes water, having him take her in his arms, cuddle her, as he'd never done before. Congratulate her. Now, it wouldn't happen. There was no way they could bring a child into their world. No way. But she did have a way out. She just had to be careful how she did it. She would be free then and so would Andrew. With some money as well if she did it before they repossessed the house. She finished her tea then dropped the mug back in with the rest in the sink.

***

'There it goes' Mal pointed at the Failsafe truck as it pulled out of the depot gates and swung slowly right. 'There's only one exit so they have to take right or left on this road. We know that the delivery will be in the morning, not before eight-thirty and no later than nine-thirty, so we can park the car on this meter at six, before anyone else arrives for work, then simply lock it up and leave it. That way we are sure of a parking place for the van. Then we wait for up to an hour. We sit in the back of the van, so no one will see that we're waiting, won't get suspicious. Then when the armoured truck comes out we simply follow. If it turns left we follow it straight off, or wait till it passes; if it turns right then call Phil to pick up the tail at the end of the road.'

'I'll be in the other car,' Phil added without a moment's breach in the flow of conversation. 'on the mobile, we then alternate the tails so they don't get suspicious, and follow them out of town. From the info we have they should be going North, so that gives them two possible routes once they reach the edge of town, Station Road or Marlin Hill; we've got a good spot on each.'

As Phil finished a dark green truck nudged its way out of the Failsafe depot, turning right as it did so. They waited, transfixed by the glare of the sun's reflection on the mesh-covered windscreen of the approaching truck. The outline of the heads and helmets of the driver and his partner were clearly visible but their features were blurred and indistinct. Instinctively Mal, Phil and Stuart turned their faces away as the truck passed them. Mal slipped the car into drive. The road was wide at this point, and the parking space they had chosen was diagonal to the kerb. Mal let two cars pass then released the brake and slipped out behind them. At the next junction the armoured truck turned right, Mal slowed, signalled then turned left. 'Well?' he asked generally.

'Seems sure enough. As long as we make sure of one of those parking spots.'

'Stuart, stop being such an old woman,' Phil replied. 'Six o'clock in the morning we'll leave the car there, the only thing up and about will be sparrows and milkmen. Then at eight we'll swap with the van. It's OK.. It'll work fine.. Let's go and have a look at the gatehouse now.'

They drove for twenty minutes before reaching their destination, taking the Marlin Hill route. Mal brought the car to a stop by a hedgerow that separated the continuous line of a high old brick wall from the lane. Some two hundred metres from them an arched gatehouse broke the continuity. 'We've got to walk now,' he announced. 'The gravel in that drive hasn't been disturbed for years. We don't want tyre tracks before the big day.'

The gatehouse had been built as an integral part of the boundary wall for a large estate. It consisted of a broad arch for traffic to pass through and four rooms above the arch for the chauffeur and his family; two rooms to the front, two to the back. The arch led to a gravel lane that took an abrupt turn to the left after fifty metres, swinging towards the distant manor house, which was totally covered from sight by the thick copse the lane cut through.

Between the gatehouse and the bend stood a suite of coach sheds, their original doors sealed with heavy black painted wooden planks. Smaller doors had been cut in the middle. Doors more suitable to the motor cars of today than the original coaches and wagons that the building had been constructed for. Stuart unlocked the chain that secured the gates. This was his third visit, the first to check the location and the security, and the second time to pick the original lock, a rusty old affair, which had given him some concern. Once he'd got it off, he had simply replaced the old lock with another old but well oiled lock of similar appearance. Everything about the gates, lock, coach shed and archway with its chauffeur's rooms, reeked of disuse and age. The entrance obviously hadn't been used for years, neither had the old coach sheds or the chauffeur's lodgings above their heads; that was why they had chosen this particular place.

They slipped inside. Stuart replaced the chain and lock, he pushed the hasp of the lock to, without actually locking it. 'This way.' He led them to the back of the coach sheds and repeated the process on a similar lock that secured the rear entrance door to the sheds. Shafts of light pierced dustily through cracks and rents in the roof and walls. Cobwebs dangled in their faces, the smell was of rotten straw, dung and mildew. 'There you are,' Stuart said smiling broadly at the obvious discomfort of the twins. 'Should do nicely for our purposes.'

'It stinks,' Phil replied, holding the front of his tee shirt to his nose.

'A week to go then,' Stuart stated absently, to no one in particular. Recently, dreams of fourteen million and what he could do with his share of that kind of money were never far from his mind.

'Plenty to do,' Mal agreed, his voice filtered through the front of his tee shirt. His own thoughts reflected on other things, another job, one that Stuart knew nothing about.

***

Marios had spent forty-eight delightful hours in Zurich with the lovely munificent Meloni. Then a further three day financial visit to Amsterdam; diamonds being one of the many diversifications he had cloaked his considerable fortune in. Confident that this particular cache was in safe and productive hands, he booked a ticket for the following day on a flight to Leeds Airport in the UK.

***

Ann hadn't dared to visit the hospital where they'd taken Derrick. That would have drawn too much attention to her. She had signed the get well card that had passed around the office and contributed to the flowers that were sent. She took a lot of ribbing from the other girls and a few sly comments from the men, but stuck steadfastly to her story, that she'd got drunk, couldn't remember much but that nothing happened, that Derrick dropped her off then went home. So visiting the hospital was unnecessary. Their relationship hadn't happened. She had no reason to visit him in hospital. Not that she wanted to visit Derrick or express any sympathy, her concern, however, was with his well being.

She knew that she had limited the dose to below a lethal level but needed some feedback to measure the success of the experiment. It came from Marlene, whose husband was an orderly at the hospital. Two cups of coffee had sufficed to learn from Marlene from accounts that Barry, her husband who was a PR Officer at the local health authority, told her that the case was being discussed all over the hospital, that the doctors were baffled. They knew it was a toxic poisoning issue and had identified the toxin by its chemical elements, but they had no idea how it had been administered or from where it had been obtained. There had been some talk of a possible suicide attempt but that had been ruled out as impractical owing to the complexity of the poison; half a bottle of Vodka and a bottle of sedatives would be more usual and much more freely available. Besides, who would submit themselves to such an exotic poison and the possibility of an agonising death. The police were briefly involved, but only as routine. Once suicide was ruled out, so was their interest. The patient was still in intensive care, but conscious and able to speak, and the latest word was that he was pulling through nicely.

It was from Marlene that Ann also learnt the circumstances under which Derrick had been discovered. Apparently, he had woken at four in the morning – about three hours after Ann had left him – with violent stomach cramps. Neighbours found him at seven o'clock, doubled up and unconscious outside their front door. He

161

had apparently been trying to get help and collapsed just short of the doorbell. They called an ambulance, which rushed him to hospital where they pumped his stomach and rushed him to intensive care, not knowing that it was to late for stomach pumping. Ann's dosage had been perfect. It hadn't been fatal, although if administered to an older of infirmed person it most certainly would have been. Ann didn't like Derrick at all, but not to the point of actually murdering him; she would kill only one person, and that she did not consider an act of murder, not even revenge, it was simply justice and she was the appointed executioner. The important thing for Ann was that he had very nearly died. Very nearly but not quite. Just a few grams more would do the trick for Alan. She had also learnt the depth to which the doctors would be able to identify the poison. That was fine.

But even after her success with Derrick, she still had doubts. She now knew for sure that the poison was safe from detection and that she had triumphantly restrained the dose to a sure but safe level, one that would be just below the minimum dose to achieve fatality. She decided to carry out one more experiment. She needed a guinea pig, and found it in the form of a stray cat, a mangy, flee-bitten creature that she convinced herself would be better off put out of its misery. She calculated that an increase of just five per cent in the dosage administered would be fatal weight for weight, then prepared a new batch. The cat died within twenty-five minutes. She curled its body into a shoebox and tied it with a double wrapping of brown string.

She buried the cardboard coffin under a thick, wild rose bush that grew at the end of their garden. Alan was asleep in front of the telly. No one saw her. She patted the soft loose soil flat with a spade. 'That'll do nicely,' she said in a whisper.

She was seeing Liam tonight, that would do nicely as well. They could have a future now.

***

Norman Hewlett-Temple MP, was in surgery. Which was more of an event rather than a regular occurrence nowadays. Since his appointment as foreign secretary his constituency had seen even less of him than ever before. He was sure they understood, after all as a cabinet minister he really couldn't waste too much time with constituents. However, surgery today had proved a blessing. He'd received a letter from a constituent, and recognised the handwriting immediately. Under different circumstances he would have responded quite openly and arranged a meeting in a public place, a pub or hotel bar. But not now, not today, not as foreign secretary. The letter was from Eric, an old flame whom he would always have strong feelings for. Eric had worked on his first election campaign and later, when he had become an established member of parliament, Eric had worked at Westminster, as a permanent member of the civil services staff that actually runs the establishment. They had become lovers then. A brief but torrid affair that had nearly ended in disaster. Funds had gone missing, party funds. It was nothing to do with either Eric or Hewlett-Temple, but the ensuing investigation had got very close to uncovering their romantic connection. Eric had resigned his post immediately, diverting all the attention to himself, saving Hewlett-Temple from certain disgrace and political ruin. In doing so Eric had deliberately taken the blame for the missing funds. No action was taken due to lack of evidence. Although Eric was innocent, mud sticks. Eric would never work in that environment again.

Eric was the thirteenth appointment of the session, a fact that did little to quell the butterflies in his stomach. He looked around the waiting room. In the centre stood a large, tubular-metal-legged glass-topped coffee table with a dishevelled assortment of magazines, each carefully selected to not contain any articles that could be considered detrimental to the local MP, the minister or the government. This reduced the selection to magazines on sport and those women's weekly magazines that had a politically safe cookery, knitting, romance and health problems format. The choice was limited and the stacks of magazines on the table quite small. An almost continuous ring of hard plastic chairs lined the walls, above which a sweep of party posters, just as carefully chosen, informed every one visiting the surgery just what a marvellous job their local MP and their party were doing for them. Cut into the wall opposite to where Eric sat was the reception desk. A recess lined with deep, varnished pine boarding contained a purpose-built reception enclosure. An ergonomically correct slate grey computer desk with retractable keyboard shelf, a raised reception counter in the same puerile grey rose to a height from which only the top of the secretary's head could be seen, and an ergonomically correct swivel chair on which sat Hewlett-Temple's constituency secretary, a sombre looking woman in her mid-forties, with hair that she regularly coloured jet black to reflect a Mediterranean ancestry countenance. She wore a deep condescending frown and carried lines to the sides of her eyes that suggested the frown was a permanent feature.

'Mr van Holt? Mr Hewlett-Temple will see you now.' Her voice was pure Birmingham and her message delivered with an unquestionable smile. Eric revised his earlier opinion, warming towards her. He returned her smile, she returned to her frown. Eric said thank you very much and opened the panelled door she directed him towards.

Hewlett-Temple rose to greet him, shaking him firmly by the hand as he leant past him to ensure that the door had been shut firmly and securely. 'Eric. How wonderful to see you. Take a seat old man. Here.' Hewlett-Temple slid the seat under Eric, then returned to his side of a sweeping mahogany desk.

'It's good to see you too,' Eric responded. 'I wasn't sure that you would want to see me.'

'Of course. Of course. An old friend like yourself. It's a delight old man a pure delight. How are you keeping? You're looking so well. Life treating you OK, is it?' Hewlett-Temple's words gushed out. Eric could see just how nervous this meeting was making his ex-lover.

'Not bad really. Health's pretty good really, considering. Remember Slatery, head of the dispatch office? That weekend we had in Bath? Well he's gone. AIDS. Six, seven months back. I was going to write and let you know but I thought it best not to. Not now, not with all this. 'Eric looked around Hewlett-Temple's office as he spoke. 'And a minister and all. I really am so proud of you.'

Eric could see Hewlett-Temple's reply forming on his lips. He held his hand up to stop him. He knew Norman. He knew what he was about to say would simply sour Eric's memories of him. The Norman that Eric remembered was a good person, an idealist who wanted to put the world right, who genuinely wanted to help people. But Eric knew how people can change, how life, especially political life could reshape a person's ideals and his character. He didn't want to listen to platitudes that would only serve to reinforce that fear. And besides, he had a new Norman now, a younger man who perhaps wouldn't enjoy the full extent of years most people enjoyed.

'Let me show you a photograph, a very good friend of mine.'

164

Hewlett-Temple took the photograph that Eric produced from his wallet. A bright young face stared up at him, full of youth and life. He could see how his old friend would be attracted.

'He's names Norman as well. Quite a coincidence really. He's a lovely person Norman. A truly beautiful person.' A tear began to well in his eye. 'Sorry,' he added, wiping his eye with his cuff.

'Is it AIDS?'

'No Hepatitis C. We don't know how exactly.'

Hewlett- Temple looked a little puzzled. 'That's deadly. Is it?'

'Can be. But not always, not like the other. It is serious though, and the cost!'

'Ah.'

'No. I'm not here for money, at least not directly. Did you think I had come here to beg, or even worse, to blackmail. You know me better than that. Both are totally abhorrent to me. Please.'

Hewlett-Temple smiled at his old friend. He had been worried. Ever since the arrival of Eric's letter he had been milling the possibilities over in his mind. But he knew Eric was right. There was no way he would put him or his career at risk. 'So, old friend, what can I do for you. Anything in my power, which is considerable now,' he added with a laugh. 'Anything.'

'I need a job,' Eric responded bluntly. 'I've been keeping myself alive with all manner of work since I left the civil service and then, a year ago I met Norman. The new Norman.' Eric tapped the photo that lay on the table between them. 'We were so so happy. Then he found out about his illness. He was mortified. At first he thought it was AIDS, then he was convinced that he must have given it to me, then we discovered that both assumptions were wrong. I hadn't caught it and it was Hepatitis C not AIDS. But then he had to give up his job, and I gave up mine to be with him, and now he needs money, for treatment, so I've got to go back to work and I can't pay for someone to look after him while I'm at work. Even if I was able to go back into the civil service I wouldn't be earning enough to cover the costs. I need a decent job, one that pays a good salary, a position like the one I used to hold but better. Please Norman, you're a minister now, can you help?'

Hewlett-Temple didn't answer for a while. He picked a pencil from a tidy on the desk and began rattling it between his teeth annoyingly. 'I think,' he said briefly arresting the pencil. 'that I can.'

Eric's shoulders sagged with relief. The Hewlett-Temple that he knew, the one who had been so close to him, would have helped. But that had been years ago, would this be a different person? Now he knew, and now he felt deeply guilty for ever doubting. 'How?' he asked meekly.

'Do you still write?'

'No. Not for a long while. I haven't had anything in print for over a decade, and then it was only one book and a few articles.'

'All on political procedures as I remember.'

'Yes. And there's no money in that. Didn't sell more than a few hundred copies in total.'

'But you can write. And you could write again. Couldn't you?'

'I suppose so, but what about? And who ever would read what I wrote?'

'Everyone my dear Eric. Everyone.'

***

Joan ran the tips of her finger along the length of Liam's bare spin, hardly touching his skin, just the slightest contact, more static than touch. Liam murmured softly. She drew her hand away. Any more and she would wake him up. That would result in only one thing and that wasn't what was on her mind. Liam however, was. He professed his love for her every time they met, in fact every time they spoke on the telephone. But? She had to make up her mind what to do. Martin knew about them. She didn't know for how long he had known but he knew. That was enough, and now she had to act, before Martin did, before it was too late. Her thoughts drifted back to the telephone call three days before. Martin hadn't heard her come into the house, he had been watching one of his stupid old films on the TV and had the volume up a bit loud. The phone rang just as she entered the kitchen and she reached the extension at exactly the same time as Martin picked up the receiver in the lounge. He answered first. It was the caller's reply that stopped Joan replacing the receiver. A woman's voice said 'Can you talk?' Martin replied 'Yes. She's out. But not for long.' The brief conversation that followed established a meeting time for that night, a time that coincided with Joan's watercolour class at the evening institute and with Martin's planned visit to the cinema, that had become a regular Monday night event. He was still going to the cinema, but obviously not alone. Joan waited until Martin replaced his receiver, then replaced hers. She walked back out through the back door of the house then back in again, slamming the door loudly so that Martin would hear her arrive. 'I'm back,' she'd shouted cheerfully.

That night she followed Martin. She'd recognised the woman's voice on the phone but had to verify her suspicions. One glimpse confirmed that is was his secretary Chloe. She told herself not to jump too quickly to conclusions, she knew that Chloe was a classic film buff as well, it might be perfectly innocent. She also knew that she was clutching at straws and wondered why she needed to do so. The marriage was all but over. She was having an extra marital affair herself, why wouldn't he be? Yet somehow she felt hurt, cheated, abandoned; after all her own affair was quite recent, and had only really come about because of Martin's neglect of her. What if he had been having affairs for a long time? Those affairs would obviously change his attitude towards her. He may have driven her into Liam's arms. Chloe's embrace as she flung her arms around Joan's husband cemented all Joan's fears. It was an affair. He was playing around, had been playing around, it was all his fault.

She'd listened in to three more telephone conversations since then. The first was from a colleague, from work, a male colleague, but the second was Chloe. They were very clipped and economic with their conversation, cautious and careful. Chloe was annoyed with Martin. It was all to do with some scheme that he had for a new apartment, for them. Listening, Joan was confused. Was he planning to leave her, to set up home with Chloe, or was this to be just a love nest, where was he going to get the money from? Martin then explained to Chloe what was happening. His voice had a worn, resigned air, as though he had been over it all before. Martin had entered the competition for the manor house apartments, the one in the newspapers. He had used a thousand pounds from their savings to buy the ticket, a thousand from their holiday cruise money. The bastard! Joan almost spat the words down the phone at them both. She just managed to control herself. Then the conversation became weird. This was the bit Chloe didn't understand and Joan could see why. Martin was going to win. There was no doubt; he had a friend; it was all set up and foolproof.

Joan listened intently. What on earth had he got himself into? For a moment she actually forgot why she was listening in. Then she was brought back, down to earth with a shattering thump. Frustrated at Chloe's refusal to accept his incomplete reasoning and explanation, Martin resorted to emotional blackmail. He told her he loved her more than anything in all the world and that he now had photographs of Joan and that ponce from the evening institute. He had an appointment with a solicitor booked for the following Monday. They would be together soon, then he would be divorced, they could marry, the house would be sold, everything was going to be wonderful.

Joan's knees almost went as she took in the full extent of Martin's statements. Divorce.. Solicitors.. Marriage.. Selling the house. She gripped the side of the telephone table and just managed to replace the handset without knocking the entire instrument clattering to the floor. She held her palms to her breast. 'Bastard! Bastard! Bastard!' she exclaimed in a voice so loud she later worried that it may have carried through the house. She staggered more than walked out of the kitchen, stumbled through the garden and out through the back gate onto the path that led between the two rows of houses.

She hadn't returned to the house for over two hours. She'd just wandered the streets during that time, desperately trying to clear her mind, rationalise her thoughts. When she did return her thoughts were still in utter turmoil. She entered the kitchen quietly; she'd been out far too long; he would be concerned about her and probably a little annoyed that she hadn't told him beforehand that she would be gone for so long. She wasn't sure how she was going to handle that, how she was going to handle anything anymore. The house was quiet. She closed the door softly behind her, took a deep breathe and was just about to call out 'Hello, I'm back' when she heard voices. The door to the hallway was ajar. She crept over. It was one voice only, Martin's. She pushed the door to, and as gently as she could lifted the receiver again, fully expecting to hear Chloe's voice, but it wasn't. This time it was a man's, a solicitor called Whet. A voice of superior tones, an arrogant voice that she took an instant dislike to.

At first she assumed it had to be the voice of Martin's divorce solicitor but then, as the conversation deepened, she learnt about the plans that had been made to cheat Rosie's Lottery. After five minutes she had learnt as much as she was going to, they were starting to repeat themselves. This Whet character obviously wanted to make sure that Martin knew exactly what he was supposed to do; which appeared to be absolutely nothing, as far as Joan could make out. Just accept the winning key, act suitably shocked and delighted, and keep as much as possible to the background. Joan had replaced the receiver and walked directly into the lounge, delighting at the look of surprise and guilt that had washed across Martin's face.

Liam murmured again and turned until his chest was flat on the mattress, the sheet slid back off the top half of his back. Joan pulled it up to his neck. His face was still turned away from her, he was still asleep.

After the telephone calls, Joan had taken a full day to really compose herself. She had looked up Whet in the telephone directory. He really did exist, she hadn't been dreaming. With the pages already opened to 'Solicitors' she'd selected one, a name she vaguely recognised from conversations at work, divorce conversations. She rang Whitney, Turnball and Crouch. She then made a second call, to a detective agency. She knew it was essential that she got in first, had the first papers served. What she didn't know was what to do about the other thing, the lottery.

She slipped out of the bed and wrapped herself in Liam's dressing gown, forcing her thoughts back to the present, to today. She had recently gone back to work, found herself a job. A good job as well. She couldn't believe her luck. Liam had introduced her to a producer from one of the regional TV companies. She'd worked in TV before, before she got married. Amazingly, the producer remembered her, which was much to her embarrassment as she didn't remember him, but he had been a junior at the time, just a runner for the crew. He needed a replacement immediately for someone he had had to fire, a remark that wasn't entirely lost on Joan. It was just for the one shoot, he explained. No future in it. But that was over a month ago and almost twenty shoots later. With all that was happening with Martin, a new job, even a new career, was just what she needed. In fact Martin thought she had been on location since yesterday. The shoot didn't start until today, somewhere in the Chilterns, a horse fair, general interest stuff for breakfast TV. The kettle began to rumble as she looked around for her watch. 7.45!

'Liam! Quick! Get up! I'm late!

***

'Well the second draw's over; yesterday; started prompt at noon and was over by twenty past. It seemed to go pretty well. There're

sixty numbers left now, including the six that Felonious Freddie and Tricky Thaddeus have rigged.

I didn't interfere. It took all of my resolve, but I stayed out of it. I'll wait for the final draw. Then we'll see.

Lisa looked a bit flustered though. The strain of it all seems to be getting to her a little. I must see what I can do to bolster her up a bit. Diane said she has a new young man, an Australian. I suppose that'll be all right. You never know with colonials. Do you?

Oh. I know. I'm showing my age, but I had an Australian beau once. Back in the late twenties. I was just sixteen and he was twenty-four; which was quite an acceptable age gap in those days; although my parents wouldn't have agreed with my choice; fortunately they knew nothing about it. Then he jilted me. Turned my head then got himself engaged to Mandy Minster, a so-called beauty from Oxford, where he was reading the classics. I was heartbroken.

Still. It's been a long time since then. I understand they have knives and forks in Australia now... In the cities at least.

Chapter 14

'It'll have to be outside,' Lisa stated with disappointment in her voice. 'I so much wanted it to be inside, here in the music room as Aunt Rose intended it to be. I know that you will think me silly, but somehow I can feel that she wanted it to be in here, because she would be here as well. Now that it's got to be in the garden, how will she know?'

Diane frowned at her. 'Don't you worry my dear she'll know and anyway the draw will be inside the house.'

'But in the entrance hall?'

'Oh. Don't be silly. Music room. Entrance Hall. What's it matter? Besides Rose wouldn't thank you for allowing an army of media into her house. No. The hallway's far enough and only then for five of them. You be firm. Five only. Two newspapers. One local radio and two from the telly. The rest can wait outside, on that platform you suggested. They can crank their nosy cameras at Newlet-Temple.'

'Hewlett.'

'Whatever. If he makes his speech and the presentation to the winners, from the front steps, as we agreed, the press will have all the coverage they need. Then they can ask him all of their silly questions over a drink and cucumber-sarnie. That should be more than enough for them. You mark my words, it's the only way to keep that lot under control.

It'll be OK, you see if I'm not right,' she added reassuringly.

Lisa gave the older woman a hug. 'What a find you were Diane. How would I have managed without you?'

'Quite nicely I'm sure. Anyway I've told you before, I had to come. Others needed me. Besides, your young man arrives today doesn't he?' Lisa's shyness over her mystery man was absolutely charming. You didn't have to be a medium to see that she was deeply smitten.

Lisa glanced at her watch, the fifth time she had done so in as many minutes. 'He's late actually. He said he'd be here at three.'

'Lisa. It's only five past.' Diane walked over to the French windows. 'If I'm not mistaken,' she said slowly. 'this must be him now.'

Lisa ran over to join her. How did she do that? Lisa had only known Diane for just over a week but they had become close in that time, extremely close, close enough for Lisa not to doubt that Chuckles was just about to arrive. A pale grey saloon car swung through the open gates at the far end of the drive. It approached the house slowly; gravel crunching under its tyres as it did so.

'Well?'

Diane's question, unanswered, hung in the air as Lisa rushed from the room into the entrance hall and flung open the double front doors. Hot sunlight blasted into the cool building.

She stopped and took three deep breaths to compose herself. It wasn't like her to behave like such a schoolgirl.

***

'Oh dear,' said Diane. 'This really does look serious.'

'You talking to me?'

'Rosie? You're eavesdropping. Stop it. It's not polite.'

'I'm allowed. I'm a ghost. It's what ghosts do.'

'You're not a ghost, haven't you realised that yet? Ghosts haunt. Rosie. They haunt. In fact they don't do too much of that nowadays, too many ghost-investigators and busybodies around. They're over rated anyway. You're a spirit Rose, a Newling spirit. Soon you'll cross over, and please don't ask me where you go I'm fed up with telling you that I don't know. Or when. That's number two on my list of all time questions that I don't want to hear again. To me a Newling is a spirit that hasn't yet crossed over, and that's everyone who dies, and a spirit is a spirit that has. Crossed over I mean. Now surely that's simple enough?'

'So what's a ghost?'

'Again?'

'I'm not convinced.'

'A Ghost is a Newling that can't cross over. Therefore it can't be a spirit and the very fact that it's been around for a long while means it's no longer a Newling. Now is that clear.'

'Not from my point of view it isn't. It's bad enough suddenly dying but not knowing how long it will be before I pass over as you put it, or where I pass over to, or in fact whether I pass over at all, is just too much. Besides you said yourself, Newlings pass over within a few days of their death. I've been hanging around here for weeks. It's like waiting for a National Health hospital appointment; it just never comes.'

'Don't be so melodramatic. I've told you why. Sometimes it

172

happens this way. Us mediums wouldn't meet Newlings if it didn't. And every time. Every time Rosie, there's a reason for it. What ever it is with you will come out eventually; sooner than later is my guess. Now go. Lisa's coming back.'

'I...'

'Go.'

***

Lisa marched Charles into the music room, her arm firmly linked in his, forcing him to follow.

'Diane,' she said purposefully with the broadest of grins, 'may I introduce Mr Charles O'Donnell from Australia.'

Involuntarily Diane took half a step backwards. The man facing her was truly handsome, of that there was no doubt and the smile he was now giving her would charm the knickers off a nun. An expression that her late husband was fond of using and that she hadn't heard or reflected on since the day he died. Charles reminded her of her late husband. Not in appearance Charles was undoubtedly handsome, her late husband was most certainly not. Ugly was the word that sprang to mind, especially on the inside. But there was a similarity. She could never read her late husband, that had been the attraction. She'd had the gift since a child and could read most people, some more, some less than others. But some she couldn't read at all, and the instant she cast eyes on Charles she knew he was one she would never be able to read. She gave a small prayer that it wasn't a bad sign after all, not all men were cast in the same mould as her late unlamented husband. She composed herself and took the hand that Charles was offering. Lisa stepped forward and whispered in Diane's ear. 'That smile. Takes your breath away, doesn't it?'

'Charm the knickers off a nun,' Diane replied.

Charles hadn't clearly heard their whispered exchange but he could guess its content. He gently pulled Diane a half step towards him, lifted her hand and kissed the back of it. 'Delighted Diane,' he said smoothly.

'I'm sure,' Diane answered inanely. Then followed in a flustered voice with, 'I'll put the kettle on.' She glanced quickly at Lisa knowing that she wouldn't be offended by her acting as if she was part of the household. 'You must be thirsty after that long journey? Or should I pour something stronger.'

'Coffee would be fine, thanks. Black no sugar. If that's OK,'

Charles replied.

'Me to,' Lisa added.

Diane retreated towards the kitchen, brushing past Lisa as she did so. 'Phew!' she whispered. 'Might become a nun myself.'

Lisa dug her in the ribs in reply. She waited until Diane left the room and turned to Charles. 'I think she likes you,' she said.

'I hope so,' Charles replied but he wasn't so sure. He had seen that first fleeting look in Diane's eyes. It wasn't exactly a look of fear, more one of concern and mistrust.

'Come on. While Diane's making the coffee I'll show you round the house. You've got to see it straightaway, the builders have already started and it's beginning to vanish in front of our eyes. But don't worry, there's still enough of the old stuff to get the feel of how it used to be.'

***

'Rosie you there? What do you think?'

'Quite a catch. A real heartthrob. But you don't look too pleased. What's the matter?'

'Oh. Nothing. Jealous, that's all. Anyway, he should be a great help for Lisa, there's only just over a week to go to the big day and the organising is becoming overwhelming, another set of hands will come in very handy.'

'What was all that about a marquee?'

'Eavesdropping again?'

'No. Just concerned interest.'

'It's the press, and the media, TV etc. Your little idea has captured everyone's imagination. You can't switch on the box without seeing the front of this house on the screen. We can't just shut them out, and besides you let them in.'

'Me?'

'Yes. You. It was you, wasn't it, who said the first two draws would be in, what is it? In camera? Well that shut them out which was like waving a rag at a bull, but for the third you said it should be witnessed by the press. That was enough to let the whole kit-and-caboodle in. So we had no choice.'

'We?'

'Don't you start. It's bad enough with my daughter, she won't stop badgering me. Why do I have to get involved? What's it got to do with me? I know what the problem is, she's bought herself a *ticket that's what it is, and she's frightened that if I'm involved and she wins someone will complain.'*

'I didn't know that your daughter had a ticket. That's interesting.'

'As if she's going to win.'

'She might, and you're talking in the positive tense. She must be through the first two rounds. She must have a very good chance.'

'Pigs might fly come Michaelmas.'

'We'll find out next week

***

Maureen was quite literally beside herself. Her blind faith that she would win had been, in a rather obscure way, somewhat dented. It had been easy to hold that belief when it was purely hypothetical, but now! Now that she was through to the last round. The whole thing had taken on a completely new ethos. She quite simply, had to win; anything else would be unthinkable. She could feel the tugging of inexorable obsession taking hold, and she had never, ever, felt quite so close to Reggie. This was a drug, just like the booze, an addiction, nothing more, nothing less. She had to talk to someone, share the pain, and get some help.

Even though she knew the answer she would get wasn't the one she wanted to hear, she still confided in her mum. Diane's predictable reaction was to close the curtains and unwrap her trusted Ouija board. Maureen's protests were brushed aside. Her mother's love was unquestionable, but why couldn't her mother just be a mother, just talk to her, perhaps even sympathise?

'Don't be silly Maureen, you know how good you are at this, it's a gift, a small gift but all the same it shouldn't be ignored, especially when you're in trouble.' Diane placed Maureen's finger on the planchette, closed her eyes, tilted her head slightly backwards and rotated the planchette three times; her limbering-up routine, she would always explain to those that asked. Without looking she stopped the planchette precisely in the centre of the antique board.

In her haste, Diane had pulled the lined curtains at the windows badly. They were meant to close out all exterior light. Light for séances was provided by a single triangular up-light mounted on a bracket half way up the wall in one corner of the room, controlled by a dimmer switch turned to a mere flicker of light of pale yellow-white light. The temperature of the room began to drop perceptibly. A damp rigour pervaded in a way that Diane had never experienced before. Maureen felt the chill oozing slowly into her very bones. The small arrows of daylight that stung into the room at the edges of the heavy curtains began to flicker and fade, even though it was still mid-morning. The light from the up-lamp changed colour. First a pulsating green, then briefly an insidious yellow ochre before slowly melding to a deep blood red. Maureen tried to pull her finger away. She had to release the grip the gnarled witch's face of the planchette had on the tip of her finger. It was as though the planchette was alive, the board was alive. The grip she had felt encompassing her entire hand now snapped to the back of her elbow, vice-like, holding her arm immobile. She pulled harder. The grip snapped to her shoulder. A dull numbing chill clutched at the base of her spine, climbing vertebrae by vertebrae, individually, on its passage between her shoulder blades, to the nape of her neck. Her head snapped backwards. Her throat uttered a silent scream. The planchette began to shudder with a soft, menacing rhythm. Its witch's finger moved slowly to the letter 'S'. Maureen let out a short stifled gasp; her chest forced forward, her rigid body locked in contraction an ever-increasing arch of pain.

'S'

Diane felt the panic inside her surge past the shock of seeing her daughter's violent reaction. It was all happening so fast. She hadn't had time to collect her thoughts,

'I'

Let alone tune her mind to making contact.

'M'

It had never happened like this before. She wasn't in control.

'O'

'Hello. Who is it?' she asked meekly.

'N'

'Simon? Stop it you're frightening me. Stop it. I command you.

The shuddering that she had previously felt through the planchette intensified, a pulsating tension increasing with every contraction until it perfectly matched the rhythm of Diane's heart. It paused for a moment, as if taking breath. The planchette began to glow with heat. Diane could smell the flesh on her finger burning from the intensity of the heat. The pulsating resumed, with each beat both it and Diane's heart beat increased. She tried to call out, to talk to the spirit, to get it to stop. No words came out. As her heart raced, her throat contracted. She was soaked in sweat, veins all over her face expanded, protruding and enlarged. Gasping for breath, she knew she didn't have long to live. Her heart rate surged. Her face began to distort to become unrecognisable as a face in human form; just a skull covered with twisted distorted flesh. She had a second, perhaps two of her life left. The blood red light collapsed. The room appeared to collapse around her, enveloped her in total blackness, then explode in a whiteness that tore at her retina. The outlines of the room were again visible, etched into distant corners. The hold on her finger broke and she was flung violently into one corner. She landed painfully but without sound, her back flat against the outlined wall, her legs stretched in front of her. She was able to breathe again. Her body was still locked, unmoveable except for her eyes and the heaving of her chest. She looked first at her finger. The flesh from the underside hung in tatters but there was no pain. She was beyond normal pain. Beyond her finger she could see Maureen, her back still arched but her entire body levitated, floating horizontally a few feet from where she lay.

Whatever had entered the room was still there. Diane could feel it circulating around the room. Recharging. '*Simon?*' She asked.

Be quiet!

The voice wasn't audible; it was as though she could see the words, as she did on the Ouija board. An evil semaphore from beyond.

Diane watched helplessly as Maureen's clothes were rent from her body, ripped into coarse strips as the spirit tore at them in an increasing spiral of lust that Diane could taste as well as feel. Invisible hands began exploring her daughters' body, the flat of her abdomen, the fullness of her breasts, parting her legs, fingers entering her, stimulating her. Maureen groaned once, then again, her head began to thrash from side to side. The groaning intensified. Diane sensed the spirit moving bodily between her daughters legs. She cried out desperately.

'Help me! Please help me!'

An overwhelming sense of panic gripped the room. The blackness, the searing white and blood red, all flashed across Diane's vision. Maureen's naked body crashed to the floor, scattering the coffee table and the Ouija board as it did so. Everything went black.

'Diane! Diane! Oh if only I could slap her face. Diane! It's me

Rosie. Wake up. Your daughter's hurt, she needs a doctor. Wake up!'

*** *

Stuart twisted the throttle back on the motor bike with a gentle squeeze. The reaction was instantaneous. The 250cc engine climbed through four, then five, then six thousand revolutions, propelling the bike past sixty and up to the speed limit in a couple of seconds. Stuart throttled back, pulling the speed down to fifty-five. 'This will do nicely, he thought.' A roundabout loomed rapidly in front of him; left to Reading, straight on for Swindon. Straight on. An extra hour would be fun.

*** *

Maureen looked up at her mother through squinted, swollen eyes. Her mother was facing away from her and appeared to be talking to someone out of Maureen's limited vision. She wanted to move, to sit up, but it hurt even to think about it.

'And what do I tell the doctor?' She heard her mother say.

She didn't hear the reply to her mother's question, but there must have been one there because her mother continued. 'Nothing's broken. It's just bruising. Bruising all over. And he didn't actually…. You know? You turned up just in time.'

Actually what? Maureen asked, but no sound came from her lips. But she knew the answer, it was there, hidden in the darkest recesses of her mind, not wanting to come out.'

'Yes. I know the word,' her mother continued.

'Yes. Alright. Yes. Rape! There I've said it. You happy now?

Whoever she was speaking to must have been happy because her mother nodded sharply and said, 'Good. That's it said then.'

Rape. Thoughts began to tickle the edges of her memory. Rape. But not rape. Yes. She remembered that she hadn't actually been raped. Simon! The name invaded from her subconscious like a searing shaft of white-hot light. Simon had tried to rape her. She groaned, the sound escaping her clenched lips as a low resonant gasp. Diane turned instantly towards her daughter.

'She's awake. She'll be OK. I told you so.' Diane smiled down at Maureen, bent towards her and stroked her fringe away from above her eyes. 'It's alright darling. You're safe now. He's gone.

Rose drove him away.'

Maureen could see over her mother's shoulder now, there was no one else in the room.

'Of course I'll have to tell her,' her mother said to the empty space Maureen was starring at. 'She was there remember. God knows what she saw while she was under. God knows what she felt, poor love. She may even have seen you. There. There.' Diane turned her attention back to her daughter. 'Rest darling. You've had a terrible experience. A truly incredible experience, wondrous that you survived, but you did and I know it must hurt all over, but trust me, nothing is broken, or damaged in any way. You're just bruised. Bruised everywhere. Nothing that a little rest won't cure. Sleep now. Sleeeep…'

***

Reggie wasn't exactly a prisoner, not detained against his will, at least not officially. But he knew they weren't about to let him out, let him back into society. He had already explored the possibility of just simply walking out of the front gate, sidling up to it in a feigned, disinterested fashion that fooled no one, especially the security guard in his neat, epaulette dark blue uniform and tidy gatehouse office. As Reggie neared the gate the guard had moved from the inspection window of the gatehouse, he reappeared a second later framed in the doorjamb, a fixed glare on his face, Reggie took the hint. Walking out was not an option. He began to plan more carefully.

***

'I don't understand?' Norman asked. 'Why does he want you to write his autobiography? And why now? He's only just become foreign secretary. He can't have that much to say yet. Can he?'

'Quite a lot,' Eric replied excitement bubbling in his voice, enthusiasm in his manner that Norman hadn't seen since that terrible day, the day they were told how ill he was. 'He gave me an advance. A retainer for my services. And it wasn't charity. He's deadly serious. Look I stopped off and bought some things. Look!' Eric held a plastic carrier bag open for Norman to inspect the contents. 'Not a tin of Baked Beans in sight. Look!' Eric spilled the contents of two carrier bags of groceries across the bed.

179

Norman's eyes opened wide at the sight of the contents of the bags. 'It's like Christmas, when I was a kid,' he replied.

Eric sat on the edge of the bed. 'He reckons that he only has a couple of months before he's thrown out.'

'Sorry?'

'Thrown out of the cabinet. Sacked.'

'But why?'

'Well it goes back a long way. Back before I knew him. Seeing him today, you know, on the telly, you wouldn't think of him as a radical, would you? And I suppose he's not really. Not an out-and-out revolutionary. But underneath that sane and sensible almost Solomonesque media persona he has managed to retain his sense of right and wrong and that's going to be his downfall. And he knows it. In fact he's even planning for it. He's not going to wait for the axe. He's going out in a blaze of his own glory. And that's where I come into the picture.'

'With a biography.'

'Autobiography. Yes. I'm going to ghost it for him. He's going to sign a pact with Iraq.'

'Lost me again?'

'He went there earlier this year. He visited villages, hospitals all the usual stuff that the Iraq's drag visiting politicians to, to curry sympathy, to get the sanctions lifted. Well. He knew he was being manipulated but he also saw the pain and the suffering and it disgusted him. It's achieving nothing. In fact it's just consolidating Saddam Hussein's position. His words not mine.' Eric added quickly.

'You mean you don't agree?'

'I haven't been there. I don't have a right to comment.'

'But Hewlett-Temple does?'

'He thinks so. He told me that ever since he started in politics he has coveted a ministerial post. He had two choices, come out of the cupboard, run as an I'm-your-local-gay MP or keep his secret to himself. He chose the second. But he knew that if he achieved cabinet level, his sexuality would get in the way. So very wisely he remained in the back benches, kept his sexuality quiet. Seniority was his greatest enemy, that and the fact that he became very good at his job. He's turned down three cabinet posts before taking this one. Not many people know that.'

'What pact with Iraq? What exactly is he going to do?' Norman hauled his feet up onto the chair, his knees tucked under his chin. He knew Eric too well. It was time to settle in for a long story.

'Well. He turned down the first ministry, Welsh affairs or something, because of what I said. This was almost ten years ago. He was a gay and gay ministers were about as common as rocking horse crap then.'

'Eric.'

'Sorry. But you know how much that sort of bigotry upsets me.'

'Go on.'

'Well they lost the next election. Norman held his seat by a narrow margin and they all had to hang on by their teeth till the next election. During that time he was also offered a shadow cabinet post but again turned it down. It was six years later, when they were back in office that the second opportunity came along. This time it was much bigger, Ministry of Agriculture, Fisheries and Food. He told me he was really tempted by that one. You should have seen the passion in his eyes as he was telling me. It was as though he was a student, back in the old days, campaigning against the bomb and proliferation of nuclear power. Ag and Fish may not sound like a very glamorous appointment, but not to Norman. He saw it as an opportunity to commit to the people, to address real issues, to improve daily lives. He almost took the job but then there was the incident with the missing party funds and, although you have always blamed him for not coming out and defending me, I wasn't the only one to lose a job...'

'But it was the only one you had.'

'I know. But he did decline Agriculture, Fisheries and Food. And I've always known that if I'd asked him, he would have risked everything on my behalf.' Norman's frown indicated his disbelief.

'That's not fair. You don't know him like I do,' Eric pouted, clearly upset by Norman's inability to share his admiration for the errant MP.

Never able to bear his lover's anguish for more then a moment or two, Norman relented. He smiled reassuringly. 'I'm sorry. You're right. Who am I to judge. Go on.'

Eric snuffled back the beginnings of an emotional tear, his heart ever worn on his sleeve. Norman crossed to him and put a reassuring arm across his shoulders. 'Go on,' he said. 'This is growing into one of your long stories, that's for sure, and if you don't get on with it soon, the canned stuff will go off, let alone the fresh.' He swept his free arm across the expanse of food covering the remainder of the bed. Eric laughed.

'Well. People,' Eric resumed, his eyes bright, almost child–like as they always were when Norman used humour to turn around an unpleasant situation; a trait that he had become quite expert at since Hepatitis C had arrived on their horizon, 'people who were politically in-the-know, other politicians, party officials etc., they all thought he'd turned down Agriculture, Fisheries and Food because he was still too frightened to take a chance. But he told me that he really was about to take the plunge. Anyway, he didn't but it got him thinking about the possibilities if he had. He was really tempted, but the opportunity was lost. He'd also lost me of course. At that time, as you know, we were an item. He was also happily married, or at least to the public eye he appeared to be, very understanding woman his Elena, I knew her at Uni. Did I tell you?'

'No!'

'Well she was.'

'That was very convenient.'

Eric gave Norman a side-ways look.

'I'm sorry'. He responded quickly, realising that he was in danger of upsetting his partner again.

'Yes. It was convenient. But the convenience was mutual, they were actually great friends. You see Elena was gay as well. She had an influential job in the Ministry of Education. Her position, especially in the earlier less sexually tolerant years, had been exactly the same as Norman's. So a marriage of convenience seemed the obvious solution. And so it was, right up to the end. Then Elena became sick. Norman's thoughts and plans about the possibilities of being a cabinet minister were put on the back burner and he even considered giving up private life, you see, they had grown to love each other dearly; sex isn't the byword to love you know.'

'I know. There's no need to lecture me. If he loved her so much why is he going to blow the whistle by writing his memoirs? What happened to her?'

'Elena died six months later. Stomach cancer. It was in the papers of course but just an inch or so on the inside pages; he was only a backbencher at the time and apparently not a very ambitious one at that, so the story didn't attract much publicity. At least not in the media. Then, about a year later, he was appointed to this committee to investigate and advise on the Iraq situation. Weapons inspectors, biological warfare, scud rockets, all of that stuff. At first he just rowed along with all the others; Saddam is a despot; Saddam has to be brought to his knees; the threat to world peace etc. The British contingent of the committee prepared its initial findings here in London and the intention was to fine tune them as soon as they had completed a field trip to Iraq; an assessment protocol, it was called.'

'Sounds like they'd already made up their mind to me,' Norman concluded.

'I'm sure they had.' Eric stepped to the kitchen unit and began to fill a kettle with water. 'Tea?' He asked, raising his voice above the noise of the running water. 'I need one.'

'Yes! Please! But carry on while you're making it.'

'Well. At first nothing much happened. They started their assessment-protocol at The Hague, then they were moved to Beirut.'

'Why? That's not in Iraq.'

'Well I know, but it was some kind of high level meeting. The Syrians and the Norwegians were trying to broker a deal between Iraq and the Americans. They didn't want the Brits to mess it up so, Norman and the other two that went with him, Sally whats-her-name and the short fat guy, the member for Harlow I think. Anyway, they were diverted to Beirut and so far it was all normal day-to-day political stuff. Meetings and press conferences and then more meetings. Norman said that at that point they were making no progress at all but no one seemed to be unduly worried; it was considered normal. Then they eventually reached Iraq and joined the Belgians, French and Dutch that formed the rest of the committee. They started in Baghdad with the Iraqis showing them all the devastation from the American bombing. Norman said it was pitiful to see. Mind you, he really believes that Saddam had hospitals and schools blown up so that he could accuse the Americans of genocide and to show the world that the technology, Smart bombs and all that, was just a sham. Norman said it was all so blatantly staged that it just hardened their opinions against Iraq. Well... after a few days the Iraqis must have got tired or something but they began to leave Norman and his colleagues alone. They still had to travel under Iraqi supervision but no longer under strict Iraqi guidance, they managed to get out of Baghdad and into the countryside, the smaller towns and villages. What they saw disgusted them. Norman's colleges' reaction was to blame Saddam and the Iraqi government even further, but Norman saw it differently. He had never witnessed such pointless suffering and he could clearly see that it could be alleviated, even stopped overnight, just by raising the sanctions that the Americans and us were inflicting, and forcing the rest of the world to inflict.'

'Us? Surely we don't have that power to influence. Not any more.'

'No we don't, at least not directly.' The kettle boiled violently. Eric poured scalding hot water over the tea bags that he'd dropped into two bright blue mugs. He dipped the tea bags a few times by their strings and then gently flipped them into the sink. They both took their tea light and black. He passed a steaming mug to Norman.

'Well,' he resumed. 'Norman explained that. You see the Americans may have awesome power but they don't like to be seen to be wielding that power arbitrarily. They need someone to join them, to agree with them, support their opinion. In their eyes it justifies their actions; legalises them. And most of the time that's us.'

'Your words or Norman's? Norman asked scornfully.

'His. But I think that I agree with him. And that's where this story starts to turn nasty. Norman really turned when he saw what he saw. He was sensible though. He kept it to himself, came back home, let the report go through; just to create the impression that he supported the government on the issue.'

'And the Americans.'

'Sorry.'

'To fool both us and the Americans.'

'Yes. Of course. Then he started to actively campaign for a ministerial post. In fact, the ministerial post. Foreign Secretary. To his utter misbelieve he got it. Apparently his earlier refusals had made him into a real catch. The PM was determined to get him into the cabinet, old rubber lips, you know Michealson, the last foreign secretary fell ill just at the right time and Norman stepped in. That's when the Americans became involved. Somehow they had become aware that Norman was not as pro government as he appeared, and therefore not as pro American on this issue, as he seemed. Norman thinks he's under surveillance.'

'What the Foreign Secretary under surveillance, by who? The CIA? Can they do that?'

'I don't know but Norman's dead worried about it. He's prepared a document, a deal with Iraq, that will effectively withdraw our support of the embargoes; it even goes as far as opening currently closed trade avenues. Once he signs it and gets the Iraqis to sign, it becomes legal and binding on the government. They won't be able to rescind it. If they try the opposition will tear them apart. As it is the government are in for a rough ride what ever they decide to do. But the damage to the Americans will be immeasurable. Their stranglehold on Iraq's economy will be severely damaged, maybe even broken. At least that's what Norman hopes. Of course he will be finished in politics. Finished forever. That's why he's going to write his book. He already has a rough draft prepared in note form. It has to be finished before the pact is signed. At least as much as can be finished up to that point. Then, as soon as all hell breaks loose we'll finish the last chapter and have it on the bookstands before anyone can stop it. It'll be a sure fired best seller.'

'But what about the Americans? If they're suspicious then they'll stop him won't they?'

'That's what he's worried about. As Foreign Secretary he has bodyguards, but you never know with the Americans. He really could be in danger.'

'Not only him,' Norman replied. 'What about you? Us? They'll just swat a couple of fags like us without batting an eyelid.

***

Brinker stared at the receiver in front of him. Another crank call? Perhaps? As the adjudicator for the lottery draw they had become quite common. However, this one had a ring of truth about it that jangled his nerve ends. He had never trusted Briskin, never would. As preposterous as the caller's story had been, the very mention of Briskin's name lent it an immediate air of reality to Brinker. The inclusion of Freddie, Thaddeus and their insidious lawyer Whet had just added credence to the entire treacherous affair.

But how?

The caller had been a woman, middle aged, her voice sounded mature and the vocabulary was dominated by a sixties lilt; Brinker had studied linguistics at university, in his second year. It had only been a single course, just to bring up his points for that year, but the topic had interested him immensely and he'd continued his observations of dialects and speech patterns ever since; on a part time hobby basis. Our speech patterns, accents, dialogue are most affected when we are young. That is what he'd been taught and observed. Ergo, the caller had been a child in the late fifties and early sixties and must therefore now be middle aged. Brinker gave himself a mental pat on the back then returned to his thoughts about the woman caller. She had known intimate details about the lottery, and in particular the draw and how it would be managed. She had said that the draw had been rigged, that the final six winning balls were being controlled by a mechanism inside the box, a clever conjuring trick that was fooling everyone.

He'd found himself arguing back with her; that the box was made from transparent plastic; that you could literally see right through it. She had told him not to be so naive. She didn't fully understand how it was being done, but he should trust her. It was something to do with the central section; the box that the balls fell through. And anyway, she couldn't explain every little detail about the damn thing. He just had to take her word for it. The anger in her voice had been the most convincing of all. Then she began to talk about Freddie and Thaddeus, for whom she didn't have names, just referring to them as two old men, cousins. It was the inclusion of Whet's name that established the link. She had heard that name specifically. He was the one organising it all. The last name she mentioned was Briskin's.

'What do I do now,' he mumbled, his finger hovered over the button on the intercom that would summon Mary Little into his office. He pulled his hand away. What was he thinking? The last thing he needed now was to have other people involved or even aware. Briskin's involvement didn't really surprise him. He hadn't expected it. He hadn't suspected that a scam was in progress at all. But the fact that the scam was under way, and that it involved Briskin, Whet, Freddie and Thaddeus did not surprise him' at all. This was a problem. A real problem. If anyone found out that something fishy was going on, that their partnership was involved, it would finish them. He banged a clenched fist painfully down on the solid top of his desk.

'I'll swing for that snivelling, stupid, greedy little erk. I know I will.' He slammed his fist into the desk again.

There was a faint knock at the door.

'Yes?' He called angrily.

Mary Little's round concerned face appeared from behind the half-opened door. 'Excuse me, but is everything all right. I thought I heard a b…'

'Only me Mary,' Brinker interrupted. 'I dropped this old paperweight on the floor.' He lifted a large chunk of polished rock off his desk. A souvenir from his younger days during military service. A genuine piece of Mount Everest his Nepalese batman had assured him. He hadn't bought the story but had kept the shiny piece of granite anyway.

'OK. As long as you're alright.' Mary Little shut the door softly behind her. 'Dropped it twice did you?' She muttered to herself in disbelief.

Brinker pulled himself together. He had to take action. Now. Immediately. First he had to check out that infernal lottery machine. Find out how they were doing it. By now he'd convinced himself that they were up to something; it made sense. If they were rigging the draw they had to have the winner under their control. They couldn't rig it to their own names, family where excluded. So who where the six bogus recipients? They had screened every single entrant, to ensure that no one was in the slightest way related to the family, or connected to anyone involved in the lottery organisation, or even related to anyone who was involved in the lottery organisation. Whoever the lucky six were intended to be, they had to be ringers planted from outside the family – by Whet.

Mary Little fussed over the papers on her desk. He would be out in a moment. She had to look busy, as though she was deeply involved in some administrative task. She mustn't let him see anything in her manner that might lead him to suspect that she'd listened in on his telephone conversation; that would spoil everything. News such as this would be bound to upset him. He'd go for a walk. He always did when he was really upset.

Brinker's office door opened. Brinker, his stride purposeful but his manner distracted, called back over his shoulder as he passed Mary's desk. 'Going out Mary. Need some fresh...' The unfinished sentence hung in the air as he departed through the outer office door.

***

Reggie peered at his wristwatch. 5.30. He slipped quietly out through his bedroom door and into the cold silent corridor. A faint smell of disinfectant greeted him as he crept past the infirmary section towards the small window at the end of the corridor that would give him a view of the gatehouse. He checked his watch again. 5.32. OK. Three minutes to go.

As he reached the window his breath frosted it over. He rubbed it with the sleeve of his paisley pyjamas; a present from his wife. He could see the gatehouse now. Nestling between the perimeter wall, the entrance driveway and a clump of flowering shrubbery that he didn't know the name off. He couldn't see the guard, but he knew he was there. There was always a guard. He glanced at his watch again. 5.37. He's late. The thought worried him. Patience was not a virtue often found in the inmates of Stalag-Rehab, as he referred to the establishment.

Suddenly the gate guard appeared at his door. Reggie rubbed the glass pane of the window vigorously, as if the extra pressure would bring the picture into closer focus. The guard stretched, batted his arms across his chest and shoulders to ward off the cold and waved to someone out of Reggie's view. The guard stepped towards the dual wrought iron gates that formed the entrance to the clinic, inserted what Reggie assumed was a key – it was too far for him to see clearly – and swung the gates wide open. A milk float appeared between the gates. Reggie could just about hear the faint whine of its electric motor and the distant tinkle of rattling milk bottles. 5.39. 'Four minutes late,' he mumbled to himself.

***

Martin knew that he'd made a grave mistake. Chloe already knew that he'd entered the lottery for Rose's mansion. She already knew that he had some scheme going, with a friend he had said, but she obviously hadn't given that much credence; he didn't think that she suspected this friend to be a crook. He had promised her that he wouldn't buy a ticket for her, only for himself, and now he had admitted that he lied. He had only bought one ticket but in her name, so that Joan wouldn't find out. Why had he thought he could tell Chloe the whole story? Perhaps it was because he knew she loved him, or because he knew she would never betray him. What he hadn't considered was her feelings, the way that she would view what he had done. Well he certainly knew now.

Chloe stood in front of him, at the end of the bed, her naked body quivering, her temples and cheeks flushed bright red with rage. 'I don't care how clever you think you've been, it's a crime, illegal. They'll catch you and throw you in prison and me as well. Can't you see that?' Chloe's face resounded with frustration and anger.

Martin looked around the cheap interior of their motel room, its ceiling tinged yellow with tobacco smoke, the cheap wallpaper curling above the cracked paint of the skirting boards, attempting to self-peel from the walls. Ever since he had discovered that Joan was having an affair he had become paranoid about his own activities. Joan mustn't find out that he too was involved with another. He had to get the divorce application in first. If he was clever, he would be able to reveal his relationship with Chloe as if it had developed after the divorce partition, as a result of and reaction to Joan's infidelity. His precautionary actions had resulted in this afternoon's tryst, at this particular low-key motel. As soon as they'd arrived he knew it was a mistake.

'For God's sake keep your voice down,' he whispered. 'These walls are paper-thin. Someone will hear you.'

'Hear me.' Chloe picked up the imitation leather folder that sat on the counter beside the TV, weighed it briefly in her hands then launched it at Martin as hard as she could. The folder flapped, spilling a creased sheet of motel notepaper and a local Indian take-away menu slip from its interior pocket before hitting Martin's outstretched arm. Chloe looked vainly around the room for something heavier to throw. Untrusting bastards, she thought to herself as she wrenched at a table lamp only to discover that the motel manager had secured all movable objects such as lamps and pictures with heavy screws into the walls and fixtures; a procedure he felt extremely necessary but one that Chloe was about to overcome. Levered by the full weight of Chloe's body, the stem of the table lamp broke away from its base. She wielded the broken lamp above her head triumphantly, its lacerated end pointed menacingly towards the bed and Martin.

Martin rolled to the floor as the lethal projectile whistled over his shoulder, smashing the lampshade against the wall and a cascade of shattered glass from its dim forty-watt bulb, over the bed. He scrambled to his feet and lunged at Chloe, pinning her against the wall with his heavier weight.

'Stop it!' he said. His breath heavy with exertion. 'Listen! It's going to be alright. No one knows that I'm involved. No one.'

Chloe pushed as hard as she could against the grip he had on her shoulders. Martin pushed back. She glared at him, unable to break his hold. 'What do you mean; no one knows you're involved?' The words were spat at him; spittle flecked his cheeks, nose and forehead. 'Those men know. Whet and Briskin. They know, don't they? And you. You blind fool. You think they are going to stand by you. When it all goes wrong you won't see them for dust. It'll just be you left holding the can. And me. Why me? Why did you have to put my name down on that ticket?

'You know why,' Martin replied.

'Oh I know what you've told me, but I don't know how you could be so stupid.' Tears began to well in the corners of her eyes, she forced them back; she always gave into him, he had that sort of hold over her, but not this time, she'd not give in, not if she could help it. 'Let. Me. Go!' She struggled anew, wriggling from side to side, dropping to her knees in an attempt to break free.

Momentarily it worked. Martins grip released as he re-adjusted his hold. He fell to the floor with her, his grip re-established. 'Chloe,' he said. His voice a silken whisper next to her ear. 'Chloe. Please believe me, you're in no danger at all. You haven't committed any crime. You haven't spoken to Whet or Briskin. You haven't even met them. You haven't signed any documents. All that's happened is I've bought a lottery ticket for you. An errant husband buying a present for his mistress. Your reputation may be at stake but little else and it's a bit late to be worrying about reputations isn't it?' Gingerly he released one of her shoulders, then the second. He cupped her chin in his hand and lifted her face to his. He gave the most reassuring smile he could muster.

The tears began to return. 'Shit,' Chloe swore silently to herself. Her head fell forward onto his shoulder, her whole body shaking with long drawn sobs.

***

Brinker walked and walked the streets, endlessly contemplating the information the woman had given him. After almost thirty minutes walking he made his decision; he would have to call for a redraw, go public and announce that there had been a mistake, an unfortunate error. That's what he had to do, the honourable thing. Nothing less. He had wondered so far that he found himself in a part of the town that he barely knew, and it took him several minutes to get his bearings and set off with a deliberate stride towards his office.

All the way back his mind was in turmoil. If he owned up and told the world that the lottery had been corrupted, it would be his fault or at least the fault of his office; Brin, Brinker and Briskin would lose all credibility, it would take years to recover their reputation, if they ever could. But he had to own up, it was the only honest course open to him and besides, who ever telephoned him knew the truth, they obviously wouldn't keep it a secret. He was damned what ever he did.

He arrived back at his office hot, tired and mentally exhausted. The quandary still facing him, tearing at his mind unabated. His resolve weakening. As a result, his pious resolve to do the right thing was beginning to fade, to fade fast. The outer office was empty, Mary Little was at lunch. The telephone console on her desk was buzzing softly, an incoming call on line one. Brinker leant across the desk pressing the line button with a preoccupied finger, his only clear thought, Briskin. Grasping, deceitful, traitorous, corrupt, Briskin. Oh how he would make that half-witted charlatan pay. Several possibilities jostled in his mind, all of which involved the application of severe physical pain and permanent mutilation. Buoyed by the thought of Briskin's undoubted, unrelenting suffering Brinker decided that his day couldn't get any worse; his assumption was very, very wrong. The day was about to become disastrously worse. He connected the incoming call through to his office.

For the second time that day he found himself staring at the telephone in front of him. He replaced the receiver, using just the tips of his fingers, as though it were a living entity, the embodiment of an evil that had just spoken directly to him. He felt quite numb, almost trance-like, drugged or anaesthetised. The voice had spoken from the past, the deep forgotten past. But that wasn't true. The voice itself wasn't from the past, it was new, a voice that he had never heard before, but one that he would never forget.

***

Martin replaced the receiver and stared thoughtfully at the telephone. He wasn't sure exactly what he had just done, or even what he had just said. He'd simply identified the caller then read the script that the lawyer Briskin had prepared for him. Not that the script had been particularly menacing in its content. But it had meaning. Sinister meaning. That was borne out by the stunned silence and the heightened breathing from the other end of the line. Martin backed out of the call box he'd phoned from and turned away. That was the last time he was going to do anything like that and it didn't matter how much anybody tried to force him; he wouldn't be doing that again.

191

***

The sun sparkled into Eric's neat and tidy office, its afternoon rays dappled by the fluttering leaves of the ancient Oak tree that guarded the entrance to the house. Their new apartment, courtesy of Hewlett-Temple's generous advance to Eric, was the entire top floor, the third floor, above a Scandinavian couple who were half way through a two-year contract; the husband worked for a merchant bank in the city. The bottom floor was occupied by the landlord, an elderly robust widower who had bulked when he first met Eric and Norman but had eventually agreed to let a gay couple into his house. Initially Eric had been a little concerned that the old man would have second thoughts and renege, but old Mr Cookson had turned out to be quite liberally disposed. Having made up his mind to accept them, that was that, subject closed. It had only been a few days since their arrival but already they'd begun to germinate a fledgling friendship with the affable landlord

Work on Hewlett-Temple's memoirs had started with a rush. The politician hoarded collected notes and diaries for several years so there was plenty to read through. Of course the main selling point for the book would be the Middle East and Hewlett-Temple's involvement with that region, but it was still to be an autobiography, so the authors' personal life, background and career would be the subject-line. Eric had discussed the form of the book at great length with Hewlett-Temple and they had decided to write the autobiography partially in reverse, to give it more impact. In the opening chapters Hewlett-Temple would outline his private policy on Iraq and the actions he would have taken just before the book was released. Actions that would shake the British government to its very core. They would then build Hewlett-Temple's private life, his childhood and his political rise to foreign secretary, with heavy emphasis on everything that Hewlett-Temple felt contributed to his final denunciation of the governments of both Britain and America; his ultimate political suicide. As a preface to the book they would include the entire text of the speech he would give on that last fateful night in Brussels.

Eric paused from his typing. His watch said 3.30. Where was Norman? Eric was worried about his partner. How could he not worry, Hepatitis C kept him worrying all the time. When he thought about it, it all became a little crazy. Especially the irony of it. Norman's illness had been discovered by a visit to their local doctors for a check-up. Norman had recently learned that a previous partner had succumbed to AIDS and, even though he was sure that he was safe from the virus, he asked for a blood sample to be taken. It had come back with the devastating news that although he was clear of AIDS he had Hepatitis C. He simply couldn't believe it. Then there were more tests, and more tests and more. No one could tell them whether it would prove fatal or not and so far he hadn't displayed any debilitating symptoms; in fact he felt and acted healthy to the extreme. But the likelihood was high, keeping both men ever alert for any sign of deteriorating health. However, Eric's current concern was in addition to this. Norman had begun to display signs of paranoia, not for his illness, although heaven knows that would be perfectly understandable. No... This paranoia was over Hewlett-Temple's book. Eric had only just started working on it. Just since they had moved into the new apartment. But with each day that Eric studied, Norman became more and more tense, nervous and touchy.

Eric pushed his new soft-fabric swivel chair back from his new desk with a resigned sigh then headed for the kitchen. He hadn't had his coffee for the day because he'd been too absorbed in his work. But now was a good time. He'd make enough for two. Norman would be here any minute now.

Eric's confidence was rewarded by the sound of Mr Cookson's resonant voice reverberating from the lobby below. A quieter voice answered. Eric couldn't make out who it was but it had to be Norman. Eric opened the front door and listened. He still couldn't hear whom Mr Cookson was talking to, then the word Norman carried clearly up the four flights of stairs that separated them.

Norman arrived at the head of the stairs a few moments later, slightly out of breath due to his exertion. Eric looked at him closely, assessing whether the shortness of breath was due to the stairs or something more sinister. Norman had a pair of white carrier bags clasped in one hand, a French stick poking incongruously out on the top of one. He pushed past Eric, into the hallway of their apartment and dropped his shopping roughly onto the floor. 'Quickly,' he said, pulling Eric by the arm, deeper into the apartment and over to the window of the office. He released the tieback that held the curtains open then folded the edge of the left-hand curtain back carefully. 'Look. Over there. The black Citroen.'

'What?'

'The car. The black one. It was outside the supermarket. Now it's here, outside the apartment. It followed me home.'

Eric pulled the curtains back and tied them off. 'Her name's Dana.'

'Whose name.'

'Dana. She lives across the road. Number 38. She drives a black Citroen and she works at the supermarket. I met her the other day, she gave me a lift home.' He gave Norman an exasperated look. 'You've got to stop this. The CIA have not marked our cards, they don't work at the local supermarket and they're not going to pop out of the black Citroen hatchback and blow us away. This isn't a movie set. No one, CIA, MI5 or any other security service are going to know anything about what Norman intends to do until he's actually done it. He'll sign with the Iraqis in private and then all anyone will be able to do is complain. The book will go to the publishers and extracts from the book will be released to the press, the same day as he signs with the Iraqis.

Dana replaced her binoculars into their case and scribbled a brief note on the notepad on her lap. 3.38 p.m. Second subject returned to apartment.

Eric returned to his keyboard and computer. The home page of a local internet service provider glowed off the screen in front of him. He clicked SEND with his mouse and dispatched eight copies of the introduction to Hewlett-Temple's biography, including the soon-to-be-infamous Brussels speech. Three copies went to three simple Email addresses he'd set up in his own name. Two went to the two Email addresses Hewlett-Temple used. But the last three went to special address he'd set up with the help of a friend who was a 'bit of an expert'. These three contained a special programme, a virus, which caused the message, and its attachments – the sections of biography – to be retransmitted to three other addresses before cancelling them from the first. It took less than two minutes to set up each address. With the help of his expert friend, Eric had set up over sixty, covering service providers based in over twenty different countries, including Iran.

The mail-received message appeared on the screen. Eric smiled, closed the link and put the computer into sleep mode.

***

I think the modern colloquialism would be 'Damn what a rush'. At least I remember hearing one of those American action heroes, in a film, shouting something like that as he blew up an entire convoy of the enemies' trucks with one flick of his little finger, but it can also happen in real life you know, not just in Hollywood. Imagine the captain of the Bismarck, just as that fatal, single shell dropped down the funnel of HMS Hood and BANG! No more Hood. Gone. Destroyed. 'What a rush'. And now I know how that feels.

Afterwards, Diane swore that she hadn't called me, but she had, although she just didn't realise it. Then when I arrived? What a mess. Maureen, Diane's daughter – I didn't know her name then, but it didn't matter, a damsel in distress she was, if ever I saw one – was elevated, suspended you understand, about waist height above the floor, between the sofa and the television. Her cloths had been ripped to shreds and swirled around her torso like spines of tall, thin pines in a gale. Her legs were spread-eagled and between them lay the most evil and malevolent thing I have ever seen. The form was male; I knew that, although I'm not sure how because it really wasn't identifiable in the human form sense; not two arms two legs etc. It was a moving entity, an elongated cyclone of mass. I suppose that I knew it was male because to me it felt so, and besides its intentions on poor Maureen where as basically male as intentions can be.

Diane lay in a heap to the far corner of the room. Her back was arched violently and her hands clawed at her throat, as if she were being strangled by invisible claws. Her breathing had stopped. A cackled gargle, bubbled from her lips, she was dying, only seconds away from joining me and I simply didn't know what to do. So I rushed in. I physically charged at the malevolence to grapple with it. I knew it was the cause of Diane's pending demise, and it was perfectly obvious what it was about to do to the poor girl beneath it, so I attacked it. Of course there was nothing tangible to grab at, or to grab with, but it worked, it disrupted him. He turned and I screamed with all my celestial – for that's how I now saw myself – might, straight into what I perceived to be his face. And it worked. His form dissolved broke into shards of cold flame, each tongue extruding long wails of pained frustration and anger as they swirled around the confines of Diane's living room. Then abruptly, they were gone. It was gone. A cloy, rank, odorous gas, translucent at its core but clearly defined by its tumbling, frayed yellow edges followed the course of the departed evil, then stopped and slowly dissipated into the natural air of the room. Although I witnessed all of this, I didn't, couldn't, actually smell the terrible odour of the gas, Diane told me about it later. She said that she would never

195

forget that smell as long as she lived. I told her to be grateful for the smell. It was that which saved her, having the same effect as smelling salts it made her cough and reach, brought her breath back with a start that rekindled her life.

I stayed with Diane and Maureen, waiting for them to recover. Diane's injuries where miraculously minor, the worst she had sustained was a bruised rib; although it was a couple of hours before her voice returned to normal. Maureen's physical injuries were more extensive but still just superficial bruising. The real problem was psychological.

After the attack, Maureen slept for about an hour, then woke wide-eyed and frightened. Diane calmed her down and eventually got her to drink a cup of sweet tea. With gentle coercing and not a few tears she started to talk to her mother. If she remembered the details of her ordeal, she wouldn't say. Eventually, and as gently as she could, Diane retold to Maureen exactly what had happened, including my part it the event. Maureen took this on board without any show of surprise. She said that she knew I was there but didn't know who I was, but she still wouldn't acknowledge that she remembered the attack. She wanted to know who I was, not what I was. It was obvious that she had previous experience of physical spirit presence, obvious to me and also to Diane.

Now cautiously, Diane is starting to quiz her daughter. Why wasn't she surprised by my presence? Had she met a physical spirit before? Was it Simon that attacked her? The answer was yes, not sure and no, but I'll come back to that later. Had he attacked her like that before?

'Can she see me? Does she know that I am here now? If I do that – I projected my presence towards her – can she feel it? I insisted that Diane ask. The answer was NO, NO and NO. Which I found very disappointing. Then she said that although she couldn't feel my presence, she could the other one.

Panic gripped me as I heard those words. I spun round through a complete circle, looking for this 'other one'. There was nothing there. 'What other one? Where?' Not being able to see it had not decreased my sense of panic at all; if you will excuse the pun, I had already reached the simple conclusion that I was being haunted, that another spirit was in some way after me.

Diane claimed that it was all clear to her now. 'Lucky Diane, because it certainly wasn't to me.' Apparently Maureen was one of a particular type of medium; a 'Portent' Diane called her. A medium, *usually with a very strong gift, that picked up only on evil; 'Portent of doom etc. That, Diane explained, was why Maureen had failed totally to communicate with all the other spirits who chatted with Diane on a virtually daily basis but, always outshone her mother when it came to talking to Simon, who was most definitely evil. And, she added, that's why she can see the other one over your shoulder. Maureen nodded in agreement to this last statement. By then she had accepted my presence in the room and the communication between us shifted from two separated conversations to a sort of second hand three way chat with Diane translating in the middle. I then asked the rhetorical question. 'If you can see this other entity, over my shoulder so to speak, then it must be evil?*

'Oh yes.' Had come the reply without hesitation. 'Very evil indeed.'

'On a scale of 1-10, say, putting Simon at 5?

'10'

'10?'

'Oh yes.'

Suddenly I'd found myself out of questions. Maureen's relaxed manner and matter-of-fact responses belayed any doubt that she was not only telling the truth but that that truth was absolute, undeniable, irrevocable.

'It must be a 'Foregoing.' Diane had announced confidently. 'Trapped in between, can't cross over. You know the sort of thing. Even the movies get that one right; sometimes. And it must know you Rose. Probably from your past, could be an ancestor I suppose, but I doubt it. It'll be someone you knew personally.'

'Can she see it now? Diane had repeated my question.

'Yes and No,' was Maureen's reply. 'It comes and goes. I think it appears when Rose is talking to you.'

I asked Diane. 'Remember the dog? When I tried to go too deep into the dog's mind, it attacked me then. Ask Maureen what it looks like. Does it have a shape?'

'Just colours really. Quite small. A bit like a halo but with just half a side.' She'd replied in a matter-of-fact tone.

'You think about that for a minute Rose.' Diane had said, then turned back to her daughter and asked. 'Now tell me about Simon. You knew him didn't you?'

This was what Maureen replied. I'll try to get it as correct as I can and it should be almost word-for-word perfect because I'll never forget what she said as long as I exist – poor child.

Maureen didn't cry, she just took a big breath and answered 'We both did mum. Simon is your husband, my father. I called him Simon because I didn't want you to know who it was all those times at the seances. I didn't want you to know his name and I never let you hear all that he said because I didn't want you to know what he was after.' Maureen had paused then, to allow Diane time to absorb what she was saying. 'He tried several times while he was alive. Each time I managed to fight him off, usually because he chose the wrong time and you would come in, or he would hear you coming to the front door. It started six months before he died.'

'Diane,' I asked. 'How old was Maureen when her father died?

'Nine. Nearly ten.' Tears had appeared in the corners of Diane's eyes as she answered. Then she drew Maureen's head into her chest and both women began to sob relentlessly.

There was nothing I could do then so I left them to their private sorrow. But I'm back there now, just to check up. Maureen's in bed. She appears to be OK. She's sleeping peacefully; I popped into her mind for a very brief minute and was quite delighted to see that instead of nightmares about this afternoon's events she was giving off a sense of relief. Obviously telling her mother about the paedophilic tendencies of her father had been a great load off her chest; in some perverse way the attack had done her good.

Diane's there, on her sofa, red eyed, staring at the blackness of the dormant TV set in the corner of her room. She hasn't noticed me yet.

'Yes I have.'

'Sorry, I didn't mean to intrude. Just wanted to see if you were alright.'

'Not really. I don't know how I feel. I've already told you that there was no love loss between Maureen's father and myself for years before he died. We only stayed together for her sake. But I had no idea that he was a…'

'Paedophile?'

'Yes… I've been thinking, and perhaps it was his illness. He had cancer. In his groin. They operated and it appeared successful but then it returned. That's terrible you know. You get the big C, beat it and then it just comes zooming back to finish you off. Perhaps it turned his mind?'

'Go to bed Diane. I'll see you tomorrow.'

Chapter 15

Teresa Stamp watched her brother punch the keypad of his mobile phone in an agitated fashion, venting his frustration on the plasticized keys. As if not satisfied with the result of his onslaught he gave the instrument a shake, defying it not to make his connection for him this time. The distant end purred gently.

'Briskin.' The reply was slightly exaggerated. Whet could just discern an edge of excitement to the voice.

'Where the hell have you been?' Whet shouted down the line.

'Sorry?'

'I said where have you been? I've been calling you for the last hour and a half.'

'Oh. Out.' Defiantly

'Out... Well, while you've been OUT, I've had a telephone call. A very worrying telephone call. A blackmailing telephone call!'

'I don't understand.'

'You don't understand. Tell me, why am I not surprised?' Whet's sarcasm caused Teresa to raise her eyebrows in agreement. 'In fact I'd be surprised if you understood anything at all.'

'Now just a minute.'

'No. There is no just-a-minute. Someone rang me to inform me that they knew everything and when I asked them what they were talking about they explained. In plain simple English. Everything; the lottery, the device in the lottery box that controls the balls, that releases the balls we want it to release, the agreement with Freddie and Thaddeus, the plans for the division of the estate afterwards. Everything!' Whet paused, collecting his breath, waiting for a reaction, then spoke again, over Briskin's tentative attempt at a response. 'Where? Where could they have got all of this detailed information from? Where?' He shouted down the receiver. 'Not from me or my sister, and we are the only ones from my side that know anything about this, even Freddie and Thaddeus don't know some of the details that our caller knew. So it has to be from your end. You've been speaking to people, haven't you? Running off at the mouth.'

'But...'

'It wasn't at that flea-pit that you call a local was it? Good grief, if it was then half the county must know by now. Don't just

199

stand there man, tell me.'

'I've been trying to. If you'll let me get a word in. The answer is NO! I haven't told anyone, anyone at all. I haven't spoken to a soul other than the people you've just mentioned and, as you say, I've never ever discussed all of the details with Freddie or Thaddeus. Whoever your mystery caller was, he didn't get any information from me. No Way!' he finished defiantly.

Silence followed. A long painful silence that Briskin could not handle. 'Well?' He said to the almost dead telephone. 'Well?'

'WELL!'

'Don't raise your voice.' Whet almost believed Briskin. The young fool was too scared to risk telling anyone. Too scared and too stupid

'What are they asking for?'

'50,000. Used notes etc. And it was a woman's voice, not a man's.'

As Whet replaced his receiver, the telephone in Freddie's lounge rang. Freddie was waiting for the call, he picked up the receiver at the third ring of the bell.

'Yes.'

'It's…'

'I know who it is. There's no need for names over the telephone. Is everything set?'

'Apart from the money, yes.'

'That will be ready this afternoon. When will you do it?'

'I'll take the down payment this evening, and it'll be in my own time. OK? Then I'll want the balance. Immediately!'

'But I'd like to know when. Exactly, and how?'

'No. That's my business, nothing to do with you. It'll be within a week from today, that I promise you. Now you make sure that you're at the meeting place this evening. Be on time.'

Softly, at almost a whisper, Freddie said 'Of course.'

'So it's actually on.' Freddie mouthed the words silently. Putting a contract out on another human being's life was not just another of life's experiences. Normal people do not hire hit men to dispose of interfering relatives and he knew himself to be normal, of course he was. He could feel the build up of adrenaline deep in the bowels of his stomach. God. What will it be like when it actually happens? It's five days to the final draw. The day of the draw? Possibly. That stupid girl Lisa had arranged quite a spectacle for the draw, what with that MP fellow being there as well. A public execution, yes, possibly. Or the day after. Everything will be quieter then. Just the tidying up going on. But they'll be no people at the manor then, no crowds for the assassin to hide away in. No. It has to be during the draw. The thought raised his adrenaline levels even higher. He didn't usually take to hard drink this early in the day but a Cognac would help to calm him down. He poured a full measure into a cut glass Brandy bowl.

'Thaddeus,' he said to himself and began to dial his cousin's number.

After a few seconds a bleak splintered voice answered. 'Hello. Freddie?'

'We're on. Don't ask for details, I don't have any, don't ask any questions over the phone either. All I can tell you is it's guaranteed for sometime in the next seven days.'

'At the manor then.' Thaddeus' comment was a statement not a question.

'Has to be. She's living there full time at present.'

'At the draw?'

'That's the obvious assumption, unless she leaves the manor for any reason. Who knows? But the quicker the better, that's for sure.'

There was a brief silence from the end of the line. Freddie could hear Thaddeus breathing heavily. He knew how he felt.

Finally Thaddeus spoke. 'I need a drink.'

'I've already got one,' Freddie replied. 'Now remember the arrangements for the payment. I'll meet you outside the bank at half past two and...'

***

Diane poked gently with the edge of her trowel. There were two days to go to the final draw and she still had to turn the Talisman for its third and final time. She should have turned it earlier, but for the last couple of days she'd not been herself. The shock of Maureen's revelations had been difficult to handle, very difficult. And she was desperately worried about her daughter. Maureen had explained that she actually felt better now that she'd told her mother the facts, and that she wasn't frightened of Simon, as she still referred to him, any more, because Rose was there to protect her. Diane didn't want to undermine her daughter's new-found sense of security by pointing out that Rose wouldn't be there forever, so she said nothing, and that made her feel even worse. But at least she had the lottery to take her mind off things. Keeping busy was the answer and the preparations for the big day had certainly taken care of that. Today had been the carpenters' day. They had erected two wooden platforms, one inside the house as a small stage for the presentation and one outside as a podium for the TV cameras. Tomorrow the marquee arrives.

She slid the point of the trowel under the talisman and eased it away from the hold the ground had on it. The bright sheen of the gold painted charm glinted in the moonlight. It was the size of a small saucer and shaped like a child's hand. Inset into the centre of its palm was what appeared to be a golden coin, a perfect circle of pure gold covered in a tight spiral of tiny runes. Diana glanced up at a clear sky above her. 'Full moon tomorrow,' she mumbled to herself. Carefully she brushed the loose loom off the Talisman then lifted it to her face. She pursed her lips as though to kiss the hand but stopped, millimetres from her mouth, closed her eyes and blew a long draught of hot breath onto its golden centre. She rotated the hand one quarter to her left and blew again, then lifted it to her forehead. She touched the hand to her flesh, a brief contact for a mere heartbeat, then placed it back into the hole she had exhumed it from, carefully reversing it from its previous lay. 'You are turned,' she said simply.

***

Marios Branchman eased his car to a halt in the restaurant car park as the Maitre'd opened the entrance door for Lisa. Marios reversed into a vacant space just a few metres from the front of the restaurant where he had a clear view through the front window. He switched off the engine and applied the hand break then sat there for a moment, in the darkness, and watched the Maitre'd lead Lisa to a secluded booth at the rear of the restaurant. She was dressed in simple clothing, a plain skirt and a loose cotton blouse, her hair was tied back in a ponytail, which she had twirled into a loop and secured with a large plastic-toothed clip. He smiled to himself.

***

Ann wrote the words Saturday PM, precisely and deliberately on the cardboard cover of the aluminium-foil freezer dish that contained

Alan's dinner for the following day. She had prepared five similar meals, all encased in aluminium freezer cartons, and each marked with the particular meal time she intended Alan to eat them; Friday PM, his dinner tonight, Saturday AM, lunch tomorrow, Saturday PM etc. She had included Sunday PM and told Alan that she would be back late from her weekend trip with the girls at the office and that he shouldn't wait for her before eating on Sunday; the meal marked Saturday PM was the one she had laced with the poison. Alan was a creature of habit, he would eat his dinner at six o'clock precisely, sitting at his chair in front of the TV with a tray on his lap and watching the six o'clock news. He would be unconscious before the first set of adverts, comatose by the end of the news and dead half way through the next programme.

She stacked the freezer packs in their correct order and slid them into the depths of the freezer. Behind her stood a red trolley-style suitcase. 'I'm off now,' she called out loudly.

'OK,' Alan's voice drifted from the lounge.

Ann poked her head round the lounge door. 'Your meals are in the freezer, as usual. I've marked them so be careful to take the right one each time or you'll end up with lunch at dinner time and you won't like that.'

'Em,' he responded. He was watching a tennis match on the TV and hardly glanced in his wife's direction.

Ann gave the back of his head one last look, picked up her suitcase, turned and walked down the passage to their front door. She'd called for a taxi and Liam would be waiting at the station. This would be her last secret weekend away with Liam at the farmhouse. It was quiet, secluded and totally safe from prying eyes, but after this Saturday PM, they wouldn't have to do this anymore. She closed the front door firmly behind her. If she'd cast just one look behind her she would have seen Alan's nose pressed between partially parted curtains, watching her leave.

***

'Time for dinner,' Alan said aloud, his spirits raised higher than they had been for, for…. Well he couldn't remember when his spirits had last been raised…. Before his illness he supposed. He shuffled towards the kitchen. Lately he had found it difficult to walk properly and this fact, combined with ever increasing periods of incontinence, the sores and interminable rashes, and increasingly intense and complete bouts of amnesia, had drawn him to the simple conclusion that both his body and his mind were slowly and inexorably falling apart, decaying, dying.

He had discovered his wife's infidelity two weeks earlier, and by complete accident. She had been careless. If he had carried out such a deception he would have been meticulous about any paper or document that could incriminate. Ann hadn't been. She often went on weekends away with her friends from work, increasingly so in recent months and he would never have become suspicious if she hadn't been foolish enough to use her credit card during her last trip. When the bill arrived Alan noticed an amount charged against a pharmacy in a place called Lower Acton. Alan was used to seeing regular purchases at pharmacies and health food shops, Ann had always been into that mumbo-jumbo rubbish but where was Lower Acton; as there was nothing worth watching on the TV at that particular moment, and out of idle curiosity, he decided to check. That's when he began to suspect. Lower Acton was nowhere near Bristol; the destination she had given him for her trip with the girls. He knew she had lied to him. There could be only one answer and the rest had been simple. Ann didn't drive; she always used buses or taxis. She went out regularly during the week, Tuesdays and Thursdays to the evening institute – her interest in evening classes had begun soon after he became ill – and on Wednesdays to her sisters who lived three streets away. On the first Thursday after he found out he followed her. Ann didn't go to the evening institute that night, she went to another address, a private address, the home of one of the evening institute teachers, Alan had since discovered, a man with a reputation for the ladies. Alan's detective work became complete with Ann's second piece of bad luck, Alan met Angela, a blond, just like Ann, in her early fifties with the sort of over-weight curves that suggested she had been quite a looker in her younger days. She had also been one of Liam's earliest conquests. They both shared the same doctor, and as Alan visited the surgery regularly and Angela had developed acute hypochondria to accompany here ample weight, it was inevitable that their paths would cross. A pile of prospectus from the evening institute had been placed with the usual year old magazines. Angela was waiting for her appointment as Alan arrived. As regulars to the surgery they exchanged 'hellos' and a little polite conversation about the weather. Then Alan picked up a copy of the evening institute prospectus and began to scan the lists of courses and the names of the teachers. Angela no longer attended the evening institute but started to read a second copy of the prospectus out of idle curiosity. It was nearly lunchtime, the surgery doors were closed and they were the last two patients waiting, with the evening institute as a common denominator, Alan introduced himself and asked Angela if she had ever attended. It was as if he had opened the flood gates. Angela may well have been a genuine hypochondriac, and not actually medically ill in any way, but she did suffer from verbal diarrhoea, and suffered badly. Within the ten minutes it took for Alan to be called as the next patient, she had told him chapter and verse about every sordid detail of evening institute life. All Alan had to do was steer her in the right direction by dropping Liam's name into the conversation, virtually the only contribution he made. It was this way that he learnt about Liam's farmhouse that he rented on the grounds of a mansion house, near Lower Acton. Angela knew all about it. She didn't tell Alan that she'd actually been there but he had drawn his own conclusions, it was all rather obvious. So now he knew where Ann was really going on her weekend trips with the girls, and with whom, and for what. Now he could plan his revenge.

Alan lifted the lid of the freezer and picked out the foil dish marked Friday PM. He peeled back the curled edge of the dish and lifted the cardboard cover.

'Liver,' he announced. 'No. Don't fancy it. Let's see what else she's prepared?' He removed Saturday PM and Sunday PM, prised open the corners of each and inspected the contents. 'Looks like Lasagne and this one's a curry,' he considered both, pushed back the corner flaps on one and placed it back in the freezer.

'Microwave next.' He twisted the back of the foil container and flipped the meal into a microwave dish. He whistled jauntily as he pressed the defrost button. Through the glass window of the microwave he watched his evening meal slowly rotate.

***

'You're late,' Lisa teased as Charles approached the table.

Charles glanced at his watch. 'Only ten minutes, and I had good cause.' He lent across the table, gave Lisa a peck on the cheek and sat on the chair opposite. 'Here,' he said offering a long thin brown envelope.

'A drink sir?' A waiter appeared silently at Charles' shoulder.

'Same as the lady please.'

'Gin and tonic?'

'Sure. Lots of ice.'

Lisa ripped the top off the envelope and avidly studied the three pages of text it contained; he'd threatened to do this but she just couldn't believe that he had. The top page included a photograph of a house, an estate agents' flyer. The house was beautiful, perfect, the implication took her breath away. Their relationship had deepened to an incredible level over the last two weeks, Lisa couldn't believe how close they had become in such a short time, she knew that if the intensity continued he would propose. Not that she actually wanted him to, marriage wasn't necessary, but she knew he was the type that would; she was sure of that. But she wasn't sure of her own reaction if he did. Was marriage the right thing, was it necessary. They were already lovers and, if as he had said several times, he was about to retire from his present profession, and if, as he had already said, he really wanted to settle down, then they would naturally just move in with each other. She had her flat in London for now, and as soon as the alterations were completed at the manor she would move into the apartment that Aunt Rose had commissioned for her, so that she could administer the estate. But they had already reached that 'what if' stage. 'What if' they were to buy a house had come up after a long dinner with plenty of wine, a week ago. Lisa had let down her guard and romanticised about the perfect home, her dream house. The flyer she held in her hands now was as close as she could imagine to the house of her dreams.

Charles waited patiently for her to finish reading. Miraculously the waiter reappeared with Charles' gin and tonic in less time than it would appear possible to even prepare the drink. 'They must have them lined up and ready,' observed Charles once the waiter was out of earshot. 'Well? What do you think.'

'It's fabulous darling. Just fabulous,' her voice teased then hardened a little. 'And it appears to be exactly what you need, and so close to the manor house, perfect.' She added with a touch of sarcasm. She looked directly into Charles' eyes, a shadow of a tear forming in her own as she registered the hurt in them. He was serious. 'Charles? What are saying?

'Read the last page.'

She read. It was a receipt, a confirmation for a deposit.

'Charles! But why?'

'What a silly question. Why? Look I may be being a touch presumptive, but we did agree that once I've completed this last job we would move in together. You did say that, agree to that.'

'Yes. But I meant in my flat or the new apartment. We've only known each other a few weeks and moving in together well, that's not so strange of course, but buying a house so that we can move in together, that's a little dramatic. What if we're wrong? What if it doesn't work out? All that money?'

'Hey! Listen. I told you I was going to retire from my old job. A guy's gotta settle down sometime, why not now, here. And besides, I've always liked England, I'm OK for funds, so it's a good choice. And if it doesn't work out with you, I can always look around for someone else,' he teased. 'There's a likely looking candidate over there.'

Lisa looked in the direction that Charles indicated. The table he referred to was occupied by an elderly woman with a blue rinse. Lisa kicked him under the table. 'Will you take me seriously for once. This is a major decision. I love you too much to let you make such a huge mistake. You have to be sure, certain, absolutely positive.'

'About the house'

'No... Yes... Don't be so obtuse. You have to be certain about both.'

'And so do you.'

The tear in Lisa's eye began to well. 'But that's the problem. I am. More certain than I've ever been about anything in my entire life. Which makes it my fault if it goes wrong.'

'Feminine logic.' Charles raised his eyebrows and shook his head slowly. 'It's beyond me.'

Lisa reached across and squeezed his hand. 'And so it should be,' she replied, laughing.

Charles reached into his jacket pocket, his hand covering a blue velvet box. 'Look,' he said softly. 'I think I know the answer to the problem. Now I'm not one for fancy speeches and I'm certainly not going down on one knee in a public place, which I suppose doesn't qualify me as one of the great romantics, but I've never felt so sure about anything in my entire life. I want you to marry me, to become Mrs Charles O'Donnell, to live with me in that little house in the English countryside...'

'Little?' Lisa interrupted in a wavering voice. 'It's got five bedrooms.'

'Don't interrupt,' he chided. 'You've no idea how much psyching-up it's taken to get this far.' He lent across the table, took her hand and placed the velvet box into her palm. 'Open it darling. Please?'

Gingerly Lisa opened the box. The ring inside literally took her breath away, a white gold scroll, encrusted with tiny diamonds that covered its upper side and surrounded the biggest solitaire she had ever seen outside of a museum or stately home. Lisa was flabbergasted. 'You do mean it don't you.'

'Of course.' Fear flicked across Charles' eyes. He wasn't used to fear, nothing ever frightened him, but the thought of her turning him down scared the life out of him.

***

'It's the big day tomorrow. The final draw. They'll all be there, unfortunately; the family, the lawyers, the VIPs, the press and of course the last twelve candidates. I've only managed to identify four of Freddie's six stooges, which is annoying as I need to know who the last two are; I'll just have to wait for tomorrow. Once they're all together it should be easy to sort out the bad apples in the barrel.

But what a week it's been. It's been exhausting just watching the preparations, to the point where I've actually had moments of doubt about the sense of the whole thing. The sense as in, was it a sensible idea in the first place. But each time I've had that thought, I just have to reflect back to the family. One minute's reflection about Freddie, Thaddeus and company – less than one minute – is always enough to fortify any lapse in resolution.

The marquee arrived yesterday and looks particularly grand erected on the front lawns. It's a long time since Southgrim Manor held an event of this magnitude, not since I was a girl in fact, not since the days of the old King, of British Empire, of privileged society. It's hard to accept that so much can change in one's own lifetime, but there you are, it does and always will do.

I've actually been quite busy myself. Not with the preparation for the draw, at least not the earthly preparations, just my own preparations. You see, I'm going soon. Moving on. Don't ask me how I know, I just do. And don't ask me if something has happened to make me feel this way, because nothing has happened at all, nothing since that terrible scene with Diane's daughter; because I haven't let anything happen. You see it's become obvious to me that

208

what ever is out there, lurking, waiting for me or Diane or her daughter or anyone else for that matter, what ever it is, it or they can't get through unless you let them in. It's your actions, not it or theirs, they haven't the strength or power; perhaps they're simply not allowed too, who knows. What I do know, and now realise, is that both Diane and her daughter let them in, and with near disastrous results – she's alright now, by the way, Diane's daughter, Maureen, she appears to have come out of it all quite remarkably unscathed. How, I simply do not understand. You'd have thought that an experience like that would have sent her completely off her trolley. Of course, the fact that her mother now knows the truth about her father must have released a terrible burden that she's been carrying almost all of her life. Mind you, I doubt that she'll ever allow herself to touch an Ouija board again, not in this lifetime anyway. But I'm digressing, and I think I've already told you that. Anyway. I know that I'm here for a purpose and assume that that has to be tied up with the draw and the lottery; I mean, I created it, it's my idea, so I'm responsible. Therefore, if I'm here for a purpose, and if that purpose is the Lottery, then it stands to reason that once its over, so am I; at least my presence here in this world will be.

I'm not thinking about what happens next. I've switched off from that topic completely. There's nothing I can do about it. So don't ask.

But before I go, I can, and will, do something about what's going on here. You'll see.

The incident with Maureen has also helped me to come to terms with my other spiritual problem, the other spirit, the colours, the presence that appears to want to contact or interact with me. It frightened me, I thought it was evil, malevolent, Diane sensed it and immediately came to the same conclusion. I've changed my mind, we were wrong. It's not malevolent at all, it's just confused, lost. It doesn't display emotions in a human sense because it doesn't have any, it never had the chance to develop any so it displays the root of all emotions, the ability to be emotional, to feel, to want and yearn, to crave and desire, to love, hate and fear and it's the last three that we saw, especially the fear, that we mistook it for evil. We were wrong, terribly wrong. The reason I am able to be so precise and certain is that I saw evil, I saw malevolence, I experienced it in a way that transcends all human experience. I saw it the day Maureen was attacked and it was at a level completely removed from the

209

other, irrespective of Diane's 10 out of 10 assessments. Which means that I now have to face the other spirit, to confront it, perhaps to release it.

Now doesn't that sound hackneyed and trite 'release it', but I'm positive that it's true. That's why I have shut that part of my world out for all of this last week. You see there is another possible scenario. I may not be here for the lottery, the draw, or any other earthly pursuit. I might just be here for the other entity and, if that is so, it frightens me. I'm afraid that as soon as I let 'it' in something irreversible will happen and I'll no longer be able to help Lisa, because she most certainly needs help and I'm the only one that can provide the type of help she needs. So I apologise to who ever or what ever sets up the spiritual timetable, if I'm delaying some celestial grand plan then I'm sure I'll pay for it later. I may no longer have any physical human abilities but I still think in a human fashion and I'm still human enough to know when I have to do the right thing.

Tomorrow will bring what tomorrow will bring.

Rosie, what a stupid and maudlin thing to say. Shut up.

***

Chapter 16

Claire moaned softly. 'Drive careful.' She pulled the hem of the duvet tight across her face to hide the alertness in her eyes and waited.

Andrew gave the bedroom door a perturbed look. He took a deep breath and pulled it closed in one smooth motion. There was a loud click as the door catch sprung into its recess. It had done that every morning. Even when he tried to hold the catch back using an old defunct credit card it still clacked home with a sharp tinny snap. It was old, worn-out and useless. Claire was awake anyway, but at least he'd tried. All he wanted to do was slip out without completely disturbing her night's rest; especially at four fifteen in the morning. He trod as quietly as he could down the wooden stairs with their threadbare carpet. At the foot of the stairs he picked up his brand new sports bag; a luxury that he had had to splash out on. He couldn't carry his Failsafe uniform on the early morning bus in a carrier bag. What if it split and someone saw him. Saw the distinctive bottle green trousers and jacket. He couldn't risk Failsafe finding out what he was doing each morning at this hour.

Andrew wasn't the only person travelling under a veil of caution that morning. Stuart's day had started just as early with an invigorating ride on the rented 250cc trial bike. Their paths actually crossed, briefly, at a junction on the edge of town. Andrew had one more stop on the bus to go, Stuart a good five miles on the bike.

By the time Stuart reached his destination Reggie was also up. He had his own private room at the clinic, so dressing without being seen wasn't a problem; as long as he was really quiet. He felt nervous, in a way that he hadn't felt since he was a kid stealing a drag during playtime. Over his clothes he stretched a fine nylon cagoule. He pulled the hood of the cagoule up over his head and tied the strings of the hood tightly under his chin; only the round globe of his face could be seen. He looked at it in the mirror above the dresser. 'God I need a drink'. He whispered to himself.

Stuart pushed the trial bike deep into the foliage that surrounded an old gnarled oak tree, fifty metres beyond the gatehouse. The ground was too soft to support the leg of the bike's stand but Stuart had thought of that. He placed a square of plywood under the leg to spread the load and gingerly let go of the bike. The leg held. He retraced his steps to the gatehouse, checking every few strides to make sure that the bike couldn't be seen. His stomach was starting to knot up. He had never felt quite so nervous about a job in his life. The diamonds worried him, the shear size of the haul quite frankly frightened him. That was healthy of course. He knew it was the worst thing possible to be over-confident. And there lay his biggest fears, the over confidence of the twins. What was he doing associating with their type? They had agreed not to be violent but would they show restraint? They had a reputation for professionalism, but as a pair, as a duo, as twins, what about Mal on his own? The prospect of Mal acting on his own, in any way at all was more than just frightening. As much as he wanted too, Stuart couldn't back out. Not now. Not at this late hour. Anyway, Phil and Mal not withstanding, it would be most unprofessional and he had both pride and reputation to respect. So he had made few alternative arrangements. Just in case.

He gave one last look back to the old oak. There was no sign of the bike in the deep foliage. He set off down the lane with a positive stride.

Down from Reggie's room the dim night-light at the far end of the corridor glowed through the two portals set in the fire doors like a pair of dull tired snake eyes, concealing the night nurse sat at her station desk. Reggie turned away from those eyes. He crept slowly towards the exit doors at the far end of the long corridor, the doors that led to the main hall and stairwell. A second night-light cast a murky yellow light across the circular entrance hall, the main entrance into the clinic. Reggie gingerly tried the main doors. Locked. He knew they would be but he tried anyway. He took the stairs to the second floor then the access passage to the rear fire escape. The door he was presented with was firmly closed by a deep steel spring bolt. Across the centre of the door was a metal bar. Reggie breathed a sigh of relief. He had never been onto the first floor, the clinic staff didn't encourage clients, as they referred to them, to wander freely about the premises, preferring to strictly control client movement. But that only applied to the interior of the clinic. Clients were actively encouraged to explore the grounds outside. Reggie had made his plans based on his external research. At the rear of the two-storey building were three iron fire escape stairways, one in the centre and one at each end. Each led to a plain heavy metal door. A door without an external handle. Reggie assumed, quite correctly as it was turning out, that on the inside would be the usual crash bar to enable an emergency exit. He lent

212

on the bar with both hands, his teeth gritted against the clatter he was afraid the noisy mechanism would make. God I need a drink! The thought tore at him. His hands shook. The bar clattered down. The door swung open with a gush of cold air. Reggie slipped through the gap and closed the door behind him as quickly as he could without slamming it. The mechanism on the far side of the heavy door clattered again. Convinced that he must have been heard, Reggie stumbled down the stairs and across the lawn and deep into the shrubbery. He stopped and looked back, his pulse racing.

'Now I really need a drink.'

The clinic was perfectly quiet. No lights had come on suddenly. No one had raised the alarm. No guard had appeared at the gatehouse door. To his right he could hear whistling and the rattle of bottles. A blue and white milk float was just pulling away from what Reggie assumed to be the kitchen area, the arm of its driver just visible as it turned along a narrow path that led to the main driveway. Reggie checked his watch, 5.38. Perfect. He was on time this morning. Reggie realised that he'd had a stroke of unplanned luck. Any noise he had made opening and closing the fire door must have coincided with the arrival of the milkman and his noisy float. He breathed out, a long languid breath of relief. At the first bend in the path the milk float flipped noisily out of sight, hid by the depth of the shrubbery. Reggie pushed back through the shrubbery, behind the dahlia beds and reached the gatehouse in a low crouching run just as the milk float rattled through the gate. He could see the uniformed hand of the gatehouse guard held up in greeting to the milkman, then a brief wave. Reggie stepped out beside the float, on the blind side from the guard. The driver, still whistling, waved back at the guard. Reggie was through. He slid away from the float and into the bushes on the far side of the boundary wall. He was free and with one thing only on his mind.

In the milk float, the driver, Andrew, caught a brief glimpse of movement in his wing mirror. He blinked and shook his head; too early in the morning, he thought absently as he rattled away from the clinic gates.

Claire turned in her sleep. Her dreams, restless and disturbed, woke her up with a start. She checked the clock 6.30. She wouldn't go back to sleep now. She lay there thinking about the last couple of days. About Andrew, what he was up too. Unfortunately for her piece of mind she had formed the wrong conclusion entirely. The tension that she had felt from Andrew was due to his moonlighting, taking a second job. Andrew had decided not to tell her the truth, and he hadn't told anyone else, either. If Failsafe found out he was moonlighting he would be fired on the spot. He couldn't burden Claire with that worry. After all it was up to him to get them out of the mess they were in. He simply told her that he was doing overtime, by adding an early shift to his normal day. She knew that was impossible. She knew that Failsafe regulations prohibited such a long day. She had read it all as something desperate and sinister, a thought that should have been exacerbated that Monday, when she had followed her husband as he left the house in the early morning. On that day he had actually taken an early shift at Failsafe, using the spare afternoon hours that shift created to visit their bank to request a new loan. A desperate move that would at least put all their problems in one basket and hopefully give them a little more time to pay. His second job was only part time but the extra money would pay the extra interest the new loan generated.

Instead of discovering what he was actually doing, Claire had concluded that if he had taken the early shift he must be doing something else in the afternoons, something desperate and bad, she had to know what that was. Following him that morning had been easy, it had been from their own home, she had known where and when he would start from. But in the afternoons it was impossible. Three afternoons she had waited, at a safe distance outside Failsafe, but he had never appeared. She just didn't know when he would be finishing. Without a positive finishing time she couldn't be there at the right time to be able to follow him to wherever he went next. She had to find another way.

***

The Viscount TV panel van pulled through the south gate of Southgrim Manor and along its twisting gravel drive. It was 7.30 in the morning. Saturday morning. The morning of the day of the final draw for Rosie's Lottery. Joan stared intently at the edifice looming through the windscreen at her. It was cold and inhospitable, constructed of block stone and styled, as you would expect a Victorian mansion to be, rectangular, solid, conservative. In front of the main entrance a large marquee had been erected, a grey/white structure, twenty five metres long and eight high, that did little to lighten the dour appearance of the manor house. The only splash of colour that assaulted her eye was a large blue tarpaulin, that had been wrapped round scaffolding erected in front of a brace of boarded windows in the east wing; temporary covering of the renovation works that Joan had read about. 'And not before time.' Joan thought.

Joan had had to call in several favours to get this particular assignment. It wasn't on her normal patch and there had been fierce resistance from her editor who wanted her to cover a Royal visit to a local children's hospital; he was like that, treating even the simplest assignment as though it were of major global importance and allotting tasks accordingly. But she had persevered, and here she was, at the scene of the crime or at least the scene of the swindle that was about to take place, the one that she had come to stop, even if she didn't know how.

And, that was the problem. How to stop it. She knew that Martin was involved, that he had bought a ticket in his mistress' name, but she didn't know the names of the other five and she hadn't a clue how she would interrupt what was obviously a carefully constructed plan; short of simply standing up and denouncing him in front of the cameras. She wouldn't do that, it would cost her job and besides the whole idea was to gather evidence against Martin that would help secure her divorce firmly in her favour. She had rung that solicitor Brunker or what ever his name was. She'd told him the lottery was fixed and it had appeared to shake him up a lot, then she'd rung the other one, Whet, and made a blatant blackmail demand, although it was only a bluff aimed at unsettling them. She had no idea whether Brunker or Whet would do anything about it all. She hadn't given her name to either of them, of course. The van pulled to a halt and was greeted by a short middle-aged woman, who stared at Joan as she got out of the van as though she already knew Joan's little secrets, Joan shuddered.

'Good morning. My name's Diane, I'm the personal assistant to Miss Lisa Going, the principle of the Rose Morgan trust. You must be...?

'Joan Welland. From Viscount TV,' she added unnecessarily as the Viscount TV logo was proudly displayed on the side of the van. 'Is that platform for us? She pointed to a section of neat, tight planking that spanned through a broad tower of scaffolding.

'Yes. I hope it will be enough. We appear to have attracted a lot of media attention. Will there be room for all the cameras?'

'Good job we're first then.' Joan laughed. 'No. Seriously. You don't have to worry, nowadays these events are syndicated. We represent five stations ourselves, and the cameras we use are mostly hand held. There'll be plenty of room.'

'Oh good.'

Joan took Diane by the shoulder and led her towards the house. 'As we are first, would it be possible to grab a quick interview with Miss Going now, before the morning gets really hectic.'

Diane stopped suddenly and for a moment Joan thought she had offended her in some way, but she smiled. 'I'm afraid things have been hectic as you put it since just after five this morning, but I'm sure that Lisa will want to speak to you.'

Joan stared at Diane. There was something in the way she had said 'you' that implied expectancy, unseen knowledge and insight. Diane took Joan by the arm and led her round the marquee and into the house.

***

Liam woke at almost the exact time that Joan and Diane reached Lisa's office. Beside him, still asleep, lay Ann. He slid his feet from the copious, mock-Tudor double bed and into a pair of battered moccasin slippers. He stretched and yawned. Ann began to stir.

'Tea?' He asked, as he patted her bottom through the thin summer duvet.

'Mmm.'

He shivered in the coolness of the early morning air that coursed freely through the shaky wooden frames of every door and window in the old farmhouse; except for the two rooms where he grew the weed, those were carefully sealed and climatically controlled. One day he intended to get round to fixing those gaps, and a thousand and one other jobs needed on the house but he never seemed to find the time; there were more important and pleasurable things to occupy him each time he visited. And besides the lease was for three more years, so he had plenty of time.

'That lottery thing's on today. 2.00 p.m. At the mansion house. Fancy going over and blacking our noses?'

'What? No. We can't. There'll be cameras there and TV and photographers. What if we're seen in the background of the nine o'clock news? I'm supposed to be in Bristol. And besides, it's a private event. I read about it in the paper. 'In camera' it said. That

216

means invites only and we haven't got one.'

'Yes we have. This place is on the grounds of the estate.

'But you only rent it?'

'Precisely. That makes me a tenant, so I must now be part of this new trust fund foundation thing they've set up. And if not, we, temporarily for this weekend at least, appoint ourselves tenants. So we get an automatic licence to go.'

'Oh. If you want, but let's make sure we steer clear of the cameras and don't blame me if we get turfed out on our ears.'

'Buy you lunch at the pub if we do. OK?'

'OK you win. Now finish making that tea and get back in this bed. I'm awake now and there's a little something I want to take up with you.'

'Little…? Bloody cheek!'

***

A light breeze rippled up the slope towards the brief copse that grew so conveniently in the grounds to the front of the Southgrim Manor. Marios was struggling to spread a thin sheet of plastic over the front seats of a hired car that he had parked deep inside the copse. He placed one knee in the middle of the plastic sheet, smoothed the sides away from him with his hands and hooked the corners into the elasticised pockets at the rear of each seat. Gently he backed out of the car, careful not to disturb the plastic sheeting. He punched a number into a mobile telephone and waited. A short burst of tone reverberated from the telephone. He keyed the number '5', behind him the rear window of the hire car dropped gently down. He punched the number '6' the window whirred back to its closed position. He grunted with satisfaction, '5' for down, '6' up, and '7' for fire. He turned to face out of the copse, across the open field to the house with its newly erected marquee outside. From his pocket he took a short cylinder of shiny metal, a range-finder. Slowly he twisted the knurled metal knob at the end of the range-finder. The two mirrors inside the device moved closer together, the split image of the columns either side of steps that led into the manor house inexorably became one. 'One hundred and thirty seven metres' he noted 'not bad, a bit long but still plausible.' He replaced the range finder with a set of miniature field glasses and scanned the front of the old building.

To the right of the main entrance stood the marquee, erected two days before in preparation for the final draw. The marquee had worried Marios at first. It was why he was here now, re-checking his position and the trajectory to the target area. He had relocated to the far end of the copse, angling the direction to target slightly. He'd been slightly caught out by the message he'd received the night before. His original instruction was to prepare and wait. This he'd done but comments made by the client had led him to believe that they wanted him to wait for at least another week. In fact those same comments had opened a sea of suspicion in his mind. This wasn't a personal contract as he'd been led to believe. This was a professional contract, political. The unexpected order to go had stopped him preparing with his usual diligence and precise care, and reduced the percentage success factor, but not by too much.

The main driveway ran at right angles to the house, turning left and east after fifty metres and forming a boundary to the lawn on which the marquee now sat. As a result the only part of the house that he couldn't see was the bottom right corner, the last three windows on that side. He focused his glasses on the main entrance. The four columns of the pediment sharpened into view. This would be his next problem. The target had to walk through that entrance, down those steps. In fact on the day the target, being such an integral part of the proceedings, would no doubt walk those steps several times. The trouble was he didn't know exactly when and he didn't want to be lying out here, in the relative open, for hours waiting for just the right moment. He had had to change his plans. He had considered making the shot from the copse, but now it would be the decoy position instead. That was why he had rented the car with its electric windows, front and rear, which he had tinted by smoothing dark window-tinting plastic across them. In the rear of the car, fixed to a tubular support, was a large bore, heavy gauge pistol, its trigger replaced with a pressure switch which was wired to a lap-top computer that sat on the floor, beneath the driver's seat. It was loaded with a single blank cartridge. It had taken him all night to set it up. This was his decoy.

Marios scanned across the left-hand side of the house, the area where the renovation and conservation work had already begun. Remodelling for the first two apartments was well underway. The two windows on the ground floor, to the immediate left of the entrance, fed light to a reception room. The room was being used as an office and it was in this room that the lottery box and all the files pertaining to Rosie's Lottery were being stored. The target would have to go to that room for sure, and the room behind that, the music room where the immediate family, the VIPs and the last twelve lucky ticket holders would meet for a pre-draw cocktail. Marios realigned the glasses on the opening of the first window. He could see quite clearly the interior of the room. If he had been firing from here, he could hit the target through the window if necessary. A difficult, low percentage shot but not impossible, even through the glass. But it wouldn't be necessary; the top of the steps would do fine. He gave one final sweep, just to check. He wouldn't take the shot from here, but there had to be a clear line of sight to his hire car pistol-decoy.

A bland, green coloured van trundled down the drive and pulled to a halt beside the marquee. Marios switched his attention to the van. 'The caterers,' he mumbled to himself. A short rather round man with dark hair and dressed in blue jeans and a red tee shirt got out of the driver's side of the van. He walked to the rear doors and opened them, letting a young girl out of the vehicle. A teenager Marios thought. From the far side passenger a tall slim woman appeared. She wore a black skirt that fitted just a little too tightly around her hips and a white blouse that accentuated pencil sharp breasts. The teenager bounced off towards the marquee. The woman called after her. Marios couldn't hear what she said but the tone was stringent, calling the young girl back, he supposed.

The man and the woman went into the house. Marios could see them talking to someone in the front reception room. They sat down on chairs in front of a desk or table and began what was obviously a pre-event meeting.

Marios was just about to put his binoculars away, when he noticed the teenager re-appear from the marquee. Her manner caught his attention, it was strange, almost furtive. She walked backwards and forwards for a moment, checking, as though she wanted to see if she was being watched. Each time she turned she was further from the centre of the house, towards the building works and the western end of the building. Suddenly, as if satisfied that she had escaped attention, she ran to the far end of the building, rounded the corner and pushed into the trees. Marios retrained the glasses, intrigued. He hadn't noticed that before. In the trees stood an old wooden shed. The girl was struggling with the door of the shed. Finally she had the door half-open. She vanished into its interior. Marios waited.

Crystel found everything just as she had left it two weeks

before. The wheelbarrow with its tar, the insecticide spray, the garden chemicals. She busied herself filling the plastic tub of the insecticide spray then gave it a few pumps just to make sure it still held pressure. She found the two chemicals she wanted, one an insecticide and the other a wood-panel treatment, both highly flammable, and placed them in the wheelbarrow. A bundle of rags completed her collection with a square of tarpaulin to cover it all. She checked that no one could see her then backed the wheelbarrow out of the shed. It was very heavy and she had to stop twice in the short distance from the old shed to the even older house. She pushed the wheelbarrow hard against the end wall of the building, wiped her hands on one of the pieces of rag. Having rearranged the tarpaulin to her satisfaction, she placed some stone on top to secure it and skipped cheerfully back to the marquee.

Marios watched her enter the marquee. 'Now what on earth was that all about?' He said to himself. He didn't like abnormalities. Not at all. They were dangerous and always potentially fatal.

***

Maureen still felt weak from her experience with the spirit of her father. Outwardly she had fully recovered but the attack had left her mentally drained. She had visited Reggie the day after it happened and that had helped a lot. Not that Reggie had been able to lift her spirits himself, it had been the site of his struggle and suffering to cope with the rigours of drying out, that had helped, Maureen could see in Reggie a person that had to be supported, constantly. She had seen a desperate soul and knew that she was the only person in the entire world that would help. Reggie needed her, desperately, and that in itself provided the basis for her own recovery. She would go and see him later, after the final draw, after she had won a wonderful luxury apartment for them to move to. Her mother had been staying at the manor house for the last few days, so she would go on her own. Maureen caught the bus as far as she could then walked the last two miles. It was a beautiful day. Slightly cool but crisp, with the sun threatening to break through at any moment. She reached the south gate, at a quarter to eleven, just as Hewlett-Temple opened his hotel bedroom door to Eric and Norman.

***

'Come in gentlemen please.' Eric and Norman entered and stood awkwardly in the centre of the room. 'This must be Norman.' Hewlett-Temple observed, taking Norman's hand and putting it to his lips. 'Enchanted.'

'Stop flirting you.' Eric rebuffed. 'He's not part of our deal so hands off.'

Norman blushed badly, retrieved his hand from Hewlett-Temple's. 'I'm very pleased to meet you. Sir,' he mumbled in a self-effacing voice.

'Of course. But I fear you won't be saying that much longer. Not after my big speech, let alone when Eric's little book comes out. The entire world will want to get as far away from me as possible. And be careful it may rub off. Failure, disgrace, ignominy. That's a good word, ignominy.'

'Don't be so morbid.' Eric replied. 'You'll be a hero to millions. Someone's got to speak out.'

'My sentiments entirely,' Hewlett-Temple smiled. 'But if we don't finish it on time, get it to the publishers in the States and Australia before my big speech next month, then it'll never see the light of day. How's it coming along?'

They sat in a row, along the edge of the bed as Eric produced a thick sheath of papers from a briefcase. 'This isn't the full book, it's about twenty five percent complete and going well, but we have a real problem getting it to print on time. I think that we will need to send the advances off just before the deadline and then the full draft as soon as we can after.' Eric laid the draft book on the floor at his feet and took another, much slimmer document from his briefcase.

'Yes. I know you're right,' Hewlett-Temple replied. 'Once I make that speech they'll clamp a gag on me so tight that I'll be lucky to be able to say my own name let alone finish the book and publish it. No... It's down to you old friend.'

'Yes I know. That's why I've brought Norman along today. He wanted to meet you in person, and as the safest thing to do is for us to leave the country now, before the authorities know that we even exist, this was his last chance.

Hewlett-Temple smiled. 'Of course, and I'm very glad to meet you, Norman.'

Eric continued. 'I'm preparing the book in this fashion. It opens with the text of the speech that you intend to make to the UN Security Council, followed by your affidavit ratifying the authenticity of the document and then, the abbreviated, hard facts from the book. The dailies will go wild. Absolutely wild. I'll send it all by soft copy over the Email, it'll be on the streets within a few hours of you delivering the speech.' Eric handed a copy to Hewlett-Temple to read.

***

Teresa and her brother travelled to the draw in the same car as Freddie and Thaddeus, the remainder of the family followed in their own cars, in convoy. The draw was to be held 'in camera' and therefore by invitation only, by travelling with the family they would circumvent that inconvenience. Teresa was in a foul mood. 'You're wrong and as usual you won't admit it,' she stated tartly.

'If you say so, sister. We'll just have to wait and see, won't we.'

'We'll all get our collar's felt. That's what we'll see. The inside of a cell block, and not just overnight. You mark my words, this is all going to go wrong.'

'Can't you get her to shut up?' Thaddeus turned from the front passenger seat, speaking to Whet directly and ignoring Teresa. 'All this mumbo-jumbo about bad signs and portents of doom is getting on my nerves. As if we didn't have enough to worry about.'

'You'll regret it. You mark my words.'

'I'll mark you with me cane if you don't shut up.' Thaddeus lifted his cane and shook the silvered end at Teresa pointedly.

'You'll need more than that strip of bamboo before this day is over. You'll see.' With that last comment Teresa stopped. She withdrew into her own thoughts, remembering the string of events that had led her to her claims, especially the cats. Five jet black kittens, newly born, that had been a bad sign. She had dispatched them all, garrotting each one – which, she had to admit gave brief but intense pleasure – but even that percussion would not guarantee to lift the dark cloud that hung over them. They were heading for trouble. Trouble with a capital 'T'.

The gates of the south entrance to the estate opened before them. They drove inexorably on. Diane stood on the entrance steps waiting. Waiting as though she knew they were coming – which, of course she did – but this was different, as though she knew precisely when they would arrive, but in advance and, what they had in mind, what their plans and schemes were.

They were all escorted into the house where Lisa and her new man Chuckles met them. Teresa shook hands with them all in turn, as did Whet. Lisa's was a normal handshake, firm for a woman of her stature and cool and dry. Diane's handshake was hot, burning into the flesh of Teresa's palm. Their grasp lingered, painfully, neither women wanting to yield to the other. Then she took Chuckles hand. It seemed to melt into hers, kindred with venom. Chuckles pulled his hand back abruptly. Elsbeth stepped forward with a dismissive gesture and no handshake, oblivious to the exchange that had taken place between Teresa and Chuckles. Helen and Charles, and Lia and Christian were the last to enter, having been at the rear of the cavalcade.

'Ah. That's wonderful.' Lisa announced with seemingly genuine feeling. 'It's so good to see you all here. It gives me a chance to show you round, let you see how the work is getting on, what's being done. I'm sure that you are all interested. I'm so glad that you have all come. Who would like to see the work they've done upstairs? Lisa bustled Lia, Christian, Helen and Charles up the main staircase, Elsbeth declined grumpily, Chuckles slid quietly into the background, Freddie and Thaddeus complained that they hadn't been offered a drink and were led off to the marquee by Diane.

'I understand that you're a rich widower?' Diane enquired, taking Thaddeus by the arm. He looked at her sharply, not knowing if she was joking or not and removed his arm from her grip.

***

Trevor slipped the gear lever smoothly from fourth to fifth.

'Clear.' Andrew stated, checking the rear view mirrors on his side of the truck.

'Clear.' Trevor repeated from his side. He punched a code into the keyboard on the dashboard of the security truck. 'All clear,' he stated flatly into the microphone he was holding. He replaced the microphone on its dashboard mounting clip. Central control would now have both their GPS position and their manual acknowledgement as well.

'Long drive this one.' Trevor stated. 'Nice to get out into the country for once.'

'Yeah.'

'You seem preoccupied. What's up?'

'Oh. Nothing more than the usual. No money, too many debts,

no future, all the depressing stuff.'

'You still moonlighting?'

Andrew looked at his friend, startled by the revelation that Trevor had guessed his secret. 'For God's sake keep that to yourself.'

'You be careful. The last thing you need now is for them to find out about that. You'd be out of a job as quick as that.' Trevor snapped his finger to emphasis the point.

'My worst nightmare. But what can I do.' Andrew replied. 'I can't think of anything worse than them finding out.'

They'd been driving for fifteen minutes when they rounded a long sweeping uphill bend. Trevor dropped the gears down one and increased the revs. The bend straightened, but the hill increased. He stayed in fourth. As the hill levelled he reached to change back to top. His ears appeared to implode. Unconsciously his feet hit the brakes and clutch, his hands flew to his head, wrenching at the straps of his own helmet. From the corner of his vision he was vaguely aware of Andrew clawing at his helmet. The noise in his head increased. It seemed impossible that it could do so, but it did, and it continued. He wanted to scream. He could have been screaming. He had no way of knowing. His vision began to blur. His last conscious thought was that the truck had crashed, not violently, just gently into the hedgerow at the side of the road.

'Plastic!' Stuart called.

Mal passed a thin paper covered rod of plastic explosive, about half a centimetre thick and five centimetres long, to Stuart.

'Detonator!' Stuart had removed the power drill from the hole he had made on the lock of the armoured car and inserted the plastic into the hole. He took the detonator and clipped it to the exposed end of the plastic. He pressed the sticky back of the digital detonator against the smooth grey paint of the door and pushed two buttons. A red light began to pulsate. 'Stand clear,' he instructed and withdrew to the safety of the rear of the van. Mal hustled in behind him. Explosives were not his area and he had a very healthy respect for them. A surprisingly soft thud, not a loud explosive noise at all, rumbled through the fabric of the armoured car. Stuart was already pulling the door of the van open as Mal appeared from behind the van. He wrenched open the bonnet and delved into the engine compartment. Within thirty seconds he had immobilised the engine immobiliser. He waved to his brother Phil who was sat at the wheel of the car they had arrived in, giving him a thumbs up sign. So far everything was going exactly to plan.

Reggie inspected each of the windows at the back of the farmhouse individually. He had to find a drink. He was in the middle of the countryside and not sure how he'd got there. He had vague recollections of catching a bus, using the small amount of money that he had; it was supposed to be for buying pieces of chocolate, to take when he had cravings. Although what that denizen of egotistical zealots at the Stalag knew about cravings you could print on the back of your thumbnail. The bus had seemed like his best chance of getting a drink. It said Aylesbury town centre on the back of the bus and that had seemed a good idea at the time, but the back of the bus carried the point of origin. On the front it said Lower Acton, and that was where he was. At least, that was where he nearly was. He had asked one of the other passengers whether they had arrived at Aylesbury town centre yet; a question that seemed to totally baffle his fellow traveller, who eventually pointed out that this particular bus had come from Aylesbury town centre. He got off at the next stop and that was when he found the gate open. It led to a house inside a high brick wall. He checked the back of the building. There were three windows. He checked each window twice. The frames were old, twisted, gapped and needed maintenance but they were all locked. His patience was beginning to wear out, and wear out fast, he needed a drink.

He picked up a half-brick from a pile of rubble in what must have originally been the vegetable garden, took a deep breath and pushed it into one of the glass lights of the back door. There was a loud clatter of glass breaking. He listened, and listened. No one shouted, there was no rushing of running feet, the house was empty. He reached through the broken window and released the bolt that secured the door.

Reggie had broken into the kitchen, and the first drink that he found was a quarter bottle of cooking sherry. He looked at it in disgust, but drank it anyway. In the lounge he faired far better, that's where he found the booze and the cookies.

***

Stuart steered the armoured car through the ivy-ridden gates that Mal held open for him. Phil drove their stolen BMW through behind him. Mal closed the gates as soon as both were through, then ran to close the stable gates of the barn that Stuart was now driving the truck into. They had made it. Stuart felt his heart racing. He began to whistle the theme from the 'Sting' as he slipped from the front seat of the van. 'Now,' he said more to himself than the two brothers who were unloading an oxyacetylene torch and gas bottles from the boot of the car. 'Let's see what we've got ourselves.

In the rear seat of the car, their heads covered in eyeless balaclavas, Trevor and Andrew were starting to come to; their heads hurt unbearably.

***

The cameraman was bored and annoyed; although he had to admit that it was his own fault for not checking out the timetable before he agreed to be up at six in the morning. When he'd asked Joan why on earth they had to be here so early – almost six hours before the event – she had just waffled on about getting a prime position for the camera and getting the first interview in. Bullshit. Every word of it. He didn't now what it was, but something had rattled her cage and he was the one paying for it. But still he had had a full breakfast for free, in the kitchens of the manor house, prepared by the manager's assistant who seemed to understand without being told that he was pissed off and needed pacifying. That had been at seven thirty, before any of the other TV crews and press had arrived, so in one way he couldn't complain, the others had to make do with sandwiches. He swung the camera across the crowd aimlessly, catching a face here and an expression there; just background footage destined for the cutting room floor. 'See anyone interesting?' He asked in a disinterested voice.

'Not really.' Joan replied. 'A couple of local dignitaries, small fry but…' She stopped abruptly. Walking across the lawns towards the marquee and the impromptu entrance that had been thrown up by the security company hired for the event – a portable chain-link fence with a single opening – was Martin, on his arm was his secretary, Chloe. Joan went pale, deathly pale. This was what she had come to see. She was expecting it but that did little to ease the pain. She began to flush with anger.

***

Liam and Ann bent down behind a thicket of brambles and peered at the old manor house. They were at the back about thirty yards from the house.

'Liam this is silly. Let's go back to the farmhouse. We won't get in there, it's all locked up and there's security guards patrolling.'

As she spoke, one of the rear doors of the house opened. A single glass-panelled French window from a room at the centre of the building. An elderly man stepped through the opening. He carried a light coloured cane and hobbled towards the rose arbour in the gardens to their left.

'Quick. Now's our chance.'

Before Ann could object, Liam had dragged her from the security of the bramble bushes and pushed her towards the house. In the rose arbour Thaddeus unfastened the last button of his fly and began to relieve himself over a beautiful bright stunning Lady Elizabeth. He grunted to himself in satisfaction. He had peed on these roses since he was a boy; it didn't seem to have done them any harm at all. He was sure that some of them were older than him, and all of them looked a darn sight sprightlier. He enjoyed peeing on the roses immensely. In some small way it satisfied his need to get one back on someone, anyone, he didn't know who really; Rose at the moment he suspected. He repaired his dress and hobbled back to the house. So much for security he thought. Anyone could have got into the house while I was out. He shut the music room doors closed behind him. Suddenly he felt cold and shuddered, his shoulder began to twitch and he looked around the room where Rose had died, in a frightened manner.

While his cousin was relieving the continuous pressure on his bladder, Freddie was attempting to relieve another type of pressure entirely. Namely his niece Lisa and the contract he had paid so highly for. The contract on her life. He didn't usually carry a mobile telephone, in fact he had never had either reason or desire to use one before and frowned on them and the entire modern technology scene entirely but, for the purposes of anonymity, he had to admit that the mobile phone was a real winner, he stabbed an impatient gnarled digit at the keypad. A soft, whispered voice answered cautiously.

'Yes?'

'Buenos Aires.' Freddie replied. A ridiculous code, but simple and effective.

'Roast Beef.' The response was even more ridiculous but the likelihood of a random conversation starting with two such abstract

227

phases had to be improbable beyond question. Total anonymity had been an indisputable pre-requisite of the hit man and one to which Freddie agreed equivocally; murder is a serious and dangerous business.

'The money has reached your bank?'

'Correct.'

'Then I expect urgent action. Urgent!'

'Today.'

Momentarily Freddie stared at the telephone, taken aback by the certainty of the reply. 'Today?'

'Here? At the draw? Inside the house?'

'Outside.'

'At the presentation?'

'Explain.'

'There's a presentation. About two thirty. She'll be there on the steps.'

The telephone went dead in his hand. There was no reply and would be no further conversation.

***

'Why do I let them get to me so much?' Lisa, almost in tears, squeezed Chuckles arm tightly. 'I mean,' she continued, her voice held back to as polite a whisper as she could muster. 'I have the upper hand. Aunt Rose handed it to me on a plate. And it's not as though I wanted to gloat, I really thought that they should see what's happening to the manor. Aunt Rose may have cut them out but it's still the family home, the Loewens seat, and for all their ugly dispositions and characters they are still Loewens.' She stamped her foot in temper. 'I wish they weren't.'

'Weren't what,' Chuckles asked, engulfing her shoulders with his arm and pulling her round to face him. 'Ugly or Loewens?'

'Weren't Loewens of course.'

'But what does it matter. They're out, for ninety-nine years. That aunt of yours didn't mess around at all. I'm glad I never had the opportunity to cross her. Formidable is the word that comes to mind. And besides all that, you do have the upper hand. They're out, you're in charge, there's nothing they can do about it and after this raffle thing is over it will all be so far beyond their control that they'll either have to accept it and just go away and die somewhere – which I might add shouldn't take too long for one or two of them

228

– or smash their heads forever against the brick wall that Rose's Will and especially the occupation of the new apartments by new outside-the-family owners, puts up. The one with the cane, what's his name?'

'Thaddeus.'

'Yeah Thaddeus looks as though he's frustrated enough to have a heart attack any minute. That'd be one less for a start.'

'Don't be so callous.'

'Don't be so soft. And besides, a moment ago you were complaining how much they wound you up.'

'Well. They do. Did. Always do. They're so callous.'

'Like me?'

She digged him in the ribs and for the first time since she had left Freddie and her family, smiled. 'No.' They're so callous, greedy, vindictive, nasty, scheming, devious, untrustworthy, spiteful, nasty and callous.'

'You said that already.'

'Well they are. In fact although I hate to use the word, evil comes to mind.' She pulled closer to Chuckles and dropped her voice. 'They deliberately kept me out of the way last month. Deliberately.'

'Well at least they got that one right. If they hadn't I wouldn't have met you.'

'Stop it.' She dug him in the ribs again. 'I know it's evil myself to have such thoughts, but if they meant to keep me away, was that just to get their hands on the Will? After all, they must have known that Aunt Rose wouldn't have left much for them, I'm surprised that she left any at all.'

'What's your point?'

'I'm afraid that they kept me out of the way because they wanted to be the last people to see poor Aunt Rose alive. The very last.'

Chuckles looked at her thoughtfully. 'They pulled the plug. That's what you're getting at. Isn't it?'

Lisa nodded. Tears in her eyes.

Chuckles took her chin in his hand and bent down to kiss her gently on the lips. If they're capable of that then what else are they capable of? The thought coursed through his mind, accompanied by a brief confused image of Lisa, in mortal danger. 'Don't be such a silly girl,' he whispered. 'You'd have to chip all the mortar out before Freddie and Thaddeus could raise a Huff and a Puff, let alone blow the house down, and as for the others, spineless the lot of them

229

and lost without the first two. Come on. Where's that agenda you drew up? What's next on the list?'

Lisa sniffed back the tears as Chuckles wiped her eyes with a white handkerchief taken from his trouser pocket. 'The caterers,' Lisa replied. 'They should be set up by now. Did you meet their daughter, Crystel? Lovely little thing. So sweet.'

***

Mary Little stared out of the window across the lawns, the rose garden, the estate and for a moment pondered the old adage 'to the manor born'. Behind her the office door opened suddenly. She gave a little start. Brinker entered at a brisk, business-like gait. 'Everything Ok Mary?' He asked. 'No one tried to tamper with the bingo machine?' It was a joke. A thin one that had worn thinner with constant repetition, but Brinker was like that. He had coined the phrase Bingo Machine and it tickled him, and when that happened he always did the thing to death. He glanced at his watch. 'Five minutes,' he announced. 'Where's that useless wastrel Briskin. It's time we moved this lot into the car, won't do to be late today. We've got to pick up Hewlett-Temple, make a grand entrance and all that. It's very good for the firm. I heard that all the major TV stations will be covering the story. Keep an eye on it all again Mary. I'll go and flush him out.'

***

Claire enjoyed the taxi ride to work each morning, it was as though she suddenly became a normal person who could afford the fare, who had money in her purse. Of course Claire had no money in her purse at all, the taxi fare was paid by the agency, a temping agency that had found her a short-term job as a cleaner at Southgrim Manor. The bus didn't go as far as the manor, so the agency paid for a taxi.

The house loomed in front of her, the walls of the marquee that had been erected yesterday wavered slightly in the breeze. Today of course, she wouldn't be cleaning, at least not until after the ceremonies had finished. She had been asked if she would like some extra work; does the Pope go to church on Sundays she'd asked herself for a split second before answering. Of course she would take some extra work, no question.

What was it?

Waiting. Waiting on guests at the reception, carrying trays of drinks and hors d'oeuvres and canapés. And did she have a black skirt, not too short, and a white blouse, nothing low at the neck, that she could wear. She hadn't but had borrowed from Trevor's wife Jan.

The lady with the strange eyes that seemed to look straight through you met her at the foot of the steps. 'Good morning,' she said cheerfully. 'Ready for a big day?'

'Oh Yes.' Claire's reply was bright, but carried a tinge of sadness, the result of her early morning fears about Andrew that Diane spotted straight away.

The older woman put her arms about Claire's shoulders. 'Don't you worry your pretty head dear. Trust me. I tell you that today will be a busy day, a big day and not just for this house. I see that it will be a big day for you as well, and for Andrew.'

Claire looked at her startled. She didn't remember ever telling Diane what her husband's name was.

'Don't look so down. It's all perfectly simple. Trust me. Now... Let me introduce you to the caterers, Stephanie and Bill, they're not a couple yet, not together you know but they will be.'

Diane's confidence in the matter broke no disagreement. Claire just nodded.

'And I want you to do me a particular favour.' Diane pulled Claire's face close to her own and whispered into her ear. 'Stephanie has a daughter, teenager, thirteen or fourteen, pretty little thing. You'd think butter wouldn't melt in her mouth. But! She's a wrong-un. Very wrong. I can feel it. Heat. Lots of heat and disaster and evil. I want you to keep a particular eye on her for me. OK,' she ended brightly, at normal voice, as though she had just asked Claire to polish an extra tray for the sandwiches and not frightened the living daylights out of her.

***

Phil cut the oxygen and the flame with a snap. Mal strained enthusiastically at the severed hinges with a large crow bar. Stuart, at a more controlled pace flexed a second long crowbar in the burnt hinges of the far side of the rear doors to the armoured car. The brace of doors eased slowly away from the back of the van, a crack big enough to thrust a child's fist into appeared. The doors held there for a moment as the two men strained, then with a rush they

231

sprang out and toppled loudly to the dirt floor of the barn. The three men stared mesmerised with anticipation into the interior of the Failsafe armoured car.

The entire length of both sides of the van had been fitted out with compartments, cupboards of heavy gauge metal that were sealed with solid, thick steel doors and ominously sophisticated locks. Stuart surveyed the scene. 'Eleven to open on this side,' he counted 'and seven on the other, that's not including that centre one there.' He pointed to an extended compartment slightly to the left of centre of the left-hand wall. 'That's the pigeonhole. The chute from the outside where deposits are put through. Nothing's stored in there, it's just the method of transfer used when they load direct from the outside, through that hole.'

Chapter 17

Well here we are, the final day. The grand entrance of Southgrim Manor. It's a long time since I've seen so many busy, bustling people at the house. All the attention is centred on the main staircase, the one that leads from the entrance hall to the gallery above. The fifth and sixth steps of the staircase now support a polished wooden platform, a temporary raised stage with a simple table. That's where the lottery ball machine has been placed. There's a small dais beside the table behind, with the Right Honourable Norman Hewlett-Temple, MP and Foreign Secretary to Her Majesty's Government standing behind it. Very refined he looks too; I remember him when he was a scruffy six year old playing in these very grounds; his father bought him a pony that year and we let him stable the animal here. Ah... a long, happy time ago. Anyway. Back to the present. Unless anything else happens to change the situation, in just over half an hour I'll have no reason to stay in this world. The lottery will be over, the winners announced, Lisa and the foundation firmly entrenched, I won't be needed, I'll have to move on: the thought frightens me witless.

As I told you before, I am now absolutely certain that the other spirit is not here to harm me, or Lisa, or my precious lottery. It doesn't bear me any malice and it's not interested in earthly matters at all. But it does represent the unknown, and it is getting impatient. I can feel it as singularly as you would hear the knocker on your own front door; at first a tap-tap-tap then rat-tat-tat now a bang-bang, a rising thump like a bad migraine. What I need to keep it out just that little bit longer, is some action. As long as I'm involved I'll be all right for a while longer and I know exactly how to become involved, Frederick! That's how.

Unfortunately I can't afford to expose myself by going into his mind, interrogating his subconscious, asking the simple question, what next, what have you hatched for this afternoon, especially for Lisa. I'm afraid that if I do the other spirit will take hold of me, and I'll be lost of this world. I can't let that happen, at least not yet. I have to see Lisa through to the end, until she's out of danger, and that means keeping a very sharp eye on brother Freddie. Of course I know that he's arranged to have the final draw fixed, just as I know that he nobbled the first two rounds. I know that he's in league with the lawyer Whet, his sister Teresa, Briskin and

233

Thaddeus, and I know how it's being done. In fact I was tempted to throw a large spanner into their little scheme earlier. My expertise in kinetics has grown considerably; I can move almost any object I choose, so shuffling those little numbered ping-pong balls around is no problem. Even the secret little mechanism that they have so ingeniously installed, the one that just fractionally decreases the size of the hole the ping-pong balls drop through, isn't a problem. No... I could have stopped their little game two weeks ago, but I didn't. Because there was something else. There was Frederick. Not the others, just him. He has something else up his sleeve, something that he alone has arranged, something bad, very bad. So I've let their little game play itself out until the end. I reasoned that six fraudulent balls out of six hundred and then out of sixty wasn't too high a price to pay, I knew I could get to them at the final draw and put the situation straight. And there lies the real danger. As soon as I foil their plans, Freddie's going to switch to plan 'B', his alternative strategy against the lottery fiddle going wrong. I don't know what it is that I can feel, but it's something very, very bad indeed. So I have to watch him know, closely, like a hawk. In just half an hour more the lottery will be over. Freddie will have lost, the families fraud come to an end, their little scheme useless; once the apartments become the leasehold property of the six winners there's nothing Frederick or the family can do. My main concern is that Freddie stays in the main hall, with the draw because I have to keep an eye on that as well, make sure the six genuine winners, win. Look at him twitch, he's not going to enjoy the next thirty minutes at all.

***

Freddie was indeed having a less than enjoyable time. One of their six stooge draw-winners had failed to show – Thaddeus was ringing the young women concerned right know; Thaddeus was the girl's godfather – Whet had brought his vampiral sister Teresa with him, whose very presence made him feel more than uncomfortable, and now that pompous autocrat Brinker was checking the lottery ball mechanism – Brin, Brinker and Briskin had been appointed by the trust to adjudicate the proceedings. No surprise there, he thought. But Brinker appeared to have found a problem. His long nose was thrust inside the barrel of the machine, probing and ferreting. The aperture for the balls to drop through was being particularly closely inspected. Freddie threw a quick glance towards Whet, who was standing close to Briskin.

Whet caught the glance, leant forward and, almost imperceptibly tapped Briskin on the shoulder. 'Get up there and stop him poking about,' he whispered. 'Quickly.'

'And what exactly do you suggest I do. Rugby tackle? A quick jab to the kidneys?' Briskin asked sarcastically.

Freddie glared at the young lawyer. 'All three if necessary. But get his interfering beak out of the drum.'

***

At the stables, by the south gate, Mal, Phil and Stuart were busy cracking open the internal compartments of the armoured car. So far they had turned out over three hundred thousand pounds in cash, plus some very interesting documentation that could well prove lucrative to anyone willing to stoop to blackmail and industrial secrets; they'd sell that on to people who specialised in that sort of thing. Mal and Phil felt no scruples about this at all and Stuart wasn't at all interested, the twins could do what they like with any documents they uncovered. Stuart thought that side of the deal was far too risky to get involved in, and besides Stuart didn't share the twin's ruthlessness, and he considered blackmail, especially personal blackmail a ruthless and heartless business. He was an expert, a tradesman, a specialist, not a common criminal. His interest was solely in the diamonds, the ones that had been so tantalisingly described in the papers he had read from that safe job a few months ago and a share of the ready cash, of course. But it was the diamonds that had forced his present and quite undesirable partnership with the twins.

Stuart was using his trusted power drill to drill out the locks on the steel compartments, Mal and Phil had resorted to more direct methods. Phil cursed as his crowbar slipped yet again. However, brute force was proving quite successful, the compartments were inside the armoured car and designed to keep the various consignments carried apart, not to protect their contents from a master crack-smith such as Stuart or the brute force of the twins. The twins had opened seven lockers before Stuart cleared his fifth, it was then that he found it.

'Hallelujah'. Stuart had pulled out a long metal box, its outer skin black and oily in colour, totally devoid of sheen. The box was sealed, Stuart had it open in less than thirty seconds. The box was full of diamonds. Six layers of double red felt sandwiching fourteen million pounds of sparkling, impervious carbon chips, none less than five or six carats. Gingerly Stuart pulled each layer of cloth back. The diamonds tumbled gently towards one end of the metal box. At the third layer, he found it. The Clinchet Star. Fifty-eight carats. One of the one hundred largest stones in the world. He palmed it quickly. Because he hadn't taken the document from the safe that day, he hadn't frightened them off; the ruse had obviously worked, because the truck was here and the Clinchet Star was in his hand. Also, because he hadn't taken the document from the safe that day Mal and Phil hadn't seen the original inventory of the shipment. They didn't even know that the Clinchet Star existed, and never would now. Stuart's back was to them, he slipped the diamond into an inside pocket.

'Here it is,' he announced. He had meant to say 'Here they are' but didn't think his Freudian slip had been noticed. He held the box of diamonds out towards Mal and Phil. The twins stared open mouthed at the layers of sparkling wealth.

***

Reggie took another bite of the cookie he had found. It was his second and the effect of the strong Hashish plus the alcohol had taken a firm hold of him. Fortunately, he had only found two cookies. He couldn't eat the raw plants that surrounded him and had now reached the point where he didn't actually know where he was or how to get back to the lounge where he vaguely remembered there was still some booze left. He staggered out of the conservatory and into the grounds of Southgrim Manor. In the distance he could hear the noise of Rose's lottery draw. He didn't know what the noises were but what little reason he still possessed told him that there was more likelihood of finding a drink where there were people than out here amongst the rhododendron bushes that shielded the farmhouse from the rest of the estate. He set off at a blind stumble.

***

Joan checked her watch. 'Five minutes to the draw,' she announced to her crew of one. 'I'll go inside now, see if I can pick up a few comments.' To reinforce her statement, she held up the recorder she was carrying. Cameras had been banned from inside the house, but a last minute reprieve had allowed six members of the press in, she had been one of those chosen. She hopped down the steps from the press platform as quickly as she could without stumbling and set off purposefully towards the front entrance of the manor house. She had more than just interviews to conduct. She couldn't believe it, but was sure that she had seen Liam, her lover, walking with the crowd up the steps into the front entrance. It was only a fleeting look, just a glance of a face, the contour of a nose and brow, but there was a strange knot in her stomach that told her it had to be him. But why? Liam wasn't interested in country manors, and especially not in the art they invariably contained; miles of staircases covered with eighteenth century family portraits were guaranteed to turn him off. He was more likely to set a torch to the place than step through its musty doors. Then she made the connection. The knot in her stomach tightened a full two turns. She had been so preoccupied with Martin, the divorce situation and that slut Chloe that she had forgotten quite where she was. The farmhouse. It was here. She had never thought of it as part of the Southgrim Manor estate but of course it was. She stopped. Looked around. Yes. It would be in that direction. That tall hedgerow of rhododendrons in the distance. Behind there. The knot tightened even more.

She was at the top of the steps now, climbing, her mind in a trance, then through the entrance. There they were, Martin with his arm round Chloe and Liam with his arm round a tall blond woman of about her own age. She stopped in mid stride and almost stumbled into the person in front of her. Her stomach began to knot; the farmhouse; the weekend; the blond! She retched, bile rose in her throat, she was barely controlling herself. To her left was a cardboard sign with an arrow that said toilets, she dashed towards it.

***

'Got to admit, we just snuck in. We're not combatants as it where. We're staying at a farmhouse, over the back there, I rent it from the estate. So, as I'm a tenant, I thought why not see what all the fuss is about? How about you. You up for a ticket, one of the finalists?'

Liam's inane chatter had immediately alienated Martin, who turned away rudely, but Chloe seemed to welcome the distraction. It was as Martin turned away that he caught sight of Joan dashing towards the bathroom.

'Shit'. He exclaimed far more loudly than could be considered polite.

'Pardon?' Liam questioned, not expecting such a strident reply to his question.

Chloe, Liam and Ann stared intently at Martin, waiting for an elaboration on his one word outburst. He became aware of the attention he had solicited.

'Err. Sorry. Someone I haven't seen in a long time. Err. Excuse me. Must go and talk to them.' He stepped away then checked, turning to peck Chloe on the cheek. 'Be back in a minute darling.' He gave her a less than convincing smile and backed into the crowd.

'Is he always so up-tight?' Liam asked directly.

'No. Not at all.' Chloe gazed at the back of Martin's head as it combined and finally vanished amongst the press of people now jamming into the entrance hall.

***

Stuart dropped the Clinchet Star into a Zippy plastic bag, sealed the bag then pushed it through the filler hole into the petrol tank of the motor bike. Mal and Phil hadn't seen him pocket it, he was sure of that. They didn't trust him any more than he trusted them, and it didn't do to think about what they would do if they found out he had cheated them. But they would never find out. They would never even be suspicious. The hoist had produced a bonus totalling at four hundred and thirty thousand pounds in cash; new bills that they would have to launder carefully. Stuart had a contact who would take them immediately; his contact would have to sit on them for a while, so they would only get forty pence on the pound but that was over fifty seven thousand each, which would keep them nicely in spending money while they shifted the stones. There was the real prize. There was the reason Stuart had risked stepping outside of his normal speciality. Valued at fourteen million pounds. Take away the Clinchet, which the inventory had valued at three point eight million and there was still over ten million to split between them. Stuart had never been completely convinced that the consignment would be as large as the inventory had stated. He had assumed that he was reading insurance values, so had told the twins the haul would be around six million. Now that he had seen them, it was clear that the inventory could well be correct. Once fenced the stone would fetch upwards of four to five million, probably one and a half million each.

Stuart rocked the bike from side to side. He could see the

plastic zipper bag floating in the half filled petrol tank. That was good, it wouldn't foul the fuel intake that way. As he replaced the screw cap he heard a noise behind him.

'What's up?' Mal asked as he appeared through the bushes. 'Got bored of counting money have you?'

Stuart recovered his composure as quickly as he could. He glanced directly into Mal's eyes and saw no sign of concern or suspicion. 'Just checking the bike,' he lied convincingly. 'Have you and Phil finished?'

"Yeah. The goods are in the back of the car. We've a change of car at Luton, then a second in Harlow. We'll be back at the flat before eight. You had better come back to the truck and see Phil before we leave.'

When they arrived at the truck Phil was just laying a blanket across the driver and guard, who were now lying on the floor of the truck.

'This one's just starting to wake up.' He pushed the rounded shape of Andrew with his foot. 'But the other one's out cold, must have tapped him a bit harder than the other one, looks like he'll be out for hours.'

Trevor lay inert under the blanket, his only sign of life being the gently in-out movement of the cloth bag over his head in the general area of his mouth. Andrew was beginning to stir, a low moaning sound coming from the brown cloth over his head. Stuart pulled the twins away, out of earshot. 'No point in letting him hear our voices,' he said quietly.

'Sure.' Phil agreed. 'You all set now? We are.'

'Yeah. Bike's fine. I'll see you back at the flat.' They had rented a two bedroomed flat, as a base for the venture. 'I'll bring the fence round at nine o'clock. Remember, stay in the back room. He'll know I haven't pulled this job on my own, but you don't want him seeing who you are, do you?'

Phil and Mal both nodded in agreement. Mal shuffled his feet, Phil fidgeted. There was something wrong, they should have been chaffing at the bit to get away from here. Stuart gave them both a hard stare. 'I'm off then,' he said.

'OK.' Mal replied but still didn't move.

Stuart turned, back towards his hidden motorcycle. He could feel the twins' eyes boring into his back, an uneasy feeling that he really didn't want at all. As soon as he reached the bike he gunned it into life. They had to hear him leaving. Whatever they were up to it wouldn't happen until he had driven away. At the gate he turned to the left, gripped the throttle and accelerated hard down the road. They'd hear that all right. At the first road junction he turned left again. The main entrance to the grounds of Southgrim Manor lay open in front of him. As quietly as the bike would allow, he drove through.

Chapter 18

Standing on the platform, Lisa leant into Charles' side, she reached down and took his hand, he squeezed hers in reassurance. 'Here we go,' he whispered, bending his lips to her ear.

Lisa felt her knees weaken, a barely perceptible sensation, that was immediately corrected by a jolt of reassurance and sinew, as though someone was standing behind her and had physically supported her. Involuntarily she looked over her shoulder.

There. There. Lisa. Don't let your Auntie Rose down. We're almost there now.

The staircase behind her was empty, everyone was in front of them. Hewlett-Temple and Brinker straddling the drum full of numbered ping-pong balls, Uncle Freddie glaring at the stage from the front of the audience below them, with the rest of the family huddled sheep-like behind them; only Thaddeus was missing, Lisa wondered why. Each ticket holder had been allowed to bring one member of their family, or a friend to the draw and Lisa had been introduced to them all a little earlier; she could therefore recognise almost every face she surveyed but their names completely escaped her. As Foreign Secretary Hewlett-Temple received the attention of a permanent bodyguard; Lisa noticed with interest how inconspicuous he had managed to make himself, standing to the edge of the family flock, relaxed, and moulded into the crowd.

Marios Branchman had also noticed the special branch officer, he had even been introduced to him, shaken his hand, exchanged names – not his own of course – this was not the usual situation he would have wished for a hit. Now here he was, thrust on a pedestal next to his victim with special branch looking on. He shivered at the thought. Thank God this job would be his last.

Brinker was talking now, restating the names of each of the twelve remaining ticket holders and asking each to identify themselves and verify their presence. Systematically he worked through them all, including a young, flustered, out of breath woman who suddenly and noisily appeared at the back of the crowd, followed by the appearance of Thaddeus. Her timing was perfect, as Brinker called out Miss Fiona Price, she thrust up her hand. 'Here,' she answered. Everyone in the room turned to look at the flustered women, except Thaddeus who glowered red, flushed and fuming.

'All present,' declared Brinker like the old-fashioned

schoolmaster he so undoubtedly could have been. He flipped a switch. The twelve balls in the clear perspex dome of the machine leapt into the air, bubbling and tumbled over each other. Brinker counted silently to himself, the faint outlines of each number visible on his lips – One… Two… Three… Six. He released the switch.

Careful now Rosie. Don't go making any mistakes. 348 no not that one 525 YES that's OK and 191, 448, 79, 259 and the last… 93, my age how appropriate. Let's see what happens now. Should be fun. Where's Freddie?

The balls stopped immediately. One by one the six final balls dropped down into the bowls of the machine to roll clear inside a transparent tube to the side. The entrance hall to Southgrim Manor was deathly silent.

'The Right Honourable Norman Hewlett-Temple will now announce the winners.' Brinker pronounced loudly, the excitement in his voice obvious, his manner suggesting that a fanfare of trumpets and a long drum roll would have been appropriate. Hewlett-Temple stepped forward.

'Thank you Mr Brinker,' he said stooping to extract the first ball. 'If I ever lose my day job, this will stand me in good stead as a bingo caller.' A ripple of laughter broke the tension that was threatening to engulf the room. Hewlett-Temple held the first ball aloft. '525'.

Freddie's head snatched round towards Thaddeus. Whet looked down at Teresa who was standing next to him, then up to Briskin who was beside Mary Little, holding six large white A4 envelopes, each of which contained a deed to an apartment and a contract for the lucky owner to sign with the Rose Loewen Trust. Mary smiled, she could see the consternation on their faces. She suspected that the family had been plotting something and something had gone wrong with their little scheme. Briskin threw Whet an I-don't-know-what's-happening look.

'What's going on?' Freddie whispered to Thaddeus.

'That's not one of ours. Is it?' Thaddeus replied.

'What's going on where? One of our what?' Helen had caught both the instant tension and the whispered exchange. 'What are you two up to?' She turned to Christian and Charles. 'I knew it. These two are up to something and we're not part of it.'

'Part of what?' Elsbeth asked urgently, leaning into the family huddle that began to surround Freddie and Thaddeus who began to twitch and scratch at his chin.

242

I knew this would be fun. A bit more scratching. Yes. That's got Helen going nicely.

'Stop that stupid scratching and twitching, you dirty old man, the shower's free you know, try using it occasionally and answer me, before I really make a scene. What's going on?'

Fortunately for Thaddeus the noise of Helen's rising voice and the palpable tension in the Loewen family group was drowned out by the spontaneous applause as a small rotund man in his late fifties threw his arms up in the air, shouted 'It's me. 525. It's me.' And was immediately engulfed by the woman beside him – his wife presumably – and a press of people all wanting to pat him on the back.

'Congratulations sir.' Brinker stepped forward. 'If each winner could just acknowledge his win…'

'As if we could stop them.' Added Hewlett-Temple to another round of laughter – he hadn't wanted to be here today but his promise to Rose had to be honoured, and now he had to admit that he was beginning to enjoy the task.

'…then, as soon as all six have been announced, my associate Mr Briskin,' he pointed at Briskin who took the six envelopes from Mary Little and raised them in the air, 'will hand you the Deeds and complete the formalities.' The crowd had quietened now. Brinker turned back to Hewlett-Temple. 'Please Mr Hewlett-Temple, carry on.'

'Number 191.'

'That's not ours either.' Freddie bristled with anger.

'You had it fixed. Didn't you?' Helen burst at Freddie. 'You and Thaddeus,' she caught Thaddeus' eye as he looked towards Whet for an explanation of the disaster that was unfolding number-by-number. Helen caught his look and the vehement glance Whet threw towards Briskin, 'and that slimy lawyer Whet. And the other one, what's his name? Bentin?'

'Briskin.' Charles corrected. He had also spotted the interchange between Thaddeus and the two lawyers.

'How many did you fix?' Helen demanded.

'It must have been all six.' Christian explained. 'Or they wouldn't be so upset with the first number called.'

'All six!' The realisation surged through Helen as a crest of anger. 'You Scheming Deceitful Greedy Parasites.'

Ooh I think she's going to hit them both in a minute – lovely! Rosie! Rosie!

Yes Diane.

What's happening? Your Helen looks as though she's having a fit.

The family are just finding out that their little scheme has gone sour. But look, I mustn't gloat. This is the dangerous time. Where are you?

At the back, near the bathroom, one of the press ladies was ill; I've been looking after her.

Is she all right now?

Well she's not sick anymore but I'm not so sure that she's all right.

Pardon?

Never mind. What were you going to say?

Keep a look out for anything strange. Whatever Freddie has in reserve he will use now. We know it's not going to be nice and I haven't got much time left. I'm not going to be able to keep the other one at bay much longer. That crimson colour's back again. Faint but back and keep an eye on your Maureen.

Maureen?

Just do it.

Diane moved around the back of the crowd, to the far side of the room where she could get a clearer view of Freddie and the family. The reporter, Joan was her name, was better now. She had seemed extremely upset and Diane had sensed a rising malevolence in the woman as she gradually overcame her physical disposition – if she hadn't been bound to watch Freddie, and now Maureen, she most certainly would have taken a stronger interest in Joan.

Martin was oblivious to the consternation of Freddie and his conspirators. Hewlett-Temple had just called number 448 and been met with a cheer from a young couple in garish clothes with rings through their noses, lips and ears. Martin assumed that this colourful pair must be another of Freddie's plants, just as he was. His would obviously be one of the last three numbers.

Similar thoughts passed through the minds of the late arriving young woman; the Asian man from Bromley that knew Thaddeus through a shaky investment deal that had gone bad the previous year; the bankrupt hairdresser from Bow whose business had gone to the wall because he had opened just one too many branches on extended credit – Whet was his lawyer; the quiet homely lady from East Grinstead who in her distant past had been a very close companion of Freddie's and still carried a torch for him; and the brash, overconfident Barry King, a local entrepreneur who specialised in shady property deals and local council bribery. They all thought the same as Martin. Their's must be one of the last three numbers.

'79.'

A cheer from a middle-aged couple in the centre of the crowd.

Six anxious minds automatically retune to theirs being one of the last two tickets.

'259.'

Six extremely anxious minds simultaneously told themselves not to worry. Someone had to have the last ticket.

'93.'

It's mine. I don't believe it. Oh God. Oh dear me...' Maureen collapsed to her knees, her head in her hands, her shoulders sobbing. 'Reggie,' she murmured. Hands grabbed at her. Lifted her to her feet. Patted her on the back. Congratulated her. She just couldn't stop the tears.

Can you see her? Is she alright?

You fixed it didn't you?

Can you see her?

Yes Rose she's fine. What am I going to do with you?

Thank me later, just keep on your toes. You sure she's OK?

I'm holding her hand now. It's just emotion. She's fine. But look at Freddie.

Freddie was far from fine. He was clutching his chest, breathing hard, rasping gulps of air.

'Give him room.' Thaddeus pushed at the crowd.

'I'd give him room.' Helen spat the words at Thaddeus. 'Room at the cemetery. Let the crooked old bastard croak.' She turned and grabbed Charles by his lapel and pulled him towards the back of the hall. 'We're going,' she stated emphatically. As soon as they had cleared the crowd she turned and headed towards the end wing of the building and the library, Christian followed but Lia remained. She had been standing slightly apart from the rest and missed the exchange between Helen and Uncle Freddie, as she missed most things really. But she didn't intend to miss the rest of the draw, she wanted to see the presentations and for the first time allowed herself a surge of excitement. She had never liked the old house but now, now that it was being split into apartments and modernised it had suddenly begun to appeal. She watched Helen and Charles leave, then Christian follow them. Uncle Thaddeus and Aunt Elsbeth were leading a shaky Uncle Freddie in the same direction, no doubt to the library and the drinks cupboard it contained. Lia waited for them to round the corner, into the passageway that led from that end of the entrance hall, then slipped over to the middle aged couple that had won with ticket number 79.

'Congratulations,' she said.

'Isn't it exiting.' The wife answered. I'm so happy for you.

'Shss. Auntie Vi. Don't say anything yet. Remember they think you are the winner. And they don't know that you're my aunt.'

'Don't worry love.' The husband replied. 'Your secret's safe with us.'

'I'm still worried about the signature though. I don't understand all of this legal stuff.' Lia's aunt, from her mother's side of the family had never been one to embrace technical or legal problems. She had mastered the telephone, after some struggle, years ago, but that had been the extent of her grasp of modern technology. Now, presented with a legal conundrum she was lost, and quite simply frightened stiff.

'I told you Auntie Vi. It's all legal and above board. The trust excludes direct relatives, but you are not related to the Loewens at all. And it allows the winners to bequeath the leasehold to their relatives. I'm your relative and I'm not a direct relative of the Loewen's either. In fact, once my papers are served and the divorce is through, I won't be related to the Loewen's at all. It's good, isn't it?'

'If you say so dear.'

"Of course she does Vi. Lia knows what she's doing. Now. Come along. Let's see that fella over there with those deeds.' They nodded to Lia as though it were a casual meeting and turned towards an inundated and extremely confused Brinker.

Lia smiled a contented smile. Thank you Aunt Rose. She spoke the words inside her head.

Lia. Lia! Are you talking to me? Can you hear me?

Lia did not respond. She couldn't hear her Aunt-in-law at all. She just felt that this sort of luck was not luck at all. That she had to have a guardian angel. She always knew she had one anyway. Perhaps they changed as you went through life. It couldn't have been Aunt Rose before she died, but it was now – she'd read the diaries – Of that she was certain. 'Thank you again,' she thought.

Lia! No. You can't hear me at all. Can you? But you're right. I

246

couldn't resist it. You see I accidentally stumbled on Lia's plan while I was keeping an eye on the family, at the beginning of all this. I was looking for Charles and found Lia instead. She was talking on the telephone to her Aunt Vi and the conversation intrigued me. I decided to follow it through, discovered that silly, daft, scatty, Lia wasn't so stupid at all. That she was planning a divorce and that she had thought of the same plan as Freddie and Thaddeus only without the dark undertones of cheating they had found so natural. I decided to help her. Why not?

Diane. I'm off to the library. The clan appear to be gathering there. If Freddie hasn't passed over before I get there I might find out what's going to happen next.

Diane! Oh never mind.

***

It took Stuart almost ten minutes to hide the bike in a clump of bushes and tramp back across the estate to the old stables. He had gambled that the twins would still be there and had been correct. They were in the barn. Mal leant casually against the side of their car but Phil was far from relaxed. 'You're mad.' He threw the words at his brother, struggling to keep his voice below a shout. 'Absolutely mad.'

Stuart could not hear the reply, but it did nothing to smooth Phil's temper. 'I'm not waiting,' he said. 'You're on your own.'

Mal lifted the palms of his hands and shrugged. Stuart pressed closer and could just make out Mal's next statement. 'A contract is a contract. That's....' The end of the sentence was lost as Phil turned and kicked an old wooden crate that lay on the floor behind him, splintering the rotten side panelling and wedging his foot in the process. Mal ignored his brother's temporary difficulty and reached into the back of the car. He took out a long plain black sports bag, its contents obviously heavy. Without another word he walked out of the barn and turned towards the manor house. Stuart followed at a safe distance. After a few moments he heard the noise of the car starting behind him. He stopped. Phil nosed the bonnet of the car out of the barn. He stopped, opened the gates to the road outside, returned to the car and drove it through, then stopped again, returned on foot and closed the gates behind him. Stuart watched this entire cycle of events in complete puzzlement. When he looked back Mal was almost out of sight in front of him, swinging the

247

sports bag at the end of his arm and striding off on foot in the other direction. 'What on earth's going on?' He mumbled to himself. 'And what's in that holdall?' Having no choice in the matter, he broke into a low run to close the rapidly opening distance between himself and Mal tripping ungainly over the tussocky meadow, grass stains peppering his knees and elbows in his haste to catch up.

***

Reggie lifted the end of the blanket. 'Oh… Allo… Ya gotta drink on ya mate?'

Andrew stared through blurred swirling vision. His ears rang painfully and although he could see the lips of this strange creature in front of him moving he had no idea what he was trying to say. He grunted a reply through the tape across his mouth and wriggled against his bonds. The creature didn't appear to notice his predicament, he just continued to ask his soundless questions.

'Ah shupose 'at's a no,' Reggie observed, then climbed into the truck and squashed himself in between a struggling Andrew and the inert form of Trevor. 'Yer mate don't say much. Do he?' Reggie remarked as he drew an empty whisky bottle from his jacket pocket. 'Ish empty,' he observed sadly, looking at Andrew, gently swaying as he did so. He appeared to notice the tape across Andrew's mouth for the first time. 'Yoou can't take a drink with 'hat across ya mouth, 'hat's 'tupid.' Andrew gasped as Reggie slowly peeled the edge of the tap away.

'Huh… Huh… Huh…'

'I know. Yer don't ave to shell me. I need one too.' Reggie took a hopeful pull at the empty whisky bottle, then in disgust threw it out of the back of the truck. 'Come on,' he said. 'There's a pub near 'ere. I 'erd em singing or shumfing. We're getta drink there.' Without giving any clue to his understanding of the situation, Reggie struggled the knots of Andrews's bond apart. 'There,' he announced as Andrew's feet and hands were finally free. 'I shink we'll leave 'im. Looks like ees had enough anyway,' he said bobbing his head towards the still inert form of Trevor. Reggie helped Andrew to his feet. Andrew collapsed back to the floor, his head still spinning, his ears ringing and the circulation in his legs telling his brain that walking would be achieved again but only in the fullness of time. Reggie reached down for Andrew again. 'I know you. You escaped this morning just like me. Didn't yer.'

Reggie remembered Andrew's face. He remembered riding the milk float out of the hospital. He remembered the face that drove that milk float. Andrews face. 'You're me mate,' he announced cheerfully. Swaying to the point of toppling as he did so. 'We's going for a drink.' He heaved Andrew to his feet.

Andrew's head hurt. Not just from the noise but also a physical pain that had resulted from being dropped unceremoniously off Mal's shoulders when he had dumped Andrew into the back of the truck. The resulting collision between his head and the hard metal floor of the armoured car was the cause of Andrew's aching head and more pointedly the route of the severe concussion he was currently suffering. His legs were beginning to respond, he followed Reggie's staggering gait away from the van and along the perimeter wall of the estate.

'I've got transport ash well.' Reggie proclaimed triumphantly.

***

At the house, Brinker was calling for order. The six winners had been gathered in front of him and presented with their envelopes full of deeds and he was trying to explain the next step but failing to rise above their enthusiastic mood.

'Please,' he pleaded. 'Please. Calm down.' He banged the edge of his hand on the dais. The noise began to subside. 'Thank you.'

'I can't believe it.' Maureen mumbled for the umpteenth time.

'Thank you.' Brinker repeated.

'Sorry.' Maureen forced herself to concentrate her attention on this man who reminded her so much of the old headmaster at her last school.

'Please open your envelopes.' Brinker waited until they had all complied. 'Now. Inside you have a rather elegant document with fancy swirls and scrolls down the sides. That's the deed to the leasehold of the apartment that is now yours.'

He even sounds like my old headmaster. Maureen thought. Suddenly she shuddered. Panic welled up in her. Something had brushed her arm. Something icy cold. Something that she recognised.

Brinker was still speaking. 'That document is the original and I suggest that you deposit it somewhere safe. It is yours, after all, for the next ninety-nine years. The second document is a contract between yourselves and the Rose Morgan Trust. It's exactly the same text as that given to you when you purchased your lottery ticket. This document has to be signed now to bring the lease into force. Please read it through and ensure that it is as I have said, the same text that you have previously been presented with. Once you have read and signed the document Mr Briskin will take two photo-copies, one for the Trust and one for the records of Brin, Brinker and Brisker, the company that I represent and that represents the Trust. We will then gather together and go outside to face the press and for the presentation of the keys by the Right Honourable Norman Hewlett-Temple.' Brinker clapped his hands together vigorously. 'And congratulation to you all,' he called, finally succumbing to the excitement of the occasion.

**

Martin had snapped. The sight of Joan, here today, was enough to confirm that his life was about to take a very bad twist. The failure of his ticket to appear, his loss of the apartment he had put so much store in, the loss of the money he had invested which wasn't really his, all these things contributed. He wanted to kill someone. Not just anyone. He wanted to kill Whet.

Temporary madness had gripped Martin's entire family. Joan had also flipped. Her catalyst had been the sight of Liam with another woman, and in the company of Chloe, Martin's tramp. Joan also wanted to kill. She wanted to kill Martin, but her resolve was not limited to a fit of spontaneous anger, hers was cold and hard and intransigent. Joan had begun to search the rooms of the house. Looking for the kitchen and a large sharp knife.

The winners all signed their contracts which had been taken away to the temporary office the builders had set up in one of the old bedrooms. Brinker was busy rounding the winners up and ushering them out onto the steps outside the house for the presentation of the keys by Hewlett-Temple. Martin saw his chance. All attention was focussed on the backs of the lucky winners as he grabbed Whet by the shoulders and whirled him round. Martin was a head taller than Whet and a full stone heavier. He lifted the hapless lawyer by the lapels of his designer suite jacket clean off his feet and slammed him against the dark wood panelling of the wall, hard. Very hard indeed.

'I want my money back,' he snarled at Whet. Peppering the lawyer's face with spittle. 'I want it back now. Right now.' Martin released his grip to let Whet sink to the floor then grabbed him again, repeating the previous process and slamming the lawyer's head even harder against the wall.

Teresa stood behind him, watching the one sided contest. Enjoying her brother's discomfort. She hadn't met Martin before but she could easily guess who he was and what his argument with her brother was about. As Martin released Whet for the third time and made to slam his head back against the wall again, Teresa decided that enough was enough. She used the umbrella that she had brought with her because she alone was convinced it would rain at sometime during the day.

The handle of the umbrella hooked between Martin's legs and encircled his manhood. He felt the brush of the handle against his inner thigh and wondered what it was. Then his world exploded. Teresa pulled back on the umbrella as hard as she could, lifting and twisting as she did so. It was a full-length umbrella, not one of those collapsible, retractable types, its length giving Teresa considerable leverage which she used to the extent of her strength. It was at this moment, as Teresa swung Martin screaming round the entrance hall and Whet collapsed in a concussed heap on the shiny stone tile floor that Joan appeared with the carving knife she had taken from the kitchen. Without hesitation Joan lunged at Martin.

At the far end of the house Crystel pulled the tarpaulin off the wheelbarrow and its contents. She prized the lid off the drum of tar using the edge of a trowel she had found in the old shed. The tar was set and hard and would not pour, that was a shame as it would have burnt particularly well when spread along the foot of the wall of the house. She topped up the tar can with weed-killer. Once that lit it would melt the top skin of the tar and ignite it, that would produce plenty of deep black, choking smoke; smoke was good, lots of it, it always created confusion, gave the fire more time to burn. She had taken the weed-killer from a large drum in the shed, it was the same fluid that she poured into the pump-up pressure spay. She pumped the spray vigorously, feeling the pressure build into a solid resistance to each forceful push. Eventually satisfied, she pulled the trigger on the long nozzle at the end of the hose. A spurt of weed killer shot high into the air. She aimed the stream at the trellis that climbed the side of the house, drenching the Wisteria in foul smelling, inflammable insecticide. The pressure spray was a large industrial version, holding a full two gallons of fluid. It took almost four minutes of pumping and spraying before it was empty. Finally the pressure dropped completely and could not be recharged. Crystel shook the spray, it was empty. She struggled the slopping, weed-killer topped tar can to the foot of the trellis, then placed the spray canister on top. From her pocket she took a length of thick string and a washer. She tied one end of the string to the washer as an anchor, then immersed the entire coil into the weed-killer. Then she draped the string over the side of the tar can as a makeshift fuse. Finally she removed the garden gloves supplied by the generous garden shed and dropped them into the tin as well. She surveyed her work, taking in the route of the Wisteria as it climbed to the second floor of the house and beyond. She struck a match, lit the string-fuse and stepped well back. Slowly the flame engulfed the thick string, not burning it away completely just charring the outer skin, but carrying the flame inexorable higher towards the lip of the tin. The flame appeared to hover at the lip, as if it were reluctant to take the last step. Then there was a whoosh, a burst of fire as the fumes that had collected in the top of the tin ignited. The base of the Wisteria caught. Flames began to flicker up the side of the building, crisping and crinkling the dry leaves of the plants. The trellis caught immediately and the first hints of black smoke began to curl from the tar can. Crystel clapped her hands with glee. Time to go. She turned her attention on the old wooden shed.

Claire stepped out from the far corner of the house. 'Hey,' she shouted. 'What you doing?' She ran forward blindly, intent on catching that wretched child, then felt herself stumble through the air. A sharp pain shot through her ankle as it turned over. She felt the tendon snap and cried out. Her head struck the exposed twisted root of the old Horse Chestnut tree that stood at that corner of the house. Unconscious blackness invaded her world.

***

Stuart was as close to Mal as he dared. The twin had reached the brow of a slight rise in the meadow that led down to the mansion house and now lay prone on his stomach as if waiting for a signal of something to happen. After a couple of minutes he must have received that signal because he suddenly rose to a crouch and began to run towards a clump of trees to their left. They were now close to the house but didn't appear to be going any nearer. Stuart was relieved, the last thing he needed was for Mal to expose himself to all the people in front of the house and in the marquee he could see.

Mal vanished into the trees and it was several moment before Stuart could locate him again. Suddenly he wished he hadn't. From the black sports bag Mal was pulling the stock and barrel of a rifle, complete with telescopic sight and tripod stand. Stuart sat back on the grass with a thud. Of course he had heard the rumours. Heard the stories about Mal and Phil but he had assumed they were just that, stories, tales put about by the twins to pump up their reputations. But it was true. The twins were contract killers on the side. After-hours assassins. Moonlighting murderers. 'So that's what all the argument was about.' He began to hum under his breath.

Mal snapped the barrel and stock together then clipped the tripod underneath. He assumed the firing position and pointed the rifle towards the house, scanning the steps and the party gathered on them. There were about a dozen people milling about, trying to organise themselves. One man, a studious type who looked like a schoolteacher was marshalling the rest into a straight line. To the left of the line stood a small group of people, he counted four, behind them, standing as inconspicuously as possible was a copper, plain clothes, Mal couldn't mistake him. The sight of the policemen gave Mal a sudden pang of panic. In the centre of the group of four stood a refined looking middle aged man in a city suit. Mal recognised him immediately. The Foreign Secretary's picture was an almost daily occurrence in the newspapers and Mal was an avid reader of the news. That's why the plain clothes copper's there – bodyguard. Mal relaxed. Next to the Foreign Secretary stood a tall well-built man in his late thirties. Mal didn't recognise him as a public figure and he didn't look like another bodyguard. He had a camera slung about his neck, a professional job, one of those twin-lens things. Probably to do with that lottery thing he'd read about. It was today, that's why they're all there. Perhaps the guy was the official photographer. He twitched the telescopic sight a notch, focusing on the two women that made up the remainder of the group. One was older than the other, much older but the younger one was the target, standing proud on the steps, just as the old man had said she would. Suddenly he had a strong feeling of not being alone. He looked around, searching for the source of his feeling. Then he saw it. Through the next bank of trees a glint of painted metal. He pointed the rifle in that direction and twisted the focusing ring of the telescopic sight. It was a car, black, small and apparently abandoned for he couldn't see a driver in the vehicle. With the rifle held at waist height he cautiously stole towards the bank of trees.

In the library Freddie was not doing very well at all. The stress of the draw had brought on a mild heart attack that was rapidly followed by a second as his cousin tried to administer a medicinal Brandy. The family gathered round him. Helen spitefully willing him to die, there, as they all looked on. Christian and Charles indifferent and Elsbeth nervous and frightened; she held a large white cotton handkerchief across her nose and mouth as though heart attacks where contagious and airborne. Only Thaddeus showed concern and even that was self-centred.

'Is he dying?' Helen asked, struggling to keep the excitement out of her voice.

'We should call an ambulance.' Thaddeus added. But no one made a move towards the telephone on the library desk.

I've locked them in. They don't know it yet but I have. I told you I was able to do most things now. Move things. Lift things. Even throw things around. So simply turning a key in a door lock was no problem – from the outside of course. I'm not sure why I've locked them in. Partially because I don't want them there at the presentation; their presence would spoil the thing completely and I couldn't keep an eye on Freddie and enjoy the presentation myself. Mind you it looks as though Freddie's no longer a problem. He'll probably be joining me soon as not.

Diane! Diane! You still in the hallway? What's all that noise?

Out on the front steps, Brinker had finally managed to arrange everyone in a straight line. Now he was busy tapping the microphone that stood on a long thin stand in front of him. The commotion caused by Joan's lunge at Martin began to reverberate through the double doors behind them. Everyone turned and for one awful moment Brinker thought his painfully assembled line was about to dissolve. Marios Branchman saved the day by stepping smartly back and pulling the double doors closed. The interrupting noise abruptly stopped. Marios lingered for a second, watching the chaos in the entrance hall. A tall red headed man with large carving knife protruding from his shoulder was being propelled spirally by a short thin woman with the ugliest face imaginable, who had the redheaded man fixed from behind by a long umbrella that was thrust between the man's legs. Another man sat with his back to the wall and his head slumped unconscious, while a blond woman knelt in the centre of the entrance hall running blood-covered hands through her hair and sobbing uncontrollably. He turned back to the assembly on the outside steps.

Lisa took his arm. 'Chuckles? What was all that.'

'Just some crazy woman. Must be one of the losers. Don't worry.'

Brinker had finished tapping the microphone and was now counting 'and a one… and a two… and a three. Eh hum. Ladies and Gentlemen. Please, your attention…'

As Brinker began his diligently rehearsed speech, Marios weighed up the situation. A glance back over his shoulder revealed that the mayhem in the entrance hall had subsided. He could see the redheaded man lying on his back on the floor, the knife still protruding from his shoulder and the umbrella draped across his knees. The women were out of his angle of vision but the other man still sat slumped against the wall. The situation looked to be on the point of getting totally out of control. Marios knew he had to act immediately. He had intended taking out the target at the end of the proceedings, as a footnote to the final speech as it were, but now he would do it as soon as the target stepped forward. Marios flipped the lid of the camera up, glanced down through the viewfinder, and turned the handle at the side of the camera as if rolling on the film. There was a faint, almost inaudible click as the internal mechanism locked into place. Marios was particularly proud of his camera, it was straight out of a Hollywood movie script but it worked perfectly and he had used it on two other occasions when he had to get close to the victim. Inside the mechanism of the camera was a small single shot pistol, with a short silencer attached. The pistol fired a .22 calibre bullet that in itself was not particularly lethal, but the cap of the bullet was cyanide tipped and that made it an extremely deadly weapon. From his pocket he retrieved a mobile phone. Lisa gave him an enquiring look. He smiled back and gestured towards Brinker who was now coming to the end of his speech.

'…so, with out more ado, may I press the Right Honourable Norman Hewlett-Temple Member of Parliament…'

Marios pressed the red key on the keypad and held it down firmly. A line of small black bars flashed across the window of the mobile phone. The word 'connected' appeared. Marios pressed the '5' key then the 'send again', with his finger poised on the '7', slid the mobile phone back into his pocket.

Hewlett-Temple stepped forward to take the microphone from Brinker.

Marios also stepped forward, pointed his camera towards the Foreign Secretary, pressed the '7' on the mobile phone, said 'Smile' aimed the camera and started to press the send button.

***

Andrew clung to Reggie's back as they careened across the meadow towards the house. He remembered breakfast, with Trevor in the canteen, a mug of tea and fried egg sandwich – Claire wouldn't let him eat those sort of fatty foods but he liked them and at work she couldn't see. Then he remembered driving the armoured truck out of the 'Failsafe' yard, but the rest of the day was a blur, that is except this morning, he remembered delivering the milk. He didn't know why he was on the back of this motorbike, but knew it was important, he had to tell someone something, that he didn't know, but it was important. The bike hit another rut bouncing them both into the air, daylight appearing between their rears and the long leather seat of the bike. With the perplexing agility of the totally drunk and the completely concussed, they somehow hung on. The house was no more than a hundred yards away now.

Mal approached the black car cautiously. He could hear a motor cycle in the distance and paused to look back across the meadow towards the house. The sound came from the left. There was a deep hollow there, Reggie and Andrew were in the centre of it so out of Mal's current view. He turned back to the car. There was definitely no driver but it couldn't be abandoned, it was a new car. The back windows of the car had been covered in the sticky film that is used to tint windows and a sheet had been hung inside the car between the front and rear, effectively concealing the back of the car. Mal circled the vehicle. There was no movement. No lovers in the back doing what lovers do in the backs of cars in dark wooded copses. As he reached the back window on the side facing towards the house he heard a click, followed by the faint whirring sound of an electric motor. Mal leant towards the black window of the black car as it gently slid downwards. An inch gap revealed only a dark interior. He leant closer, following the path of the window as it dropped into the door of the car, his nose pointed downwards. He lifted his head slowly.

Marios pressed 'send' for the third time, removed his hand from his pocket, steadied the camera that was a bare two metres from Hewlett-Temple, counting as he did so, 'and two and three.'

***

Stephanie had been looking for her daughter for at least five minutes and was beginning to become both worried and annoyed. It was not like Crystel to vanish like this, not as their part of the day was about to go into full swing. That lawyer fellow had been speaking on the microphone for ages, and now he had stopped. She reached the end of the manor house and stopped herself. Black, acrid smoke was billowing up the end wall of the building, fuelled by a core of bright flickering flames. She turned and screamed 'FIRE' as loudly as she could.

'…and four.' Marios pressed the shutter release.

The large, round muzzle of the pistol mounted in the rear of the black car exploded in a cacophony of noise and flame, removing all of the hair from Mal's face and most of the hair from his forehead and the front of his scalp in the process. There was no bullet, no velocity to the blast, Mal's violent propulsion backwards was purely as a result of his own reflexes, as his face, and in particular his eyes took the full brunt of the searing heat of the blast. He had lost the end of his nose and was totally blind. His normal hearing had been replaced by a sea of crashing explosions. He rolled on the grass clutching his face in his hands.

Except for Marios every head turned at the sound of Stephanie's alarm. Her shout checked Hewlett-Temple's step as he approached the microphone and the turn of his own head towards her cry, was sufficient to save his life. The cyanide tipped .22 bullet shot across the heads of the watching crowd towards the platform erected for the press. Joan's cameraman had the whole thing on tape and couldn't believe his luck, till the .22 bullet shattered the centre of the lens on his camera wrenching it from his grip in the process.

Lisa was thrust violently aside as the bodyguard launched himself through to Hewlett-Temple, bundling the MP to the floor. Clutching him in an unappreciated bear hug, he rolled them both painfully off the steps and onto the driveway below.

What the hell's going on? That blond haired woman has just stabbed the redheaded man in the entrance hall. The man that Whet's sister was molesting so successfully with the end of an umbrella. Someone's just taken a pot-shot at poor Norman and now the buildings on fire. Diane! Diane!

The smoke was now billowing above the roof of the building, the flames threatening to take hold on the ancient timbers of the roof. People were panicking, and running in every direction at once, even towards the fire. Stephanie found Crystel wandering back towards the fire, she had been hiding behind the old shed at the end of the building, which had really caught by now and resembled a huge November the fifth bonfire. Her eyes were transfixed by the flames that were now licking high towards the dark sky above. Stephanie grabbed her daughter and spun her round to face her. Crystel's eyes were ablaze. The red glow of the flames shone in her pupils, tinting the clear white skin of her teenage face to a deep pink hue. Stephanie saw in those eyes something she had never seen before, something she had never even dreamed could exist. She grabbed her daughter's hand and snatched her away from the flames.

Reggie was also transfixed by the flames. Somehow he had managed to return to the clinic, to his prison. He didn't know how he had done it, but he could see that he had. The realisation that he was about to return to the horrors of that drinkless mausoleum made him brake, as he did so the bike began to slide and would have crashed into the rose garden had he continued to apply pressure to the brakes. But the flames momentarily saved them. It was on fire. But why was it on fire? Reggie had dreamt of seeing the detestable building destroyed, had prayed for it. But he hadn't started the fire. Someone else must have. He released his pressure on the brake peddle, but not his grip on the throttle. The bike corrected itself as it careened past the rose garden off the grass and onto the gravel of the drive. Stones flew in all directions. The back wheel slid to the left then violently to the right Andrew looked up over Reggie's shoulder, just as they whipped through the entrance of the grand marquee. They were doing over fifty miles an hour as they hit the astro-turf that covered the ground inside the marquee. Reggie and Andrew slide across the shiny artificial grass, veering in different directions either side of the central pole that supported the marquee, the trial bike smashed into the foot of the pole, snapping it cleanly at ground level. Reggie flew past the pole to the left, hitting one of the catering tables a glancing blow with his shoulder that snapped his collar bone like twig and spun him round so that he hit the far wall of canvas with his back. Andrew went to the right and should have dashed his brains firmly on the pole, except that the pole was no longer there. It spun violently away, pivoted by its connection to the momentarily upright apex of the marquee. Andrew hit the far wall of canvas face first; his arms and legs splayed and would have slid gracefully down the canvas to the floor if the marquee hadn't collapsed on top of him.

That's when it started to rain.

The storm had been building all morning, gathering millions of gallons of moisture over the nearby Chiltern Hills. By midday its epicentre hung above the town of Aylesbury before a chance wind blew it directly into the path of Southgrim Manor. The first of the thunder rolled out of the skies just as Marios and Lisa pulled Whet clear of the entrance steps to the building. The end wall of the building was ablaze in a spectacular flurry of flames and smoke, but apart from the end wall where the fire had started, the structure of the house was as yet untouched, protected by the very stone from which it was constructed. However, this situation would not last for long. Once the flames found their way into the interior of the house, with all of its combustible materials, that would be the end. No one would be able to save the house.

***

Lisa and Marios laid the still inert form of Whet out on the grass, in the meadow beyond the rose gardens, the same meadow that Reggie and Andrew had careered across a few minutes before. The twin lens reflex camera was still slung round Marios' neck, swinging beneath him as he stooped to inspect Whet. There was a gurgling sound coming from his throat. Marios felt for his pulse.

'His pulse is strong, but he's not looking too good. Looks like he banged his head and knocked himself out, but before he did that someone had a really good go at crushing his windpipe. Look here, see the bruising. Here's where he banged his head.' Marios parted the hair to the back of Whet's scalp. 'See. Blood.' The skin was torn and a deep blue-black bruise had formed. Behind them another couple were struggling to carry Martin clear of the house. The knife was no longer in his shoulder and there was no sign of the original umbrella. There was a lot of blood and although Martin was obviously still alive, the best he could contribute was a low moan. An attractive young woman in her late twenties rushed up to him and collapsed in a heap beside him. She lifted his head gently and slid her legs beneath it until it was resting squarely in the centre of her lap.

Mal had reached the edge of the meadow. He stumbled as the ground beneath his feet changed from tussock to gravel. He groped forward, hands and arms outstretched, blinded by the flash of

Marios' decoy pistol, the sight in his left eye completely destroyed – he would eventually gain back the sight in the right eye, but only partially. After the blast, once he had managed to pick himself up, he had followed the sound from the Manor house and staggered off in that general direction. Stuart had followed. Not because he wanted to help Mal or because he wanted to make sure that Mal didn't get himself picked up by the police. Stuart had followed because that was the way the Clinchet Star had gone in the fuel tank of that bike. He slid round to the back of the collapsed marquee then stepped into the crowd that had gathered there, at a safe distance from the roaring flames. It was starting to rain. Gentle rain that increased in intensity with each drop. 'There are people under the marquee,' he shouted. 'They'll suffocate.' Around him onlookers stared, numbed by the shock of events. 'NOW!' he yelled. 'Help me get them out.

***

There you are Diane. Do you know what happened?

It's that little brat from the caterers. She started the fire. I could feel that there was something wrong with her the moment she arrived. If it hadn't been for all the other things going on I'd have kept a closer eye on her.

How do you know it was her?

Saw her going back to the scene. Her mother collared her and whisked her away; they're in that catering van of theirs now. The girl had tar on her dress and all that smoke, that's tar. You can smell it.

But why?

Prank. I suppose. But at least Lisa's out of danger.

Is she?

For the moment. The gunshot must have been for her. Who ever it was missed and they won't have hung around with all this lot going on. Besides, it was Freddie that organised it and he's not going to be organising much of anything from now on. I know a heart attack when I see one.

My. You have been busy. I don't doubt you at all but how do you know it was Freddie that organised it?

Overheard him whispering with the other one…

Thaddeus?

Yeah. Him. I didn't understand what they were saying at the time. It was just an argument with Thaddeus telling Freddie that he

260

was going too far and Freddie telling him that if one of them didn't have the stomach for it, their last chance was gone. As I say it didn't make sense then. Did you start the rain?

Me? If only I could.

Thought it was asking a bit much. Still. However it started, it's doing the job. The roof's soaked, It's just the east wing, where that little vixen started it, that's still burning.

It's getting stronger Diane.

No. It's Ok the fires being held ba...

Not the fire. I can leave that to the hands of providence and the local fire brigade. Besides the house is covered for millions. It was only the Trust Fund that I under valued not the insurance. It's the other spirit. He's coming and I won't be able to stop him this time.

Who is it Rosie?

My son. Robert.

***

The cold sting of the rain snapped Joan out of her trance. She still held the bloody knife that she had wrenched from Martin's shoulder. It had twisted as it came out, emitting a fresh jet of bright scarlet blood. She smiled at the thought. 'Bastard.' Now she had to find Liam. He was with that blond tart. He was just as bad as Martin. Worse. At least she wasn't in love with Martin. She looked around to get her bearings. The loud clang of the fire brigade rent the air as a huge fire engine rumbled past her and ground to a halt. She was at the front driveway. Liam would have to be outside with the other spectators. She'd check the front of the building, if he wasn't there then she'd go across to the farmhouse. It must be within walking distance, beyond the meadow to the front of the house. She slipped the knife under the folds of her jacket.

Teresa was already in the limousine when the bodyguard dragged Hewlett-Temple to it. He wrenched open the rear door. 'Who the hell are you?' he demanded, on the point of slamming the door shut again – assassins can be male or female.

'Teresa Stamp. From the lawyers. We were introduced earlier. For God's sake get him in the car and let's get out of this mad-house.'

The bodyguard hesitated. The shot had come from the trees in front of the house. Teresa had been in the entrance hall, he had seen her fighting with that crazy redheaded man. She couldn't have fired the shot. 'OK.' He pushed Hewlett-Temple groaning, into the car. 'His got a couple of bruised or cracked ribs and I'm not sure about his left leg. See if you can make him comfortable.' He slammed the door then jumped into the driver's seat. The limousine was the second vehicle to leave. Stephanie, Bob and Crystel escaped a bare two minutes earlier, both were safely out of the grounds before the first of the police cars arrived; Hewlett-Temple to have his bruised ribs bandaged and his leg plastered in time for his turnkey speech at the Hague; he had also gained a new personal research assistant, Teresa, although at that particular moment in time he was unaware of the fact; Crystel to be frog-marched by her mother to a child psychiatrist, presenting that particular expert with the challenge of his lifetime.

In the library everyone was in panic. The builders, in preparation for the renovation works had completely blocked in the library windows. In the absence of Freddie, who sat inertly in a corner chair, a faint drizzle of saliva dribbling down his chin, his life close to an end, Thaddeus had taken charge. Banging on the locked door had proved useless and as the heavy door open inwards, all attempts to break it down had failed. Black acrid smoke had begun to permeate from behind the bookcases. Thaddeus ordered Charles and Christian to pull the cases forward but they were built into the wall so the best they could do was scoop the books off the shelves and into the centre of the room. The wall behind the empty shelves was hot to touch and becoming hotter. Charles and Christian used chairs as clubs to smash away the solid shelving. The smoke was coming from a crack in the wall that grew until it formed the outline of a doorway. Elsbeth screamed at the sight, as though she had seen a ghost but it was only because she remembered that when she was a child there used to be a doorway from the library directly into the music room. It had been boarded up and hidden behind the bookshelves. The realisation that they did not have the protection of a solid wall between them and the fire had made her scream. The boarded doorway gave way. Flames rushed into the room.

Christian and Charles batted at the flames, holding them back long enough for Helen to pull back the square of rug that had covered the centre of the library floor for as long as Helen could remember. Starved of flammable material the flames licked at the tiled floor and stone walls, temporarily held at bay. But the hard cold stone could not hold back the smoke. Gradually the room filled with deep, churning, acrid smog. It burnt their eyes, blackened their clothes and skin, choked their thoughts. Freddie was the first to go, followed by Elsbeth who had collapsed to the floor close to the doorway and choked to death on the fumes.

Thaddeus, Charles, Christian and Helen lay on the floor at the far side of the room. Their faces pressed as hard as they could into the tiles, trying to breath beneath the thick veil that began to completely engulf them.

***

The fire brigade found Claire curled into a ball beside the old horse chestnut tree. They had directed their hoses at the end wall of the house, ploughing jets of water through the thick smoke, unable to see the extent of the fire or its grip on the building. As a result Claire, who was still unconscious with her face lying in a hollow formed by the roots of the old tree, very nearly met an untimely end through drowning.

Claire felt strong hands roll her backwards. She was shivering uncontrollably from the coldness of the water and coughing and spluttering from the taste of it.

'You're alright now love.'

The voice was far off, distant. She coughed and retched and felt the strong hands gently unfolding her legs from underneath her. She cried out in sudden pain as the hands straightened her left leg.

'Looks like you've ricked your ankle love.' The voice paused as she felt the hands gently searching her leg from the knee down. At the ankle the sharp pain shot back. She bit her lip to stop herself crying out. One of the hands stroked her hair. 'Nothing broken, but you won't be ice skating for a while.'

Her eyes were open now and her vision clearing. The hands belonged to a heavy set man in a dark uniform with a strange helmet on his head. A fireman. Memories began to return; the fire, the young girl; she called out to her; then everything went black. 'It was the girl,' she murmured. 'She had an apron on, the other waitress. She set the fire. Deliberately.'

The expression on the fireman's face changed suddenly. 'Say that again please?'

'When I tripped, knocked myself out. It was because I rushed forward to try and stop the girl. She'd lit the fire to the house just before I got here, but she was going to that shed.' Claire looked round in the direction that the shed had been but there was only a cloud of water spray and smoke to be seen. 'She must have done the shed too. Diane told me to watch her. I'm afraid I didn't do a very good job. Did I?'

'Don't you worry about that.' The fireman replied. 'This waitress, do you know where she'll be now? And who's the other person, Diane?'

"Diane's in charge. She's doing all the organising. The girl belongs to the catering company. I think she's the daughter of Stephanie, the lady that's doing the catering today. I really messed up. Didn't I?'

The fireman smiled at her reassuringly. 'No you didn't. Don't you worry at all. Look. Let's get you out of here and get that ankle seen to. OK?'

'Thank you.' Tears were rolling down Claire's cheeks now. Tears of relief and pain.

'We've a couple of ambulances standing by. You just sit there and I'll go and get a couple of the lads and a stretcher.' He gave her another reassuring smile and started to turn away, then stopped. 'Did you actually see this girl light the fire?' He asked.

'She did.'

'I know. I know. But did you actually see her do it, or set that shed alight.'

'Well. Not striking the match exactly. I'm sorry.'

'Don't be sorry love. It's not your fault. Now... Let's get you that stretcher.'

Claire watched the fireman's broad bake as he ran back through the swirling smoke. She didn't hear him curse under his breath. 'I don't believe it. If it is that Jenny Hellfire kid, we'll need more than placing her at the scene for a conviction. Shit.'

Behind him the flames were beginning to subside. The fire was firmly under control but only the trained eye of the firemen could appreciate that. To the rest of the people around the manor house the intensity of the smoke, which had increased with the application of several thousand gallons of water, made the fire seem infinitely worse than it was. An observation that was not lost on the press.

Joan's Viscount TV crew of one had abandoned his smashed camera and joined Stuart's crew pulling the buried victims of the collapsed marquee clear of the canvas melee that engulfed them. Eighteen people had been extracted and were being inspected by the ambulance staff and a few volunteers from the crowd, for bodily damage. So far the worst was a broken arm, caused by the erratic swinging of the central tent pole in those last few seconds before the marquee collapsed. Another victim had sustained third degree scalding from the shower of steaming hot water created as Stuart's trial bike had spun off the severed central pole and crashed into a catering table scattering cups saucers and the boiled urn of water for the tea. A third victim nursed a bruised forehead having been struck by the lid from that same urn as it flew through the air, but that was a minor injury. The rescuers were straining with the folds of one corner of canvas in an attempt to get to the remaining six people inside; which included both Reggie and Andrew. Stuart was leading the effort, shouting for everyone to lift at once as he just managed to wriggle under a cascade of heavy canvas folds.

Although the Viscount crew were out of action the other TV crews were not. Four handheld, high-tech TV video cameras whirled incessantly as their operators pushed as close to the fire as they could, their reporters beside them speaking as fast as they could into their recorders, except one. 'Event TV' were a small independent outfit from Harlow in Essex who wouldn't normally have managed to get on a restricted list of invited media except that their CEO happened to be playing squash with a middle level PR man from CNN, three weeks earlier and had convinced the CNN man that although the lottery of Rosie's estate obviously didn't carry a global news attraction or weight, it was a very unusual novelty story that they might want to put on file as a possible filler, for a quiet day. His pitch had worked and resulted in the 'Events' crew having the only satellite uplink facility on the day.

It was a rather excitable and completely misplaced programme manager in the Belfast studios of CNN that picked up the broadcast from Southgrim Manor and asked the simple question – Is this a terrorist attack?

The result, in colloquial terms, was – BREAKING NEWS.

***

Mal's face screamed in pain. Mal was screaming in pain as he blindly staggered to and fro. He hadn't been spotted by the firemen, ambulance crew or anyone else, simply because having reached the gravel of the driveway, and relatively close to the house he had lurched hard to his left and not stopped until he'd literally hit the end wall of the house; the far wall at the distant end from the fire. Using the wall as a guide he had circumnavigated the house, eventually passing Claire just after the fireman had left her. Claire saw him coming out of the smoke and spluttering flames as he rounded the corner of the building and screamed out in panic. She wasn't sure what it was walking towards her but it was the most horrific thing she had ever seen in her life. It was a person, not an animal, she could see that. And it was too large to be a woman so it had to be a man. Its clothes were ripped and torn around the upper chest but from the waist down appeared to be a normal pair of jeans held up by a thick leather belt. It was the face that she couldn't define, it just wasn't there. Where it should have been hung a globule of red bloody tissue. The tip of the nose appeared to have melted away, the right cheek, which had been slightly nearer the blast of the pistol had a jagged hole in it that revealed two lines of stained teeth but it was the eye above that cheek that was really scary; it wasn't there at all.

Claire tried to back away from the thing as it approached her but her injured ankle slowed her down and she was only able to move closer into the tree trunk as the thing was upon her. She screamed. She screamed as loud as she could, as loud as she ever would in her entire life. The thing stopped. Tottered in front of her and for one awful moment Claire thought it would fall onto her. Then it turned. Wavering with its weight on one leg, a deep pitiful cry gurgling through what was left of its burnt shrivelled lips and staggered back towards the building.

It was blind. Claire called out to it. Tried to stop it as it walked straight into the smoke, back towards the flames. That's when the pressure of the water, which actually did more damage to the manor house than the fire did, collapsed one of the roof timbers. The heavy length of wood crashed to the ground with a force that would have ended Mal's misery instantly had it struck him, but it didn't. The debris drawn behind the timber did. It included a section of lathe and plaster cladding from a temporarily repaired area of wall between the eaves. The cladding was on fire. It hit Mal across the shoulders and although quite heavy caused little damage except to set his hair ablaze.

The blow from the cladding material caused Mal to change direction again. He hadn't yet felt the extra discomfort of having his hair on fire. His other injuries were paramount on his pain level. His burning hair kicked in just as he rounded the corner of the building and came into view from the chaos at the front. Someone shouted. 'Look.' There was half a heartbeat of universal pause then screaming and shouting and fireman running with blankets to throw over Mal's head. He charged. Through the noise, through the firemen, almost tripping as he ran between the line of slightly injured at the rear of one of the ambulances, and straight into the flattened marquee.

Stuart could see the shinning polished chrome of the front wheel of the trail bike about two body lengths from the end of his out stretched arm. Behind him people were straining with the heavy canvas folds and he could feel the drafts of air they were creating each time they hauled at the canvas. He dug his heels in and pushed. Nothing. The canvas on top of him was too heavy. He waited for the next heave from behind.

A waft of fresh air. Push. Yes. Half a yard. He waited.

The team lifting the canvas for Stuart, stopped in mid pull as Mal appeared. Mal hit the edge of the canvas at a full terrified run, his mind completely lost in the sea of pain that engulfed him. The toe of his trainer caught the edge of the canvas and pitched him headlong towards the middle. His head hit the ground, cushioned by the folds of petrol stained canvas that covered the trial bike. The fumes seeping through the canvas ignited, as did the fumes and petrol inside the breached petrol tank on the bike. There was an explosion. Not a huge explosion. A localised bang held back by the same folds of canvas that pinned Stuart firmly to the ground and probably saved his life. The blast tore through Mal, relieving him of both his earthly presence and his pain, rent the petrol tank apart and shot the Clinchet Star like a bullet across the driveway and into the air.

**

Jesus. It's getting crowded up here.

First Freddie then Elsbeth. Thaddeus appeared briefly for a split second then went back. I didn't know you could do that. He must be hanging on in there. Now this one. Who on earth he is I don't know. And why he set himself alight and run amok like that is beyond me.

Look at them all.

Freddie's been here the longest, just a couple of your minutes more than Elsbeth but it shows. I can see him looking around, trying to get his bearings whereas Elsbeth and this new one are just groping aimlessly. I don't think he can see me though. Not yet.

Diane! Diane! What's going on now? Who's this new one?

267

Mal's fire raging charge and apparent self combustion had flashed around the world on CNN almost as quickly as his own life had vanished in the blast. The Prime Minister was alerted and became particularly alert when he asked the question where was this all happening, to be told Southgrim Manor, where the Foreign Secretary was making a presentation.

'Did they get him? Did he escape? Get me Special Branch.'

As the attack was in the UK and didn't appear to involve American citizens the President wasn't woken, but the First Secretary was, and the head of the CIA.

At London's four airports, flights were grounded as a precaution and not resumed for over one hour.

***

Alan was watching the Saturday afternoon football programme. They weren't showing any football, just a group of ex players, who were watching the games, reporting on events as they occurred. The programme was interrupted by a news flash reporting a suspected terrorist attack and attempted assassination of the Foreign Secretary the Right Honourable Norman Hewlett-Temple MP. Alan wasn't interested. 'They won't put on the News Flash that I want. I bet,' he mumbled to himself. On his lap he had a tray with his lunch. He'd changed his mind about which meal to have and in the kitchen lay the discarded tinfoil dish his lunch had been stored in and its lid marked Saturday PM. He chuckled to himself. I wonder if they're gone yet. He thought. He closed his eyes, picturing Ann and her gigolo rolling a joint each with that funny tobacco she thought she had hidden from him. Alan had laced the leaves with a second kind. He didn't know the name of the new plant but had taken enough interest in Ann's ramblings to know that it was deadly. He plunged his spoon into his meal and ate heartily.

Another two! Where are they all coming from? These two weren't from the house. Ah. I remember. These are the two at the farmhouse, the one we lease. Lionel. No. Lance. Liam! That's it. Liam. Don't know her name. They're a bit young for up here. I wonder what happened.

Marios dropped his camera onto the backseat of his car. Despite the mayhem of the last hour, the fact that he had failed in his attempt on Hewlett-Temple meant that the police wouldn't be looking for an alternative weapon and he would get rid of the camera as soon as possible; he had a genuine twin lens that he could produce if asked. He wasn't even that bothered about messing up the kill. He hadn't wanted the job in the first place, his principles only knew of him as a voice on the phone, he'd just credit the deposit back to its source and leave it at that. If they really wanted to top Hewlett-Temple they would have to get someone else. He'd retired. And besides he had a new occupation helping Lisa rebuild the manor house. Which was going to be quite a task after the events of the last hour. He stopped to recap. Camera was OK. The car in the copse was clean and the pistol untraceable. The SIM cards he'd bought for the mobile phones were pre-paid type and he'd used a false driving license as identification to buy them. It all seemed OK. Good. He could look forward to the rest of his life. He smiled broadly and laughed out loud as he stared back at the smoke and ambulances and sirens of the police cars that were know arriving in droves.

'I don't see what's funny mate.' One of the firemen had caught his laugh and smile.

'No. Nor do I. A bit of delayed shock. That's all.'

'Better join the queue at the ambulances then.' The fireman trudged off. All thought of Marios gone from his mind.

Reggie stared at the canvas roof above him. His head hurt and his lips were dry and parched. For some reason that he couldn't explain he was having trouble breathing. 'Hello Maureen,' he said as though his wife had been with him all the time. 'They've got it back up then.'

Maureen looked down at him, wondering if he was delirious. 'Got what up Reggie?'

'That big tent. The one that fell on me.'

Maureen laughed. He liked it when she did that. It wasn't as good as a drink but it helped and she hadn't laughed at him for a long, long time. He wondered what he'd said that was so funny.

'It's a temporary shelter. They put it up because there's no room left in the ambulances. How are you?'

'I'm not sure. I need a drink.'

Maureen ignored the request. 'How did you get here? And that motor bike, where did that come from?'

Reggie stared up into her eyes and smiled. 'I escaped. I fooled them all and escaped. I found a farmhouse but they didn't have much to drink. Then I got hungry and all they had was biscuits, big thick brown things; burnt I think. Where's the milkman. He escaped as well.'

Maureen knelt on the ground beside him. Tears dripped from Maureen's cheeks. 'Oh Reggie darling. You're delirious. Don't worry. We'll have you back at the clinic in no time. They'll soon get you better and the builders, the builders here at the manor, they'll soon have the house back to its old glory. The fire didn't do too much damage. The fire brigade have put it out now and it's really not that bad at all. Plus it's all insured. I read it in that contract they gave us. So in a couple of months we'll be able to move into our own brand new apartment.'

Reggie was drifting in and out of a fitful exhausted sleep. His cracked ribs hurt like hell and it was easier to sleep than try to draw enough breath to answer his wife. 'Back?' He mumbled.

'Just think. A place of our own, all paid for.'

Two of the volunteers arrived carrying a woman in a plastic garden chair. Her foot was in a splint, supported by a board that she was sitting on that pushed her leg out in front of her. The volunteers placed the woman and her plastic chair across from Maureen and Reggie. Maureen smiled at her. 'Are you OK?' She asked.

'Yes. Just my ankle. Stupid really with all of this going on I managed to trip and sprain it. I've torn a ligament they tell me. And you?'

'I'm OK. But my husband here has broken ribs and a bad shoulder. You'll have to excuse him. He's a bit delirious.'

Claire smiled in reply. 'So's mine. They're bringing him now. I don't know what he's doing here but he's had a bad bump on the head and they say he's concussed. Here he comes now.'

The same two volunteers that had carried Claire in the plastic seat reappeared carrying a stretcher. They placed the stretcher on the ground and lifted Andrew off onto a blanket next to Reggie.

'It's the milkman. They got you too?'

Andrew squinted his eyes. Peering at the voice. 'Oh. Hi,' he replied.

Maureen and Claire stared at each other.

Claire put her hand in her pocket and felt the cold hard surface of the Clanchet Star, which had landed next to her as she lay waiting beside the old chestnut tree, he was delirious she thought, but he'll be OK and now all their problems were over.

270

Joan stared down at the bodies of Ann and Liam. She looked at the knife in her hand and the blood on her clothes. Realisation surged back to her consciousness. She dropped the knife with a clatter to the floor and sank to her knees, crying loudly. Around her the air held that cloy sweet smells of hashish that she vaguely remembered from her student days. Liam had shown her his pottery. He'd offered her the thin flimsy joints that he rolled so delicately with his artist's hands but she'd refused. Those days were far behind her and she didn't need stimulants of any kind where Liam was concerned. The thought hung there, in front of her eyes. She should have seen it before. It was all part of the game Liam played. The drugs, the women. Oh how she hated him. How she hated herself. Even more than him. She looked up at his body. He looked ugly. So did she. The blond. It was the grimace across their faces that created that impression. It must have hurt. Their death. It must have hurt. She reached out to feel Liam's pulse. A useless exercise because they'd obviously both overdosed; although she didn't think you could on that weed stuff he grew. Not by smoking it at least.

Martin? What about Martin? He wasn't dead. She'd tried to kill him but only stuck the knife in his shoulder; he may have bled to death though. There was a lot of blood.

'No. I don't think so,' she said aloud.

Joan cleaned the knife in the kitchen sink and hid it by simply including it in the knife draw with the other knives in Liam's kitchen. In the bathroom she stripped and inspected her own wounds. There was a bruise to her forehead but the skin wasn't broken and several scratches and abrasions to her legs and arms from her lung at Martin with the knife and her demented flight across the estate to the farmhouse. But there was nothing to explain the blood that covered the front of her clothes and face.

Naked, she stuffed her clothes into the pot-bellied boiler that stood in one corner of the kitchen. She rummaged round till she found a packet of firelighters then light the boiler and watched as her clothes vanished in the flames. She showered. Rubbing her skin till it hurt to remove the stains of blood and the stain of the cause of that blood, dried herself then searched through Ann's small weekend bag for a change of clothes. Fortunately Liam's perchance for middle-aged women of a certain build ensured that the clothes she found fitted almost perfectly. She dressed. Went out to the front of the house. Checked around to make sure that no one was watching then rolled and rolled on the ground to dirty the new clothes she'd put on. Eventually satisfied that she looked as though she'd just escaped from the fire she made her way back to the manor house, holding her head and feigning delirium.

***

Lia had been searching for Christian for almost half an hour before she started to panic. She'd last seen him with the rest of the family, just after the draw finished. She'd been too exited to join them. She was afraid that her excitement would show and that they'd become suspicious. She'd save that surprise till later. Probably tell them the same time as she had the divorce papers served. The thought exited her even more. But now she'd found all their cars still there. They hadn't left. Then she realised how stupid she'd been. They'd have gone to the library. Uncle Freddie would have demanded a brandy and they'd have begun arguing. They always drank and argued when they lost and they most certainly had lost today. They must still be in the house. She looked round for someone to raise the alarm. Then saw four stretchers being carried at a run to the back of the ambulances. An arm hung from one of the stretchers. Aunt Elsbeth's arm. Lia recognised the jewellery on her wrist. She ran to the ambulances.

***

Another one. There won't be any room left up here soon.

Oh. It's Elsbeth.

Nice to see you dear. Had a bad day?

She can't hear me but Freddie can. That's got him going. Either he doesn't recognise the voice or... What am I saying? We aren't actually talking anyway. He doesn't know who it is.

Diane! Diane! Can you hear me?

I think its time for me to go. The colours are coming, there really pressing now. And besides I don't like the present company at all.

Diane? Are you there?

Yes. Yes. It's a bit busy down here at the moment.

I know. Sorry. But I really am going this time. Tell me everything's OK.

Everything's OK.

No. Properly.

It's Ok. Believe me. The fire's out and the damage is not more than the builders would have done as they stripped the old place apart. Except for that shed at the end of the house that's completely gone.

Meant to get rid of that years ago. How's Lisa.

Fine. That new man of hers is a real tower of strength. He's going to look after her fine. I thought there was something wrong about him at first but he seems to have turned up trumps. The police are starting to organise everyone who isn't injured; for questioning and that sort of thing. You've never seen so many police in your life. I heard one shouting something about finding the terrorists. Where they got that one from I don't know. Someone said that there has been an assassination attempt on that MP fellow. But he was OK. Left straight away though. I caught the lawyers Briskin and Brinker having a right old barney over something but I don't know what...

Blackmail

Pardon?

Briskin, the younger one. He's blackmailing Brinker. He's got photographs of Brinker, compromising photographs. He's using them to push Brinker out and try to take over the partnership. I had meant to do something about that but got too busy on other things. Too late now.

Well. They're with the police now along with Lia and the Australian and all the others. Being interviewed.

So how did the fire start?

It was that young girl. Crystel was her name. The daughter of the woman running the catering. The other waitress saw her. We've been on the telly!

TV?

Yes CNN. Some idiot sent the report to them. I think that's why they think it was a terrorist attack. There was that big bang, like a rifle shot, while the MP was making his speech. I suppose that him being Home Secretary and all it's understandable.

Foreign

Is he? I didn't know. Did you see what happened to Freddie?

Freddie? And Elsbeth and two others that I don't know. They're all here. It's like Clapham Junction at the moment.

Gotta go Rosie. The police want to interview me as well.

Diane! Wait! Thank you. For everything. I've got to go as well... Robert....

Bye Rosie

Chapter 19

To say that the room, the building, the entire assembly were stunned into silence would be a total understatement. Hewlett-Temple his leg in a gleaming white plaster caste, gazed across the sea of vacant faces before him. 'I've got you now. Haven't I?' His thoughts filled the brief pause he had allowed before winding up the speech, and his career.

'And may I conclude by saying, that as Foreign Minister for Her Majesty's Government, I am delighted to have had this opportunity to present this signed document,' He waved a thin sheaf of paper in the air, 'and deliver the clear message contained in my speech to this security council and in fact to the entire world. Ladies and Gentlemen. Thank you.'

He sat down very slowly and carefully, his heart racing, his blood pressure so high his head throbbed violently, his forehead felt as though it was encased in a seething band of fluid, adrenaline coursed to every extremity, he literally felt as though he was going to burst.

Sir Malcolm Talbert-Flock, Principle Private Secretary to the Foreign Minister, civil servant of six different administrations, was also experiencing high blood pressure, excessively high and rising. His normal, extravagantly articulate demeanour completely dispossessed by the Foreign Minister's speech. He started to stammer, something he hadn't done since he was four years of age. Yet he felt as helpless as that four year old. 'De... De... Debacle!' Was all he could manage.

The silence contained by the circular array of foreign ministers and their aids facing Hewlett-Temple and Talbert-Flock was to say the least, palpable. The French stared in disbelief, their only comment coming from the Second Secretary to the Principle Secretary to the French Foreign Secretary who broke the silence by simply whispering the word 'Merd.' The Russian Foreign Secretary was the next to react turning dramatically to his aids, flaying his arms and demanding confirmation that the interpreter translating into his headphones had said the same words to him as Hewlett-Temple had said to the assembly. The Chinese broke into a cackle of timorous Cantonese and the Americans, in unison, rose from their seats, turned, and walked abruptly from the chamber. For them the business of the day was firmly concluded even though the agenda carried several, as yet undisclosed, issues. Bob Dorf, Senator for Ohio and representative to the Security Council, member of the select committee on third world industrialisation and adviser to the President himself, on Islamic affairs, waited until the double glass doors to the assembly chamber had closed behind them then turned to his two colleagues. He addressed them both, but particularly the shorter of the two, Grant Merchason, who, with his CIA connections, was possibly the only person listening to the speech who had not been totally surprised.

'Something will have to be done about this.' Dorf stated.

'Decidedly.' Merchason replied.

Behind them, back in the Assembly Chamber, Talbert-Flock had turned an uncommonly vibrant shade of blue around his lips. He dragged at his collar, fumbling to release the tiny button beneath his stripped silk tie, gasped, and collapsed forward. His face slapped noisily into the bright, polished redwood of the table in front of him. Hewlett-Temple looked down at him disdainfully. He had never liked the man anyway.

Chapter 20

In the garden of their villa, nestling quietly in the steep Ligurian hills, Eric, Norman and Norman Hewlett-Temple sat in relaxed conversation. Each had a glass of good Italian Bardalino wine in his hand and each had a contented smile of his lips.

Hewlett-Temple, who they now referred to as Norm – Normal Norman, a pun that he particularly liked under the circumstances – had resigned from the post of Foreign Secretary three weeks before; on the very same evening of his now famous speech at The Hague. He'd had to face an extremely acrimonious and upsetting meeting with the Prime Minister, who although he had lost his temper and had at one point threatened to have Hewlett-Temple thrown into the Tower for treason, was powerless to stop the process his erstwhile Foreign Secretary had put into place. The British Government would have to swallow the pill and then, in the fullness of time, slowly pull the situation back to the status quo that existed before the speech; about six months the PM estimated. But they, Eric, Norman and Norm, had put pay to that assumption. One week ago they had released the autobiography that Eric had hastily put together. The first edition had gone onto the shelves in Sydney in the morning and sold out by lunchtime. They hadn't bothered to try and have the book released in Britain. It would surely have been barred. But they serialised it to German, French and Italian periodicals and then released the full version in Canada a week later. The book was a sell out, a best seller.

Eric had done a masterful job, or so Norm said, to produce the book in such a short time. Especially as the events at Southgrim Manor came out and added a beautiful post script to the first edition. The discovery of Teresa and her subsequent hire as a research assistant had revealed the plot by Freddie and Thaddeus to fix Rosie's Lottery, and the involvement of her brother; who Teresa seemed to have no compunction putting in the frame. Criminal proceedings were not levied but an investigation was carried out by a private agency hired by the Rose Morgan Trust Fund who discovered that the scam had gone completely wrong, and that not one of the bogus ticket holders set up to win had in fact won. The draw was declared valid. Teresa also helped to unravel the mystery of the shot that had, at first assumption, been fired at Norm. She pointed the finger at Freddie and his unsuccessful attempt to have

Lisa killed; a fact that greatly relieved the world's international criminal agencies who, upon discovery of the car in the copse and the carefully planned and intricate decoy had recognised all the hallmarks of the Python, Marios Branchman, whose original name and 'modus operandi' were the only things they actually knew about him. They let the press run with the local story about Freddie and when the police quickly came to the conclusion that the whole thing was a botched affair by a local heavy called Malcolm Prentice, a known felon with a violent past who had managed to shoot himself instead of his victim before throwing himself into the path of an exploding 250cc motorcycle, they breathed a long sigh of relief. Special Branch informed the Prime Minister's Office, and the CIA informed the President. Both were of the opinion that if public curiosity had been assuaged, and a culprit found who was now conveniently dead, then best to let things lie. As for Hewlett-Temple, the decision was easy. He'd resigned. He was no longer part of the government, even though he was still technically an MP, if someone was still after him, they'd commiserate, afterwards.

Because they were afraid to return to Britain, Eric had to rely on Teresa for all his research into the Southgrim Manor Affair. And she proved tireless.

The lawyer Brinker, who had adjudicated at the draw ceremony had retired and his place taken by Teresa's brother Terrance Whet. The Uncle Frederick Loewen, who was accused of orchestrating the botched assassination of Lisa Going, the manager of the Rose Morgan Trust and goddaughter to Rose Morgan, had suffered a heart attack and conveniently died. His cousin Thaddeus, also implicated in the murder plot was in hospital in a coma that he wasn't expected to come out of, brought on by smoke inhalation during the fire at the Manor house; Thaddeus' sister Elsbeth had also died from the smoke of the fire but she was not implicated in the murder attempt. Three other members of the family had been hospitalised with the same problem, but, probably because they were much younger, had survived the smoke. They had been released from hospital three days after the fire. An interesting footnote to the Loewen family involvement was the announcement that Helen, wife of Charles Loewen, son of the comatose Thaddeus, had filed for divorce and was currently taking her husband for seventy five percent of his wealth; which appeared to consist entirely of his recent inheritance from the late Rose Morgan. But the Loewen family troubles ended on a happier note. Lisa Going announced her betrothal to Charles O'Donnell, a retired businessman from Australia. Norm had received an invitation to the wedding, via Teresa. He wouldn't be able to go but he would send flowers and a present.

The local police had also announced that they had identified the person responsible for starting the fire at Southgrim Manor, but as the arsonist was a juvenile they were withholding the name. Charges were not being pressed but psychiatric counselling was taking place.

Rumours of a knife attack during the lottery draw were investigated, but investigations had petered out when the alleged victim declined to identify his attacker. However, the two bodies found in a farmhouse on the estate were identified and seriously investigated. This story did make a splash, all over the daily papers. The man found was identified as Liam Chesterton, an arts teacher at an Evening Institute in Sevenoaks. He had rented the farmhouse the previous year and according to the local village shopkeepers, was a regular weekend visitor; although, it was said, with a different woman on each occasion. Mr Chesterton, it was reported, was illegally growing Hashish in the farmhouse and it had been a concoction of Hashish and, an as yet unidentified poisonous herb that had been the cause of both his death and that of the woman's – Mrs Ann Banks. But it was the discovery of Mr Banks, found dead, slumped over a poisoned TV dinner of vegetarian curry that really fuelled the fires of the nation's curiosity. Unfortunately, as all the involved parties were dead, investigations quickly ground to a halt and the police moved on to other more pressing things; the coroner recorded death by misadventure for all three. Finally there had been the Clanchet Star and the highjack of over fourteen million in jewels from an armoured truck that had been found abandoned, with the driver still unconscious in the back, on the grounds of Southgrim Manor. The only thing that stopped the press going wild with this last seemingly unbelievable twist in the events of the final draw day, had been the recovery of the Clinchet Star by the young co-driver of the van, one Andrew Winter, who had been declared a hero for pursuing the robbers onto the estate and recovering the precious gem. There was a rumour that he was to be called to the palace to receive a decoration from the Queen, to accompany the reward he had been granted by the owners of the gem. In the last chapter of the book, Eric had wanted to speculate on both the whereabouts of the remaining gems stolen and the mysterious deaths at the farmhouse.

But stopped himself, as it really had nothing to do with Norm or his life and therefore shouldn't be referred to in his autobiography.

'It's another beautiful day.' Eric remarked.

Norman raised his glass, squinting at the sanguine reflection of the soft Italian sun reflecting through the deep red wine. 'Absolutely glorious,' he said.

Norm looked at them both. His ex-lover and friend. His friend's lover, who was now his friend too.

'It is now,' he agreed.